Praise for *The Daed...*

"A true genre-bender. It mixes alche........., and historical figures in ways you haven't see.. ...ore. […] adventurous, original, and a blast to read."
—Tor.com

"Genre bending often come at great peril, but Martinez pulls it off with an assurance that makes all the pieces slot together perfectly."
—BuzzFeed, selected as one of "The 14 Greatest Science Fiction Books of the Year"

"An ambitious and fun romp."
—SFSignal

"On a five star scale, gets six. […] One of the most enjoyable reads I've had all year."
—GeekDad

"A thoroughly enjoyable, swashbuckling romp through worlds in which I would happily spend more time."
—Fantasy Faction

"Martinez's debut is a triumph of genre-blending, as steampunk adventure merges with modern space opera. With a cast of superbly drawn characters, Martinez's title is a mesmerizing tale of two universes that briefly cross paths, leaving both worlds forever changed."
—*Library Journal* (starred review), included in "Best Books 2013: SF/Fantasy" year-end wrap-up

THE ENCELADUS
CRISIS

Books by Michael J. Martinez

The Daedalus Incident
The Enceladus Crisis
The Gravity of the Affair (novella)

THE ENCELADUS
CRISIS

BOOK TWO OF THE DAEDALUS SERIES

Michael J. Martinez

NIGHT SHADE BOOKS
NEW YORK

Night Shade books may be purchased in bulk at special discounts for sales promotion, corporate gifts, fund-raising, or educational purposes. Special editions can also be created to specifications. For details, contact the Special Sales Department, Night Shade Books, 307 West 36th Street, 11th Floor, New York, NY 10018 or info@skyhorsepublishing.com.

Night Shade Books® is a registered trademark of Skyhorse Publishing, Inc.®, a Delaware corporation.

Visit our website at www.nightshadebooks.com.

10 9 8 7 6 5 4 3 2 1

Library of Congress Cataloging-in-Publication Data is available on file.

ISBN: 978-1-59780-504-9

Cover illustration by Lauren Saint-Onge
Cover art and design by Victoria Maderna and Federico Piatti
Interior layout and design by Amy Popovich

Printed in the United States of America

For my mom and grandfather,
who always encouraged me to dream big

PROLOGUE

4,137 B.C.

Mars would soon be dead.

Standing on the balcony of his fortress, the warlord knew—despite all his efforts and his brilliance—that the battle on the fields below would end in crushing defeat. The flanking gambit backed by his most aggressive general had failed, as he knew it would; the eldritch machines of the enemy made short work of his massed armies. But it was not a gambit designed to win. It merely bought time.

The warlord clutched his scimitar in one tightened, green fist. This war was all but over. Another was beginning. A new front. A terrible and uncertain front…but potentially a winning one.

"My lord, it is time," came a voice from behind him. "The subjects are ready."

He turned to his chief disciple and aide-de-camp, Rathemas—a fine warrior in his own right, and an even more adept mystic. Rathemas bore a look of grim determination on his face, but his black-eyed gaze remained steady. His hand rested lightly on his own scimitar, sheathed now but ready enough should the defenses finally break.

Once again, the warlord turned back to the blasted plain for one final look. Dark yellow blood marred the rust-red plains—the blood of heroes, the warlord knew. It would be avenged, though not in this lifetime.

But the warlord was no longer interested in such short time spans. He watched his final lines of beast riders fall to the lightning strikes of a terrible war machine—such a beautiful, horrible creation it was!—before turning back to Rathemas. "So it is," he said finally. "Begin the power sequence. I follow shortly."

Rathemas bowed and left quickly, the claws on his feet clacking against the bare stone floors.

Sharp, dissonant shouts floated up from the battlefield, and he knew without even looking that the time was shorter than Rathemas knew. The human vanguard had been crushed, and the enemies' war-cries were shrill and piercing. It *must* be now.

The warlord turned and followed his disciple through the halls of the fortress. His fellows cleared a path for him immediately, pressing their backs to the stone walls and saluting crisply, even as many struggled to stand under the weight of exhaustion and injury.

Outside the skies were black, roiling masses of alchemical cloud, pierced by the erratic, failing electrical currents linking his citadel to others across the planet, others now likely in ruins. The once verdant plains below were ground to dust, the metal of sword and armor now rusting amid the blood and ichor. Nearly the entire planet's water supply had slowly been blasted out into the Void during the year-long onslaught. It would be mere hours before the last citadel fell.

But improbably, it would be time enough for a final masterstroke. What the enemy thought would be the end of the war was merely the opening of a new stratagem, one that would come to fruition over centuries.

The warlord strode down corridors, hurtled down stairways, brushed past the dead and dying, all while bringing his mind into focus for the task ahead. His will had to be as sharp as the long-hafted blade in his scabbard, and he had many opportunities to practice such concentration in the years since he assumed the mantle of leadership on behalf of his people.

Finally, in the lowest dungeon of his tallest citadel, he arrived in the massive stone chamber set aside for this ritual and began surveying the preparations of his acolytes and disciples. The room was a vaulted, circular space nearly more than a hundred yards wide, with cunning arches supporting the high domed ceiling and arcane sigils carved in the walls providing the only décor. In the dim electrical light, he could see the subjects were indeed ready—a band of some two hundred humans, along with another sixty enemy beings, their low harmonic moans bringing sweet minor chords to his ears. Thirty reptilian beasts from the second world, barely sentient and scraping futilely at their iron bonds, were in a third area. Together, these groups formed a triangle, in the center of which was the semi-circular altar, hewn of black stone and covered in ritual accoutrements—the symbolic tools of high occult practice and the gears, switches and knobs that represented the pinnacle of his people's technology.

Finally, streams of warriors and acolytes entered the room, chanting as he had prescribed. Dozens, and then hundreds, flowed through the doors, forming a circle around the altar—and another circle, and another. A thousand strong, the massed horde began to sway to the susurrant drone of their own voices, enraptured by the chance of final victory.

Naturally, they were not told of this victory's cost, or of its time frame. But they were loyal, and they would see its value in the days and years to come. No matter how long it took.

The ranks of the faithful parted for the warlord as he strode, full of purpose, to the altar, his faithful Rathemas by his side. "You need not be here," he told his disciple with solemn paternal pride. "You are free to go and die in defense of this working."

Rathemas gave a shadow of a smile. "There are plenty outside left to die, my lord. I want to be part of the final victory to come."

The warlord could not help but smile in turn. That was Rathemas, true to the end. He was the only other creature in the universe who knew of the full extent of the warlord's plans, and yet here he was, ready to give far more than one single life for the cause. He placed a long, spindly hand on his disciple's shoulder. "Then it will fall to you to lead them, when the time is nigh. You will know the hour and bend all to your Will."

Rathemas nodded and stopped at the foot of the dais leading to the altar, leaving the warlord to ascend the steps. Upon the altar, he saw the two most precious components there, awaiting the necessary infusion of physical and occult energies needed for the plan to work—two books, one with a cover hewn of the finest emeralds left upon his world, and the other shielded with the blackest onyx, the pages stained with the blood of both ally and enemy alike.

Chanting softly to himself, the warlord began. He poured noxious liquids over these books—containing the most powerful magical, alchemical and technological processes in the Known Worlds—powered up his etheric generators and ritually cleansed the souls of those present according to the ancient ways.

Then, just as the citadel shook violently under the enemy's siege engines, etheric lightning shot from the altar in every direction to pierce the souls of every being in the room, save the warlord. He closed his eyes and savored the screams—the first notes of his magnum opus—before a final stroke of energy shot through his own body.

"In here!" cried the sergeant, his slug-projectile weapon pointing through the doorway into the massive basement chamber. The melodies of his voice were martial, staccato, and hopeful, all at once, and were audible despite the heavy armor that covered him from head to toe.

Quickly the squad entered and fanned out, weapons at the ready. But there seemed to be little need. The room smelled of ozone and blood, and the broken husks of long, green-skinned bodies were strewn about, as if thrown around by a giant hand. Yet in other areas, the squad found their fellow soldiers, prisoners now, unconscious but alive. The humans and lizard-creatures also seemed to avoid whatever had slain the warlord's allies.

The officer walked in and quickly identified his quarry. "There. Bring the chains," she sang excitedly, pointing to the green-skinned figure slumped over the console in the middle of the room. "And fetch the healers. We should repatriate these captives to their homeworlds."

Within moments, the figure was bound hand and foot, lying on the floor unconscious. "The carnage," the officer sang dolefully, quietly, an elegy to the fallen. "What has this madman done?"

A cough from the floor drew everyone's attention as the warlord—the enemy of many worlds—sputtered and awakened. "It is...victory."

The officer stepped forward to tower over him. "No, it seems you've failed, Althotas," she sang, her voice carrying minor chords of contempt and rage. "Only your compatriots have fallen."

The squad pulled the warlord Althotas to his feet, roughly, supporting him under their arms. Althotas did not respond, instead allowing a small, strange smile to appear on his bloodied, yellow-streaked face.

Mars would be dead soon.

CHAPTER 1

July 21, 1798

Allah, be merciful. It is like lambs to the slaughter," the young man said as he surveyed the flat plain far below. His was, perhaps, the finest vantage point one could muster—atop the Great Pyramid of Cheops itself—and yet one neither side from the battle below had seen fit to use.

Far below and far away, the young man and his companion watched the first line of mounted mamelukes charge forth across the desert toward the arrayed forces of infantry and artillery before them. The cries of the horsemen could be heard faintly over the desert wind, their words not quite discernible, though both men knew that among the cries, many of the mamelukes would be shouting *allahu akbar*—God is great.

Wisps of smoke erupted from the lines of the European infantry, followed shortly by the sound of gunfire reaching the observers' ears. The Europeans, in actuality, were not in lines per se, but had arranged themselves in squares, with artillery pieces in the center of their formations. It was a canny move, for it allowed more muskets to be deployed against the charging cavalry. Thus the mamelukes fell in waves, as if harvested by an invisible scythe. Barely a handful of riders made it to the European lines, and these few were handled expediently by the soldiers and their bayonets.

The second line of mamelukes charged, this time trying to take a different tack by aiming for the spaces between the squares. Perhaps they had hoped to peel off at the last moment before getting caught in the crossfire, but that experiment never came to fruition, for the cavalry riders and their horses fell just the same. It was an exercise in utter futility and, perhaps, the very end of a storied era of warfare in this part of the world.

"Murshid, I feel I must warn someone," the youth—barely a man of 16 years—said to his companion. "Should we not ride to Cairo?"

The older man, who appeared to be a very hale and healthy forty, merely shrugged under his robe and turban, which seemed an odd pairing with his sandy hair and thinly drawn face. "Cairo knows, Jabir. The mamelukes rode forth from there, after all, and the city is far closer to the fighting than we are. They'll see it from the battlements, and know the extent of the defeat when no one rides back afterward."

Jabir studied his mentor intently. The older man sat serenely on the stones of the pyramid, some four hundred feet above the valley floor, as he watched the defenders of Cairo shredded before the modern European army, which had arrayed itself in massive squares of men, muskets, and cannon protruding from all sides. Surely, the great *murshid*—"teacher" in the Arabic tongue, a sure sign of respect for a foreigner—would be keen on learning the kinds of alchemical shot the Europeans used, the tactics they employed and, in the end, what their purpose was. But to Jabir, Cairo was his one and only home, and he knew it would fall to these new crusaders within days, perhaps less. He wanted to do something—anything—but exactly what...he knew not.

"So it's true," the murshid murmured to himself, still in Arabic. "They've come all this way. But why? Why Cairo? Why now?"

Jabir cleared his throat. "The traders in the *suq* say this Frankish general wishes to cut off the English from India. He hopes to hurt them so they sue for peace back where they came from."

The murshid shook his head. "A likely story," he said, standing and stretching his long limbs, his robes fluttering amid the winds that graced the slopes of the ancient monument. "You might as well direct your attention toward a gnat when your enemy stands before you. There are other reasons for this."

The murshid started climbing down the steep rocks of the pyramid, leaving Jabir scrambling to pack up their gear and follow. "Where are we going, murshid?"

The older man turned to his student, a compassionate look upon his face. "Cairo is lost, Jabir. I'm sorry. The best we can do now is head north.

I doubt the English will have allowed the French to simply sail across the Mediterranean without contest, and I'll wager the Royal Navy will be at Aboukir Bay before long. There's 25,000 Frenchmen down there, and they're just about done cutting the heart out of the mameluke army. So we'll go and tell the English what has happened here."

Jabir frowned as he slung their gear over his back. "Why? So that they too can come and launch a new crusade?"

"No, Jabir," the murshid said. "The English have India. They rule the sea and the Void, and they have little quarrel with the Ottomans. But this French general...he is canny. Last I heard, the Royal Navy is all that's keeping him from launching an invasion of England itself, or taking flight beyond Earth. And should this general reach land, as you can see, there is no stopping him. He must be contained to the Continent, lest England fall."

The two continued to pick their way down the side of the crumbling limestone pyramid, occasionally stopping to watch the fighting rage on. "I thought you did not care about England, murshid," Jabir observed.

"It is true that I left home a long time ago," the man replied. "But there are still friends whom I care about most dearly. And they will be among those who will be told to fight this General Bonaparte. I must tell them what happened here, so they may be prepared."

Jabir nodded; friendship he could understand. "I will defer to your wisdom, as I do in all things, murshid."

That brought a small, wry smile to the man's face as he replied in quiet English. "Good luck with that," said Dr. Andrew Finch, formerly of the English Royal Navy—one of the finest alchemists in the Known Worlds.

July 28, 2134

A single rust-colored rock sits upon red soil, shrouded in darkness. It begins to tremble, slightly at first, but then starts to move of its own accord. It rolls...uphill. Gaining speed, it ascends a hill of rubble, then moves vertically up an orange cliff face. It reaches the top, piling atop other stones. There are tears and sadness from somewhere, shouting and vengeance. The stones rise higher, the cliff surrounded by a purple sea. Suddenly, the sky turns black, and from nowhere, snow bursts in a whirling fury.

"Ow! Damn!"

Lt. Cmdr. Shaila Jain shook herself out of the momentary reverie at the sound of Stephane Durand's voice. He was grinning sheepishly as he rubbed the back of his head, turning to examine the culprit—a protruding electrical access hatch, the corner of which caught him squarely on the crown of his head. He gave it a sharp slap with his hand—which in turn sent him floating away in the opposite direction, prompting another oath, this one in more familiar French.

Shaila couldn't help but giggle. The French language was sexy as hell, even if it involved swearing and a rather comical attempt at zero-g movement by a mostly naked Frenchman. She had been enjoying some well-deserved afterglow when the little half-trance overcame her, and her laughter now was equal parts relief and genuine amusement. "Hey, this was your idea," she teased. "I told you it wouldn't be easy."

She watched as Stephane managed to grab one of the overhead conduits and arrest his sudden flight, blushing furiously. "We didn't have this problem when we were doing it, yes? So why now?"

Shaila launched herself toward her coverall-slash-uniform, twisting her body mid-flight so she could slide the lower half on as she progressed down the storage bay toward her boyfriend-slash-shipmate. "I'm just better at this than you are. And I can multitask better, too." She arrived just in time to loop an arm around his waist, ending her zero-g flight with a caress and a hug, her black hair flowing all around them, dark Indian skin contrasting with his paleness.

"You mean? While we were…you were making sure we hit nothing?" Stephane asked, brushing aside a strand of his blond hair from his eyes. "I thought I did a better job than that!"

She slid up his torso and planted a kiss on his face. "Don't worry. You were fabulous, as usual. I wedged myself in before you really went at it."

"All right," he demurred, returning her kiss with one of his. "Thanks for this. I always wanted to try."

"Was it what you expected?" she asked.

He laughed quietly. "Yes and no. It was…different. Parts were very good. Parts were just confusing."

Ever since the Joint Space Command Ship *Armstrong* launched four months ago for Saturn—humanity's first manned mission to the ringed planet—Stephane had been asking to give zero-gravity sex a try. With manned spaceflight well into its second century, they weren't really breaking new ground, except on a personal level. But Shaila, a Royal Navy pilot and the ship's second in command, had heard all the stories about zero-g antics, and knew that the fantasy wouldn't quite measure up. Stephane could be awfully persuasive, however. And today seemed like a good day to experiment.

"Happy two years together," Shaila said.

"Give or take," he replied. "Funny you measure our relationship by what happened that day on Mars. You were not even out of medical for more than a week after that."

Unbidden, Shaila's memory raced back two years, to the longest three days of her life, during which the red planet was wracked by earthquakes, her mining colony nearly collapsed around her, and her life was nearly taken by the first alien species ever to come into contact with humanity.

On this side of the fence, she reminded herself.

"Sometimes really bad shit has to happen before you realize how lucky you are," she said, reaching up to snag Stephane's coverall, which was languidly floating past over his head. "I thought you were some asshole playboy."

"I am," he smiled. "The planetary geology thing, this is just a fake."

"Yeah, well, then you had to go and save my life a few times. Cat's out of the bag, darling."

Stephane's reply was cut off by the ship's intercom: "Archie to Jain, Archie to Jain, please report to command. Over."

Shaila looked up at the comm speaker in surprise; it was Dr. Dean Archibald's watch, but for months, all a watch entailed was running diagnostics, relaying communications, and staring out the window as Saturn began to get larger day by day. What would he need her for? On the other hand, he didn't sound an alarm, so it's not like the ship was in trouble.

Shaila turned to see Stephane with a wide-eyed, oh-shit look on his face. "Do you think he saw us?" he whispered incongruously, looking as if he got caught with his hand in the proverbial cookie jar.

It was enough to make Shaila laugh. "We're not the first people to have sex in space, you know," she said, shaking her head as she launched herself across the cargo bay toward her socks and shoes while sending various articles of Stephane's clothing back at him as she went. "And it's not like JSC can up and fire us out here. We're a billion clicks from the unemployment queue."

She turned to look at Stephane as he struggled into his coverall, which produced a series of cartwheels along with another bout of swearing in surprisingly lyrical French. Zipping up her own coverall, she quickly slid her socks and shoes on. "I'll catch up with you later. Don't forget you're on mess duty tonight—don't make me write you up for tardiness!" As she pulled open the access hatch, she plugged the camera's feed line back into its socket—a little joke, one of many on this trip, at Stephane's expense. He generally took them well, and Shaila had no idea why she insisted on pranking him. Sometimes she wondered if she was so unused to actual happiness that she subconsciously tried to sabotage it.

Whatever. Stephane was a good sport—and besides, it would take a minute for the system to reboot and his indecency broadcast to the entire ship. He'd be fine.

Shaila quickly propelled herself down the access corridor that spanned the ship's length, using regularly spaced handholds to guide her flight. Behind her were the two cargo bays, which were positioned just fore of the ship's reactor room and engine core—the very latest in nuclear propulsion technology that made the trip to Saturn a reasonable length. After the cargo bays were the access hatches for *Armstrong*'s landers, which would be used when they arrived in the Saturn system to explore the four moons on deck for this mission—Titan, Iapetus, Enceladus, and Tethys.

She quickly flew past the ship's hub, where four access tubes spun idly around the central axis of the ship. These tubes led to the ship's outer ring, which rotated around the axis in order to create artificial gravity aboard. Crew quarters, labs, and the medical berth all spun around the ship at 2.5 rotations per minute in order to give the crew about 85 percent Earth gravity. Combined with exercise, a carefully constructed diet and a regular dose of pharmaceuticals, it was enough to stave off the worst effects of space travel on a two-year mission.

Shaila grabbed a handhold just before the door to the ship's command center, which was an ambitious name for a glorified cockpit. She pulled open the hatch and entered a hemispherical space about three meters in diameter, with enough seats for three people; the three other seats were on the zero-g science lab and observation lounge, located directly under the command center.

Inside the command hemisphere, Shaila found Dr. Dean Archibald, one of the foremost nuclear engineers in the world, a certified mathematical genius with a second Ph.D. in physics to boot. He was 90 years old and still fit enough to pass muster with JSC's medical staff. That was a good thing, because not only did he design the *Armstrong*'s next generation nuclear propulsion system, but he was one of a bare handful of people qualified to run it.

And at the moment, the wiry engineer with the handlebar mustache and snow-white hair was sitting in the command center as if he were suspended in space itself, his gloved hands outstretched and fluttering in the darkness. *Armstrong* featured the latest in holographic command-and-control software, which essentially projected the space around the ship on the surfaces inside the command center. The goggles Archie was wearing projected holographic controls into his field of vision, while the computer measured where his hands were in that holographic space and the gloves provided tactile stimulation. Archie could be plotting the course of a rogue asteroid, running a diagnostic on the ship's reactor, or simply writing an e-mail to his girlfriend, about whom Shaila had already heard far too much. He *was* old, after all, no matter his conditioning.

"What's up, Archie?" Shaila said as she floated into the room, grabbing a pair of goggles hanging off the armrest of the command chair next to Archie and sliding into the seat. She buckled herself in and slid the semitransparent headset on. Immediately, her surroundings included her piloting controls, a communications panel, a general computer workstation and her lucky holographic fuzzy dice. She looked over at Archie and saw he was working on a communications diagnostic. The headset also gave her the latest on Archie's workflow for the watch; he was efficient as usual, it seemed.

With a practiced wave of his hand, Archie slid his holographic screen closer to Shaila's seat and widened the view. "We were just getting our usual data dump from Houston when we had a seven-second interruption in the feed."

Shaila studied the screen intently. *Armstrong* kept in constant contact with Earth through the latest in laser-guided communications. Houston sent data destined to the ship to any number of satellites situated in Earth orbit, in the Earth-sun Lagrange points, and around Mars as well. *Armstrong*'s communications suite would seek out signals from each of these sources every second and recompute their positions vis-à-vis the ship, which was hurtling through space at nearly 11,000 kilometers a second. When the computer latched onto a signal, laser beams would send microsecond pulses across space with startling accuracy, forming the ones and zeros of data packets. While it took a lot of pulses to create a full data packet, it was still a lot more efficient than old-fashioned radio.

Archie's screen showed the typical cascade of data packets—the pulses of light transmitted from Houston—and then a strange millisecond cutoff. From there, a different set of data packets had taken over before a second millisecond blip. The normal feed had resumed after that.

In data terms, seven seconds was a very long time. Shaila could see numerous parallel tracks of data being sent, in packets large and small. It was enough for a couple thousand e-mail messages, a few dozen vid-mails and maybe a snippet of a holovision show. "It wasn't just an interruption. It was a different signal," she said quietly. "Who else besides Houston would be trying to talk to us?"

"No idea," Archie said. He widened the view again so that only the interfering data packets were showing. "These are encrypted to hell and back, and they're not using any key that we have. I've got the computer working on it now."

Shaila nodded. *Armstrong's* quantum computers were expensive as hell, but the multistate hardware would make short work of most encryption schemes. "It's probably some kind of stray transmission from the Moon or Mars. Pop a message off to JSC to let them know that we caught this. They'll probably want to run some diagnostics on their comm gear, and get some military folks to do the same on their end." She smiled over at Archie. "It's not like anybody else is out this far."

The old engineer began composing an e-mail message to Houston, copying and dragging the image of the data interruption into his message screen. Shaila gazed out at the star field in front of her, her gaze being drawn to Saturn, about half the size of the Moon as seen from Earth and getting closer every day. The computer immediately highlighted the view and provided the ship's course and distance to the planet. Just twenty-three days to go.

Suddenly, a second message popped up in her field of view, and a soothing female voice sounded in the room. "Partial decryption completed."

"Show us," Archie said. Immediately, the message screen widened to accommodate the decrypted data from the comm feed interruption.

They were Chinese characters. Several dozen of them.

Shaila and Becker looked at each other in surprise. "Well, I'll be damned. Translate," Archie ordered.

A moment later, the pictograms were replaced with English words.

...has gone to Shanghai to find work. It is about time he left that horrible village. In the meantime, Mei-Lien misses her daddy and says to say hi. She hopes you will bring her ice from Saturn's rings and...

Shaila sat there in shock. *Ice from Saturn's rings?* "Where's the rest of the message?" she demanded.

"This was the smallest partial data packet available for decryption and translation," the computer responded. "The others will take anywhere from several minutes to eight hours."

Shaila's fingers flew across her holoboard, pulling up intelligence reports and maps of orbital Earth and Mars. She studied the data silently for several minutes while Archie—whose security clearance was far lower than Shaila's—updated his message to Houston and logged everything carefully.

Finally, Shaila had her answer, and it wasn't one she was happy about.

"I think we're getting company," she said, a look of despair on her face.

August 2, 1798

HMS *Fortitude* plunged through the dark night sky, her helmsman struggling valiantly to keep her ruddersail true. Attempting the descent from Void to sea was hard enough during the day, but at night, in the middle of a seeming gale, with a battle raging below? In all of the great naval battles of history, there was no record of a ship making keel-fall from the Void onto the sea in the midst of combat. And yet that is exactly what HMS *Fortitude* and her captain, Thomas Weatherby, were about to do.

Not everyone aboard was excited about making such history, however.

"Wind's picking up!" Folkes called out. "She'll be setting down hard at this rate!"

The officer next to him simply nodded. "Understood, Folkes. Straight on until the captain says otherwise."

Folkes' arms were getting quite sore, and he could see the tiny flashes of green and red alchemical shot from the sea below. There had to be thirty ships down there, and it was nigh impossible to tell friend from foe. "Can ye not at least tell him, Mr. Barnes?" he pleaded quietly.

Second Lt. James Barnes frowned, but still stood ramrod straight, staring ahead across the deck toward the ship's bow and the sea below. "Mind your station, man. The captain has sailed into far worse."

A blast of wind shook the *Fortitude* violently—no mean feat for a 74-gun ship of the line, one of the workhorses of the British Royal Navy and home to more than six hundred souls. Even the officer shifted his stance in order to keep his feet. After a moment, once the ship stopped heaving, the second lieutenant walked away from the wheel toward Weatherby, who stood stoically at the very back of the quarterdeck, the gold piping on his uniform and hat signaling his mastery of the ship.

"Captain, the wind's getting worse," Barnes reported. "Can we not tack in sail?"

To Barnes' very great surprise, Weatherby gave him a small smile. "She can handle it, Mr. Barnes. Besides, you were right. I've made keel-fall in far worse conditions than these. Come with me a moment."

Weatherby immediately strode forward, Barnes in tow. They clambered down the stairs to the main deck, quickly walking forward amid a flurry of salutes from the men, all of whom were secured to the ship with body lines in case their descent proved more violent than even the captain had wagered. Finally, they clambered up the stairs to the forecastle, or fo'c'sle, where another officer stood watch with a looking glass.

"Any luck?" Weatherby asked the first lieutenant, widely considered to have the best eyes of any man aboard. There were few others whom Weatherby trusted so closely as he.

"I see two lines moving on either side of a third, sir," Lt. Patrick O'Brian replied. "The third is caught in the crossfire between the two, but they're returning fire well enough. The southern line is quite close to shore, though. I imagine one or two might run aground if they're not careful."

The captain nodded grimly. "That sounds like Nelson. He always enjoyed taking risks. Any room for us to make keel-fall?"

O'Brian offered the captain his glass. "Southern line. It appears one of ours is out of the fight at the moment. We could splash down right next to the two largest French ships. Could be rather difficult, though, sir."

Weatherby eyed the scene below. "I see it. 'Tis a tight fit, Mr. O'Brian, but we'd rake the French before they knew what hit them." He snapped the glass shut and handed it back. "Mr. Barnes, beat to quarters, if you please."

The younger officer turned and shouted back down the length of the ship. "We shall beat to quarters! All hands to stations!" He then quickly left the fo'c'sle and began seeing to the ship's readiness as one of the marines began drumming a martial beat. Men quickly pulled their cannon away from the hull and began loading, while the rest of the marine detachment—with body lines firmly secured—began climbing up to the tops, their muskets slung around their bodies.

"How bad do you think?" O'Brian asked quietly, once again peering out toward the battle below. Nearly twenty years in service together brought forth a familiarity that extended beyond rank.

"Us? We shall do our duty," Weatherby said. "Them? Hopefully far worse than we."

With a clap of O'Brian's shoulder, Weatherby made his way back to the quarterdeck. They would splash their keel upon the Mediterranean Sea in mere minutes. Thankfully, the men of *Fortitude* were well drilled, and Weatherby expected they should be ready to fire as soon as they made keel-fall. But it would be a close thing. Such a descent took an incredible toll on the ship's timbers, not to mention exhausting the alchemical workings that kept it aloft in the first place. They might turn the tide in this engagement, but it would take some repairs before they were fit for the Void once again. They had been en route to Portsmouth when a chance meeting with a Sunward Trading Company sloop brought them news of Rear Admiral Sir Horatio Nelson's pursuit of the French through the Mediterranean. From there, it was simple deduction as to the French destination, and a decision to beat them to it. The French, however, were already there. As was Nelson.

Just as Weatherby ascended to the quarterdeck, the four men on the wheel lost their grip upon it. The captain rushed forward, driving his left shoulder into the space between the spinning spokes. A sharp jab of pain told him he was successful; he knew then that he and the ship's alchemist-surgeon would meet later on.

"Captain!" Wilkes cried as he once again regained control. "I'm sorry, sir! We couldn't hold her!"

Weatherby gingerly straightened up, his left arm now dangling limply at his side. "Then ask for help next time," he said, trying to make his tone paternal despite the pain and frustration. "It'll do us no good if we land upon our allies."

"Aye, captain. Sorry, sir." Wilkes immediately shouted for two other men to come join their efforts.

Weatherby turned to see O'Brian had followed him astern. "Shall I call for Dr. Hawkins, sir?"

"No, I think not," the captain said, managing a small smile through the obvious pain. "He'll be nervous enough as is. I should be the least of his worries about now. Guide us in, Mr. O'Brian, and have the larboard battery ready to fire on my command."

The sounds of the battle below could be now be heard—cannon fire, mostly, punctuated by the occasional explosion as a ship's powder magazine succumbed to burning timbers. Weatherby was thankful that they were still too far aloft to hear the inevitable screams of dying men.

He would hear those screams soon enough, however. "We're close!" O'Brian shouted from his post along the quarterdeck railing, where he leaned out to determine their best landing point. "Two points to starboard, thirty degrees up on the planes!"

Immediately, the six men on the wheel began cautiously turning to starboard, while the men on the *Fortitude*'s four planesails—two on each side, running outward at a square angle from the hull—were brought up to catch the winds and soften their decent.

"Larboard battery, make ready!" Weatherby shouted, trying desperately not to clutch his throbbing shoulder. It would do no good for the men to see him weakened mere moments before engaging the enemy.

The men on the left side of the ship complied with his order, running the guns out and bringing their flintlocks upward. But they looked to the quarterdeck with fear, and rightly so. Not only were they to be the very vessel to try to drop from the Void straight into an engagement, they were also aiming for a spot uncomfortably close to shore, at night, and with only an educated guess as to their opponents.

"Attention all hands!" Weatherby cried out as he approached the front railing of the quarterdeck. "Englishmen are dying down there at the hands of the damnable French! We cannot—will not—allow this to go unmet! Stand fast and show these frogs what Englishmen can do when they show their *Fortitude*!"

The men below cheered and rejoined their work with a grim determination, while Weatherby took a deep breath and tried to ignore the throbbing pain in his shoulder. It wasn't his first speech by far—he'd commanded ships for over a decade now. In fact, he remembered his first such rallying cry as if it were yesterday, even though it was nearly twenty years ago, and he was barely past boyhood then.

The fact that his ship at the time was destroyed shortly thereafter was something he preferred not to dwell upon.

"All hands, brace!" O'Brian cried out. Weatherby immediately grabbed on to the rail before him with both hands, ignoring the pain that lanced through his shoulder as a result. He looked to larboard, where the tops of other ships began to fly past…then the sails…the rigging….

With a deafening splash and a bone-shaking collision that sent the entire crew sprawling, the *Fortitude* arrived on the seas of Earth once more.

Water cascaded over the sides of ship, primarily upon the maindeck, but even the officers aft were soaked. The cries of men could be heard—on *Fortitude*? The other ships?—as everyone was tossed about violently. Weatherby fell backwards, slamming his back into the mizzenmast. One of the marines in the tops fell, his body line failing him, and landed upon the main deck with a sickening smack of flesh upon planking. The fo'c'sle nearly submerged itself entirely into the waters of the Mediterranean as the ship's momentum carried it forward, and dozens of men skittered forward across the deck, desperately grabbing at ropes and railings.

Fortitude continued to bob and sway upon the sea as her captain regained his feet, his shoulder throbbing anew from the lashing his body had taken upon keel-fall. "Run out the guns!" he cried, not even sure of where they landed at this point, but knowing he must be ready. Weatherby looked toward his left once more and saw *Fortitude* had been lucky enough to come alongside a slightly larger ship, a third-rate with a few extra guns. He quickly scanned her stern.

The French tricolor hung there.

"Larboard battery! FIRE!" Weatherby shouted.

Almost as one, thirty-seven gun crews responded, sending streams of alchemical cannonballs hurtling toward the French vessel. The captain looked on as the glowing shot broke through rigging, planking and men. Most of the French crew was engaged on the other side of the ship, and had only began rushing to their starboard side to engage this new threat that had seemed to materialize out of nowhere.

It didn't matter. *Fortitude*'s guns fired true, and many Frenchmen died painfully under their wrath. Weatherby saw that the enemy vessel was likely out of the fight, her quarterdeck a smoldering ruin and her guns askew throughout.

"Rudder amidships, full sail!" Weatherby shouted. "Reload! We shall engage the next ship in the line!"

The men flew into action, and a moment later the *Fortitude* surged forward, her captain looking forward to the next French ship—a massive first-rate ship with three gun decks. It was likely *L'Orient*, as the French had very few ships of that caliber, and she was their best. Fortunately for *Fortitude*, the ship already appeared to be in dire straits, with fires seemingly spouting from every gunport.

But *L'Orient* was not dead yet, as the report of her cannon soon attested. Thankfully, her full complement of guns were not available to her—only twenty or so managed to get off shots toward *Fortitude* as she neared. This was more than enough, however. The crew ducked as shot careened through the ship, boring holes into the upper and lower gun decks, blasting part of the fo'c'sle into shards and cracking the ship's foremast, which nonetheless managed to hold.

"Return fire at will!" Weatherby shouted, and the *Fortitude*'s guns responded quickly, shredding *L'Orient*'s lower gun deck with cannonballs laced with mystic alchemical formulae. Some pounded through the oaken planking like a knife through butter, while others followed to set all ablaze as if it were mere tinder. Still others exploded within the ship itself, causing splintered wood and ensorcelled iron to cascade through the air and turning the interior of the ship into an abattoir.

Weatherby saw the fires raging through the blasted gaps in the French flagship's hull; she was not going to last much longer. "Mr. O'Brian, twenty degrees to starboard, if you please, and post lookouts to keep us away from those shoals. Fire teams make ready."

Just as quickly as she arrived, *Fortitude* peeled away from the French line—joined by many of the French ships seeking to escape the wreckage of *L'Orient*. The fires on the French flagship were spreading, and the men aboard—she had a complement of at least a thousand men—were streaming over the sides and swimming for shore, for their fellows, and even for the English ships. Weatherby dispatched his more junior lieutenants and midshipmen to oversee the recovery of any man overboard; the laws of sea and Void required no less.

"Sir?" O'Brian said quietly.

The captain turned to see his first lieutenant peering back toward the French line before handing him the looking glass. "The first ship we engaged, sir," O'Brian said.

Looking through the glass, the captain saw that their first target was trying to move off from *L'Orient* along with the rest—and the rest of Nelson's fleet was doing an admirable job of making it difficult for any of the French to find room to escape. Weatherby focused on the ship's aft.

Emblazoned there, below the French tricolor, was her name: *Franklin*.

A moment later, fire filled the captain's field of vision. The powder magazine aboard *L'Orient* blew, turning the proud flagship into a pile of tinder. But by this point, only a few flaming shards made it to *Fortitude*, and the crew quickly extinguished the fires.

Weatherby somberly handed the glass back to O'Brian, his mind filled with thoughts of an old, wise friend from his youth, one who put aside politics and rancor in the name of a greater good. "Come about, Mr. O'Brian. I want to take *Franklin* as a prize before the rest of the fleet blows her out of the water," he said.

"She deserves no less."

CHAPTER 2

July 28, 2134

With less than four weeks to go until their scheduled arrival at Saturn, the mood of the *Armstrong* crew had been improving daily. Their mission checklists had started going from the banal repetition of routine shipboard duties to experiment diagnostics and increased observation of Saturn and its moons. The six members of the crew were going to be the first-ever human beings to survey Saturn first-hand.

Or would they? Everyone had already received word about the Chinese intercept, and the faces around the table were pretty glum. Shaila wondered how they'd take to this briefing. There was even more going on than they realized.

"All right, people, let's go," said the ship's commander, Col. Mark Nilssen, U.S. Marine Corps. The wiry, crew-cut skipper was every inch a Marine, from the tattoos to the muscles to the weathered eye. "Three hours ago, Archie discovered an interruption in our comm feed. Normally, this wouldn't be such a big deal; we'd just run a diagnostic, find the source of the interruption, fix it and request the data again. But this wasn't just an outage. The comm signal was interrupted by another signal entirely, and the computer decrypted it and translated it from the original Chinese. What we got were several personal vidmails and e-mails, some basic ship-update commands and about twenty minutes of a popular Chinese reality holoshow." This prompted a few smirks and raised eyebrows around the table as the skipper continued. "But those personal messages contained a few references about Saturn which surprised us. So Jain ran some queries through our intelligence database. Jain?"

Shaila nodded at the colonel and turned to address the rest of the crew, unconsciously giving Stephane a slight smile as she did so. "According to JSC reports, there are only a handful of communications stations that can relay laser-comm data and only a few long-range survey ships that can receive it—that we know of. They can broadcast from Earth, of course, their base on the Moon, and from a pair of satellites at the L4 and L5 Earth-Sun Lagrange points. And right now, there are three ships out there that could receive that data. One's in the shop, one's around Venus and one's supposedly in the Jovian system."

Shaila paused to call up a hologram of the Solar System, which sprung to life above the conference table for all to see. "As you can see, Venus is on the other side of the Sun from us, so there's no way they could miss their ship that way. Jupiter is at least in the right direction, but still a good 40 degrees away. They'd have to have a major technical foul-up in order to cross our signal streams."

"I think there is a 'but' coming here," Stephane said. "This is too easy to explain away."

Nilssen nodded. "Naturally. The Chinese ship *Tienlong* was supposed to be surveying the Jovian system for the past month or so. Our satellites there caught it entering the system and swinging around toward the far side of the planet. We assumed they were using the planet's atmosphere for braking, but we never caught them entering a stable orbit. We assumed they plotted a course away from our assets, like they usually do, but we always manage to catch a peek somewhere. This time, no luck. At first, we thought they may have skirted the atmosphere too close and took a dive into the planet, but the Chinese assured us that their mission was fine—and of course, told us to mind our own goddamn business."

The Chinese were notoriously insular and private about their space activities, a tradition going back more than a century. They had even taken to using holographic cloaking and light-dampening coatings for some of their near-Earth assets. Naturally, such reticence made the Chinese immensely popular for congloms—shorthand for multinational conglomerates—to partner with. Space exploration and, more importantly, exploitation was the next frontier in big business, and would likely stay that way for decades to come.

Nilssen nodded over to Archie, who picked up the thread. "With Jain here looking up China's assets in place, it was easy to figure out where the laser comm might have been going," Archie said. "It's a simple point-A to point-B thing. Logically, however, there was no way that any of their Earth-based or Lagrange assets could've been sending that signal to anybody unless they had a major technical fuckup. Unless…"

Archie stood and gestured within the holographic image of the Solar System. "We know when *Tienlong* left Earth, about two weeks after we did. We also know from its course that it was headed for Jupiter, and we saw it arrive there last month before it disappeared. However, what if they didn't stop at Jupiter, but used its gravity in a slingshot maneuver to head to Saturn?" Archie traced a path with his finger, which the computer dutifully illuminated in the hologram. "We know their speed from the time it took for them to get to Jupiter from Earth. And we can extrapolate their Jupiter approach from what our satellites there caught. The boost they'd get would place them about here." Archie jabbed a gnarled finger at a spot on the hologram, which began to glow red. "Now, take a look at China's L4 comm satellite, the position of the *Armstrong* and that big red dot." Archie traced a line between the three points.

A very straight line, one which the computer dutifully animated.

"We got lucky," Nilssen said as Archie took his seat. "If this were some random intercept, the odds would be huge. But seeing how their orbits worked out, they probably should've known we'd be in their way at some point, and they didn't do a good enough job on their security."

"Actually," Archie interrupted, "I don't think it was security. I think they didn't get as much of a boost from Jupiter as they thought. The idea would be to *beat* us to Saturn, after all. As it stands, we're going to arrive pretty much at the same time."

"Which means there's a very good chance we could run into them, literally," Shaila added. "Lord knows they can be pretty cavalier about respecting other people's space out here. I wouldn't be surprised if they maneuver just to edge us out of our orbit, since they're behind schedule."

There was silence around the table for several moments until, finally, Dr. Maria Conti, the ship's medical and biology officer, spoke up. "Why did we not slingshot around Jupiter and save a few weeks?" she asked.

"Safety, mostly," Nilssen said. "Cutting it that close around Jupiter requires a lot of extra shielding and energy. Sure, you shave a few weeks, but if you're off your game for a minute, you end up either diving into the planet or shooting off target into nowhere. The magnetic and gravitational fields play hell with your sensors at high speed. And don't forget, until now we didn't realize this was a race. Now we're stuck playing a huge game of chicken with a really big planet, and the Chinese had the element of surprise."

"But now they will play chicken, as you say, with us, yes?" Stephane said.

"Possibly," Nilssen said. "As you can imagine, Houston's having kittens about this, and they're doing everything they can to get a firm track on *Tienlong*, if it really is *Tienlong* out there in the first place. Once we get them pinpointed, we can at least make some adjustments to our course before we get there so we can avoid them. Archie, how's our reactor output looking?"

"We're running at about 85 percent," he said, running a liver-spotted hand across his face. "I suppose I can get you to 95 percent, but any more than that and we start having to worry about fuel consumption. We need some wiggle room once we get there in order to rendezvous with the depots."

Prior to *Armstrong*'s launch, JSC had sent three depot ships on a slow course to Saturn. By sending food and fuel ahead, the *Armstrong* could get to Saturn faster without carrying the cargo necessary for the return trip. In fact, they only needed to rendezvous with one of the ships to get home safely—the other two would simply allow *Armstrong* to extend its mission and survey more of the Saturn system if the situations warranted.

"What about their fuel situation?" Conti asked. "Any sign of depot ships from them?"

"Great question. Hard to say," Nilssen responded. "The Chinese wouldn't let anybody get close enough to the ship in orbit to get a good look, and the intel is pretty spotty. It's possible they simply brought enough food and fuel for the entire trip, or maybe the depot will launch once they're there safely."

"They could always try to refuel after arriving," said Dr. Elizabeth Hall, the mission's corporate specialist. Hall was executive vice president for extraterrestrial resources at ExEn Corp., the world's largest energy conglomerate and the mission's corporate underwriter. Unlike most corporate specs, she had a Ph.D. in geology as well as an M.B.A., and thus was actually qualified to be aboard; she had even taken on additional training to serve as emergency pilot.

"Exactly," Nilssen said. "Between water on Enceladus and pick-your-hydrocarbons on Titan, refuel is a definite possibility." He didn't need to mention that *Armstrong* had emergency procedures in place to refuel on site as well, in case the rendezvous with their pre-launched fuel depot didn't go as planned. "For now, we just don't know. In the meantime, though, we got about three and a half weeks to get ready. Jain?"

As second in command, it fell to Jain to let everyone know just how much their workloads would be increasing as they approached Saturn. Funny how the number two person aboard ship never got to be the popular one. "All right, then. Archie, we need to get some short-range comm gear up and running. We don't have an extra laser-comm on board, so we'll have to use good old-fashioned radio waves. I want digital, analog, holo, 2D vid, audio-only, and text. Throw in Morse code while you're at it. English and Chinese. Let's say hello, ask them their intent and offer assistance if they're off course."

Archie nodded. It was highly doubtful, at this point, that the Chinese were off course. "I'll put it on a repeat loop so they're absolutely sure we're here."

Shaila smiled. "Well done, then. Maria, there's a chance that their sling-shot move didn't go so well, since they're not ahead of us, so let's double check our medical stores and make sure we can actually offer assistance if they need it," Jain continued. "Stephane, research everything you can about their landers and their docking systems, then request some docking simulations holos from Houston. If we need to shuttle over to them, we need to be sure we can dock with them safely."

She looked up at the table, trying to catch the gaze of each of her colleagues. "I know we're going to be busy with experiments and observations as we get closer to Saturn, but with another ship out there somewhere, God-knows-where, we're going to have to squeeze in some additional drills, particularly evasive and collision drills. Some of them will be unannounced. I'll apologize now so that I can freely tell you 'tough shit' later." This got the laughs that she had hoped for. Always deliver bad news with humor. "Our first announced drill will be tomorrow at oh-nine-hundred, to start things off civilized. Everyone else, try to think of your worst-case scenarios and come up with procedures for dealing with them. Colonel?"

Nilssen nodded. "All right." He took a deep breath before continuing. "There's one question that still doesn't have an answer: Why?"

Hall frowned a little. "Obvious, isn't it? They got a backer who wants to go head-to-head with ExEn in trying to stake a resource claim. And the Chinese love sticking it to JSC whenever they can."

"True," Nilssen allowed. "But…there's more. A lot more. I was just briefed on this stuff a couple hours ago, and I'm still…well, I'm going to hand it off to Jain and Durand. Go."

With a quick look over to Stephane, who gave her a smile of encouragement, Shaila cleared her throat. A sudden wave of nerves came over her, and she was grateful for the holopacket she brought with her on the voyage. The just-in-case had become necessary.

"You're right, Liz. The Chinese do have a backer. Corporate registry for the *Tienlong* is Total-Suez, the French-Hong Kong conglom. Turns out we know one of the senior execs signed on as a manager. His name's Harry Yu." Shaila pressed a button and the image of a handsome Chinese man sprang to life in three-dimensional light above the table. "Harry's been there less than two years, arriving just ten months before *Tienlong* launched. Turns out Total-Suez bought out his old company, Billiton Minmetals."

"How do you know him?" Conti asked.

This is where it gets tricky. "Harry was the senior Billiton mining exec on Mars more than two years ago when…well, when things went down," Shaila said. "Chances are, he walked off-planet with a briefcase full of highly classified information that would've made a Saturn mission suddenly look amazingly interesting to a more ambitious conglom. While this could simply be a case of corporate one-upsmanship, it's been decided that there could potentially be more here. You were scheduled to receive this briefing only once we made Saturn, and only if we discovered things there that warranted it. With the Chinese and the congloms involved, though, it's been determined to get you up to speed now, so you'll know what to look for."

Shaila pressed a few more keys on the table, calling up a large vidfile.

The image of Harry Yu was replaced by that of a middle-aged Hispanic woman in a U.S. Air Force uniform with a pair of stars on her shoulders. She greeted the room with a curt nod. "*Armstrong*, I'm Major General Maria Diaz, executive director of Project DAEDALUS. If you're watching this, then something's gotten really interesting out there in Saturn space. I promise this will help you deal with it, but it's not going to be easy to digest. I'm going to ask Jain to put this presentation, and the accompanying reports and holovids, on your personal servers for you to review at your leisure.

You're going to have a lot of questions, but a lot of the answers are in those files—the contents of which, by the way, you're not to share with anybody. You already know we're reading your comms, so really, don't even try it.

"What you're facing today in Saturn space has its roots in something that we've taken to calling the *Daedalus* incident, something that happened two years ago at McAuliffe Base near the southern ice cap of Mars. To put it very bluntly, the area-of-operations around McAuliffe was the location of history's first recorded extraterrestrial—and extradimensional—incursion."

Archie, Conti, and Hall all leaned closer, almost in unison, looking both surprised and highly skeptical. Nilssen watched dispassionately—this was his second viewing, and he'd spent all his emotions after the first one. Shaila caught a glimpse of Stephane with a small smile on his face. He was a good bluffer in poker, but not here. Not now.

"By means which we're still trying to understand," Diaz continued, "Dr. Yuna Hiyashi came into contact with an extradimensional being known as Althotas, who claimed to be a warlord from Mars' ancient past. And he was—in his dimension. Turns out this other dimension is very close to our own in many ways, running almost parallel except for a few key points.

"One, the other dimension was about 350 years behind our timeline; their year was 1779. Two, they used an unknown kind of technology to propel sailing ships through space. Yes, actual three-masted sailing ships with cannons and everything. They called their technology 'alchemy,' and it appeared to work far better than the historical antecedent in our own dimension."

Shaila smiled, remembering the day Diaz recorded the holo. She had stumbled over the word "antecedent" five times. A small pang of emotion hit her suddenly. Diaz was her mentor, her role model, and a real friend. Shaila missed her.

"Three, the worlds of *their* Solar System are far different from ours. For whatever reason, most of them are habitable. As far as we know, there's indigenous life on Venus, Mars, several Jovian moons and," Diaz paused for effect, "an actual advanced civilization of non-human sentients living in cities built on the rings of Saturn."

"Oh, bullshit," Archie said quietly. Shaila just smiled a bit broader. She knew what was coming next.

"All of these strange new worlds are unconfirmed, based almost entirely on the journals of one Thomas Weatherby, acting captain of HMS *Daedalus*, a 32-gun frigate in the English Royal Navy. He's the guy who crashed his ship into Mars, smack dab in our ops area. He was chasing another ship, led by a guy who wanted to free Althotas from some kind of pocket dimension. Thankfully, Weatherby was able to stop him—in cooperation with Jain and Durand here, and a few other folks, including myself.

"I imagine you're still skeptical, so I prepared a holovid for you. It was edited together from our suit cameras, as well as handheld footage taken by Yuna Hiyashi right before her death."

Shaila watched as Diaz' face disappeared, replaced with a Martian landscape. The computer automatically lowered the lights and boosted the sound. She could hear the *pop-pop* of musket fire already—and a terrifying, utterly unnatural scream.

"What was *that*?" Hall asked, eyes wide.

"Martian sand beast," Stephane said. "You'll see."

Shaila got up from her seat and, tapping Stephane on the shoulder, headed for the door. It would take them a few hours to go through all the videos and reports on the *Daedalus* incident. She'd seen it all several times. She occasionally still had nightmares. Not to mention those annoying semi-dream things that kept nagging at her. Those kept changing, and whatever they were, she was sure there wasn't a good answer for them.

"Why are we leaving?" Stephane asked once they left the common room.

Shaila shrugged. There were a lot of reasons, but few worth getting into at the moment. "I've seen it all before. I lived it. So did you. There's at least two hours of vids alone in there. And someone has to watch the ship. So let's give them some time to wrap their heads around it."

"I'm still trying," Stephane said, giving her a slight grin. "Some days, it even works."

Shaila gave him a small, tired smile in return, but her mind flashed back to the images she had seen in her mind's eye a few hours ago. They had been occurring ever since Mars, anywhere from days to months apart, always different, always keyed on what occurred there, and yet…different.

She hadn't told anyone. And she was damned if she was going to start now.

"Come on," she said. "We have a lot more work to do."

August 4, 1798

Weatherby waited outside the great cabin on board HMS *Vanguard*, his hat tucked under his arm and his full dress uniform chafing him in the heat of the afternoon. The occupant of said cabin knew very well Weatherby was waiting outside, but seemed to take no further notice, despite the fact that it was he who summoned Weatherby from *Fortitude* to report.

Finally, after several minutes, a gruff voice barked, "Come."

With more than a little relief, Weatherby opened the door to the cabin, closed it behind him, and saluted the man sitting behind a simple desk. "Reporting as ordered, admiral."

Rear Admiral Sir Horatio Nelson nodded briefly, but did not look up from his writing, which appeared to be slow and laborious for him. At first, Weatherby thought it was the bandage wrapped around the admiral's head, which seemed to obscure his left eye somewhat. But finally he saw the true reason—the admiral's right hand was not his own.

"My apologies, Weatherby," the admiral said. "I'm still getting used to this damned contrivance."

"Not at all, sir," Weatherby responded. "Alchemical replacement, is it?"

Nelson finally put the quill down and arose from his seat, coming around the desk to formally greet Weatherby with an outstretched hand. Aside from the graying hair and the replacement arm, Nelson was nearly as he was when Weatherby first met him nearly two decades ago—a small, thin man with a surfeit of energy and bravado.

"Lost the arm at Santa Cruz de Tenerife last year," Nelson said. "When I swore to give body and soul for England, I didn't know it would be piece by piece."

Weatherby laughed as he took the admiral's hand—the artificial one, as it turned out. It was harder than a human hand, the clay comprising its "flesh" having been made from specially foraged soils on Venus, mixed in with sulfur-iron from Io and crystals harvested from caves upon the Moon. The arm made a very soft clicking sound as Nelson disengaged from the handshake. "Clockworks within it, then?" Weatherby asked.

Nelson lifted his hand to regard it. "So they tell me. The surgeon who made this presented his work to the Royal Society, I'm told. Of course, it was damned expensive, but worth the cost, I'd say." Nelson dropped his hand and gave a grin. "I should think I'd look ridiculous with my right sleeve pinned to my chest or some such." The admiral waved Weatherby to a chair opposite the desk. "You were late," he noted, but without rancor.

"Aye, sir. I do apologize, but the currents between Mars and Earth were particularly sluggish, even for this time of year," Weatherby said. "When we received word of the mysterious French fleet coming out of Toulon and your pursuit of them, I immediately set a course for Earth. Once we arrived, it was a simple matter of putting together likely landing areas, then using our telescopes to find signs of activity."

Nelson nodded. "All sound moves on your part. 'Tis a shame we can't communicate better with our ships in the Void. I should imagine it rather useful to have a pair of eyes in the sky, looking for the French." Nelson stretched a bit before continuing. "Saumarez is a bit upset with you."

Weatherby raised an eyebrow at this. Sir James Saumarez captained HMS *Orion*, the ship that had tacked away from the engagement, giving *Fortitude* the space it needed to drop into the fight. "I don't think our arrival put *Orion* at risk, sir."

"No, not at all," Nelson said with a dismissive wave of his hand. "James led the vanguard on his line. I think he merely wanted to put some shot into *L'Orient* before you did, that's all. You may want to smooth his feathers should you see him before you depart for Portsmouth."

"Portsmouth, sir?" Weatherby asked, surprised. He had assumed that he would remain in the Mediterranean after the battle, as it seemed Napoleon would either attempt to bring in more supplies by sea, or seek escape from Egypt. Returning to England was quite a change from the prospect of continued action.

Nelson handed over one of the papers on his desk. "Your orders. You're hereby promoted to commodore, with *Bellerophon, Majestic* and *Swiftsure* under your command. You're to take the prizes from this engagement back to Portsmouth and see to it that they're refitted for duty as soon as possible. From there, your squadron will be dispersed and you'll take new orders from the Admiralty."

Weatherby nodded and scanned the orders, trying to keep his anger under wraps. Nelson was famous for many things, including loyalty to the captains under his command—his "band of brothers," as he liked to quote from Shakespeare. Weatherby, however, was not part of this fraternity; he had never actually been assigned outright to Nelson's squadrons. He couldn't help but wonder if this assignment—mere escort duty—was done to help assuage Saumarez' ego. Or Nelson's, for that matter. *Fortitude*'s arrival likely made the battle shorter and more decisive than it might otherwise have been, and it was Weatherby's initiative that made it so.

Furthermore, *Bellerophon* and *Majestic* were heavily damaged in the battle; *Fortitude* and *Swiftsure* would be the only two ships to defend them all. They would be ripe pickings should another French squadron come calling.

A rap upon Nelson's door interrupted Weatherby's thoughts. "Come," Nelson called.

A young lieutenant, looking half-scared and quite apologetic, poked his head through the door. "Pardon the interruption, admiral, but there's an Englishman here says he's from Cairo, says he has news of the French troop movements there. Asked to talk to you and Captain Weatherby, both."

Nelson and Weatherby exchanged a look of bemused surprise. "Well, he's well informed," Nelson said. "Show him in."

A moment later, an incongruous sight walked into Nelson's cabin. The tall, lanky man was dressed in the *galabia* and *abaya* of the local Muslims, complete with a loosely wrapped turban, yet his features were plainly those of a European, despite the tan. With him was an Egyptian teen, similarly dressed.

Weatherby studied the man carefully, even as the latter looked at him with something akin to amusement. Then it hit him and he jumped to his feet: "Finch!"

The captain of HMS *Fortitude* and his former shipmate quickly met in a crushing hug. "Well, then," Weatherby said once they were disentangled. "Don't you look charming. All the rage in Cairo this season?"

Finch smiled broadly. "Of course! I wouldn't expect a man of your poor breeding to understand."

The two laughed while Nelson looked on. "It's *Doctor* Finch, isn't it?" the admiral said, rising from his desk and extending his hand. "I remember you from *Daedalus*."

Finch took the proffered hand. "Indeed, Admiral Nelson. Thank you for seeing—" Finch paused and looked down at Nelson's right hand. "This is well done, indeed," he remarked. "Who was your doctor?"

"Bateman," Nelson said.

Finch smiled as he ran his hands and eyes up and down the length of Nelson's arm, oblivious to the admiral's discomfited gaze. "I tutored him at Oxford. About time he stepped up."

The lieutenant brought in a chair for Finch, leaving the boy to stand. "So you have news for us?" Weatherby said.

"I do. Cairo was taken two weeks ago. Jabir and I saw the conflict from the pyramids themselves," Finch said as he took a seat, with Jabir standing behind; Finch saw no chair was forthcoming for his protégé and, with a slight scowl, continued. "Five divisions, roughly five thousand men each, plus cannon. They deployed into massive squares. Here." He pulled out a sketch of the conflict, made en route from Cairo to Alexandria. "This should give the army something to think about."

Nelson studied the drawings. "And I should think this stymied the mamelukes greatly. Probably just rode up against it and were mowed down like grass."

"Exactly," Finch said. "And there's more. The French commander is Napoleon Bonaparte, of whom you're likely aware. I've heard word he's quite the up-and-coming general. They say he aims to cut us off from India, but I have my doubts."

"And why is that?" Weatherby asked.

"Jabir and I wandered through their camp that evening. In the dark, even I can pass for Egyptian dressed this way. The French brought *savants* with them—an entire society of alchemists, scientists and scholars. Dozens of them."

Nelson harrumphed. "What is that to us?"

Finch shot Weatherby a knowing look, which was returned in kind, before explaining. "I've spent nearly five years here, exploring the ancient Egyptian ruins. From what we learned from our Saturnine neighbors on Callisto whilst we were there back in '79, humanity's alchemical knowledge may be of extra-Earth origin, given to us in ages past by the ancient denizens of Mars, the Xan themselves, or both. Egypt *is* ages past. If you bring an army of alchemists with you, then they're here for a reason."

"And you think something is out there for them to find," Weatherby said. It wasn't a question.

"My own research suggests it. There are two ancient texts that have been rumored to exist for millennia now—the Emerald Tablet and *The Book of the Dead*. Both are said to have originated in Egypt. Both could have ties to the ancient practices of either the Martians or the Xan. Both are said to contain unequaled alchemical insights—and terrible power. Nobody knows where they might be found, or even if they are nothing more than myth. But those who have heard of them invariably come looking for them. I believe the French *savants* plan on their own search. There are precious few alternative reasons for their presence here."

"And you've been looking for these relics as well," Nelson challenged.

"Of course."

"For England?"

"If you wish," Finch replied with a smile.

Nelson frowned. "I swear, Thomas, I've no idea how you put up with this scoundrel aboard your ships."

Weatherby shrugged. "He's the finest alchemist to come out of England in ages, sir, despite his ill temper, aristocratic snobbery, and ill-conceived researches." Weatherby's grin took the edge off his critique, and Finch merely smiled once more.

Nelson was not amused. "So, then. You've been here for some time, then, Finch. You're known in Cairo?"

"Quite so, sir." He nodded toward the Egyptian boy. "So much so that the local authorities have placed their own sons with me in order to learn alchemy."

"Then you should make haste back there at once and ingratiate yourself in with these *savants*," Nelson said. "You might learn something of what they're up to. We've a few merchants in Cairo who have supplied information for us. You can report in through them."

Finch smiled. "Yes, everyone in Cairo knows who the English spies are. Actually, in Arabic, they're called the English-spy-merchants. Never subtle, are we?"

"So you'll do it?" Nelson asked—demanded, really.

"Only because I want to find these items first," Finch said. "I'll see to it that you remain informed of Bonaparte's activities. But the alchemy—leave that to me."

Weatherby looked over at his old friend, a frown upon his face. "Finch, remember what's important here."

Finch's smug demeanor softened. "I know, Tom," he said softly. "Rest assured, I will act appropriately should greater threats arise."

Weatherby nodded, relieved, though Nelson looked decidedly unimpressed. "You had better, Dr. Finch," the admiral growled. "There are rumors, sir, of the reasons you left the service."

Finch gave Nelson a wicked smile. "Then let me assuage you, admiral. I left the service to join with friends and comrades in the revolution in France. And then I left when I saw that revolution come to naught under that fiend Robespierre. That, sir, should answer you."

"And what guarantee do we have that you won't side with the frogs now?" Nelson demanded.

"Because France has squandered its promise and is now sliding toward either anarchy or totalitarianism, depending on the day," Finch countered. "At least England is consistent and, for the most part, agreeable when it must be. I am English, sir, I assure you. And moreover, I bear my responsibilities as a practitioner of the Great Work most seriously. I cannot with certainty say the same for these French invaders."

Hours later, having finally calmed Nelson to some small degree, Finch had joined Weatherby aboard *Fortitude* for a private dinner between two old shipmates. Lt. O'Brian had also been invited, having also been posted to *Daedalus* as a midshipman during the extraordinary events of 1779, but the younger officer declined graciously, knowing that there were some bonds that should be renewed privately. Indeed, only Weatherby's valet was allowed in and out of his great cabin, and even then only to deliver dishes and wine.

"You've a Venusian for a valet now?" Finch asked as the servant—a three-foot tall bipedal lizard creature with a pronounced sharp beak and three-fingered hands, left after bringing a second bottle of wine for the two.

Weatherby nodded as he filled their glasses. "The Venusians are surprisingly hard workers when the poor creatures aren't enslaved," he said. "Gar'uk is the most efficient, fastidious valet I've ever had in the service, his attempts at humor notwithstanding. He still has yet to fully grasp idioms, it seems."

Finch smiled broadly. "I love the Venusians. I wish I had more time to be in their company. I did a survey there back in '89, just before leaving the service. Fascinating people. It would be wise to learn their ways before we destroy their culture entirely." Finch paused to take a swig of wine. "Do you take Gar'uk home with you? How does Margaret like him?"

Weatherby smiled and glanced at the small portrait of a little girl at the edge of his table. "She believes him to be the best sort of toy, and Gar'uk suffers her patiently, though perhaps not with great enthusiasm. She is coming of an age now where she must learn that living, intelligent creatures should not be considered playthings."

They both laughed at this. "How old now?" Finch asked.

"She shall be seven in two months. My sister tells me she grows smarter and more beautiful each day," Weatherby replied with evident paternal pride. "And as much as Nelson's assignment infuriates me, I must say that if I can actually bring these prizes home in one piece, I will rejoice in seeing her again sooner than expected."

"It is well that your sister does so much for the both of you, but have you thought of perhaps seeking marriage once more?" Finch said, perhaps too bluntly.

Weatherby, however, was used to Finch's lack of boundaries and good taste in such matters. "I've not the stomach for it, old man," he said. "I've loved twice in my life. The first time, I was in the wrong and paid the price. The second time, I lost Mary to childbirth. I'm not sure I could weather a third attempt."

Finch nodded. "I've heard news of Anne, should you wish to hear it."

Weatherby's jaw tightened a moment before he relaxed once more. "Would've been better had you not mentioned it. Now that you have, damn you, out with it."

Oblivious as usual, Finch continued to dine. "She remains in the company of the Count St. Germain, it seems, though they've changed their names. Again. Last I've heard, they are somewhere on Venus, in the Dutch holdings."

"And that is all?" Weatherby asked.

"All I know," he replied. "But if nothing else, she is still out there."

Weatherby nodded and stared into his half-empty glass. "I was a fool, you know."

Finch nodded. "Absolutely. But it's been nineteen years, Tom. Time to let it go."

"And how do I do that?" Weatherby asked, a small, sad smile upon his face. "It's not as if those years have helped matters."

"Gar'uk!" Finch called, noting the sullen look on his friend's face. "I think we need more wine!"

CHAPTER 3

August 1, 2134

Mars: a bleak, frigid dustbowl; a has-been planet that saw its best years back when the Sun was still new. The first landing happened nearly a century ago, and since then, it was probably the most explored planet in the Solar System after Earth itself. There were even high-priced tour groups making landings there now.

And yet Dr. Evan Greene couldn't imagine being anywhere else.

"McAuliffe to Greene, come in. Over," squawked his comm.

The astrophysicist keyed the appropriate button on his suit gauntlet to respond. He hoped he wasn't going to get more crap for being outside when the experiment was conducted. Yes, it made more sense to be back at McAuliffe Base, nice and warm with a cup of coffee in hand, instead of in a pressure suit out in the middle of nowhere.

But the people on base now hadn't been there two years ago. They didn't see what he saw. If something was going to happen, he wanted to be out here, responding to it, recording it, experiencing it again.

"Greene here, go ahead."

"Jimenez here, Doctor. Our board is green. Just give the word and we'll light this candle."

Greene smiled as he went over the multiple streams of figures on his data-pad and the heads-up display on his helmet visor, confirming that everything was in order. He then glanced around at the rust-red surface of the planet before him, the vaguely pinkish sky—and the massive mechanical tube be-fore him that stretched off hundreds of kilometers in either direction. It was nothing less than the largest particle accelerator ever built, and it had taken less than two years to complete. This huge ring, some 250 kilometers in diameter, could be the key to unlocking the secrets of the universe. Actually, Greene thought, the *multiverse*. As he scanned the length of the accelerator, the HUD in his visor ticked off the various diagnostic programs that had been up and running for weeks now. All systems were in order.

"Looking good, colonel. The word is given," Greene said into his comm.

"Roger that. Commencing startup sequence," responded Col. Javier Jimenez, a U.S. Air Force officer and the commander of McAuliffe.

Greene looked down at his datapad and watched the readout being fed from the base, comparing it with his own sensors on the HUD. The cycles were beginning as expected. How it would end was anybody's guess.

Normally, a particle accelerator would simply send electrons or protons colliding into each other, and sensors would collect data on the sub-atomic particles created in the collision. In some cases, the accelerator would collect positrons, or anti-protons, to smash into regular protons. But in this case, they were taking huge, complex molecules and sending them onto a collision course with each other over and over again, stripping them down repeatedly into fields of highly energetic particles that, ultimately, would be reduced into the smallest of sub-atomic particles—a slew of positrons, antiprotons and antineutrons. Finally, the antimatter particles would collide with their positive counterparts, creating a matter-antimatter annihilation. The energy, focused at a single point over and over, would start to produce gamma rays and, theoretically, Cherenkov radiation. If the latter happened, that *might* signal enough energy had been created at a single point in space-time to create a fracture.

And that's where the fun would begin.

Two years prior, with little more than spare parts and a keen knowledge of physics, Yuna Hiyashi created a particle accelerator near McAuliffe Base, under the Martian terrain itself, and managed to open a portal between our world and…another. That other world, Greene believed, was related to our own, and may have been split apart in a kind of quantum singularity ages ago. It had taken the better part of a year to scrounge up the funding, but Greene had finally been able to convince the Joint Space Command to allow him to begin accelerator experiments that would try to replicate the conditions surrounding the dimensional rift—though ideally without the aggressive alien warlord that they encountered last time. Half of Mars had been closed off to resource exploitation as a result, and there were more than a few folks—Greene's boss included—who felt the idea was pretty dangerous. But Greene, a former Peabody-winning science journalist and holovision star, could be pretty convincing when he needed to be.

"Peak power," Jimenez reported, confirming Greene's own readouts. "We have a strong Higgs field now. Ready to knock it down?"

Greene nodded, unnecessarily given that nobody was watching. "Let's do it. Go for final sequence."

The last several positrons were gathered and sent flying into the anti-positrons collected by the previous collisions within the accelerator. By aiming this collision at a magnetic suspension of Higgs bosons—another byproduct of the multiple collisions within the great metal tube—the matter-antimatter annihilation would tear apart the Higgs particles as well, destroying the last structure of physical reality within the testing chamber and, ideally, creating a rift in space-time that would re-open the portal between dimensions created on this spot two years prior.

Greene stopped looking at his datapad, instead staring off at the testing chamber some 100 meters away from his position. His HUD zoomed in on the chamber while readouts at the edge of his vision showed the buildup of energy surrounding the intense collisions, now occurring every nanosecond. Waves of energy started leaking out of the containment chamber, and Greene smiled as his HUD and datapad both started to flicker slightly.

"Tachyon emission!" Jimenez said over the comm. "Repeat, we have a tachyon emiss—"

A sudden surge of light from the testing chamber filled Greene's vision as the comm cut out. His HUD winked out, his datapad went dead and he felt the rust-red ground under his boots begin to quake. This...*this*...this was what he was looking for! Even as he staggered backward, the grin on his face grew wider.

And then the light winked out just as quickly as it surged, and all was quiet. Greene stood silently, looking around, struggling to peer out at the testing chamber and particle accelerator without the zoom and data readouts his helmet usually provided.

A hiss of static erupted in his ears. "....McAuliffe...systems...repeat. McAuliffe to Greene, systems are offline. What's your status? Over."

Greene stabbed his comm button again, just as his HUD winked to life once more. "Greene here. Lost electrical, but my systems are rebooting as we speak. What about the experiment?"

Jimenez sounded subdued. "We have a lot of data to analyze, doctor. Meantime, why don't you come on in. We'll send the techs out to look at the accelerator."

In other words, we just spent billions of terras to create a pretty light, Greene mused silently. *Again.* "Roger. Heading in. Greene out."

Minutes later, Greene was in his rover, speeding past the Martian terrain en route to McAuliffe, passing by several now-abandoned mining efforts. Just two years ago, Billiton Minmetals had a team of sixty miners here, primarily after deuterium from the Martian ice cap, but also mining everything from uranium to gold. Now, the base—most of the Martian south pole, really—was under a strict JSC quarantine as Greene and his team tried to recreate the rift between worlds.

Between worlds, Greene thought. *That's the trick, isn't it? It's between worlds. Not one forcing its way in on the other.* He thought back to the immense alien structure that arose from the Martian desert, the archaic mysticism that the people on the "other side" had used in place of science, how dupes on both sides of the dimensional rift had worked in concert, without even knowing it, to almost unleash an ancient evil onto both worlds.

By the time Greene arrived at McAullife, a giant once-white dome turned pink with a thin layer of Martian dust, the physicist's fears and theories were confirmed. He knew intuitively what the data would say. He parked his rover and headed into the airlock. Once the woosh-hiss of air came over him, he lifted off his helmet and entered the garage-like ground floor of the base.

Waiting for him was Jimenez, the Spaniard's black hair perfectly in place, his slight frown another confirmation. The colonel handed Greene a datapad. "Same as before," Jimenez said simply.

Greene walked over to the suit lockers and set the pad down on a bench so that it would project the data holographically as he unsuited. By the time he pulled off the top half of his suit, he had seen enough. "Three tachyons this time?" he said with a rueful smile.

"New record," Jimenez said. "At this rate, we'll achieve interdimensional travel in about four thousand years."

"It was sixteen thousand last week," Greene said as he stepped out of his pressure suit. His coverall wasn't the typical red-and-black of McAuliffe's assigned personnel. Instead, his black uniform bore patches of the American flag and of Joint Space Command—and a third emblem, that of Project DAEDALUS.

The name was originally in homage of the events that occurred on Mars two years prior, and moreso to the other people involved. But someone at JSC managed to make it an acronym that actually worked: Dimensional And Extraterrestrial Defense, Analysis & Logistical Unified Services. Greene remembered there had been some debate about the S, but he didn't care at the time. Still didn't, actually. Those events prompted him to leave his highly rated award-winning holoshow and rejoin JSC as DAEDALUS' science lead. For the first time in decades, he was doing *real* science, cutting-edge science that mattered.

But he and DAEDALUS were going to need some help. Getting it would be the hard part. There were only so many failures the higher-ups would tolerate.

"Unless we can generate more power—exponentially more—we're stuck," Greene said. "What made it work here before was that the folks on the other side were working on the same problem at the same quantum spacetime point, give or take."

"So why aren't they doing experiments as well?" Jimenez asked. "I mean, they seemed to be pretty smart, right?"

Greene smiled as he thought back to the alchemists and mystics he met. "Brilliant. But they also needed some pretty rare materials to make their rituals work. A few, apparently, were the work of lifetimes. Even considering the different temporal flows, I'm not sure they'd be right here doing it anyway. They could be doing it anywhere."

Jimenez took his datapad back. "And I assume you guys are looking for signs elsewhere, yeah?" His question, and the grin that accompanied it, was familiar to anyone working in space or military circles—the signs of someone trying to find out information that he wasn't cleared for.

Greene simply smiled back. "I better report in."

"We sent the data back to Washington. Diaz already sent a vidmail back. I have it up in conference two, waiting for your DNA key," Jimenez said.

The two men climbed the stairs leading up out of the "garage," past the labs and common areas on the second floor, and up to the command center atop the dome. While Jimenez checked in on his crew, Greene ducked into a small room off to the side. Sitting down at the conference table, he opened a holostation and keyed a button. *To think this base used to have actual keyboards and screens two years ago.* "Greene, Evan. Access vidmail."

A small line of red light flashed over three separate areas of his body, scanning and decoding his genome and matching it to the encryption key. The computer cleared Greene's DNA and a holoimage of his boss, Brigadier General Maria Diaz, U.S.A.F., sprang from the center of the conference table and began talking.

"Hey, Evan," she began, sympathy in her voice. "We thought third time might've been a charm. We're going over the data now, but by the time you get this, I figure you'll come up with the same conclusion we will. No dice. Not sure how we can ramp up the power without blowing a hole through Mars, but you'll have some time to ponder it on your way back home."

Greene's eyebrows shot up. He wasn't due to leave Mars for another three months.

"BlueNet is gonna be operational in about four weeks' time, and I want you back here when we switch it on," Diaz continued. "I know your project brief isn't complete there, but if your both-sides theory is correct, then you're not going to get anywhere on Mars unless we get some kind of sign that the guys on the other side of the fence are working on it too. This way, if you're here and BlueNet gives us a ding, we can jump on it with our best guy and maybe make some progress."

Flattery gets you everywhere, General, Greene mused.

BlueNet was DAEDALUS' first major initiative, a network of sensors blanketing the Earth—on the ground, in orbit, on the Moon—all designed to detect unusual levels of Cherenkov radiation. Non-ionized and harmless, Cherenkov radiation appeared as a blue light that occupied a very narrow band on the visible light spectrum. It was commonly found in and around fusion reactors, but it was also a telltale sign of the passage of a tachyon. During the *Daedalus* incident, it seemed half of Mars was turning blue.

BlueNet's sensors would detect Cherenkov radiation from nearly anywhere on the planet and feed that data back into DAEDALUS' headquarters in Washington. Those "hits" would be measured against known producers of Cherenkov radiation, including fusion reactors and cosmic ray activity. If the incident passed those filters, then the DAEDALUS team was ready to head to wherever the Cherenkov radiation was coming from in the hopes that the people from the other side would be using their alchemy to reach our world.

What to do from there…that was the real sticking point. Greene wanted to try to recreate the events of two years ago, possibly using an experimental portable particle accelerator. Others, including Diaz, wanted to take a far more cautious approach, perhaps only generating enough power and subatomic disruption in order to establish communications, rather than create a full gateway. Given that the first incursion into our dimension was decidedly unfriendly, Greene could see her point…in theory. The problem was in the matter of degrees, since it was highly unlikely that the energy needed to send a message would be huge orders of magnitude less than the energy needed to open a full-fledged portal. At that point, why send a note in a bottle when you can just walk over and say hi?

It was the biggest sticking point in Greene's relationship with Diaz since he left his show. He was doing real science, but he had nothing so far to show for it. And now it looked like Diaz was pulling the plug.

"I see here that there's an outbound cargo flight leaving Chretien Base in two days, and we'll get you a seat on board," Diaz continued. "I'll have Jimenez set you up a flight over there tomorrow. Safe travels. See you in D.C. Diaz out."

The vidmail winked out and the room lights obligingly grew brighter. Chretien Base was another mining operation near the Martian equator, just off the Ius Chasma. It was far smaller than McAuliffe used to be, highly automated with only a dozen people supervising the robots that mined the walls of the chasm for precious minerals. It would be small and cramped and likely smell bad.

On the bright side, they were miners. He might be able to cadge a drink off someone. After today, he needed it. For now, he settled in and started sending some vidmails. He needed to have something to show for all the effort up on Mars, after all, if he ever wanted to try again.

August 18, 1798

"A proper drink would go well right about now," Wilkes commented from the wheel. "An ale, or even a bit of wine, then. Something besides grog, at any rate."

Weatherby smiled as the pilot chatted amiably with the midshipman twenty years his junior. It was the mid's watch—Welling, was it? Yes, Welling. Fine lad.—and Weatherby was merely taking in the morning breeze upon the quarterdeck with coffee in hand, as was his wont at sea. Gar'uk knew to have a cup ready upon the compass table by eight bells, and the rest of the crew knew to leave it be until the captain was ready for it. Rank, Weatherby would readily admit, has its privileges.

The captain gazed out across the waters to the rest of his tiny squadron. *Bellerophon* and *Majestic* managed to limp along as best they could, though there was barely enough time in Egypt to patch their hulls before Nelson insisted they leave for Portsmouth. The crew of *Bellerophon* managed to erect a single working mast, to match the one left unscathed on *Majestic*. As a result, they were barely doing four knots despite a breeze that seemed to make *Fortitude* outright jittery, as if she could taste the wind and wanted to let fly.

Bellerophon and *Majestic*, along with the relatively hale *Swiftsure* to the north, still kept their guns out and trained upon their French prizes. Within the perimeter of these four English ships was, first and foremost, *Franklin*, now under the command of O'Brian, with a double compliment of marines from various other parts of the fleet to aid him. Given the multitude of prizes and the scarcity of English sailors to bring them home, *Franklin* in particular was partially given over to its former crew to sail, under the very watchful eyes of the marines. Weatherby had hoped to personally inspect *Franklin* and its crew—he had something of a knack for weeding out potential trouble-makers among any crew, captive or not—but he had spent his last hours in port trying vainly to smooth over James Saumarez' ruffled feathers. Saumarez was, of course, perfectly courteous and mannered during their rather lengthy luncheon, but ultimately faulted Weatherby for taking *Orion*'s place in the engagement. The higher in rank you rose, it seemed, the more your peers and fellow officers disguised their true intentions behind thinly-veiled smiles and curt public displays of respect.

By the end of it, Weatherby simply wished Saumarez would punch him and be done with it. He had done as Nelson suggested, and to no avail. Politics were not his forte, nor would they be, he felt. Give him enemies who fought honestly and honorably, and he would be the happiest man alive.

Weatherby regretted not being able to inspect *Franklin* before they departed, but he knew O'Brian was fluent in French, and would easily overhear any rumblings amongst the crew. Given that O'Brian planned to be generous with both rations and grog, Weatherby imagined the French would be subservient enough for the voyage home. Only two of the French officers remained aboard—both spoke English, and both were fairly junior. The situation was not uncommon in the slightest among the navies of the Known Worlds. In exchange for their best behavior, the French sailors would be paroled and allowed their freedom—and if those worthies took advantage of this freedom and failed to report back to the French navy for further duty, so much the better.

It seemed O'Brian and *Franklin* were good for each other, for the repairs to the French ship were happening apace. Already, the main and mizzen masts had been replaced, and Weatherby could see workers bringing a new foremast up from the ship's hold. The same could not be said for the other three prizes in the squadron. *Tonnant, Aquilon* and the ancient *Conquerant* were all third rates, and all were underway with but a single jury mast. There were very few French who wished to stay aboard, even with the promise of a return to France, and Weatherby could not entirely blame them. *Conquerant*, in particular, was a sorry ship indeed. While technically a 74-gun third-rate, she had a compliment of but 400 men and mere 12- and 18-pound guns prior to the battle, and was quickly decimated under English fire. Those that survived the battle seemed quite happy to be paroled to the deserts around Alexandria, where Napoleon's troops were said to be welcoming them into the army, rather than chance another voyage aboard the creaky ship. So these other prizes were manned by skeleton crews from Nelson's fleet. There was no dearth of volunteers among the English, of course, given the chance to return home and be first in line for prize money.

Far ahead of the convoy was the sloop HMS *Mutine*, scouting their course for signs of another French squadron. Thankfully, it seemed the French had most of their Mediterranean fleet at Aboukir Bay, but one could never tell whether there would be a second wave, or a squadron newly arrived from the French colonies on Venus or Ganymede, to give them trouble.

"Good morning, sir," Barnes said with a salute, which Weatherby returned with a small smile. "I hope you've found everything in order this morning. Any discrepancies have been noted in the log and are being dealt with."

Second—now First, actually—Lieutenant Barnes was a good man, if somewhat…unimaginative, perhaps, was the right word…when it came to anything except the maintenance and order of a ship. "I see that, Mr. Barnes. A thorough job of it, as always," Weatherby replied. "The only thing that concerns me on such a fine morning is our alchemical stores. You note that we are low on a number of things, particularly shot and curatives."

Barnes looked somewhat chagrined at this, though Weatherby knew his comment was a bit unfair. His broad face grew slightly ruddy, and his eyes widened a touch. "Well, I know Dr. Hawkins has been working very hard to replenish our supplies, sir. Of course, we used quite a bit of shot in the engagement, and we sent our extra curatives off to the French once the battle was won."

"Of course, and rightly so," Weatherby murmured. "You know as well as I that law and custom require it. But now," he added, "I see we're low on many things. Please have Dr. Hawkins report to the quarterdeck, if you would, Mr. Barnes."

A few shouts and roughly three minutes later, a skinny, slightly disheveled alchemist appeared before Weatherby, looking exhausted and terribly nervous. There was no doubt that Dr. Charles Hawkins was a competent alchemist. He knew the *Royal Navy Handbook of Alchemical Praxes and Policies* (the seventh edition, edited by one Dr. A. Finch) like the back of his hand. He spent his off hours deep in research and experimentation. He was, by all appearances, thoroughly dedicated to the mystic sciences. But by God, he was something of a wreck at all times: Nervous, jittery, wide-eyed, slightly sweaty, and seemingly ready to cry out at any moment, all for no good reason. His countenance was pale and drawn, his thin lips pressed into a kind of permanent grimace, and his broad forehead was often dappled in dewy perspiration…as it was now.

"Dr. Hawkins reporting as ordered, Captain Weatherby," Hawkins said formally.

"At ease, doctor," Weatherby said, shocked at the sight of the man, for he looked even more ruinous than usual. "Do you wish to sit? Have you been getting enough sleep?"

Hawkins managed a slight grin that, surprisingly, made him look even more distressed…and distressing to the viewer as well. "I am well, thank you, sir. The casualties are recovering well, and the last should be out from under my care in a week's time."

"Very good, very good," Weatherby said, still unable to tear his eyes off the man. "I'm sure the care of our good, brave men has taken you away from your other duties, and rightly so. Can you apprise me of the status of our stores? Your usual praxes?"

Hawkins did, haltingly and with more than a touch of angst. There were precious few curatives left, and indeed, the doctor had been spending his nights creating more, in case they should be set upon en route to Portsmouth. Soon, however, the raw materials necessary would be in short supply, as they had little time in Egypt for resupply. The Venusian extracts and dried leaves—the most efficacious ingredients in most healing elixirs—were quickly being depleted.

Likewise, the ship itself was in short supply of Mercurium, a most remarkable substance—named for the planet upon which it could be found—that gave speed and maneuverability to ships and allowed them to rise from the seas to the Void without having to catch the solar wind within the aurorae at the poles of the Known Worlds. England had something of a monopoly on Mercurium, making the Royal Navy nigh-dominant in the Void, let alone at sea. For the French, it was a rare prize, used sparingly—if at all.

Finally, Hawkins reported, the ship's alchemical shot was likewise in short supply, though not as much as their other deficits. This was, to Weatherby's mind, the least of their problems, as any three vessels of frigate size or larger would result in the loss of his prizes anyway. Their best hope was to simply get home to England with all haste, and pray to avoid all other ships until then.

Naturally, Weatherby and the rest of Nelson's fleet had scoured their prizes for any kind of alchemical treasures aboard, and some of their stores had been replenished that way. But curatives, especially, were always of short supply after an engagement such as Aboukir Bay.

With Weatherby admonishing him to mind his own health and welfare, Hawkins was dismissed to continue his work. Weatherby knew he had been spoilt working alongside Finch for much of his career. From *Daedalus* in '79, through his post as first officer of *Invincible,* then the command of his own frigate, HMS *Brilliant* in '84, Finch had been there by his side, regularly working alchemical miracles and making them seem effortless.

But when Weatherby took command of HMS *Intrepid*, a 60-gun fourth-rate, in '89, Finch had already decided to leave the service as he had become enamored of the political changes occurring in France, and had sought to encourage the societal experimentation there. It had been a sore point between the two men for a number of years, but not so sensitive that it had threatened their friendship overmuch. Finch had always been something of a political creature, despite his aristocratic upbringing and his study of the Great Work. He once called politics "the alchemy of governance," a term to which the late Benjamin Franklin had introduced him.

Yet it seemed the French Revolution was far too leaden to turn into gold. Now, Weatherby mused, at least Finch was back working for the Crown. Despite their close ties, the Navy man had often wondered whether the alchemist would one day go too far in his researches, whether they be political or alchemical. Finch, he knew, would make a terrible enemy, though certainly one with an appreciable cunning and a great deal of panache.

"Captain!" Barnes shouted from amidships, starboard side, breaking Weatherby's reverie. "Something's wrong with *Franklin*!"

Weatherby quickly moved to the right-hand railing of the quarterdeck, nearly upsetting his coffee in the process. He put his cup and saucer down and brought out his glass, aiming it at the larger, 80-gun ship that had begun to drift to the north, away from *Fortitude* and toward *Majestic*. Weatherby could see a number of crewmen dashing back and forth on the main deck, and could even make out O'Brian talking animatedly to one of the French officers, gesturing wildly toward the sails above....

...which were unfurling. *Franklin* was not only turning away from the squadron, but she was gaining speed as well.

"Beat to quarters and make full sail!" Weatherby yelled. "Wilkes! Four points to the north! Come about and make for *Franklin*!"

The decks of *Fortitude* were quickly awash in frenetic activity, as the night watch poured out onto the main deck and began climbing to the tops in order to unfurl all the ship's sails. Marines likewise began their ascent, muskets slung across their backs, while below decks, Weatherby could hear the gun crews readying their weapons. Meanwhile, Wilkes turned northerly and began to pursue the *Franklin*, which was now heading nearly due north and aimed directly for the water between *Swiftsure* and *Majestic*.

Weatherby turned to the young mid, who was doing an admirable job of directing matters on the quarterdeck, as he had not yet been relieved. "Walling, I shall take this watch now. Well done," Weatherby said. "Signal *Swiftsure* to intercept *Franklin*. I fear that there are a few too many French left aboard."

That was, of course, the problem with prizes, especially large ones. It takes too many hands to sail them, and they are too slow to outrun enemy ships wishing to retake them. So one depends on the former enemy crew to bring the prize home, with the promise of good treatment and a quick repatriation. Most of the time, it worked well.

But every now and again....

"Smoke from the *Franklin's* stern!" Barnes reported, his glass still trained on the fleeing French ship. A moment later, the unmistakable bass *whoosh* of a cannon ball careened past *Fortitude's* port side. The French had enough control of the ship, then, to fire the chase guns aft, aiming for the one vessel that could stop her in her tracks—*Fortitude.*

Weatherby frowned deeply, knowing his next move would endanger the life of his first lieutenant, a man who served with him since he was a mere boy. "Fire the forward chase guns," Weatherby said to Walling, who relayed his orders with a shout.

Moments later, cannon fire erupted from under *Fortitude's* bowspirit, and the captain could see two lines of alchemical fire streak toward *Franklin.*

"Planesails!" Barnes barked from his new position at the bow of the ship. "She's heading aloft!"

"Damn! How the hell are they doing that?" Weatherby growled, snapping his own glass open. Yes, the French ship had unfurled two sets of new sails, hanging off the port and starboard sides of the ship. These plane sails were critical for navigating in three dimensions, both in the Void itself as well as on ascent and decent to one of the Known Worlds. Apparently, the rarity of Mercurium amongst the French fleet was something of a fallacy, at least in this instance.

The captain also saw that his two chase guns hit their mark, smashing through the lower glass of the *Franklin's* stern and ripping through its nameplate. Every ship was most vulnerable at the stern—there were precious few ways to fortify the endmost part of a ship without weighing it down overmuch—and Weatherby knew his alchemical shot was likely wreaking bloody havoc inside the French gundecks.

But it was too late. The *Franklin* began to emerge from the waters of the Mediterranean and quickly began its ascent into the skies of Earth, buoyed by mystical alchemy and a great deal of daring. Weatherby had a decision to make, and quickly.

"Walling, signal the *Swiftsure* to take command and seek safe harbor immediately," Weatherby ordered. "Rig the ship for the Void and begin your ascent as soon as possible."

Wide-eyed and altogether beside himself with excitement and fear, the young midshipman nonetheless relayed Weatherby's orders quickly and efficiently. Weatherby meanwhile watched the minute adjustments the *Franklin* made as she climbed out of Earth's skies, stopping only to glance at the orrery of the Known Worlds contained within the compass table in front of the ship's wheel.

"Venus, perhaps. Mercury, possibly. But not Jupiter," Weatherby mused to himself. "Of course, they could simply circle the Moon and try to come back down."

He heard Barnes clear his throat next to him. "Sir, this would leave our prizes unprotected," he murmured, so as not to be overheard questioning Weatherby's authority by the rest of the crew.

"Which is why they were told to seek safe harbor," Weatherby said, a touch of impatience creeping into his voice. "Meanwhile, we have a conundrum on our hands."

"The escaped ship is certainly vexing, sir, especially with Mr. O'Brian aboard..." Barnes began. Weatherby snapped his glass shut, however, and wheeled on him.

"'Tis more than just vexing, Mr. Barnes," Weatherby said sternly. "It is outright infuriating that we somehow allowed enough French men onto one ship to become a problem, and that they have enough leaders aboard to rally their men. It is unforgiveable that we managed to somehow miss the fact that there was a quantity of Mercurium on this ship that we did not take for ourselves, which not only failed to bolster our stores but gave the damned frogs a rapid means of escape!

"And what's more," Weatherby continued, realization dawning upon him, "it is intolerable that we should somehow fail to notice all this, given that Napoleon's invasion of Egypt seemed to be a terrestrial affair. Why would he even equip a vessel, let alone an 80-gun third rate, with Mercurium when it is so damnably rare and expensive for the French? No, this ship was meant to leave Earth and go somewhere else as part of a greater plan, Mr. Barnes. And our bumbling efforts in her capture have allowed her to continue upon this course!" Weatherby spun 'round once more. "Mr. Walling! Why are we not in the Void yet?"

The young mid now looked quite terrified, given his captain's tirade. "Sir! I—"

Walling's sentence was cut off as the *Fortitude* suddenly nosed up and began her own climb toward the stars. Buffeted by the winds, the men quickly hunkered down lower and began tying their body lines on. Weatherby, however, stood tall and began peering after *Franklin* once more, leaving it to the unflappable Gar'uk to tie the captain's body line around his waist.

"Where are you going, *Franklin*?" he muttered. "And why aren't you more like your namesake?" Then again, he remembered that particular namesake as a brilliant, cagey man. It seemed the ship had aspirations of emulation after all. Mostly, however, he felt immensely guilty he had not seen to the ship's security in person, having instead tried to engage in the politics of the service. He could only hope it would not cost his first lieutenant his life.

June 16, 2132

"I still can't find them!" Stephane groused he scanned the space around *Armstrong*. "They must be using some kind of camouflage or shielding or something. Sensors aren't picking up anything!"

This had been the case ever since *Armstrong* detected the errant transmission from the Chinese weeks ago. Multiple searches along their possible trajectory—from Earth, from Jovian satellites, from the *Armstrong* itself—resulted in nothing.

But while the search turned up nothing new, their situation was very different—the *Armstrong* was minutes away from a series of complex maneuvers to enter the Saturn system. And the last thing they wanted was to hit an errant Chinese spaceship en route to Titan.

"Keep scanning," Nilssen ordered. "Shaila, how we doing?"

Shaila smiled, her hands gripping the holocontrols firmly thanks to force-feedback gloves. She wore the visor that allowed her to see space in a nearly 360-degree configuration, with the bulk of the ship behind her outlined against the black of space and Saturn's bright rings. "We've a good wind at our back, sir," she quipped. "All systems nominal."

"Incoming message from Houston," Archie said, switching his holocontrols over to comms. "Want to hear it?"

Nilssen nodded and a quick headshot of Admiral Hans Gerlich, chief of the U.S./E.U. Joint Space Command, appeared at the corner of Shaila's field of vision. "*Armstrong,* this is Gerlich. You're on approach, so I won't take up too much of your time. Nothing new on the Chinese—the government's still denying they're even there, and we certainly can't find them. In the end, I hope you guys are still first. Either way, you've already done us proud. Good luck and safe travels. You're go for insertion into Saturn orbit. Gerlich out."

The headshot winked out, leaving Shaila to scan the horizon in front of her once more. Below her, through her HUD, she could see some of the larger individual chunks of ice that made up Saturn's rings. Those chunks quickly coalesced into a flat plane of rings stretching out before her. *Armstrong's* course was taking the ship just 10,000 kilometers above the ring plane at its closest point. The ship would then slip in between the rings and Saturn itself, using the gravity of the gas giant to slingshot around and, with a timely jolt from *Armstrong's* engines, place the ship into an elliptical orbit that, in a few days' time, eventually take it to Titan, where history—and an orbiting food and fuel depot ship—awaited.

Stephane's voice chimed into her headset from his sensor station below on the observation deck. "Remember, cherie, you are *not* a leaf on the wind."

Shaila's grin grew wider. She had used that phrase a lot in training, until Stephane reminded her of what happened to the character who once said it, long ago in a 2-D space flick. "Roger that. I'm still going to soar," she replied.

"Cut the chatter, you two," Nilssen said, though he bore a faint smile himself. "I need all aboard to keep eyes open. You see something out there, you flag it, even if it doesn't look like it'll impact insertion."

This was, of course, somewhat redundant, as the ship's computer was also scanning the space around the ship far more frequently, and with greater thoroughness, than the crew could possibly manage. Shaila knew that Nilssen believed in keeping all hands busy during stressful periods, even when 99 percent of the mission was in the hands of the computer and the pilot—Shaila herself.

The ship vibrated slightly and, a moment later, Shaila saw a chunk of ice explode into shards several dozen kilometers below her. The HUD zoomed in dutifully for a moment, and Shaila quickly scanned the readout next to the image. The ice had been roughly the size of a chair, and would have come within two kilometers of the ship. The computer thus used its high-frequency microwave emitter to blast the ice into snowflakes.

The emitter was a legacy of JSC's 2128 voyage to Jupiter aboard *Atlantis*. A routine survey of the Galilean moons turned into a nightmare when a small meteor slammed into the ship as it emerged from its braking maneuver. Of the eight crew, seven were lost, most succumbing to intensely painful radiation poisoning due to the loss of their rad shielding. The surviving crew member managed to place the ship in a long, slow orbit back to Earth, but it took nearly thirteen months to return home.

It took Shaila, the sole survivor, another three years—and a brush with another dimension—to put it all behind her. Mostly. She tried not to flinch at each emitter burst, but couldn't help gripping the holocontrols a little tighter. In the back of her mind, she hoped the force-feedback gloves wouldn't short out.

"Coming up on main engine burn in thirty seconds," Shaila said, prompted by the notification in her HUD. "All systems nominal."

She flicked a holoswitch and her flight path appeared before her, superimposed against the looming mass of Saturn and the plane of its rings. They would alter course slightly in order to slip in between the planet and its innermost rings—roughly 6,000 kilometers of space between the innermost D-ring and the upper reaches of Saturn's atmosphere. The trick here was to fly over the D-ring without causing any major perturbances within its structure. The D-ring was made of very small, fine particulates, primarily ice, that would easily scatter in the wake of *Armstrong*'s approach if they weren't careful. The result could be a shower of particles spinning planetward at several hundred kilometers per second—potentially endangering the ship.

Snow swirling across a starry sky.

Shaila shook her head to clear it. Not now. There was too much to do, too much to monitor. She blinked several times and flexed her fingers. There wouldn't be an issue, she told herself. The flight path took them more than a thousand kilometers over the inner edge of the D-ring, and any particles dislodged from orbit would rain down upon Saturn well behind the ship. At least, that was the idea. If they rained down on *Tienlong*, well…the Chinese should've filed a bloody flight plan, then, shouldn't they?

"Go for main engine burn in three…two…one. Main engine burn," Shaila intoned, once more fully focused on the task at hand. Immediately, the ship's preprogrammed flight plan fired the engines, and the ship's attitude adjusted slightly, headed for the dark gap between planet and ice.

"Signal detected! Incoming object!"

Stephane's voice echoed in Shaila's ears a moment. Immediately, her HUD drew her attention to a point above and to her left. Something was racing toward the planet just as quickly as *Armstrong*.

"What is it?" Shaila demanded, throwing protocol out the window for a moment. She was, after all, the one flying the damn ship.

"It's the God damn Chinese," Archie said before Stephane could respond. "Got some kind of antireflective coating on the ship, but we're close enough to get sensor readings. Titanium, electrical and…yep, there's their engine burn."

"Projected course, Archie," Nilssen said. A moment later, the other ship's course was highlighted in yellow on Shaila's field of vision.

The two flight paths would cross roughly 3,000 kilometers above Saturn.

"Shit," Nilssen swore. "Hall, take over on comms and get on the horn. Tell those fuckers to adjust course. All comm protocols."

A moment later, Hall's voice came through their headsets: "Attention, unidentified ship. This is the JSCS *Armstrong*. You are on course to impact this ship. Our flight plan is pre-approved by the U.N. Space Treaty Directorate. Divert immediately. Repeat, divert immediately." She then launched into a carefully pronounced Chinese version of the broadcast, helpfully translated by the ship's computer. Of course, the Chinese would probably have a translation subroutine aboard as well, but nobody was taking chances.

Seconds ticked by in silence, with Shaila splitting her attention between the *Armstrong*'s systems and the little red dot that was drawing closer and closer.

"No response," Hall said.

"Put it on a loop and repeat ad nauseum," Nilssen ordered. "I want them to be sick of it by the time all is said and done. Archie, time to go to plan B."

"Already on it," the engineer said. While not technically the ship's navigator, nobody else on board could wrangle the computers as quickly as he could, and his reflexes tested out as second only to Shaila's despite his age. "If we deviate much, we'll lose Titan," he said. "It's gonna be close."

"That's why Jain gets the big bucks," Nilssen said. "Give us options. We've got our second engine burn in three minutes."

Shaila thought about remarking that she really didn't get paid well enough for this, but figured she'd been hanging out with Stephane far too long and kept her mouth shut.

A moment later, three white tracks appeared on their holodisplays. "Primary still gets us to Titan, but a day or two late," Archie said. "Secondary and tertiary put us into a different orbit that takes us past Rhea and Enceladus first. Primary is gonna be real tight, and it depends if they change course or not."

Shaila zoomed in on the primary course adjustment. It looked like the two ships could come within a few kilometers of each other. "Close doesn't begin to describe it," she muttered. "If they blink, we're either shooting off to Uranus or diving into Saturn."

"That's our course," Nilssen said simply. "Hall, broadcast our updated course to our friends out there and advise them to stay on their present heading. If they don't, tell them they'll probably kill us all."

Shaila turned quickly to see Nilssen frowning at his display, his forehead creased with worry despite the nonchalance in his voice. "Think they'll play ball?" Shaila asked quietly.

"Depends if they feel like being assholes or not," the colonel responded. "Or maybe they don't have enough fuel to change course. Maybe they *want* us to skip Titan. Who the hell knows? Bastards."

"Colonel, if we don't hit Titan first, we could lose out on the rights," Hall said from the observation deck. "That makes this mission a huge wash."

Shaila and Nilssen traded a look. "I recognize, Liz," Nilssen said. "Right now, I just want to get us into orbit in one piece. If they screw us over, you can sue the hell out of 'em."

"We'll do that anyway. And....OK, sir, getting a lot of comm traffic off the Chinese ship now that we're close enough," Hall said. "They're sending a lot of signals back to Earth."

"Can you hack in?" Nilssen demanded.

"It's encrypted to hell and back. It'll take a few hours to decode."

"Record it," the colonel said. "At least we can figure out what their deal is."

Shaila saw the timestamp in her HUD ticking down. "Looks like fifteen seconds to new engine burn," she reported. "Still go for primary alternative course."

Suddenly, alarms sounded throughout the ship, and a pulse of red drew Shaila's attention back toward the Chinese.

They were adjusting course, heading straight for *Armstrong* at 5,000 kilometers a second. And their own microwave emitter was powering up.

"Colonel, recommend evasive. Now," Shaila said, the coolness in her voice masking all else as she flipped holoswitches and prepared to wrest control away from the computer.

"Go for evasive," Nilssen said. "Archie, get the comp to recalculate a course ASAP."

"Love you, Stephane," Shaila muttered before grabbing the yoke and sending *Armstrong* into a dive straight toward Saturn.

CHAPTER 4

August 20, 1798

The glass beaker bubbled with an angry percussiveness, each pale blue sphere disappearing with a pop and releasing a fine mist into the air as the flame below continued agitating the mixture. The elixir was nearly complete, and the dozen young faces surrounding the table upon which the beaker lay were rapt in wonder and attention.

"Now, let us remember the key steps," Finch lectured slowly, in Arabic, to his students. "First, we must break down the substances, which we did by placing the Ioian ores and Venusian *ur'lak* root into the sulfuric acid. Then the purification, which is what we've done with the flames here, and that bit of Europan ice. What's next?"

Four hands went up at once, but Finch looked for the stragglers, settling upon one bored looking boy of perhaps twelve, the one whose father didn't believe would make a warrior. And so, he would learn alchemy. It was those that gave Finch the hardest time. "Mohammed?"

The boy stared at the floor and recited the words from rote. "It is the *rubedo, murshid.* The final stage in which it is refined."

"Indeed it is, young one. So given these ingredients and processes, what do you think should be applied to generate a healing elixir for wounds?" Finch asked the class.

Another flurry of hands were raised. Finch pointed to another of the boys—they were all boys, of course. "It is jasmine flower!" the boy said proudly.

Finch smiled. "Not unless you want to fall in love with your doctor," he said, which produced a slew of giggles. "The properties of jasmine are far too weighted toward Venus for our purposes. Anyone else?"

Mohammed raised his hand tentatively. "What would the blood from a Martian sand beast do?"

The *murshid* frowned at this, memories coming back quickly and unbidden. "Most likely your internal organs would instantly explode," Finch said sternly. "That is, of course, if you survived the experience of harvesting the blood in the first place!" He reached out to give the boy a rap on the head, but this did little to erase Mohammed's grin, for the thought of exploding innards was universal in its appeal to boys his age.

A third hand shot up, this from a boy named Fareed. "Salamander's tail?"

"Yes! Very good," Finch said, his smile returning. "Remember, alchemy does not necessarily require us to harvest the rare and unusual from the Known Worlds. At times, a simple salamander's tail will suffice." Finch pulled a small, desiccated strip of reptilian anatomy from a box atop the table and dropped it into the beaker. Immediately, the color seeped out of the mixture, leaving a clear, bubbling liquid.

Finch pulled the candle from under the beaker and blew it out. "We leave this cool for an hour and it's ready to use," he said. "Remember, the ingredients are important, but it is less about the individual items and more about what they can do together. An alchemist with the knowledge and Will can produce wonders from the simplest things."

Another boy—Finch forgot his name at the moment, for he was new to the class—piped up. "And what of the Franks, *murshid*? Do they bring powerful alchemy with them?"

Finch was surprised it took the class that long to bring up the French. He had been back in Cairo for more than a week, and this wasn't his first session with his charges, many of whom had families directly affected by Napoleon's invasion. More than half the boys had already lost a father or brother to the Battle of the Pyramids, or subsequent battles. The rest found their families' power and wealth in varying levels of distress; the merchants, naturally, had the easiest time of it, as not even the French could simply walk in and take what they would.

"The French question is interesting," Finch allowed. "I have seen many scholars with them, but I do not know how skilled they may be in the

Great Work. And remember, alchemy is named for Egypt itself. Surely the knowledge of Al-Khem is on par with any the Franks may bring, yes?"

The faces before him broke into wide grins, especially that of Mohammed. Perhaps, Finch thought, the boy might find a way to use his burgeoning knowledge to pursue his dreams after all. He wouldn't be the first warrior to study alchemy for its battlefield applications.

Finch's attention was drawn to the doorway of the study, where Jabir stood looking anxious and holding up a small piece of paper. "All right," Finch said. "We're done for today. Thank you."

The boys each left their coins upon the table—as with other scholars, Finch charged by the lesson—and dashed from the room and out of the house. They were excused early today, but Finch felt that the lesson had been a good one. Besides, they would each get a small vial of the curative tomorrow.

"What is it, Jabir?" Finch asked in English. The boy needed work on his language skills anyway.

The boy looked worried. "There is a Frank here to see you. There are two soldiers with him."

Finch, however, smiled broadly. "About bloody time. This Frank is dressed well?"

Jabir nodded. "He looks like a peacock."

"Excellent!" Finch rubbed his hands together. "It seems our English spy-merchants have done well enough. Let's go and say *bonjour*."

Jabir led the way through Finch's house—a large one for a foreigner, and a sure sign of the beys' favor—until they arrived in an open-air parlor. Two French soldiers, looking distinctly uncomfortable in their wool uniforms, flanked the door and kept watch over the gentleman, who was peering at one of Finch's bookshelves.

"*Monsieur*, welcome to my home," Finch said in passable French. "What may I do—why, Dolomieu!!" In his surprise, Finch lapsed into English. "What in God's name are you doing here?"

The gentleman smiled most broadly at Finch's surprise, and it was a charming smile, writ upon a handsome face. Deodat Gratet de Dolomieu was perhaps one of France's finest alchemists of the *materia* school, special-izing in the alchemical properties of minerals. He was also something of an adventurer and ladies' man, and when Finch first met him a decade ago, they had developed common kinship over the Great Work, good wine and questionable women.

"Andrew!" the Frenchman said, striding toward Finch with arms out-stretched. The two met in a ferocious hug, punctuated by kisses on each cheek. "Look at you!" Dolomieu scanned Finch's kaftan and robes with a broad grin. "Don't you look perfectly native!"

"I should have known you'd be among these *savants* I've heard so much about," Finch said, equally pleased. For a man of forty-eight years, Dolomieu remained the picture of health, thanks to numerous mountain treks in search of minerals and, perhaps, a few alchemical treatments in a nod to vanity. He was a short, wiry man with a shock of graying hair atop his head, and his coat and breeches spoke of fine tailoring, with the cut of his linen offering a hint of panache. "So you've come to divine the secrets of ancient Egypt, have you?"

Dolomieu laughed heartily. "Oh, goodness, I very much doubt we will do so much, Andrew. We are a company of lost men, scholars and bookworms thrust into the desert with hot clothes and bad wine. And why are you in such a place where alcohol is forbidden by law? Not to mention how the women are covered head to toe in bedsheets!"

And comments such as these are why the French will not make friends, Finch thought. *No matter how many proclamations Napoleon issues saying he is a fellow Muslim.* "I do hope you keep such opinions to yourself on the streets, Deodat. These comments are likely a stoning offense. And you will not have enough time to analyze the rocks before they hit your head!"

"Like I said, we are lost men, all of us," Dolomieu said, though the brief shadow that crossed his thin, angular face showed the truth of his words. "General Bonaparte has scholarly ambitions along with his military ones, and so we come to fulfill them. Now, Andrew, will you leave me standing here, or will you get me something to drink? I am parched!"

A few minutes later, the two were sitting in the shade of a fig tree in Finch's modest courtyard, with Jabir serving tea. A small fountain in the center of the courtyard bubbled agreeably, helping to mask the hustle and bustle of Cairo's streets outside the walls of the house. The two men chatted amiably and excitedly about their activities since they last met, the fates of old acquaintances and what life was like in Cairo.

"You must understand, Deo, the Muslims here, they take it all quite se-riously," Finch said. "Insulting their religion and customs will mark you as an enemy far more than simply occupying the land. The fruits of the Enlightenment are all well and good, but they cannot be positioned as being better, but rather just new and different. Something to add to life here, not to replace anything."

Dolomieu nodded. "We have seen as much already. Not a day goes by where one of the *savants* insults a merchant or imam or some such. We have invited many of their scholars to attend us, but they have not taken up the opportunity thus far."

"Maybe you should be attending them," Finch replied pointedly. "This land is old. Alchemy got its start here. Surely, they've not our scientific methods, and their works are cloaked in superstition and religious trappings. Only the truly wise, they say, may know the secrets of Al-Khem and still walk with God."

Dolomieu snorted at this. "Which is why it was all too easy for Napoleon to invade, Andrew. As you well know, any man who considers himself a scholar knows something of the Great Work, even if he hasn't the aptitude for its higher secrets. And we have worked hard in France to strip away these cloaks of folly. Alchemy is science, not magic, and it should be treated as such!"

"And this is why you will not be met with welcome here," Finch said. "You must understand these people, not try to change them."

"Spoken like an Egyptian," Dolomieu said. "How long have you been here?"

"Five years. And I came as a student, not a master, which is why they have welcomed me," Finch said. "I have made some little headway in teaching alchemy to others here, even as I learn from their greatest workers. But I walk a fine line, and I show the utmost respect for their imams and priests when I cannot steer clear of them entirely. You would be wise to do the same."

"Wisdom, I'm afraid, does not come easily to us," Dolomieu said sadly. "But we are here, and we have things we are set upon doing, so they must be done. Or tried. Do you know of Claude Louis Berthollet?"

Finch nodded. "A fine alchemist, said to understand both *materia* and *vitalis* quite well. He is here as well?"

"He is why I'm here, despite your agreeable company," Dolomieu said. "He is perhaps foremost among our little company, though Gaspard Monge is the leader of our group appointed by Bonaparte. But it is Berthollet who has excited the scholars here as to the wonders of Egypt, and the secrets that lie between the desert sands."

"And what secrets are these, Deo?"

The geologist merely shrugged in that perfectly equivocal way so common to all Frenchmen. "He has yet to say, really. But he has asked for you. More precisely, he has asked me to determine whether you are trustworthy."

Finch laughed at this. "You know I'm not."

"This is what I have told him," Dolomieu said, grinning. "You were a friend of the Revolution for a time, but you are English. I told Berthollet as much, if only to dissuade him from dragging you into this. But from what we are told by the natives here, there is no other European in Cairo who knows both the country and the mystic sciences as well as you. And so I must ask, Andrew, how is your relationship with your homeland?"

Finch knew the question was coming. He'd been crafting his answer for days, with all the care and precision usually given over to his workings. "You know I supported the Revolution, Deo," he replied cautiously. "I've no love for the Crown and the politicians and the bankers who pull their strings. But you also must know that I feel France has squandered its opportunity. Look at what happened on Ganymede. They threw off the English yoke and have made for themselves a nice little democracy. No beheadings. No Robespierre."

Dolomieu's smile dropped as he nodded grimly. "I agree with you, *ami*. But France may yet make things right. For now, however, I must simply be assured that we may…shall we say…consult with you as we begin our explorations here."

And that is the opening, Finch thought. "Scholarship and alchemy should have no borders, Deo. You know that. So long as your band of *savants* is here for the right reasons, I shall be glad of your company."

This actually gave the Frenchman pause. "I cannot say whether the reasons are right, because I've not been told enough," he said, echoing Finch's caution. "There are plans afoot that only a handful of us know. The fact that I am to secure your cooperation tells me only that they are intimately intertwined with Egypt itself."

Finch polished off his tea. "Then leave it to me to determine whether you are in the right or not," he said. "Rest assured, I am a scholar first. Should your reasons be sound, you may count on me."

Dolomieu smiled as he rose from his chair. "I know you, Andrew. That is more than enough. There is a meeting six days from now, the first of what we are calling *l'Institut d'Egypte*. I invite you to attend."

Finch rose and extended his hand. "And so I shall. Thank you, Deo. I look forward to it."

With a few more formalities and off-color jokes, Jabir ushered Dolomieu out, leaving Finch to stare idly at the fountain, deep in thought until Jabir returned.

"*Murshid?*" the boy asked.

"Yes?"

"This man, he is a friend?"

Finch smiled up at the boy. "Yes, he is."

This seemed to trouble Jabir. "Then you lied to a friend?"

"I lied to a friend, yes," Finch sighed. "The French have come with an army of scholars, and I do not know why they are here. So I must find out." He took up a quill and paper from the table and scribbled a note. "Go to the *suq* and give this to the spice merchant, Mr. Gregory. For now, I will keep Nelson apprised of what's happened."

The boy took the note. "And later?"

"We'll see."

June 16, 2132

"Maria, we're talking about an ongoing scientific experiment here, one that cost several hundred billion terras to construct and maintain! 'We'll see' isn't exactly something I can run with," Greene complained as he struggled to match strides with Maj. Gen. Maria Diaz, USAF, despite being several centimeters taller than her.

The general, a short Hispanic woman with a powerful build and the barest streaks of gray in her hair, couldn't help but smile at the charismatic Greene's unusual fluster as she walked toward the conference room at DAEDALUS headquarters. "Evan, we have four trained quantum physicists at McAuliffe now. Your baby is in good hands. Fact is, I need you here and now to help us make sense of the BlueNet data. You know that."

Greene did indeed know that, but wasn't about to concede the point. "Maria, I'm the science lead for DAEDALUS. The science is happening

69

on Mars." For the third time in the past two days, he tapped on his data-pad to send her the results of the latest particle accelerator experiment. "I had a chance to review all the data en route from Mars, and I've spelled out a number of new ideas for future experiments, experiments that could conceivably regulate the interaction between two dimensions. That's real science. This…this is running down a bunch of dead ends!"

Diaz wheeled around and fixed Greene with a hard stare. Despite having to look up at him, the general suddenly seemed a lot taller than the physicist. "Listen, Evan. You know damn well our first job is defense, not experimentation. If there's another invasion into our Solar System, we're the ones at the front lines. And that means I need my best brain here, on Earth, fully engaged when we power up BlueNet and try to figure out when and where those incursions might happen. Why do we keep having his conversation? You knew what you signed onto. You're the science lead, but I'm the one in charge, and I'm answerable to a lot of people who feel the same way I do."

Greene stood his ground well, considering. "OK, fine. But say we see the people on the other side opening up something. Our experiments on Mars can teach us how to close portals as well as open them. Yes, it's risky, but right now, we have no defense other than to be able to say, yes, they're coming. Then what? The basic science needs to be better understood before we can defend anything. And what if Weatherby and his crew are trying to reach us? They had a better grasp of the situation than we did last time."

"Evan, I know you. You want to open the door and see what's over there," Diaz replied. Her words were quiet, but carried accusation as well.

"Yeah, you're right, I do. There are entire new worlds out there. And if we can figure this out, we can go see them. That's what this should be about."

They both stared at each other a moment. This wasn't the first sparring match for either of them, though it was perhaps the most honest one they had in a while.

"You know that can't happen, Evan," Diaz said with an air of finality. "We'll talk later. Right now, I need you in there. Let's go."

The general didn't wait for an answer, instead wheeling around again and striding off, leaving Greene at an uncharacteristic loss of words. Defeated for the moment and feeling more than a little chastened, Greene slowly walked behind Diaz as they headed to the BlueNet control center, parked incongruously in a simple office building along the Potomac River in Washington, D.C.

All four of the DAEDALUS team's BlueNet techs were at their holostations around a large central holoimager. The walls flickered through a variety of two-D readouts, and it took but a glance for Greene to see that all systems were nominal. The last of thirty-four satellites had been launched yesterday, and they were now linked to each other and to various tracking stations around the Earth and Moon. The satellites were not solely dedicated to BlueNet—most were commercial or military sats with a little bit of extra comm and sensor gear attached. When the government offers to pick up some costs in exchange for a bit of payload—for scientific purposes, of course—most companies don't ask too many questions.

The result was a network that blanketed the Earth, Moon and surrounding space with Cherenkov radiation detectors. If there was so much as a blink of Cherenkov radiation anywhere within a million kilometers of Earth, they'd know about it in five seconds or less.

"Huntington, report," Diaz said.

A young African-American woman, wearing the uniform of a U.S. Marine captain, turned to her. "All systems go for network launch, general."

"Thanks, Maggie. Greene, how we doing on our databases?" Diaz asked.

Greene had already settled into his station and didn't bother turning around as he responded. "We have U.S. Department of Energy and IAEA databases up and running, along with CIA, MI6 and UN Security Council intelligence reports," he replied. "All fusion reactors, public and classified, should be ready to map against the results. Same with all your potential 'anomalous' sites."

Greene finally turned around and shared a quick smile with Diaz at this, their earlier animosity temporarily forgotten. At Diaz' insistence, the BlueNet monitoring system included a database of carefully selected sites including the Pyramids of Giza, Machu Picchu, the Nazca lines and any number of sites that may have been a landing point for little green men in ages past.

Two years ago, Diaz would have laughed herself out of government service for even considering such sites. Given what she'd been through, however, she figured better safe than sorry. When she delved into the slew of "ancient astronaut" theories that had cropped up over the past century or so—actually, she had a junior officer do it, but still—she found to her great surprise that some of the seemingly spurious evidence of earlier ancient visitations by "aliens" actually dovetailed with some of the architectural images she had seen in the Martian "temple" that appeared two years ago. There were elements in Weatherby's journal that likewise had surprising links to many of the various conspiracy theories, even the more outlandish ones.

Another voice piped in. "General Diaz, we have our observers online and ready, ma'am," said Flight Lieutenant James Coogan of the U.K. Royal Air Force. He was Diaz' logistics officer and all around gopher, and she figured DAEDALUS would collapse under its own bureaucratic weight without the good cheer and fanatical organization of the British officer.

"Thanks, Jimmy, and hello out there to any and all observing," Diaz said. She knew the higher ups at JSC, the EU Defense Forces, the Pentagon and a few political folks would probably be listening in. She specifically asked Jimmy not to show her the list; she was nervous enough as is. "We've gone through our final system checks and we've laid in our database work. Thank you everyone who helped us with the intelligence and information we needed to make this system reliable." She took a deep breath. "Captain Huntington, deploy BlueNet."

The young woman nodded and began working her holocontrols, the images of which glowed faintly around her hands. "Initiating startup sequencing. Network links active...sensors responding to diagnostics...all sensors in position...and all sensors now active, ma'am. BlueNet is active and feeding data, ma'am."

Diaz thought there should be a cheer or something, but everyone just kept hunkered down. Probably for the best—the work was just beginning. "All right then. Greene, go to work."

Now this was a role Greene was accustomed to. He took a holographic model of the Earth-Moon system and transferred it across the room to the central holoimager, then stood up and followed it there as the image grew larger and blue dots began to appear all around the two worlds. "All right, then. The idea here is to identify any and all sources of Cherenkov radiation currently active anywhere in the Earth-Moon system. And so far, we've got some pretty good C-rad hits already," he said. "Let's take away the DoE and IAEA stuff first."

A few seconds later, several of the blue lights winked out. "OK, those were the registered fusion energy sites around the world operating at reported capacity. Next, let's throw the military sites out there." More lights winked out, including every single ocean- and Moon-based light. "OK. Those are the subs and ships at sea, all the lunar colonies. Nothing around the Moon?" Greene reached out and gave the holoimage of the moon a quick spin in his hands to check. "Good," he said as the Moon righted itself in orbit once more. "All right, let's put the black stuff on there now."

The "black stuff," as Greene liked to call it, represented the highly classified sites that would be producing fusion energy, such as research labs and top-secret military installations. For some, even DAEDALUS—an ultra top-secret program in its own right—was given only a location and a rough sense of the fusion energy output…and nothing else.

More lights winked out. There were precious few left on the globe. "All right, that should be everything. It looks like we've got a hit in Bolivia, another in the Congo, two in China, one in Russia and one in the middle of the Egyptian desert."

The holoimager collated the material into a readout on the far wall of the conference room. "Let's see," Diaz said, walking over to it. "Bolivia and the Congo…plenty of crap going on both those places. Figure some portables? Jimmy, let's get some intel on those places."

"Yes, ma'am," Coogan said briskly. "Shall I also try for the Chinese and Russian sites? We've nothing at all there."

Diaz smiled grimly. "You can try. If you get anything, I'm transferring your ass to CIA. They could use the help."

"Very good, ma'am, though I'd prefer double-oh status with MI6 if you don't mind," Coogan said. "What about Egypt? Looks like it's some kind of misread on an existing site?"

Diaz used her fingers to expand the view on the Egyptian site. The hit was on a power plant along the newly-created Siwa Bay in the middle of the Egypt-Libyan desert. It was supposed to anchor an effort by the Egyptian government to create a new resort city, much like Dubai or Abu Dhabi before they fell under the rising oceans—the same rising oceans that created Siwa Bay in the middle of the desert.

"Jimmy? This data fresh?" Diaz asked. "Says here they're not up and running yet."

The operations officer checked his readout. "Latest reports are in this morning. They're still months away, but I suppose they could be testing."

"Who's they?" the general asked.

"It's a contract player," Coogan responded. "They have a license from the Islamic League government to set it up. Financing from the Chinese, apparently. Any more than that and we run up against the Corporate Protection act. That means we have to ask directly. And nicely."

That prompted a deep frown from the general. "Corporate Protection Act, my ass," she groused. "Fine, go ask. And give me some creativity on the alternatives. I want to know more about it."

Coogan smiled. "Creativity" and "alternatives" had quickly become DAEDALUS codewords for a great deal of chicanery and shenanigans, so long as they were ultimately plausibly denied. Being a multinational task force made such things modestly easier, given the different laws and ethics of the countries involved. "Yes, ma'am," Coogan said primly.

"And same goes for the other sites," Diaz said. "Everything and anything we can find out, we find out. Better safe than scaly." She turned to gaze at the holoimage of the Earth and Moon again. The unknown blue lights remained; no others appeared. "All right, then. Nice job, everyone. Observers, thanks for being online. Seeing as you're cleared for this, you're probably cleared for whatever we find via BlueNet, so we'll keep you posted should anything come up. I feel confident that if there is an incursion, we'll be able to respond to it quickly and effectively. Thanks for your support. Diaz out."

The general strode out of the command center and made for her office, just around the corner, but she noticed Greene quick on her heels. "Maria?"

Diaz let herself enjoy a small grim smile before turning on her heel and reassuming her command demeanor. "Yes, Evan?"

Greene looked both embarrassed and slightly excited. "We got one."

"One what?"

At this, Greene looked genuinely perplexed. "Your database. We got a hit on one of the anomalous sites you logged in."

In all the excitement, Diaz had forgotten about that. She had Huntington link all her favorite ancient-astronaut sites into BlueNet's filtering systems, so that any Cherenkov radiation detected there would immediately be upgraded to the next level of scrutiny. In all honesty, despite all she had seen on Mars, she really hadn't believed they'd get a hit—but she ordered everyone on the DAEDALUS project to leave the database out of their presentation to their backers…just in case.

"No shit? Where's the hit?" Diaz said.

"Teotihuacan."

"You mean to tell me there's a potential Cherenkov hit in the middle of suburban Mexico City?"

"Well, there is a rather large Aztec temple complex there," Greene said, calling up the data on his pad. "Looks like…huh, interesting. It's a pretty old ruin, and the walls include substantial amounts of mica. The ancient-astronaut nuts think it could've served as both heat and radiation shielding."

Diaz couldn't help but raise an eyebrow at this. She'd read up on enough ancient-astronaut theories to know that whatever the question was, the answer was aliens. She took Greene's datapad and scanned it quickly. There was just enough Cherenkov radiation there to warrant an investigation. "Well, I'll be damned," she said, handing it back. "Well, I suppose we should check it out."

Greene grimaced. "I was afraid you'd say that. I was hoping to grab a few weeks off after the BlueNet launch, recharge after Mars."

Diaz smiled, knowing full well she was taking a crap all over Greene's day. Again. "I know, but I need you to track this down first. Take Huntington with you. Chances are, there's a plausible explanation for it, so let's not start with the human sacrifices, got it?"

"Yes, ma'am," Greene said curtly before retreating, likely afraid Diaz would add something more unpalatable to the mix. She felt bad about riding herd on him—he'd been talking about getting some R&R ever since he left Mars—but she figured he'd enjoy debunking whatever pseudoscience he came across. And if there *was* something there, he'd be the right one to identify it.

Diaz scribbled an order into her datapad and sent it along to Coogan. He'd set up their flights and gear, and let Huntington know she was signed onto the goose chase. As soon as she sent off the message, a chime went off on her pad. There was a new message waiting for her.

"ARMSTRONG IN TROUBLE. CHINESE ARRIVED WHEN THEY DID. WILL KEEP YOU POSTED. –GERLICH"

Diaz swore under her breath. She immediately accessed all the data she could on *Armstrong*. They had last heard from the ship more than twenty minutes ago.

There had been nothing since.

"Communications are down. Repeat, link with Earth is lost," Hall reported as the *Armstrong* dove nose-first toward the salmon atmosphere of Saturn. "Telemetry is down. We're cut off."

Shaila nodded reflexively, concentrating fully on the ship's controls. She barely noticed the Chinese ship zip by at a distance of 127 kilometers—close enough for it to be seen as a shooting star off the port side. In the grand scale of spaceflight, with ships traveling at thousands of kilometers per hour, it was nothing short of a near-collision.

"I need a heading, Archie," she snapped as her HUD popped up with multiple warnings. "We're forty-five seconds from atmospheric entry."

"Well, then pull the hell up!" Archie groused from below. "Get us into some kind of orbit, then we'll figure out the damned heading."

Shaila had already began to arrest the ship's dive, but it would be close—they'd skirt the outer reaches of the planet's atmosphere, putting further drag on the ship. Not to mention the potential friction.

Nilssen saw it too. "Prepare to deploy heat shield," he ordered. Immediately, the ship's computer produced a small set of holocontrols off to Shaila's right. The inflatable heat shielding was more a precaution at this stage, but had been included in the *Armstrong*'s construction for other types of missions. "Chart possible headings for deployment."

A pair of lines entered into Shaila's view. One put the *Armstrong* a little deeper into the atmosphere, while the other would require a steep climb—now. Shaila jerked the controls upward, sending all aboard sinking into their seats as a temporary bout of gravity took hold. If she could avoid the atmosphere, she would.

She heard metal groan as the thrusters fired, testing the structural integrity of the ship. Swearing under her breath, she pivoted the *Armstrong* to put as much of the planet under her as possible. Looking up for a moment, she saw Saturn's rings neatly bisect the void above her. The ship was slowing considerably—too slow. Warnings started popping up in red in her HUD, followed by an alarm sound.

"We need main engine burst ASAP," she said. "Archie, help me out!"

Moments passed in what seemed like eons before Archie's voice came back on the comm. "Main engine burn in three…two…one. Go."

Shaila pushed the holographic throttle forward and the ship shuddered even more as it struggled to free itself of Saturn's immense gravity. She looked down and saw the clouds begin to recede somewhat, though the planet still stretched off toward the horizon. "Heading?" she asked.

A fuel warning added to the chaotic display before her. They had cut it too close, and they were burning far more of their reserves than they should. "A real close heading would be good," she added, though Archie and the rest of the crew were seeing the same warnings she saw.

"Come to heading 164 mark 8," Archie replied. "If we're lucky, we'll make Enceladus."

And there goes Titan, Shaila said as she adjusted course. The ship rose up further as the navigation thrusters fired, and soon there was black sky and rings before her. "How much room we going to have over those rings?" she asked.

"Enough. Quit your bitching," Archie snapped.

Nilssen was busy next to her doing his own calculations. "About 750 kilometers," he said. "Don't miss."

At this, she actually grinned. "Roger that. Heads up for rogues. I don't want to get smacked with an ice cube." As if on cue, the microwave emitter lashed out at an errant piece of Saturn's rings, destroying a chunk of ice the size of a small car.

"We're out of Saturn's gravity well," Nilssen reported. "Engines stop."

The roar that filled the ship's command center came to an abrupt halt, leaving everyone in a shaky, relieved silence. Shaila swatted away the various warnings in her holographic display until the ones she wanted remained. "We are on course for orbital insertion around Enceladus. ETA in 23.5 hours."

"Fuel status is iffy," Nilssen said. "We'll end up dipping into reserves to get into orbit. Hall, how are we on comm?"

It took a moment before the exec came back. "We've reestablished contact with Earth. They're going crazy looking for us."

Nilssen smiled. "Tell them we're fine and send them the recordings and telemetry. I'll file a full report later." He turned to Shaila and gave her a pat on the shoulder. "Nice driving, kid."

Shaila gave him a nod, but wasn't in the mood to say much more. She let go of the holocontrols and felt her hands cramp and tremble. There was no governor on the force-feedback gauntlets she wore, and she felt the effects of white-knuckling the yoke.

"All hands, this is Nilssen," the skipper said—unnecessary, since they were all on the same commlink, but to Shaila it seemed appropriate. "We're on course for Enceladus. I know we were all excited about hitting Titan first, but it looks like our Chinese friends will get there ahead of us. That's fine—Enceladus is just as interesting. Looks like we're going need a refuel op when we get there to top up. Hall, ask Houston whether the depot ship has enough juice to break orbit and meet us there. If not, we'll have to go on rations for a couple weeks. At least we'll have plenty of water. Until then, let's do a full ship diagnostic and get back to work. Nilssen out."

They were lucky. Enceladus was small, but it was perhaps the second-most interesting moon around Saturn. In orbit within the outermost of Saturn's rings, the little moon was covered in a crust of ice—with an ocean of salty water just 40 kilometers below the surface that was rich in deuterium. Thankfully, they wouldn't have to drill down that far—the moon's southern hemisphere was a hotbed of cryovolcanism, spewing water from the oceans below into space on a regular basis. Their "refuel op," designed for just such an emergency, basically entailed putting a hose up to one of the geysers and letting it flow through a filter to separate the deuterium. The deuterium would flow into a storage take in one of the landers, which would then be flown back up to *Armstrong*. It would take at least a dozen lander trips to make a meaningful dent in *Armstrong*'s fuel situation, but it was something. Actual hydrocarbon propellants would've been far more efficient—they had similar procedures in place for refueling from Titan's hydrocarbon oceans—but deuterium would do the trick as well.

Plus, they'd at least get some drinking water, once properly desalinated and purified. Half-rations would stretch out their remaining food stores for a month, which was probably a week more than they needed. Still, Shaila hoped Houston could maneuver the depot ship from Titan to Enceladus. She didn't feel like dieting.

Shaila peeled her visor and gauntlets off and slipped them into the pouch on her chair. The 360-degree view of space immediately winked out, replaced by the dull gray of the command center. She looked around to see the rest of the crew likewise powering down. Archie was frowning considerably, probably worried about how the new mission profile would affect his engines. And Nilssen…he looked pissed.

"Durand, do we have a track on that Chinese ship?" he demanded.

"Yes, sir. They've pulled out of Saturn's gravity well and appear to be on course for Titan."

"Fuckers," the marine spat. "Hall, aim a comm at them and remind them in no uncertain terms that the depot ship there is JSC property. If they approach it, we'll consider it an act of piracy under the U.N. Space Charter."

Nilssen unbuckled his harness and floated out of the command center—likely heading to his quarters to begin filing what would be a lengthy report to Houston. Archie soon followed, muttering about his reactor and the stress on the ship, leaving Shaila to stare out the forward window, looking at the stars and the expanse of Saturn's rings beneath the ships, stretching out toward the horizon. She let her mind shut down, instead losing herself in the scene before her. It may have been messy, but they arrived. Intact.

"Next time I drive," came a comforting Gallic voice from behind her.

She turned and grinned up at Stephane. He looked pale; she knew from their mission training that he had something of a sensitive stomach, and the gyrations of their maneuvers probably had him reaching for the ubiquitous barf bag in the pouch on his chair. "Oh, please," she teased. "Remember our trip to Paris? You nearly drove our damn scooter into the Seine."

Stephane floated above her chair, coming to rest upside down in front of her, his face even with hers. "And you nearly drove us into a planet."

"But I didn't," she said, the pride coming out. "I surfed those rings like a champ."

"You did," he replied, kissing her gently. "You were amazing."

"Thanks," she said, sheepish. "Now it's your turn."

"I know. Enceladus," he grinned as he righted himself and settled into the seat next to hers. "I admit, I was looking forward to Enceladus more than Titan. The geologic factors at play are far more interesting. And the water. The possibility of life! And we get to go first."

This had been a frequent topic of discussion late at night for the two of them. Titan was ExEn's primary objective, the entire reason they helped finance the mission. A world larger than Mercury, with oceans of hydrocarbon fuels to make Earth's dwindling resources look like a dripping faucet?

Even if it took another century to fully exploit, it was a giant ball of cash floating in the heavens.

But the scientists wanted a hard look at Enceladus. Europa, the icy moon of Jupiter, hadn't yielded any signs of life yet, so Enceladus was the big hope for alien lifeforms in the Solar System. *Well,* this *solar system,* Shaila thought.

"Liz is pissed?" Shaila asked.

"She adjusted quickly," Stephane allowed with a bemused grin. "She is already planning the details of her lawsuit against anyone who tries to claim Titan's resources. Something about flight plan filings and right of first intent. Honestly, it all seemed very legal-ish and silly, but she seems all right with it. Plus, if you claim water on Enceladus, you claim a lot of potential resources there, too."

"Let them fight it out," Shaila said. "I'm just happy to be here."

"Yes," he said quietly. "We did it. We made it to Saturn."

The two of them simply floated together in silence, holding hands, as the rings of Saturn passed below them.

CHAPTER 5

August 23, 1798

Weatherby and Dr. Hawkins sat in the courtyard of a weathered hacienda, drinking thin wine and attempting to pass the time congenially. This was difficult, however, and not simply because of the wine's poor quality. This was Venus, in the town of Esperanza, and in the intense heat and humidity of the cloudy afternoon, Weatherby felt that the town was poorly named indeed. His own despair, subtle and quiet and visible to only those who knew him well, may have further colored his impression of the town.

His company was only slightly more agreeable, though not by much. Hawkins had traded his customary uniform for the garb of a respectable gentleman—as did Weatherby, a veteran of clandestine visits to the Green Planet—but the new, more comfortable attire did little to strip the alchemist of his anxious demeanor. Furthermore, the sweat upon his brow was even more prodigious now, and his face even more drawn and pallid than before, which was quite a feat of coloration indeed.

"You are sure, sir, that your valet simply did not wish to be with his own kind, rather than continue in your service?" Hawkins asked, his mild presumption in the matter of Gar'uk's absence an obvious sign of his discomfort with the heat and humidity of Venus, especially a settlement so close to the planet's midsection. "I mean to say, sir, I have no doubt you have treated him most splendidly. But I can't imagine these savages would prefer to remain with any but their fellows."

Weatherby raised an eyebrow at this before checking his pocketwatch; Gar'uk was indeed a bit late, but not unduly so, and it wasn't as though the Venusian lizard-people could tell time adeptly to begin with. "What do you know of the Venusians, doctor?" the captain asked, trying not to make the question pointed.

"Certainly not as much as you, of course, sir," Hawkins demurred. "I know that they are tribal and rather uncivilized, far beyond the most remote tribes of men in Africa. I know these tribes are sometimes differentiated by sub-species, others seemingly by culture or language. And I know you had personal contact with the Va'hak'ri, the tribe of lore-keepers. Their religion is a very primitive anima-based system that knows nothing of God or His Son."

Weatherby nodded. "All true, doctor. Of course, despite the Venusians' primitive state when first discovered, you will find that many have mastered our language to the degree which different anatomies will allow, and some few, such as Gar'uk, can be taught to read and write. But perhaps most importantly, their grasp of the mystic sciences, I am told, exceeds their knowledge of other matters, and is tied closely to the alchemical nature of Venus itself."

"Due respect, Captain Weatherby, but that latter statement is merely theory," Hawkins said, warming to the argument to the point where an actual hint of color touched his cheeks. "It is true their shamanistic rituals take advantage of known alchemical substances, or rather, the plants and animals from which they may be derived. But most researchers to date strongly doubt that there is much more to their rites than lore and legend, and any alchemical wonders derived from such primitive workings is the result of rote repetition born of some ancient happenstance, rather than systemic explorations of the kind that produces true alchemical knowledge."

Weatherby thought back to his first encounter with the Venusians and merely smiled at the doctor. "As you say, Hawkins. I do believe that if mankind were to approach the Venusians without bias or condescension, a more systemic approach to the mystic sciences may be realized." Weatherby then raised his glass in salute. "Of course, I'm a mere ship's captain, not an alchemist like yourself. Ah! And here is Gar'uk now."

The two men sat up as the diminutive lizard man approached, his neck frills in full spread and his reptilian eyes even wider than normal. "Am I late, Captain?" he said, his beak clacking slightly around the words.

"Not unreasonably," Weatherby said. "What news?"

Gar'uk bowed quickly toward Weatherby, then Hawkins, his tail swishing excitedly behind him the whole while. "There is one of my tribe here, and he knew another of another tribe who speaks your French-tongue. And it was he who heard the French-tongue from the ship that came here two days past."

Weatherby turned and gave Hawkins a wicked grin; they had been searching for *Franklin* for the better part of five days. "The French must be worse off than we thought, Doctor! This is good news indeed. Go on, Gar'uk."

The little Venusian was jumping up and down now, and his clawed fingers seemed they would tear through the little shirt and breeches he wore. "And so the French-tongue-men, they went out to see the village human-doctor. They came back after night, got back on their ship, and left."

"Human-doctor?" Hawkins asked.

"Alchemist," Weatherby replied. "That would make sense, especially if their stores were fully depleted upon arrival here. Gar'uk, do you know the way to the human-doctor?"

As it happened, Gar'uk did not. But the little valet dutifully led his captain to his Venusian kinsman, who then led the party to the laborer who knew French, who then led the now-larger party out of the city proper, up a small road through the dense jungle and, about a half-mile later, to a house situated upon the edge of a swamp, built in the Oriental flood-plain style with stilts and a pitched roof on all sides.

"Hask'ara ura'sk na!" came a woman's voice from inside, illustrating a surprising aptitude for Venusian linguistics, it seemed. "Na cela'sk agar gesh'ak!"

"She says the human-doctor is not here, but she can help us if we have ills," Gar'uk replied.

Weatherby nodded at Gar'uk and then cupped a hand to his face. "I say, we're quite well, but would much appreciate a word, if we may," he called out.

"Ah! Just a moment, then!" a muffled woman's voice called back. "I'll be right out!"

Hawkins looked disparagingly at the house. "Who would live upon the edge of a jungle swamp?" he muttered quietly. "Surely an alchemist would do better for himself within the town itself."

Weatherby, for his part, grew pale, for surely, the voice from the house struck him as surely as lightning from a storm. He had assumed Finch's gossip was just that—ill-founded rumor meant to assuage him. And yet…

"That would be true if the alchemist in question sought to make a business of his abilities," Weatherby said finally. Were it any other occasion, the captain might have marveled at Hawkins' seeming lack of imagination. If it wasn't in a text or manual, Weatherby often felt his ship's alchemist would be at quite a loss. Yet Weatherby's mind was elsewhere "There are those who devote themselves to research," he added quietly, "especially here, with Venus being rich in so many different materials, as you know."

"And we are among the latter, sir. A fine deduction," the woman called out from the house. "I should think, then, that you are not—"

The woman's voice stopped suddenly, prompting Weatherby to turn to look up at the home's railed porch. The sight stripped him of words as well.

The woman brushed a strand of blonde hair from her eyes, to join the rest that had been swept up casually in a bun. Her face was lightly tanned, as many were who spent a great deal of time on Venus, for even the clouds could not completely conceal the closer distance from the Sun. The woman wore a simple blouse and a long skirt that reached to the very boards of her porch, and had an apron haphazardly tied around her. Her eyes shone as she regarded the party below, especially Weatherby. A faint smile escaped her lips.

She looked to be no more than twenty-five years old, though Weatherby knew that she was a decade older than that, for he had been but seventeen when they first met, she merely sixteen or so. And they had experienced much together in a brief time.

"Hello, Tom," the woman said, her smile gaining a twinge of sadness. "It is you they set upon the trail then?"

He nodded. "More or less," he replied, finally finding his tongue. "'Twas the ship named for our old friend, was it?"

She smiled broadly now, genuinely. "It was. It made me think of him. And you, I must confess."

Weatherby's face grew red and he straightened his waistcoat unconsciously. "I can say the same." He then noticed his ship's alchemist and three Venusians all looking confused, shifting their gazes between the captain and the woman above in the stilt-house. "Dr. Hawkins, please return to *Forti-*

tude and have Mr. Barnes prepare to make sail. We leave with the tide. And take our helpers here with you, if you please. Gar'uk may stay with me."

Hawkins prepared to protest, but the look in his captain's eye was nothing like he had seen prior—a look of wistfulness, perhaps a touch of sadness, but also steel. "Very well, Captain." After some fussing about, the doctor was picking his way back down the jungle path, two diminutive lizard-men croaking and chirping at his heels.

"*Captain* Weatherby, is it?" the woman said, straightening up. "Do come in."

"Thank you, Miss Baker," he replied, making his way to the steps of the home.

"It is no longer Baker, of course," she replied, leading him into the home, which was decorated with Spartan furniture and a surfeit of books, along with plain tables covered in alchemical laboratory fixtures, boxes and glassware. "Tea?"

"Thank you, yes," Weatherby replied, surveying the general disarray of the home. As the former Miss Anne Baker seemed not to be troubled by it, he would not make anything of it either. "So what shall I call you then?"

The woman rolled her eyes at this. "Please, Tom. After all these years, the formality is hardly required." She took a beaker of water and placed it under a strange apparatus. With the flick of a switch, a gout of flame covered the bottom of the beaker—the water would be ready in mere moments.

"My apologies, Anne," he said. "Old habits, I suppose. And to be fair, we did not part well, and for that I must apologize."

Anne pulled two teacups off a shelf and, sweeping away a pile of papers with her arm, placed them on one of the tables. "I suppose nineteen years is better than not at all," she replied. He was about to protest when he caught the twinkle in her eye and the grin on her face. "It wasn't meant to be then, Tom. And I would not trade my life now for it."

Weatherby blushed again, for he was thinking exactly of such a trade, and felt ashamed for it. "Of course, neither would I," he replied, "though my behavior then…I was a young man, and foolish besides."

"And now?"

"Merely foolish, I suppose," he smiled. "Enough to still be chasing the French across the Void."

Anne nodded as she used a pair of tongs to pull the beaker off the flame and pour the water into the teakettle. "I had assumed you would come," she said. "Well, you as in the English, at any rate. You specifically, that was a surprise."

"What did they want?"

Anne placed the kettle on a tray, along with the cups, and brought it over to where Weatherby was standing. "Oh, damn your manners, Tom. Sit!"

She may have looked twenty-five—no doubt the result of her own precocious knowledge of alchemy—but she spoke like a true matron. He dutifully sat upon a low sofa near one of the tables.

"And as to your question, they wanted my husband," she continued. "And they got him, too."

Weatherby stiffened at this. "Good Lord, they took him?"

Taken aback, Anne fixed her gaze upon Weatherby oddly. "No, goodness no! He went freely, of his own accord!" she replied. "I heard but a little of it, but there was to be a journey and embassage of some kind, and they needed his talents. It was, he told me, quite an opportunity, though he would not share many of the particulars."

Weatherby took the tea she offered and sipped; it was a fine blend of Indian and Venusian teas, perhaps one of the finest he had tasted, which perhaps made the disheveled house even more of a conundrum. "You know not where he went?"

"Even the most agreeable husband does not always tell his wife what she wishes to know," she sighed. "And you know mine. He can be particularly obstinate when the mood strikes."

Weatherby halted in mid-sip, stunned a moment before he finally drew his tea away. "I know him?"

Anne fixed him with a bemused, perturbed stare. "Thomas Weatherby! Was it so difficult a parting that you had not thought to seek out word of me for nearly twenty years?"

It was, actually, and it had taken him at least half those two decades before he finally married another, only to lose her in childbirth. "I'm sorry…I had heard that the Count St. Germain had been mentoring you, and that you had traveled extensively across the Known Worlds. You met Finch back in '93, if I remember."

She shook her head at this. "Damn him, that scoundrel, Finch," she said, but with a small grin. "Of course he would omit such things with you.

You're lucky he's a friend, you know. My husband is indeed Francis, the Count St. Germain."

It took Weatherby several moments for this to sink in. When he had last seen Anne, their differences seemingly had been too great to reconcile. And yet, through the years, Weatherby recognized he had been in the wrong. Despite his own subsequent marriage, and the birth of his daughter, his one, true unreserved joy in life, he had always felt remorse over how they had parted. It was, he felt, a missed opportunity—one that her mentor, the Count St. Germain, had not missed at all.

"I see," Weatherby said, struggling to regain focus. "So the Count....wait, does that make you a Countess, then?"

Anne laughed at this. "You do realize, Tom, that the title was self-appointed. He's no more a count than you're a king. But...when you have a man who could conceivably turn lead to gold or find immortality, few argue the point. So yes, I suppose I'm a Countess!" She straightened her skirts and apron in an exaggerated, fussy way, prompting Weatherby to laugh despite himself and, in the process, completing his mind's journey back to the present.

"The Count is now working for the French," he said simply, with a sense of finality. "That is...problematic."

"Not necessarily," Anne cautioned. "Francis and I have made a point never to involve ourselves in the conflicts of nations. If there's something going on between England and France, I'm quite sure that Francis is not involved in it."

Weatherby set his cup down upon the table and rose. "I'm sorry, Anne. The *Franklin* took part in an invasion of Egypt by the French. We captured it and were returning to Portsmouth with it when the prize crew was overcome and she made for the Void. You remember young midshipman O'Brian?" She nodded, concern growing upon her face. "Well, he is my first lieutenant, and he is aboard *Franklin*. At least, I hope he is, if he's still alive at all.

"Given all this, I must conclude that *Franklin* is off upon some errand of the French general, Bonaparte, and this has everything to do with the conflicts on the Continent. I am sad to say that I must find this ship and see what they are about, because I doubt it is merely embassage, and Dr. Finch—who is now investigating in Egypt itself—agrees that this invasion may conceal greater motives." Weatherby drew nearer and knelt upon one knee before her chair. "I promise you, Anne, I shall do my best to see to the safety of your husband. One of my oldest friends is also aboard that ship, and I've no desire to shoot such a nobly-named vessel from the Void or sea."

Anne nodded. "Thank you, Tom. I believe you." Her voice was quiet, and her eyes glistened. "I do not think I can help you, however."

There was little more to say. They both struggled through the cruel civilities of saying good-bye, but Weatherby eventually extricated himself from the house and, with Gar'uk in tow, made his way through the jungle by the dimming afternoon light, arriving in Esperanza and back to *Fortitude* just as the lanterns around the city had begun to be lit.

"Captain Weatherby, sir, I trust you'll find all in order," Lt. Barnes said once the formalities of bringing the captain aboard were finished. "Your efforts went well?"

Weatherby frowned slightly, and the gloom of the cloudy evening sky was mirrored by his countenance. "I fear not, Mr. Barnes. The *Franklin* was here, but she's two days ahead, and we've no word of her destination. Gather the officers and Hawkins and have them meet me in my cabin. We need to chart the quickest route to the pole and see if there's a port along the way they may have stopped at."

Weatherby turned and stalked to the door of his cabin, tucked under the quarterdeck at the stern of the ship. He opened it and entered, with Gar'uk right behind him, ready to gather his coat. However, the Venusian stopped suddenly and grabbed Weatherby's hand. "Not alone," the lizard-man said quietly, seemingly sniffing at the air. He was right. A dark figure was sitting at Weatherby's table, silhouetted by the window's at the ship's stern. Another seemed to be standing up next to the chair.

"Identify yourselves!" Weatherby shouted.

A moment later, Gar'uk had lit a lamp, revealing the face of Anne St. Germain sitting at the captain's table. Next to her was a boy of about twelve, perhaps thirteen years of age.

"It would seem I need your help, Tom," she said simply. He face had changed; where she was gentle and smiling just an hour prior, here now she was grim and determined. It was a look with which he was well familiar.

"You know where he's going, but not what," Weatherby replied. He had an hour's walk to mull things over, and that was one potentiality he had come upon. Alchemists by their very nature were orderly people, and it struck Weatherby that the home of perhaps the most legendary alchemist in history would be a bit more well-kept. It looked, when he pondered the matter further, as though someone had been rifling through it in search of...something. Given Anne's lack of excuse for the state of her home, he was left to conclude she had been the one to do the rifling. Which meant she had her own questions.

It didn't even occur to Weatherby to ponder how they arrived ahead of him, nor how they stowed away aboard a ship of His Majesty's Navy. He was thoroughly convinced of Anne's alchemical mastery that she could do as she wished.

"What you told me worries me more than you can know," Anne said. "I need to know what he's become involved in."

Weatherby nodded. "And this young man?"

"My son."

Indeed, Weatherby could see Anne's soft features in the boy's face, but also his father's sharp Roman nose. "And you are?" he asked.

"Philip Thomas St. Germain," the boy replied in the manner of the young seeking to impress their elders. "I have heard much about you, Captain Weatherby."

Weatherby spared the boy a brief smile before turning back to Anne. "And you know where he's going?"

"I believe so. I overheard enough to piece things together, I think, combined with what he took and what he left behind," she replied. "I had tried to find out more, but he said little, other than that he might be gone for a year."

A year....

A rap on the door was followed later by Barnes peeking his head inside. "Captain, I....oh, we have guests?"

Weatherby turned. "Indeed we do, and they will be coming with us. Dr. Hawkins will make berth in the wardroom while our guests share his quarters. Have all hands make ready to sail immediately, if you please, and rig for Void-sailing. Set a course for....?" Weatherby turned to Anne.

"Saturn," she said simply.

Of course. The Xan. "Saturn," Weatherby repeated. "At once."

CHAPTER 7

June 17, 2134

We're a few hours away from insertion over Enceladus, and so far it's going as well as can be expected," Lt. Cmdr. Shaila Jain reported, her holographic head hovering over Diaz' desk. "I mean, there's a ton of crap out there that we have to sail through to get there. As you get farther out from Saturn, the rings grow wider and more diffuse, the particles get smaller. Our electromagnetic shielding is crackling several times a second now. It's like flying through a popcorn machine. And the microwave emitter pops off every few minutes or so to take care of the bigger debris. It's made for a stressful watch, but the automated systems seem to be doing a good job of it so far.

"Of course, if we hadn't been pushed off course by the bloody Chinese, we wouldn't have to slog through the worst of the E-ring, now would we? Haven't heard a word from them yet, despite our constant broadcasts. Houston says they've filed a formal protest, for all the good that'll do them. Turns out we can't bring the Titan depot ship here, so we're on rations for a while. Thankfully, if we wait a week or so, Enceladus and Titan will be lined up well for a quick transfer orbit. Meantime, we'll have to work double-time to fill the fuel tanks and get our drinking water desalinated. I wonder what Enceladus water will taste like. I'll try to save some for you.

"We definitely think the Chinese arrival is no accident. Who knows? They may have timed things perfectly to throw us off track and get to Titan first. Weatherby's journal hinted that Titan was the Xan homeworld, after all. I think we have to assume that the Chinese know about Mars, and may even have an idea about your DAEDALUS ops. They're very good at hiding behind the corporate shield laws. Anything you can get us on their ship, and their corporate sponsors, would help. I want to know who's out here with us and why.

"That's it from here. Wrapping up my watch now. Stephane says hi, as usual. He always pesters me to say that." At this, Shaila broke into a genuine grin, which prompted Diaz to smile back at her recording. "*Armstrong* out."

Diaz thumbed off the holoemitter and called up the latest intel on the Chinese ship. The People's Army Survey Ship *Tienlong*, "heavenly dragon" in Chinese, launched for Jupiter last year. Like most planetary survey vessels, *Tienlong* was constructed in orbit. Unlike most vessels, the Chinese had erected a giant shroud—nearly a half mile in diameter—around the ship in orbit, standard procedure for the vast majority of their space endeavors. That made it tough for spy satellites—U.S., E.U., and corporate alike—to see exactly what they were up to. Intel reports were able to trace some unusual components, such as larger fuel and cargo compartments, but at the time they were assumed to be part of a longer Jupiter mission.

It was, Diaz reflected, a dearth of imagination on the intel analysts' part. Sifting through report after report, she could see the pieces of the Chinese mission coming together. A Chinese survey satellite reported "off course" that would end up heading straight for Saturn. The very tight system entry by *Tienlong* that would ultimately see them slingshot around Jupiter for a speed-boost to Saturn. The lack of in-country publicity, even considering the usually tight-lipped Chinese media. And no corporate sponsor announcement....

Corporate sponsorship was a fact of life in 22nd century space exploration and colonization. It made sense, really; Christopher Columbus was looking for a trade route, not a new continent. ExEn was aboard the *Armstrong* in hopes of laying claim to Titan's hydrocarbons, and Diaz' last command, McAuliffe Base on Mars, was financed at the time by Billiton Minmetals, the Australian-Chinese mining concern. Most sponsorships were loudly trumpeted by the respective companies' PR arms, but not all; competitive advantage was hard won around the world, leading to the corporate shield laws that Jain had mentioned. So it wasn't unheard of that the *Tienlong's* sponsor would remain under wraps.

Thankfully, DAEDALUS wasn't bound by such restrictions. More precisely, they were empowered by their sponsors, the United States and the European Union, to take extra-legal steps "when necessary as part of its mission to investigate extradimensional phenomena that may potentially harm the Earth." The language was broad enough—and Diaz' legal team talented enough—to allow for most anything.

Thus, through the incredible information-gathering talents of Coogan, Diaz already knew *Tienlong* was sponsored by Total-Suez, and by her old acquaintance, Harry Yu. She called up an image of him, which sprang to life over her desk. The black-haired Asian man in the expensive suit smiled out at her. Harold A. Yu, senior vice president of new business development at Total-Suez—and formerly of Billiton Minmetals' Martian operations.

Harry Yu had spent a whole lot of time making McAuliffe Base's mining operations consistently profitable, only to see the entire thing collapse in the wake of the extradimensional incursion. But he did in fact *see* nearly everything that occurred—and what he didn't see, he likely copied from the base computers. Those were strange days, and security wasn't what it should've been, what with the whole ancient Martian temple appearing on the slopes of the Australis Montes range, complete with resident Martian trying to conquer multiple dimensions. While most everyone on Mars spent months in quarantine and debriefing, Harry's Chinese citizenship and corporate privileges let him off pretty easily. Hell, Diaz figured he might not have even been physically searched, let alone interrogated.

So she had to assume, for the sake of security, that Harry Yu knew everything about the *Daedalus* incident. And given that, Total-Suez knew. And since they were sponsoring *Tienlong*....

"Jimmy, I need you," Diaz said. Less than twenty seconds later, Lt. Coogan entered the room.

"Ma'am?" It always sounded like "mum" to Diaz, which made her feel her age. The fact that Coogan always wore a transparent HUD visor and earpiece didn't help either.

She swiped at Harry Yu's file on her holoimager and literally shoved the data toward her assistant. "I need to know where this man is right now."

Coogan's eyes flickered and blinked inside his visor; Diaz could see tiny bursts of light in front of the young man's eyes. "Most of my queries are coming up blank, ma'am. All I know is he has a Nexus-cleared corporate passport."

Diaz frowned. It was getting easier to track actual government spies than to locate corporate executives anymore. "Get on it. Everything you got. I want to know where he is, what he's doing right now. Don't much care how you do it."

"Very good, ma'am. I—wait a moment," Coogan said, his eyes darting around the room once more. "I have Dr. Greene on vidcall for you. Shall I put him through?"

Diaz leaned back in her chair. "Sure. Let's see how he's enjoying Mexico." A moment later, Harry Yu's face was replaced by Evan Greene's. While Diaz was expecting either ironic humor or actual pissed-off-ness, what she saw was genuine concern. "Don't tell me you found something," Diaz said, motioning for Coogan to remain and observe.

"Not what you think, Maria," Greene replied. "But BlueNet's working. There are above-average levels of Cherenkov radiation present at Teotihuacan."

"Source?" Diaz demanded.

"That's the real pisser," Greene said, holding up a piece of electronics that looked like a cyberpunk version of a bowling pin. "Know what this is?"

"Enlighten me."

Greene grinned slightly; he loved to get his lecture on. "This is, in essence, a radiation magnet. It takes ambient radiation in a given area and refocuses it. There are thirty-seven of these here, forming a ring around Teotihuacan."

"Yuna Hiyashi built a ring of gizmos around McAuliffe Base two years ago and we ended up with a frigate in our ops area," Diaz snapped. "Get to the point."

"This isn't like that, Maria. These won't focus enough Cherenkov radiation to do anything at all except to have it show up if someone's looking for it. It boosts the ambient levels to above-ambient, nothing more."

Diaz' frown grew more intense. "That makes no sense. Why do that?"

"Well, if there were folks on the other side of the fence looking for us, there's a non-zero chance these devices might capture a tachyon or two—maybe just enough for them to notice we're here, and maybe send a message in reply. Honestly, it's kind of clever, but not really well conceived."

"Define non-zero."

Greene shrugged. "Global lotto odds, I suppose."

"Then it's useless. What else?"

"Only other thing I can think of is that it took Huntington and I a day and about a million terras to come out here and investigate, so it makes for one helluva distraction."

"And someone put them there."

"That's right," Greene nodded. "On the bright side, this gave me a few neat ideas to play with on the plane ride back."

Diaz exhaled sharply and ran a hand over her face. "All right. Bring every scrap of unauthorized tech back here ASAP. We're gonna find out who put them there and why. Diaz out."

Coogan immediately jumped in. "There are twenty-seven different vendors for this kind of technology. Once we have serial numbers, or even part numbers, we can track down who bought them and when."

"Good man," Diaz said. "For all our top-secret clearance, I think someone's onto DAEDALUS in a big way. And if they know about us, they know about everything else."

"Your friend here…Harry?"

Diaz nodded and rose from her seat. "I want something really fast put on 24-hour standby. Once we track him down, or whoever put that tech out there in Mexico, I want to be there in his face."

Coogan blinked a few times into his HUD. "I can get an executive-class transport in forty-five minutes, but there's no pilot available."

Diaz shot him a look and pointed at the wings on her uniform. "I think I can manage."

August 22, 1798

Cairo can be particularly unkind to Europeans in the summer heat, and despite the early hour, there was plenty of sweat on the brows of the scientists and soldiers gathered in one of the city's newly abandoned palaces. Finch had opted to wear more traditional European attire for the meeting, but his coat and waistcoat were made of far lighter materials than the wool many of the Frenchmen boasted. A few of the savants had taken to wearing Egyptian robes and coats…*on top of* their European attire, and Finch idly wondered which one of them would be the first to pass out.

To make matters worse, the newly formed *Institut d'Egypt* had somehow decided that the first-floor harem room would make the most picturesque setting to launch their endeavor, even though the cooling breezes were hampered by the intricately carved geometry of the *mashrabiya* latticework covering all the windows. Downstairs, Finch could hear a fountain gurgle in the courtyard, which would have been far more preferable.

"You are Dr. Finch, I presume?" came a voice in French from behind him. Finch turned to see a man in a French revolutionary army uniform, with a great deal of braiding and rather impressive-looking epaulets.

"Ah! You must be General Bonaparte," Finch said, smiling and extending his hand. The other man nodded and smiled as they shook; he was evidently pleased to be recognized, though there were few other military men who would make the time for such an endeavor when much of the countryside still required pacifying. But the Institute was Bonaparte's idea, and it seemed he fancied himself a scholar as well as a warrior. Finch knew as much, so the assumption was natural, though he thought the general would be somewhat shorter.

"Dolomieu tells me you are a friend of the revolution, Doctor," Bonaparte said. It was less a question or a statement, more a challenge.

"I am a friend of knowledge and liberty, General," Finch replied, "and foe to any who would curtail either."

Bonaparte nodded and smiled, seemingly quite pleased with the nuanced answer. "Then you are most welcome here among us, Doctor. Now if you'll excuse us, I believe the Institute is about to meet. Where is Monge? Let us begin!"

And with that, the Frenchmen filed into the harem room, leaving Finch outside in the open corridor outside. If there were any question about whether Finch should attend, the stern looks from the French soldiers guarding the doors answered them most assuredly.

Despairing of his mission, Finch sat down upon a bench...and waited.

From his perch, Finch could hear muffled French from inside the room. There were smatterings of applause here and there, and then Napoleon himself took up a fair amount of time, his unusual Corsican accent distinctive even if his words were muddled to Finch's ears.

Finch stood. And paced. Then sat down again. Then stood. All the while, the guards at the doors regarded him warily, if idly. He felt for all the world like an unwelcome suitor, and he was beginning to think Dolomieu was in the wrong for inviting him to begin with. Or that he was in the wrong for taking the offer. Perhaps there were other ways of discerning the motives for the French invasion.

In the midst of wrestling with peevish doubt, and an hour after Finch was left to do so, the meeting in the harem room adjourned, and the *savants* streamed out. Finch waited, arms folded across his chest, as Dolomieu hurried up to him.

"I am so sorry, my friend," he said, looking genuinely contrite and concerned. "I had no idea they would go on for so long. The general," he added, looking around and lowering his voice, "has us worrying about producing enough bread and clean water to feed his armies, rather than any sort of study."

"Then perhaps I should leave you to it," Finch said, trying not to snap at his friend but succeeding only partially. "I'm quite hopeless in the kitchen."

"No, please, Andrew, I've been asked to introduce you to Berthollet," Dolomieu said hurriedly. "Come, please."

Silently, Finch acquiesced and allowed his friend to take his arm and lead him into the harem room. There, an older man wearing the finest clothes was shaking hands with some of the other attendees as they left.

"You must be Andrew Finch," Berthollet said in heavily accented English as Finch approached. "Deodat has told me much of you."

"Hopefully only the best parts," Finch said as he accepted Berthollet's outstretched hand. "Otherwise, I shall be forced to deny it all."

"Deny nothing, young man!" Berthollet responded, a broad smile lighting up his florid face. He was a larger man, with an obvious love of food, but he was barely a few years older than Finch. Both were, in many ways, contemporaries and rivals in terms of aptitude and talent; Finch knew that Berthollet was one of the few Frenchmen to be made a Fellow of the Royal Society in London, as was Finch. "Of course I have heard of you, Dr. Finch, and I am pleased to find you here in Cairo after all. There is much to discuss between us, I think."

"Oh? And what is that, Dr. Berthollet?" Finch asked as innocently as he might muster. *Let the chess game begin*, Finch thought, smiling inwardly.

"I believe our General Bonaparte will wish to be part of this discussion, yes? Ah, there he is now. Come, Doctor," Berthollet said motioning toward the courtyard beyond the harem room. At least, Finch thought, it would be cooler there.

And when they rounded the corner and Finch spotted a table with morning tea, set with four places, he understood why the larger meeting was elsewhere. The general was no fool when it came to the sun.

"Dr. Finch," Bonaparte said with a smile. "Come, partake with us."

With a nod, Finch took his place at Bonaparte's left hand, with Berthollet at his right—a most natural place for him, Finch thought. "I find it interesting, *monsieur general*, that we three are the only ones invited to tea with you," Finch said, helping himself to the tea. "I assume, then, you have other things in mind."

Finch winked at Dolomieu, who looked pale and slightly shocked at Finch's lack of decorum, but Berthollet merely smiled, while Bonaparte let out a short bark of a laugh. "I like you, Dr. Finch!" the general said. "You speak plainly, as I do. So I shall return the favor."

"And I welcome it," Finch said, sipping at his tea and reaching for a piece of toasted bread with jam. Someone took the time to spread the jam on the bread already, which Finch thought was a nice touch, and perhaps telling of the comforts these men were used to.

"You left the English Royal Navy, and England itself, to participate in the events of our glorious revolution," Bonaparte said. "And then you left seven years ago to come to Egypt. Why?"

Finch smiled graciously at this. "You know full well what France was like when I left, *monsieur*. Robespierre's Terror was a betrayal of all that we fought for. France squandered its opportunity. Just look at the United States of Ganymede to see the difference."

"You might have stayed to try to prevent it," Bonaparte said, though with no hint of malice. It was, for all Finch could tell, a simple question, though of course it was anything but.

"I am an alchemist, and a terrible politician," Finch demurred. "I assisted how and when I could, but there comes a time when the waves grow too strong to navigate. And I had no wish to meet Madame Guillotine in the event I was accused of being an English spy."

"Were you?" Berthollet asked brusquely, though with a grim smile upon his face.

"I am also a terrible spy," Finch said. "And I think my move to Cairo, rather than back to England, is telling in that regard."

"Berthollet and Dolomieu say you are among the foremost experts on

Egyptian lore, as well as an alchemist of some renown," Bonaparte said. "We hope, Doctor, we may rely upon you."

"For what, may I ask? I can certainly facilitate some introductions to those among the local populace who have some alchemical training, or knowledge of ancient myth," he said, hoping to strike the right balance of innocence and aid.

Dolomieu actually laughed at this. "Do you think, Andrew, that we have come all this way searching after myths? I think the real alchemy of Egypt shall be prize enough!"

With a sidelong glare at Dolomieu, Bonaparte smiled and rose, prompting all at the table to do the same. "Doctor, it has been a great pleasure," he said, extending his hand. "I have other matters to attend to. Berthollet, you may proceed. Dolomieu, a moment if you please."

Looking excited, Dolomieu quickly shook hands with Finch and bustled off after the Corsican, whose strides quickly took him out of the courtyard. That left Finch alone with Berthollet. "Will you meet me this afternoon at the Mosque of Ibn Tulun? Before the final prayer of the day?" the Frenchman asked him.

Surprised, Finch nodded, and shortly thereafter took his leave. Ibn Tulun was Cairo's oldest surviving intact place of worship, and while it had been improved upon over the years, much of the interior hailed from the 9th century A.D. The mosaic work inside was said to be centuries ahead of its time, and Finch himself had spent more than a few long afternoons there, enjoying the art and consulting with the learned imams there with regard to alchemical practices that would meet with the approval of their customs and laws.

The imams, generally speaking, were highly skeptical of the French intentions to begin with; how Berthollet managed to gain entrance was a mystery. If he had done so at musket-point, then all of Cairo would literally be up in arms, and Bonaparte would not have had time for his little scientific society this past morning.

Finch returned to his home and his tutoring, but was distracted through the rest of the day, and admittedly gave his charges less attention than they deserved—one of them nearly created a massive explosion through an incorrect admixture, but ever-watchful Jabir quickly stayed the boy's hand just as the final errant ingredient was to be added. Chagrined yet grateful,

Finch gave his protégé half the coins from the class, as well as an afternoon at liberty. This served a two-fold purpose: To reward the boy's actions, and to send him off whilst Finch met with Berthollet. Jabir did not understand Finch's agnostic views when it came to politics (or religion, for that matter) and continued to voice his opinion that the French were little more than the newest wave of Western crusaders. Finch had to admit, there was a chance the boy was right.

Now dressed in his customary Egyptian clothing—far better suited to the summer heat—Finch took a leisurely path to the mosque in order to better gauge the Frenchmen's activities in the city. Life, it seemed, continued apace in the sprawling honeycomb of byways and alleys, with vendors hawking their wares and porters moving quickly with their oversized burdens. There were street preachers here and there, as was their wont, and some few were stark naked under the glare of the Sun, barking loudly at passersby. While not entirely common, these individuals were largely tolerated under the beys, as they were believed to be touched by Allah and given license by Him to question the ways of mankind.

Likewise, alchemists of all stripes and talents (or lack thereof) plied their wares alongside the vendors of livestock and bread, cloth and metal. Finch nodded to a few of better repute, but got fewer acknowledgements in return. It was not that he was a Westerner, though he imagined that he might be lumped in with the French should the latter make gross missteps, but rather that he was an accomplished alchemist who taught a rigorous, demanding path to the Great Work, one that was done with the tacit approval of the imams. In Egypt, the teaching of Al-Khem was considerably more secretive, with masters accepting one student at a time, and applying their own unique—some might say eccentric—twists to the Work. Some held it to be nothing short of a religious practice, sharing the ecstatic worldviews of the twirling Sufis, while others felt it was completely unrelated to Islam, which would draw the ire of the imams if said publicly. And still others secretly hewed to the ancient Egyptian rites, calling upon Isis and Osiris and Set in their Workings—something that would get them summarily stoned to death if it came to light.

But for all the secretiveness, the wonders of Al-Khem were on full display. Elixirs and potions of varying levels of authenticity were on offer in many stalls around the city, while the windows of wealthy homes allowed alchemical light to seep forth from shadowed corners. Tools and blades of alchemical steel glinted brightly in the sunshine, and occasionally a rich merchant or wife thereof would glide by on a flying carpet. Finch thought the carpets were highly ostentatious and utterly useless as a great Working, but did on occasion fashion them when the price was right—and he charged a great deal indeed for such luxuries.

The alchemy stalls grew less frequent as Finch approached Ibn Tulun Mosque, for even the least devout amongst the Workers rarely chanced the anger of the imams in such things. In the heat of the afternoon, the approach to the mosque was sparsely populated, and as Finch passed under the minaret into the courtyard proper, there were fewer still inside. He walked slowly to the dome in the center of the courtyard where the ablutions fountain was housed; Finch was careful to show respect to Islam, even though he was not a believer, and after his walk, the cool waters of the fountain felt good upon his face, hands and feet. Thus purified, Finch continued toward the prayer area, where the Muslims would pay homage in the direction of Mecca, as signified by the *mihrab*—a ceremonial alcove—along the rear wall.

He could see Berthollet leaning against a pillar, just inside the hall, as he approached. The Frenchman had at least eschewed his frock coat and cravat, but still looked quite uncomfortable, beads of sweat dotting his broad face, patches of wetness apparent under his arms. Yet he smiled as Finch approached and extended his hand.

"Thank you for coming, Doctor!" Berthollet said. "I am sure you are familiar with this mosque?"

Finch shook hands and smiled. "I am, sir. 'Tis one of the oldest in all Islam, they say. A thousand years, give or take. Is Deodat coming as well?"

"Dolomieu has other matters to attend to, and does not know of our visit here. He is young, and does not know when to speak, and when to be silent, though he is a good, smart man despite this," the Frenchman said, ushering Finch into the prayer area, a columned affair of impressive length, with soaring ceilings and intricate mosaics on the floor. "I have been to many, many mosques since arriving, Doctor, and found this one to be particularly interesting. Have you paid much attention to the architecture here?"

Berthollet's professorial demeanor gave Finch pause; there was something in the man's tone that hinted of a discovery, perhaps. "Not as much as you, I'll wager," Finch replied.

"Perhaps," Berthollet said, his smile widening. "I do not know if you're aware, *monsieur*, but prior to coming here, I had assisted in the cataloging of the Vatican Archives on behalf of General Bonaparte when he liberated the Italian peninsula. There was much knowledge in that storeroom that had been kept out of our hands for centuries, all in the name of religious orthodoxy! Can you imagine?"

Finch could, of course. The relationship between practitioners of the Great Work and the Roman Catholic Church was far more strained than within most Islamic nations. The Church had even produced mechanical orreries that showed the Sun and the other planets going around the Earth—even though these were utterly useless for navigating the Known Worlds. Thankfully, it seemed the Church was at least coming around to the fact that the Sun was central in the Void, for it had been quite obvious for three centuries of exploration.

Berthollet led Finch to the very center of the long, rectangular prayer room, facing the *mihrab*. "This is the very direction of Mecca, to the south-southeast, yes?" Berthollet asked.

"Quite so, and they did a fine job of it, considering the age of the place," Finch said.

"Now look closely at the floor, if you would, doctor," Berthollet said.

Finch looked down at his feet. The floor was tiled in an intricate geometric pattern, one that showed advanced knowledge of mathematics. There were numerous green and blue lines on a white background, intersecting regularly. Finch attempted to discern a pattern beyond that of geometry, but to no avail. There was, sad to say, a great deal of damage done to the floor over the centuries, and it was cracked in places. He knew the imams there were considering doing away with it entirely, in favor of a simpler stone floor.

After a minute, Finch looked up, slightly annoyed. "There is clearly something more here, sir, though I cannot say what."

A cat with a fat mouse could not have looked more satisfied than Berthollet at that moment. "Do you have something that might allow you to filter out colors before your eyes?"

Finch gasped slightly as he grasped it; he had walked across this floor dozens of times over the past decade! Immediately, he began rummaging around in the small bag he carried with him. He pulled out a pair of eyeglasses, one with several different colored lenses on swivels attached to the frame.

"What have you found?" he muttered, all pretense at formality lost. He settled the glasses onto his nose and began flipping the lenses back and forth, filtering out white, then blue, then green....

Until the faint outline of a red line appeared before his eyes, snaking away to the very western corner of the room.

"What do we have here?" he said, immediately walking forward to follow the line, cannily embedded in the tiles below. So focused on his trail, Finch nearly careened into not one, but two of the columns in the room before he reached the corner, several dozen yards away. There, he saw a bright red dot, partially obscured by dirt and dust.

"A map," he breathed.

"Yes indeed, Doctor. A map!" Berthollet said. The Frenchman had followed him to the corner of the room, and now stood smiling, hands clasped behind his back. "But to what, do you think?"

Finch could not help but cast a profoundly irritated glance at the man. "Without a sense of scale, monsieur, it is quite difficult to say, but –"

Then he saw another red line behind the other alchemist, one that deftly snaked across the multiple entrances to the prayer room. Finch set off again, following this line. It was far more jagged than the last, dipping and swooping in places, but still relatively straight. It stopped perhaps three yards past the *mihrab*, then curved up and disappeared into the courtyard.

Finch looked back, then down, then back again. "I know this, somehow."

"You should. You've been here many years now."

Then it struck him. "Egypt!" Finch exclaimed. "This is the coastline!"

Berthollet actually clapped his hands a few times. "Very good, sir! And so that alcove there, that would be this very spot, Cairo. And thus, that line?"

Finch pondered a moment. "It goes almost directly east, which would take it into the very depths of the desert." He put his hands on his hips, deep in thought. "But that leads nowhere."

"Surely, in all recorded history, someone from the West has made that journey, would you think?"

It took a full two minutes of thinking and staring before Finch came upon the answer, and it stunned him to his core. "Surely not," he said quietly. "Alexander?"

"I believe it to be so," Berthollet said. "The scrolls I read in the Vatican Archive were taken from Alexandria's library itself. I believe this is the route Alexander and Ptolemy took to the temple of Amun-Ra more than two thousand years ago.

"And," he added solemnly, "is it too much to assume that, situated so far from the Nile and the wars of the ancient peoples, this temple may be where some of the greatest alchemical treasures of the Ancient World reside, perhaps knowledge from the Xan or the Martians themselves?"

Finch marveled at this, and a small smile grew upon his face.

CHAPTER 8

June 18, 2134

Shaila fired the *Armstrong's* braking rockets a final time, causing a minor tremor to wash over the ship before it settled languorously into orbit around the tiny snowball of Enceladus. With a circumference of less than 1,600 kilometers and an exceptionally minimal gravity, Enceladus wasn't going to make maintaining orbit easy, but Shaila managed to get the ship into something steady, just 50 kilometers from the surface. Even so, they'd be zipping around the little moon once an hour or so, which would be dizzying if anyone had the time to look out the window.

The orbit also had to avoid the moon's southern pole, which erupted frequently—they observed three such eruptions on their day-long approach from Saturn. The amount of water spit out of Enceladus' "tiger stripes"—fissures on the surface that led directly to the salty ocean underneath—was minimal, but the ship's electromagnetic shielding was already working overtime as they traveled through the more diffuse E-ring, and they didn't want to get hit with any more ice particles than absolutely necessary.

Two hours later, Archie was still reminding her about the dangers the ice posed. "You'll have to take it slow getting down there," he said as she prepared Lander One's checklist. "No more than 100 kph until you're within 25 clicks of the surface. Otherwise, the ice crystals could cause structural damage." He sounded grouchy as usual, but he kept running his gnarled hands through his white hair—a sure tell if there ever was one. Shaila liked to think of him as the gruff-but-lovable great-grandfather she never had... or really wanted.

"I know, Archie," she smiled, but not without a hint of frustration. "Moon's not going anywhere. We'll be nice and safe about it."

"This is why you're driving," Stephane chimed in as he loaded his gear into the lander. He had pre-loaded it for Titan, but with plans having changed, he had to swap it out for his Enceladus gear. Conti and Hall were likewise bustling back and forth as they prepared to become the first humans on a moon of Saturn; if nothing else, the longer distance to Titan meant the JSC crew would at least have that distinction.

"I'm driving because your simulation work was horrible," Shaila teased. "You crashed the lander, what was it, six times?"

"Five," Stephane grinned as he loaded a container into the lander. "That sixth time, I just broke the landing gear."

Shaking her head, Shaila dialed up the manifest on her datapad and triple checked everything as it was loaded up. Conti was in charge of assessing organic molecules near the tiger stripes, while Stephane handled the geographical and tectonic surveys. Hall would check on water quality and the presence of any other potentially useful—and marketable—materials. Shaila had to give Hall credit for that; most corporate reps wouldn't be caught dead in a spacesuit, but Hall was game for it, and she was one of the few "suits" with the scientific cred to back it up.

The *Armstrong*'s two landers were roughly the size of cargo vans, featuring a cramped crew compartment and a spacious cargo area for fuel and equipment. Much of the cargo area in Lander One had been taken up with a giant, empty inflatable tank capable of holding 1,200 liters. Once they ascertained that the water below contained enough deuterium—something of a formality given the plethora of orbiters and landers that had surveyed the moon for more than a century—they would filter out the heavy water and fill the tank for the flight back to the ship. Then they'd spend the next 48 hours ferrying additional deuterium back and forth—and *that* would be just enough to get them to Titan, where their depot ship awaited them...if the Chinese hadn't messed with it first.

To be fair, Shaila didn't think they'd go that far. Beating JSC and ExEn to Titan was one thing—possession was nine-tenths of the law, and Titan's hydrocarbons were a rich prize indeed—but the laws of sea and space still applied to most astronauts, despite their national and corporate allegiances. Just last month, a Chinese lunar cargo hauler came to the rescue of a commercial passenger ship that had a malfunction and failed to make its lunar transit orbit.

She didn't expect that level of consideration from the *Tienlong*, but she didn't think they'd go for outright piracy either.

"Shay? It's time," Stephane said.

She looked up from her work to see Nilssen and the rest of the crew gathered in the zero-g of the passageway, smiles on their faces. Nilssen clutched four drinking straws in his hand.

"Short straw gets the honors," the commander said. "Let's get picking."

Shaila looked at the four plastic straws in the skipper's fist and felt her heart start to race. Amazing to think this is how they'd decide who would be the first person to set foot on Enceladus and, in effect, go down in history as the pioneer of Saturn exploration. It seemed far too surreal.

Nilssen floated over to Hall, who surprised everyone by crossing her arms and shaking her head. "Corporate sponsors get enough crap from the media," she said with a smile, one tinged with a bit of regret. "I don't want to be the poster child for corporate exploitation of the solar system."

The skipper nodded and gave her a pat on the shoulder. "Understood. Tempted to make you first now, but so be it." Nilssen deftly removed one of the straws and floated over to Conti. "Doctor?"

Grinning broadly, the Italian surveyed the straws carefully before choosing—a long one, as it turned out. She flicked it across the room in mock disgust, but didn't seem too put out. That left Shaila and Stephane.

"You go," Shaila told him. "I can't do it."

Stephane quickly floated over to the skipper, almost crashing into him, and drew a straw.

The short one.

"All right then, Durand's the first human being on Enceladus," Nilssen said, extending his hand toward the grinning planetary scientist. "Don't do anything stupid."

Stephane shook his hand eagerly. "I guarantee nothing, but I'll try."

Shaila, for her part, was inwardly disappointed, but quite happy for Stephane. He had come a long way from the slacker playboy he had been when they were posted together on Mars. She floated over and gave him a big hug, which he returned in kind. "I can't believe it," he whispered in her ear. "We are going to Enceladus together."

"Wouldn't have it any other way," she replied quietly, giving him a final squeeze before disengaging. "All right, people," she said to the group. "Everyone going to Enceladus, suit up. Everyone else, back to work!"

Shaila was the first to be suited, having far more experience with EVA gear than the rest, and even took a moment to help Stephane into his suit, tsking at him for taking too long, before entering Lander One through the top hatch. She started the power-up sequence and ran through the inflight checklist carefully. She had been running diagnostics on both landers every few days since they left Earth, and all was as she expected. Unlike the controls of *Armstrong* itself, there was little in the way of holotech on the landers—most of the controls were touchscreens, except for the old-fashioned stick-and-throttle in the pilot and copilot seats. Hall would be her copilot on this run, with Conti and Stephane right behind them.

"We good?" Hall asked as she floated down into her seat.

"Board is green," Shaila replied. "You want to give it a try?"

Hall smiled that regretful smile again. "Not this time. You'll stick the landing better anyway."

"You know, for a corporate stooge, you're OK," Shaila said, not for the first time. While the two weren't particularly close, despite the close quarters and long journey, they developed an easy rapport that included its fair share of commentary.

"And you're not so bad for a slack-jawed space jockey," Hall replied. "Besides, I need to get ready to do the real work once you chauffeur us down there."

"Roger that. I'll keep the meter running."

Moments later, Conti and Stephane floated down into the crew compartment, the final bits of their equipment stored. Conti also brought with her six flags: those of the United States, Italy, France and the United Kingdom, as well as the United Nations and Joint Space Command. There had been some argument as to whether to plant a flag at all—Stephane particularly found it to be just more unabashed 22nd century colonialism—but Shaila felt it was a nice touch, especially since so many nations were represented. Besides, she thought, the Chinese sure as hell were going to stick a big red one in Titan.

"All right, everyone," Shaila said. "Buckle up. *Armstrong*, this is Lander One. Request permission to begin landing procedures."

Nilssen's voice came on over the speakers. "Lander One, *Armstrong*. You are cleared for departure. Godspeed."

Nobody ever says Godspeed anymore, unless it's in space, Shaila thought idly as she sealed off the airlock. "Good seal," she reported. "Disengaging docking clamp."

With the flip of a switch, Lander One was free of *Armstrong*, hovering mere inches from the hull. Shaila teased the docking thrusters slightly and pulled away slowly from the ship. With a handful of small thruster bursts, she slowly navigated down the length of *Armstrong*'s hull. The ship looked surprisingly good after her long voyage; Shaila's mind flashed back to the thin layer of red dust that covered everything on Mars, and was grateful she wasn't there.

"*Armstrong*, Lander One. Ship looks pretty. We're good to go," Shaila reported.

"Roger that, Lander One. Dropping shields on my mark," Nilssen said. "Three...two...one...mark!"

There was no visible change to the view outside the lander's windows, but Shaila knew that the electromagnetic energy field around the *Armstrong* would short out the Lander's electronics, leaving it dead in space. So for each lander's departure and arrival, the ship had to drop its protection for a moment. While there was always the off chance a few particles would get through, it wasn't as though they were in orbit around an ice storm. They would, of course, do a thorough inspection before leaving Enceladus, and make any patches necessary. And the EM emitter was still active, too, which would take care of the bigger stuff anyway.

On Nilssen's "mark," Shaila hit the ship's engines and roared away from *Armstrong*, clearing the ship in mere seconds. By going in the opposite direction of the ship, Lander One would not only get clear faster, but also begin to slow down so that it could descend to the surface without the micrometeor and ice impacts Archie had worried over.

"Decelerating rapidly," Hall reported. "Looking good."

"Roger that. Starting our descent. I'll try to aim for the t-shirt kiosk," Shaila replied.

The next hour was pretty quiet aboard Lander One as the four astronauts were more than satisfied to gaze out the windows at the icy moon below. At first glance it appeared smooth, but as the little ship drew closer, they could see an intricate pattern of valleys and gorges spread haphazardly across the surface, punctuated by the pock-marks left by asteroid impacts over the millennia.

Shaila looked back at Stephane and took immense joy in seeing his rapturous face practically pressed up against his window. The fact that he was brilliant was unquestioned; she thought she deserved a bit of credit, though, for getting him to focus. Of course, the events on Mars probably had more to do with it, but she still staked her claim to his improvement, and he never denied it.

Catching her watching, Stephane turned to her and said in a fake baritone, "That's it. The Rebels are there."

Combined with his French accent, the impression was more comedic than perhaps intended. At least, Shaila thought with a smile, he was paying attention when she made him watch all those *Star Wars* movies. She always thought the 150-year-old originals were the best, but Stephane had been partial to the 2107-2115 holo remakes, probably from seeing them when he was a kid. But he was French, and there was no accounting for taste.

"I don't see a shield generator," Shaila said gamely.

"That is the system. And I'm sure Skywalker is with them," Stephane replied, his Vader-voice dissolving into a chuckle.

That lightened the mood considerably, and soon all four of them were talking about the things they'd do when they landed. Conti was particularly interested in her pet experiment, which would set up a laser drill that, over the next day, would melt enough ice to reach the interior ocean of the moon. From there, a handful of tennis-ball-sized probes would be dropped in—and the search for life would be on. She didn't expect to find anything, but it would make for a very pleasant, and extraordinarily historic, surprise.

On the topic of history, Stephane was surprisingly quiet about what he would say when he set foot upon Enceladus. From Neil Armstrong's "one small step" speech to Yuna Hiyashi's two-word statement on Europa—"Nice view!"—there was a proud tradition of memorable sayings. Part of Shaila was pretty happy that she hadn't drawn the short straw, because everything she came up with during the voyage sounded awful and trite.

"Lander One, *Armstrong*. You're coming up on the landing zone. Looking good. Over."

Nilssen's voice brought Shaila back to the present. "Roger that, *Armstrong*. We're ready to roll. Over."

"Copy, Lander One. Good luck. Out."

Shaila began to descend more steeply now. Their landing zone was a good five kilometers away from the edge of the outermost tiger stripe, and had been selected using nearly a century of probe data. Of course, *Armstrong* was also running sensor sweeps of the area, and Shaila had to be ready to fire thrusters and get the lander up and out in case the ice there wasn't the kilometer-thick crust they thought it might be.

She needn't have worried, however. The landing procedure was textbook, and the lander slowly settled down on the surface of Enceladus. It was a surprisingly long process—the moon's gravity was barely 1 percent of Earth's, so Shaila brought the ship to a halt five meters above the surface and cut the engines. It took a few minutes until the ship gently touched down upon the ice, and Shaila fired a very slow, gradual thruster burn in order to prevent the lander from literally bouncing.

And then she cut the engines, and all was silent for a moment. Her heart racing, Shaila finally keyed the comm. "Lander One to *Armstrong*, landing procedure successful. Preparing to EVA," she said, making sure each word was spoken with a steady voice.

"Roger that, Lander One. Nice landing," Nilssen said.

"Thanks, *Armstrong*. Lander One out." Shaila turned to her compatriots. "All right, let's get sealed up and get out of here."

The crew put their gauntlets and helmets on, sealed them tightly and turned on their atmospheric units and individual visor HUDs. Shaila checked each suit personally, and had everyone check hers as well. Then, one by one, they went through the tiny airlock in the ceiling and out on top of the lander itself.

Shaila was the last to leave, and found all four of them silently admiring the view. The horizon was impossibly close, and beyond it, the rings of Saturn spread out before them covering half the sky, with three-quarters of Saturn itself looming before them. To the right, the Sun shone brightly, though from that distance, it looked more like a very ambitious star than the blazing orb seen from Earth.

"All right," she said. "Stephane?"

She saw him look down at the surface, as if weighing exactly how to go about it. She walked carefully over to him—a wrong move would send her tens of meters straight up—and put a hand on his shoulder. "Go ahead," she said quietly. "It's all yours."

He turned and smiled at her, and they touched their helmets together. She found herself smiling like a giddy teenager in that moment. How many couples got to do something like this?

Then she felt his hands on her arms...lifting.

"What are you doing?" she asked, the grin instantly dissolving.

"This," he said simply. He picked her right up off the top of the lander—she weighed little more than a backpack in Enceladus' gravity—and carried her to the edge.

Then he dropped her.

It took her a good five seconds to fall to the surface of Enceladus—enough time for her to wonder whether to kill him or kiss him.

And then her boots hit the fine granular ice on the surface.

"*Armstrong*, this is Durand," she heard over her comm. "Change of plans. I have given my honor to Lieutenant Commander Shaila Jain. She is the first person to set foot in the Saturn system. Over."

There were a few seconds of silence before Nilssen replied, sounding amused, "Roger, Durand. Conti caught it on the holocam. Status, Jain?"

Oh, God. Now I have to say something. "*Armstrong*, this is Jain." She paused, trying to come up with...anything. "It's a pretty little moon," she stammered. "Let's leave it the way we found it."

That sucked. That sucked so badly! She turned to look up at her colleagues, all of whom were smiling down at her. Stephane gave her a thumbs up; she resisted giving him the finger. "All right," Shaila said. "Enough with the history books. Let's get to work. And Durand?"

"Yes, Commander?" he said, already floating down to the surface. He only ever used her rank to tease her.

"You're in serious trouble when we get back to the ship."

He landed in a little cloud of icy powder. "You're welcome," he grinned. "How many men can say they gave the woman they loved an entire world?"

"*Serious* trouble," she replied, his grin sparking her own.

"Christ, you two, get a room," Hall teased. "The suits don't come with airlocks."

Before Shaila could retort, she felt a vibration through the soles of her boots. Immediately, her HUD lit up with sensor warnings. "Seismic activity," she reported, immediately back to business. "Epicenter is six klicks ahead."

Stephane started tapping commands into the pad on his wrist gauntlet. "It is the tiger stripes," he said. "They're about to blow."

The four astronauts turned away from Saturn and watched as a plume of icy crystals erupted into the sky above them…and began heading their way with surprising speed.

The night sky erupted in a blizzard. And with it came a tide that would envelop them all…

Shaila shook her head, but the image—and the feeling of dread at seeing the cloud of ice—was all-encompassing.

"Take cover!" she yelled.

Sept. 15, 1798

"These sails, Captain, they are treated with the typical admixture of mercury, sulfur and goldenrod, yes?" the young man—little more than an older boy, really—asked the captain of HMS *Fortitude* as they stood on the quarterdeck, admiring the view of the Rocky Main as the ship carefully picked its way through the boulder-islands.

Weatherby smiled at the boy, remembering the curiosity of his mother, so many years ago. "I cannot say what is typical or not, Philip. You already know more of alchemy than I've the patience or ability to learn," the captain replied. "Perhaps Dr. Hawkins might oblige you with an answer."

The boy looked up at Weatherby and gave a bemused smile, quite similar to the one his mother often wore. "Dr. Hawkins is often busy with his duties, sir. I don't think he particularly likes company, nor many questions."

Weatherby barked a short laugh. "No, I dare say he does not. But he's a good man. I'll have him make time for your questions soon enough, Philip."

To be fair, Philip Thomas St. Germain was not ill-mannered, especially considering the typical curiosity and rambunctiousness of most 13-year-olds. Indeed, he seemed to have inherited the best of both his parents—his father's self-possession and rigor and his mother's compassion and gentle humor. The intellectual acuity and prowess, Weatherby reasoned, was a toss-up between the two, or perhaps even greater than the sum, which would be formidable indeed.

As for the boy's mother, Weatherby found himself intrigued and entranced all over again, despite his initial attempts at showing remove and resolve. It did not help, of course, that she was just as beautiful as he remembered, perhaps even more so. Gone were the last vestiges of adolescence, but otherwise the tide of time was forestalled in her face and form. Intellectually, Weatherby knew that the Count St. Germain had unlocked many secrets to longevity and health, and the hale man he had met in '79 was, by then, well into his sixties but looked no more than forty. But to see Anne there, in the full flower of youthful womanhood…it was something for which he was wholly unprepared.

Weatherby's looking glass was somewhat less kind. The scar across his cheek—gained over Mars during those fateful days—never fully healed, and a life in service to His Majesty's Navy had left a slightly crooked nose and a few more scars upon his weather-beaten face. Yet Weatherby liked to think that responsibility and command suited him well, and that his bearing had grown with his confidence. That is what his late wife, at least, told him, and he was more inclined to believe her now than when she was alive, may God rest her soul.

"Good day, Captain," Anne said as she climbed the stairs of the quarter-deck, her marine guard in tow. A formidable alchemist, yes, but she was still the only woman on a ship with six hundred men aboard, at least half of them pressed into service. Hence the armed escort. Ever mindful, Gar'uk appeared with a cup of tea in hand, which Anne accepted gratefully. The valet had been ordered to attend to the needs of Anne and Philip whenever possible—a charge he took so seriously that Weatherby had to remind the Venusian that the captain still needed a valet now and again.

"Countess," Weatherby said by way of greeting. "I trust you continue to find ways of passing the time?"

"Your lodestones belowdecks are well ensorcelled, though a touch more elemental fire may be required once past Jupiter," she said simply. "And it smells to High Heaven down there. How you put up with such rancid odors, I cannot say."

Weatherby's smile was genuine; part of him worried the crew would begin to talk. "I shall communicate your recommendation to Dr. Hawkins when next he reports," the captain said. "As for the odor, I'm sorry to say there's little to be done for it."

Anne grimaced slightly. "I'm afraid I may have already offended Dr. Hawkins," she said. "I tried to show him a few new procedures to improve upon the workings in his manuals, but I think I may have unduly upset him."

Weatherby could readily see the two clashing. While Anne looked merely twenty-five years old, she was in her late thirties, and her tongue was stayed for no man. And if that man was the overly sensitive ship's alchemist.... "I'm sure Dr. Hawkins will be quite fine. Eventually."

The two shared a secret smile. It was all too easy to pretend that the years were never spent away, though Weatherby knew that Anne was married now, and to the most renowned master of the mystic sciences in all Earth's history. A ship's captain was far less a prize than that.

"You didn't mention you had a daughter, Captain," Anne said, with the barest hint of...something...in her voice, something Weatherby could not place. "I could not help but notice the portrait of her upon your table below. How old is she?"

Weatherby felt color seep into his face. "Nearly ten years, now. Elizabeth. Her mother died in childbirth," he said quietly.

Genuine concern and remorse appeared on Anne's face. "I'm sorry, Tom. I didn't mean to pry."

"Not at all, Lady Anne," he said, tempering his mood with a small smile. "Elizabeth is my *raison d'etre*. I had hoped to see her when the prizes were returned to Portsmouth. She is...well, we all dote upon our children, I suppose. But she is frighteningly intelligent, and fully of questions. I cannot help but be reminded of...."

He stopped, catching himself staring into Anne's eyes a bit longer than was entirely appropriate. The fact that she met his gaze for the same amount of time was...well, it was too much. He quickly looked down at his shoes, while she turned to look larboard at the boulder-islands of the Rocky Main.

"Lights spotted!" came a cry from the top of the mainmast. "Two sets, one larboard, one starboard!"

Never was a sighting so welcome as in that wholly uncomfortable moment. Weatherby immediately drew his glass and raised it. There...along the boulder islands massed to the left, was a blinking light. He swiveled right...and saw a light blinking in response.

A code.

"Beat to quarters! All hands, prepare for battle!" Weatherby shouted. "Lookouts to their stations right away! Identify those ships at once!"

He then turned to Anne, who had immediately taken charge of Philip. "Anne, I need you to go...." He stopped, looked at her, and saw the gleam of readied anger in her eye. If it were any other woman and child, they would be sent to the bowels of the ship for relative safety. He could instantly see this would not stand. "Report to Dr. Hawkins and assist as you are able."

She flashed him a winning smile. "You've a fine memory, Captain. Come, Philip. We've work to do," she said, handing her teacup to Gar'uk and hustling back down the stairs toward the ship's forecastle, where the alchemy lab was housed.

"Sir, might I suggest that the fo'c'sle isn't the safest place for a woman?" Lt. Barnes said quietly from over his shoulder.

Weatherby turned and smiled. "If you wish, you may go and try to convince her, Mr. Barnes. Then go and wrestle a Martian sand beast whilst you're on about it."

The second lieutenant smiled. "I understand, sir. Lookouts will be in place momentarily. We're also checking beneath and behind as well."

That gave Weatherby an idea, and he quickly rushed over to the map table, where the chaos of the Rocky Main was charted out. An orrery of the thousands of boulder-islands in the Main was hardly feasible, but there were somewhat stable routes mapped through them. "Where are we, Mr. Barnes?"

"Here, sir," he said, pointing to a relatively clear point on the chart. "I imagine the lights we've seen are coming from this cluster of stone here, and this one ahead to starboard. Perhaps pirates, sir. They'll likely turn tail and run soon as they see us."

"Perhaps," Weatherby allowed. "But the French do a brisk business between Earth and their Jovian holdings. They may have found some of their fellows to bring to bear against us. I want every gun loaded and ready to fire, if you please, Mr. Barnes."

"Straight on, then, sir?" he asked quietly, trying to gauge Weatherby's intent.

The captain shook his head slightly. "I want each of those ships identified as soon as possible. If one of them is *Franklin*, I want that ship captured. Otherwise, we shall try to out-race them and make for Saturn with all due haste." Weatherby pointed toward a point toward the starboard cluster of boulder-islands. "We make for these. Full sail, royals and stud'sels, if you please."

Barnes paused a good three seconds, confusion writ upon his face, before giving the necessary orders and course. It was only after that he turned to address his captain once more. "Within the cluster, sir?"

Weatherby gave the man credit for posting his orders first before questioning them. "A gambit, Mr. Barnes. If they're a pair of frigates, then 'tis folly to race them in the clear. We shall even the odds greatly within the cluster, as they will have to slow down or be crushed."

"As will we, sir."

"We shall see about that, Mr. Barnes," Weatherby said, giving his first lieutenant a smile that only deepened the junior officer's frown.

The captain watched as the royals and studding sails were unfurled across the ship, wrapping the *Fortitude* in a swath of sailcloth. The solar winds filled them almost immediately, and the ship's gain in speed was felt underfoot, prompting Barnes to issue an order for safety lines. A wise course, given what Weatherby had in mind.

"Ship identified! French flag!" came the shout from one of the lookouts. "She's coming straight at us!"

Weatherby nodded; it's what he might have done. If the aggressor were to get off a few lucky shots, *Fortitude* might be slowed enough for the other enemy ship to join in. At that point, the battle would be in the French's favor.

"Four points to starboard! Ready the larboard guns! Two points up on the planes!" Weatherby shouted. Immediately, the ship turned toward the right, while the guns on the left side of the ship were readied to fire at the oncoming French vessel. *Fortitude* began a shallow climb higher into the Void, for the higher ground, as it were, would make her broadside count all the more.

The French ship, however, would have none of it. It tacked to follow *Fortitude* and likewise climbed higher. Lookouts immediately counted forty guns on the enemy ship; a rather large frigate, but no match for *Fortitude*'s seventy-six. Of course, if the frigate's compatriot was likewise armed, the odds would be evened considerably.

Weatherby watched closely as the two ships sped toward one another. Unlike naval combat upon the seas, battle in the Void was a much faster affair. Two vessels would speed past each other and fire quickly, or they would vie to come alongside one another—without colliding, no mean feat in that—to continually exchange blazing alchemical shot. The cluster of boulder-islands now looming ahead only served to complicate matters. And there was the open question of the location of the other French ship.

"The frigate is positioning itself to come up upon our larboard side," Barnes reported, "and we're about to enter the boulder cluster."

Weatherby nodded but said nothing, instead pulling out his glass in order to look ahead. Timing would be critical for the maneuver, as would his calculations. He could only hope there were no large boulders flying freely around inside the cluster. Not, at least, until he passed through.

Barnes stood next to him, fidgeting with his hands and occasionally rising onto the balls of his feet. "Sir," he finally whispered, "they will be on us in no time."

"Thank you, Mr. Barnes," he said. "We just need wait for our opening."

Barnes nodded, then turned to look ahead at the rather larger boulder looming straight ahead of them, and the French frigate coming around their larboard side. "Sir, they're almost in range. Should we –"

"Four points up on the larboard plane! Now!" Weatherby shouted.

The ship immediately curved away from the French frigate, turning to move around the right side of the boulder-island ahead. Weatherby heard shots ring out from the French frigate; they would try to shoot at *Fortitude*'s keel, but the range was still too far for their guns. It was a futile gesture.

"Four points up on the starboard plane!" Weatherby commanded, and soon the ship righted itself, its keel less than three hundred yards from a boulder roughly the size of London. Weatherby turned aft and peered through his glass; the French frigate had given chase.

"Excellent!" Weatherby exclaimed, snapping his glass shut. "Mr. Barnes, set up additional lookouts for the pilot, and go to half sail. We shan't wish to be struck in transit."

Looking mildly exasperated at this point, Barnes nonetheless issued the orders. At half sail, the frigate would be upon them quite quickly, and it was only good fortune that the ship didn't appear to have chase guns.

Weatherby caught his lieutenant's look. "Mr. Barnes, do we have a sighting of the other ship? Unless she's particularly fast, I imagine we'd see her about three points to larboard, two points below horizon." Barnes alerted the lookouts and soon the voices from the tops reported back; Weatherby was off by only a point on either axis. The other French ship—another frigate, this one of thirty-two guns—was on a bearing to intercept the *Fortitude* in the middle of the cluster.

The captain ordered additional sail—just enough to keep ahead of the speedier frigate behind them—and began poring over the charts again, murmuring minute course corrections to the seaman at the wheel. He would look up, scan the horizon with his glass, then consult the charts and make more corrections.

"Very well, there's nothing more to be done," Weatherby said finally, snapping his glass closed. "Ready all guns to fire broadsides on my command."

"All guns, sir?" Barnes asked. "Even the starboard side?"

"Every gun we have, Mr. Barnes. No alchemical shot needed."

Even more confused, Barnes nonetheless dutifully carried out his orders. Weatherby knew the man was trying his best to comprehend, but simply wasn't arriving at the matter quickly. They would walk through this engagement over a glass of claret later…should they survive.

Even so, Weatherby felt the man deserved something. "Have you ever played at billiards, Mr. Barnes?"

"I'm afraid I haven't, sir," he replied, coming full circle in his confusion so as to simply answer the unexpected question with something approaching equanimity.

"Are you familiar with it?" Weatherby asked.

"Only in passing, sir."

"You should take it up some time, Mr. Barnes. You may find it most illuminating."

"I shall gladly take your advice, sir," the lieutenant noted. "In the meantime, there's our other adversary." The younger officer pointed off to the starboard side. "It appears she's turning to attempt a broadside. Another frigate, roughly thirty-two guns, I should say."

"About time," Weatherby responded. "She's running late. Three points down on the planes, if you please, Mr. Barnes."

The *Fortitude* dove deeper into the Void, prompting the other two vessels to change course. The ship's pilot swore as he saw a number of boulder-islands on either side of the ship. "'Tis a tight fit, cap'n, sir," the man said. "And I trust you're the man to fit us through," Weatherby said, clapping a hand on the man's shoulder. "Straight on, the tighter the better."

Unlike Barnes, who at least attempted to maintain decorum at all times, the crewman was unsparing in his look of incredulity. "As you say, sir, but this'll be tight enough."

Within moments, boulders began speeding past the ship on either side. Some were small, the size of cannon shot, while others were half again the size of the ship itself. A few pebble-sized pieces of rock started raining down onto the ship's deck, caught by the *Fortitude*'s gravity, which was fueled by the ensorcelled lodestones in the bowels of the ship.

"They're still with us and closing fast, sir," Barnes said. "Almost within range." More quietly, he added: "We're not well positioned to return fire, sir. Suggest we come about to engage?"

Weatherby nodded, then cracked another small smile. "Fire all guns now, Mr. Barnes."

"Sir?" the lieutenant asked, completely bewildered. "We won't hit anything!"

Weatherby strode forward and placed his hands on the quarterdeck rail. "Fire all guns!" he shouted at the top of his lungs.

Immediately—with a reaction time far greater than Barnes had a moment prior—all seventy-four cannons aboard *Fortitude* fired their shot into the Void.

And at least three-quarters of those shots hit boulder-islands. The iron shot smashed into boulders big and small, near and far. A bare few were smashed entirely, with most of the smaller rocks split in two and sent careening away from each other. The larger rocks—including several half the size of *Fortitude* herself—likewise spun wildly through the Void after being struck, and went on to strike other boulder-islands, which in turn struck others with the same prodigious force.

"Planes full up!" Weatherby shouted.

With a chorus of creaking wood and groaning lines, *Fortitude* began a sharp climb out of the boulder cluster....

...leaving a wake of careening boulder-islands behind her.

Weatherby and Barnes both turned to look aft with their glasses at the two ships now behind them. The *Fortitude*'s cannon fire had prompted a chain of reactions throughout the cluster, sending boulders askew in their paths, bouncing off each other and generally creating a blizzard of speeding stone all around the two frigates. They watched as one of the ships lost a mast in the onslaught, while another already appeared to be on fire, likely from a direct hit into its underbelly, where the powder was stored.

A moment later, that ship burst into flame, while the other worked arduously to clear out of the hail of stone.

Weatherby snapped his glass shut, and turned to Barnes. "Keep the lookouts at their posts, and have the guns reloaded, Mr. Barnes. There may be more of them out there."

"Sir, I..." Barnes began, "I must apologize. I—"

Weatherby nodded and interrupted. "Faster, next time, Mr. Barnes. And in the interim...billiards."

The captain turned and started walking down the stairs toward the main deck, and his cabin, when he was met by Philip St. Germain. "That was amazing, Captain!" the boy exclaimed. "I've never seen anything like it!"

Weatherby couldn't help but smile. "Thank you, young man. But aren't you assigned to assist Dr. Hawkins?"

The boy was immediately flustered. "Well, yes. Sorry, sir."

Weatherby saw Anne walk up behind him. "It's all right, Philip. You're not actually *in* the Navy," she said with a smile. "Though I will say, the service has proven to be more imaginative than I would have given it credit for, Captain."

"Thank you, Lady Anne," Weatherby said with a slight bow and a smile. "It was not always so."

"No, it wasn't," she replied, with a fair share of weight behind it. "But it's nice to see some adaptability at long last. Come along, Philip. Let's help Dr. Hawkins recover his nerves."

The two turned and walked forward once again, leaving Weatherby feeling less like a victorious captain and more like an eighteen-year-old second lieutenant once more.

CHAPTER 9

June 19, 2134

Maj. Gen. Maria Diaz jumped at every chance to fly she could get. Sure, an executive-class supersonic business jet wasn't the same as her old Lightning VII stealth fighter-bomber—or a Mars lander, for that matter. But beggars can't be choosers.

"Wheels up, control," Diaz called out as she pushed the aircraft down the runway. To her right, Coogan managed the rest of the comm with the tower at Andrews Air Force Base. Between her rank and her security clearance, she didn't even need to talk to the tower at all, but she knew the controllers preferred knowing just who the hell was in their airspace.

Diaz pushed the throttle forward and the little jet sped up…fast. She noticed Coogan giving her a look, but she merely grinned and pushed it forward a bit more, then pulled back on the yoke a bit more than strictly necessary. The jet practically leapt into the air, pressing everyone aboard a bit harder into their seats.

Ninety seconds later, a boom echoed through the jet's hull—they were supersonic. Diaz keyed in the course and took the headset off. "You got this, Jimmy?"

Her aide smiled at her. "Gladly, yes," he deadpanned, as only the British know how. "I'll let you know when we're twenty minutes out so you can plan an appropriately 'cowboy' landing."

"Smart ass," she chided, chucking him on the shoulder as she rose from the cockpit and made her way toward the passenger area, where the rest of her team awaited her.

"General, ma'am, you drive like a maniac," Greene chided, though he wore a sympathetic smile on his face. Capt. Maggie Huntington smiled slightly at this, though she also looked a bit pale, and Diaz noticed the barf bag discreetly placed on her armrest. Perhaps her landing wouldn't be so cowboy after all.

"As you were, Doctor," Diaz said, winking at him conspiratorially while flipping on the comm so Coogan could listen in. "And thanks, everyone, for packing up on such short notice, and without the faintest idea where we're going. Any guesses?"

Greene shrugged and looked at the others. Huntington finally spoke up. "Egypt."

Diaz' eyebrows raised. "Not bad, Captain. How'd you get there?"

"Ma'am," the Marine officer said formally. "The only initial BlueNet site left unaccounted for in either neutral or friendly territory was the one on Siwa Bay. If we were heading for the unknown sites in either Russia or China, our current transport would be unsuitable."

"Right. Invading Russia or China isn't on the agenda today. Anything else?"

"Only the fact that you and Lieutenant Coogan were burning up comms for more than six hours before ordering us to pack up. So it seems to me there's something at Siwa worth seeing."

"Well done, Mags," Diaz said. "We've been working on a couple leads on the intel front, and it turns out they're all related. First off, that gear you found at Teotihuacan. Serial numbers were almost entirely stripped except for a single sensor inside a heap of casing. They'd have to break the whole damn thing to rub that number off, which kind of defeats the purpose. Of course, we broke 'em. Traced the part to the piece, and the piece to an outfit called Orion RadTech. Three guesses which conglom owns Orion?"

Greene beat everyone else to it. "Total-Suez?"

"Bingo. So now you have this particular corporate entity not only playing chicken with *Armstrong* around Saturn, but also planting red herrings around major ancient astronaut sites," Diaz said.

"Or boosting the Cherenkov signatures at those sites in order to make contact with the other side," Huntington added. "Even Dr. Greene thinks that's possible."

Greene rolled his eyes. "Lottery odds, remember?"

Diaz dismissed the discussion with a wave of her hand. "Total-Suez. So why Egypt?"

Coogan chimed in from the cockpit. "The new fusion reactor there that gave us the BlueNet positive is run by Total-Suez."

"Right you are," Diaz said. "So we have unauthorized tech creating Cherenkov false positives, we have a sponsored Chinese ship making for Titan like a bat out of hell, and we have possible unauthorized tech out in Egypt. All being run by the same company. So we're going to go have a look."

"Is Harry there?" Greene asked.

"God, I hope so," Diaz replied, "but we still can't find the bastard. Meantime, here's our cover story for Siwa…"

Walls surrounded most of world's coastal cities, humanity's reaction to global warming and the resulting rise in ocean levels. Without them, New York would be inundated up to 45th Street, while half the Mall in Washington—including the White House—would be swallowed by the Potomac River. Miami, Hong Kong, Mumbai, London, Buenos Aires—all were in a battle with the ocean and, in some cases, were barely hanging on.

There were a few places which welcomed the rising oceans, however, and none as much as Egypt. Where the Libyan Desert once stretched from Cairo to Tripoli with a bare handful of oases between, today there was Siwa Bay, a massive inlet that stretched more than 300 kilometers to the sea. The Egyptian authorities, enthused at the notion of having hundreds of miles of developable coastline, encouraged native wildlife development and added desalinization, irrigation and a wide array of completely unindigenous plant life.

Then came the investment, primarily from fellow Islamic League nations on the Arabian Peninsula, but also from any number of Western and Asian congloms. The Chinese, in particular—having claimed most of Africa as client states over the past century—fueled development of new "seaside" resorts and more than a few casinos with ties to Macau. Conservationists, already feeling rather ineffective in the face of a century of warming, provided only muted warnings, and there was little in the way of historical preservation, even among the towns, like Siwa proper, that managed to avoid the floodwaters.

Diaz thought the place looked like a goddamn eyesore. As her car rolled through the freshly paved streets of Siwa City, surrounded by new blocks of hotels, apartments, casinos and shopping centers, she could practically feel her own character seeping away from her in the face of such generic, bland construction. The absence of crowds—there were bare handfuls of people out, even in the morning hours when it was cooler—didn't help matters. It was a glistening ghost town, a representation of fervent hope awaiting a validation that might or might not arrive, for there was little else besides the calm waters of the bay to recommend the place. Waterfront property in the desert was still…in a desert.

"These are our IAEA badges," Coogan said coolly as he passed out the identification to Diaz, Greene and Huntington. "We're doing a spot inspection of the Total-Suez plant. Captain Huntington and I will play the lead investigators, which should allow General Diaz and Dr. Greene to spot anything out of sorts that might be related to their…past experiences."

Past experiences. That's an understatement, Diaz thought.

"General, you and Dr. Greene should keep your hats and sunglasses on as much as possible, in case your friend Harry's looking out for you," Coogan added. "If we're found out, then the game's up and we'll be sent packing."

Huntington, meanwhile, was looking up information on the area, the readout appearing in his own sunglasses. "Place was an oasis since at least Ptolemaic times," he said. "They've uncovered temple ruins here that some believe is the ancient temple of Amun-Ra."

"What's the significance of that?" Greene said, challenge in his tone.

Huntington gave him a shrug. "The temple of Amu-Ra is where Alexander and Ptolemy visited back around 331 B.C., where Alexander was anointed a god and shown the secrets of the ancients," she said.

"Well, he was anointed," Greene said, flipping through his datapad; Diaz noted with some amusement that Greene was actually checking on Huntington's assertions. "I don't see anything about secrets."

"Well, they *are* secrets," Huntington smirked, clearly enjoying herself. "It's probably not like he wrote them down."

"Can it, everybody," Diaz ordered as she tried to hide a smirk. "I don't think Harry needs an ancient temple to make mischief."

Huntington sat forward in her seat, showing a touch of genuine concern. "But there was a temple on Mars, ma'am. And if there's a counterpart temple to the one here—"

"Then yes, in theory, it wouldn't be a bad place to try to break though," Diaz allowed. "Fine, but let's not get ahead of ourselves. Facts first, guys."

Huntington nodded dutifully and leaned back in her seat, looking out the window at a line of fast-food eateries, including the venerable Starbucks and McDonalds lines. There were a bare handful of people in each.

The Total-Suez fusion power generation plant was on the outskirts of the city, 40 kilometers to the south and east of the city's Americanized boardwalks. It was a surprisingly innocuous structure, looking more like a warehouse complex than the potential source of electrical power for millions of people. Like many modern fusion power plants, the facility fused hydrogen atoms into helium, creating immense amounts of heat used to generate steam in order to spin highly efficient electromagnetic turbines.

"Looks like we're here," Diaz ordered. "Jimmy, make sure Washington knows where we are before we head in. And remember, we're inspectors and colleagues. No ranks, first names."

"You got it, Maria," Huntington smirked. "Always wanted to say that."

Diaz reached across to whack her in the arm playfully as she pulled the van up to the guard post. As she rolled down the window, a blast of hot, dry air hit her face...followed by the sound of a bored, irritated Arabic-speaking man a moment later.

"What the hell do you want?" he asked, the translation program in Diaz' earpiece doing wonders to capture his tone. The HUD in her sunglasses showed that the man wasn't similarly equipped, so she tried to pronounce the Arabic translation provided by the computer. It must have sounded awful, because after a few seconds, the burly guard held up his hand and shook his head. "You try English," he said.

"Thank God," she muttered. "Unannounced IAEA inspection. We're to have full access."

The guard took her proffered paperwork, scanning it idly. "We did not know there was inspection today."

"That's why it's unannounced, chief," she replied, which earned her a dirty look.

It took about ten minutes for the guard to scan the paperwork, call his supervisors inside and then wait for them to get authorization. Diaz wasn't particularly worried; IAEA had long worked with intelligence communities around the world to help stem the proliferation of nuclear weapons, and it was the matter of a few e-mails and a hastily arranged conference call before the flight in order to set up the inspection back-story.

Finally, the guard came back. "You park there," he said, pointing to a space near the entrance. "Go inside. Someone will be there for you."

Diaz nodded and pulled through the gate and across the lot. Coogan and Huntington were busy on their handhelds, likely recording and filing everything they saw, while Greene recorded the proceedings with a holocam. Despite an immense facility for computing to go along with his scientific work, Greene was a bit curmudgeonly when it came to HUD technology in glasses or contacts. That officially made him the old man of the team, even though Diaz was technically two years older.

They quickly hustled out of the air-conditioned van and into the building, where they found a small lobby space that could reasonably be called industrial-corporate. There was surprisingly bad wood paneling, brand-new plastic furniture, a few 'Net access tablets on a glaringly white coffee table, and a desk with a smiling woman behind it, dressed in a modern business suit with a hijab. "Welcome!" she said, standing as they entered. "You are the inspectors, yes?"

"We are," Huntington said, smoothly taking charge and shaking the woman's hand. "Chief Inspector Margaret Huntington. Pleasure to meet you."

The two exchanged pleasantries and pertinent information for a few moments, leaving Diaz to marvel at how lucky she was to find such a talented field officer. Huntington had spent time doing both infantry and intelligence work, and knew her way around computers, too. She was the kind of Swiss-army-knife body Diaz loved to work with. Coogan was the one who set things up, but Huntington specialized in getting them done on the ground.

A few minutes later, they were walking through the outermost parts of the plant, with the Egyptian woman providing a very adept tour of the facilities; Diaz figured she had done this dog-and-pony show dozens of times already. The place was spotlessly clean, and if there was such a thing as "new fusion power plant smell," it had it.

As they walked, Diaz saw an IM pop up in her HUD:

SHOWING POWER FLOW BENEATH THE PLANT. –C

She turned to Coogan, who had sent the message, and shrugged. With a subtle but visible roll of his eyes, he resumed typing on his handheld. A moment later:

POWER FROM GENERATOR SHOULD ALL FLOW OUT, NOT INTO THE BASEMENT!

Damn if he didn't have to be a dick about it, Diaz thought. She tapped out an order to the team:

START OPENING DOORS. NEED BASEMENT ACCESS.

"Hey, wait a sec. What's that over there?" Huntington said a moment later, pointing to what for all the world looked like a broom closet.

"That?" their guide replied. "That is maintenance." Nonetheless, Huntington was already striding over. She opened the door to find several mops, a slop sink and a shelf of cleaning chemicals. With a grin and a shrug, she fell back into the group.

The next several hours were ripped straight from a holocomedy, with the team opening nearly every door in the complex. All they discovered were various hallways, monitoring stations, closets, restrooms, locker rooms and the occasional office. The main control room was of particular interest, and Coogan spent at least forty-five minutes scrolling through every permutation of the plant's holographic controls and peeking into every available file.

"Anything?" Diaz asked Greene and Coogan sotto voce while Huntington prodded the woman for details about the plant's emergency containment systems.

Both men shrugged. "Sensors are definitely showing the flow of power into the basement," Coogan said. "The rest of the lines run straight out of the building. It could be nothing, but most plants of this type siphon power off an outgoing trunk line; they don't dedicate a line to loop back in."

Diaz turned to Greene. "Blue?" It was their shorthand for Cherenkov radiation.

"Only where you'd expect," Greene said. "Could be that when we got the hit off BlueNet, they had a power spike of some kind."

"But what about Harry?" she asked.

"Hey, I agree it stinks. But whatever we're looking for, it might not be here."

"Jimmy, give us a map. Where haven't we been?" Diaz asked.

A moment later, a map of the facility popped up on their HUDs and screens. The plant was connected by a corridor to an office complex about fifty meters away. That was the only place left to search.

"All right, let's go to the office, then," Diaz said.

With an increasingly confused tour guide now in tow, the "inspectors" made their way toward the office building, a two-story affair that seemed as generic as the rest of Siwa City. On the bright side, the décor was markedly improved, reflecting Total-Suez' wealth and influence as a global purveyor of electric power, water and petrochemical energy sources.

As they did in the plant, the team helped themselves to every available door, and there were considerably more of them in an office than in the power generation facility. It was a Friday—a fortuitous turn of events, given that most of the lower-level employees had the day off, as was Muslim custom. Still, there were more than a few people still there, primarily Europeans and Chinese. And most were surprised to see a team of inspectors probing their offices with sensors.

One office on the second floor stopped all of them in their tracks. The name on the door read: HARRY YU.

"What do you think?" Greene asked.

Diaz shrugged. "Maybe he took the day off," she said. "If not, he's not in a hurry to say hi." She turned to the tour guide. "This one, too."

The guide opened the door, and Harry Yu looked up from his desk, then immediately went wide eyed. "What the hell?"

Diaz turned to Greene. "Or, you know, he could be sitting there the whole time like a spider in the center of a web, but that would be really cliché."

Harry narrowed his eyes, then looked at the group's tour guide. "Who are these people?"

The now-nervous Egyptian woman bowed slightly as she addressed Harry. "IAEA inspectors, Mr. Yu. Their papers are in order."

Harry leaned back at his desk, scanning holocopies of the fake IAEA documents forwarded by their tour guide. "Huh. Pretty impressive. Scanned through cleanly, too," he said with a growing smile before turning back to the woman. "Why don't you leave these folks here with me for a while. I'm sure they have questions."

The woman nodded, bowed and quickly left, and Diaz heard the door close behind them with a click.

Then all her tech went blank.

A quick look at Coogan and Huntington confirmed it—they were cut off from the rest of the world.

"C'mon in. Have a seat," Harry said, motioning toward a conference table in the corner of the room, overlooking the brand new city off in the distance. "You can tell me what the fuck you're doing here."

October 10, 1798

Never was a setting sun more welcomed than on the road to the temple of Amun-Ra. Finch smiled at the thought of lamplight in the cities of Europe, or the chill of winter nights upon Ganymede. In rural areas, sunset was a time to lock doors against the night's predators. And certainly, the Libyan Desert had its predators, animal and human alike. Yet the sun's rest was cause for celebration, for Finch could finally stop sweating for a few hours.

And Finch was perhaps the one man most acclimated to the desert climate, except for young Jabir. The French, certainly, were perhaps even more relieved—bordering on rapturous—to see the light fade. It would make their night's journey that much more bearable.

There were a half-dozen *savants* in the caravan, mostly younger scholars who served as Berthollet's assistants, along with another dozen servants and a platoon of soldiers wearing the finest French wool uniforms. It took Berthollet, the caravan's nominal commander, only a single day and two deaths to realize that marching in the heat of the afternoon sun would result in a severely foreshortened journey. Thus, they marched from roughly five in the afternoon to seven in the morning, taking their breakfast before marching two hours in the lingering day and the rest under the Moon and stars. And in the chill of the desert night, the wool uniforms were actually useful.

Their first two weeks saw them march to Alexandria along the banks of the Nile, followed by another three weeks of travel along the coast. This was not, of course, the exact route depicted in the mosque's hidden map, but rather seemed to be the safest route to get to its destination. For all their political posturing—the caravan's soldiers and scholars still shared a great deal of revolutionary fervor nearly ten years on— Finch trusted the French when it came to geometry and geography. Now, they were well into the desert, ideally less than a week away. Travel was excruciatingly slow among the dunes of the desert, especially with all the water the caravan had to carry. Prior to leaving, Finch had argued for a smaller group, one that might travel more quickly, but Berthollet insisted upon the soldiers, given the encounters the French already had with the Bedouin tribes of the desert whilst marching on Cairo.

The mornings before sleep had been most convivial for Finch, engaged in conversation with Berthollet, Dolomieu and the other *savants*. Berthollet was, of course, a premier alchemist, on a par with Finch's ability and—if he were being completely honest with himself—perhaps surpassing him in certain areas, especially those related to the *materia* school, something modernists had taken to calling chemistry. This complimented Finch's own strengths in the *energia* and *vitalis* schools, and both men had a keen interest in the burgeoning *mechanica* school of thought. Both spoke fondly of the late alchemical master Benjamin Franklin, for Berthollet had once met the genial Ganymedean just prior to his departure from Paris, where he served as the United States of Ganymede's ambassador. Finch, for his part, had his own fond memories of Dr. Franklin, but these had less to do with alchemical mastery and far more to do with simple humanity.

"Another lovely night, is it not?" Berthollet said as he rode his horse up to Finch's side. Finch had been offered a horse as well, but preferred the surer footing and languorous pace of a sturdy camel. Given that the drovers guided the camels, this perch also gave Finch more time to brush up on his reading; most of his investigations into Egypt's past had to do with kingdoms four and five millennia old. He had paid little attention to the Ptolemaic dynasties, much to his chagrin now.

"It is, monsieur," Finch agreed, though he personally found the nights somewhat monotonous, despite the clarity of the Void above that seemed to entrance the French. Then again, the British weren't letting too many French ships out of Earth's grasp of late, whereas Finch could point to a planet above and describe conditions upon them from first-hand knowledge. "I have been disappointed with the quality of my collection, I fear. There is very little regarding Alexander, and most of it has to do with the Pillar of Hermes, which of course, may not exist at all."

Berthollet smiled and nodded sagely. "I agree, doctor. If anything, I believe the Pillar of Hermes is something of a ruse to throw the scholar off the scent." He handed Finch a piece of paper. "One of our *savants* has been translating a variety of scrolls while we journey, and just finished one such work. It is, shall we say, interesting reading. Perhaps you might enjoy it?"

Finch took the paper and scanned the first few lines, then looked up at Berthollet in shock. "Where did you get this?"

The Frenchman's smile grew wider. "We have engaged in much scholarly research amongst the Mohammedans since we arrived in Cairo," he said. "This was among the papers of an old mosque, though I can't remember which at the moment."

Finch frowned at this, for he knew that the parchments kept safe among the imams of Cairo were considered part and parcel of the history of Islam itself and of Egypt before it. Some scrolls, it was rumored, could trace their origins back to the burned Library of Alexandria, if not before. And Finch knew, from his own repeated and respectful inquiries, that most imams were exceedingly reluctant to let any Westerner, even a respected *murshid*, view their troves. Finch feared that Berthollet's research collaborations were likely conducted at musket-point.

Nonetheless, the translation was in his hand, and it was not as though *not* reading it would somehow set things aright.

The document in question was an account of Alexander the Great's conquest of Egypt, which had occurred more than 330 years before the coming of Christ. Apparently part of a larger narrative, the papers in Finch's hand dealt with Alexander's near-legendary pilgrimage to the Temple of Amun-Ra—which made sense, of course.

There were two things, however, that stood out as Finch quickly skimmed over the translator's work. One, the narrator seemed to be none other than Ptolemy, Alexander's chief deputy and the future pharaoh of Egypt and founder of the Ptolemaic dynasty.

The second was even more unbelievable. Ptolemy wrote of Alexander departing from his private audience with the Oracle of the Siwa Temple of Amun-Ra, and how the experience changed him and his plans for Alexandria, the city he would build into a font of learning.

"My friend," the mighty king said unto me, "I have been entrusted with the secrets of the world, the secrets of science and history, all of it. I have seen it in that temple as if I had been there myself. The gods once fought across our world, and sundered it in twain in ages past. One day, they shall return. And we men must be ready for them, lest our very lives be lost in the coming battles."

The king, the son of the gods himself, placed his hands upon my shoulders and then said unto me: "My city is the key. When it is finished, it will fall to you, my most trusted ally, to gather the greatest minds in the world there so that, when the time comes, we may defeat the very gods themselves!"

There, in that moment, I confess I fell to doubting the words of this great king, to my eternal shame. I said unto him: "It is not enough to make the Mediterranean ours? For the world is large, and we would spend our lives, and our children's lives, and their children's lives besides, in trying to conquer it all."

Yet Alexander, the great son of Zeus, took pity upon me and said unto me: "None of it is truly ours unless we can unite the very world in opposition to the gods. They hewed Atlantis from the rest of the world, covering the world in water. They hewed the heavens from us. And they will hew us from our lives and send us all to Hades itself should they renew their war. So we must build for the dark time to come. My city is but the first step in our long quest."

Finch handed the narrative back to Berthollet, still going over the words in his mind.

"This would confirm some of my theories regarding Xan and Martian involvement in human affairs in the ancient past," Finch said slowly, almost absently. "But you do realize, *monsieur*, we truly have no idea what is there. Alexander may truly have seen the secrets of the universe, or he simply was drugged and made to see visions."

Berthollet nodded. "And yet the temple was, as you say, kept apart from all of Egypt, kept hidden from all but those who were chosen."

"And how are we chosen, then?" Finch asked. "Our most singular accomplishment has been to discern a map laid down in a mosaic. And there is no guarantee that anything Alexander may have seen even remains there some two thousand years later."

Berthollet paused, as if assessing Finch for a moment. "You will simply have to trust me, sir, for I feel that our expedition will not be for naught." And with that, the Frenchman turned back toward the other *savants*, leaving Finch's mind reeling.

The secrets of the world. Alchemists had scoured Egypt for centuries, seeking the roots of mystic science, said to be found enscribed upon the Emerald Tablet and *The Book of the Dead*. Yet few had ever tried to make for the Temple of Amun-Ra, for the location remained closely guarded by the Bedouin tribes, and the journey was hazardous.

Yet...perhaps one or both of these mythical relics were indeed there.

The trick, Finch surmised, would be to ensure he got his hands on them before Berthollet.

CHAPTER 10

June 19, 2134

In a matter of twenty seconds, the surface of Enceladus had been transformed from a quiet, star-lit satellite to the epicenter of the strangest blizzard any human ever experienced—and one that shook Shaila to her core. It looked exactly like her vision, and while she knew in her head that ice crystals and snow wouldn't bother their ops one bit, her heart's drumbeat in her chest and ears said something else entirely. The four astronauts were hunkered alongside the lander, placing the vehicle between themselves and the swirl of ice and snow—yes, snow—that had come roaring toward them like a wall. Shaila knew that there was no wind, but rather it was Enceladus' own rotation, combined with the direction of the tiger stripes' eruption, that made the event seem so oddly reminiscent of Earthly winter storms.

"Durand, report," she said curtly, doing her best to keep the edge from her voice. Stephane had the entire voyage out to study Saturn's moons, and Shaila was very certain the planetologist had done his homework—they had practically shared quarters together the entire time.

"Impressive display of cryovolcanism," Stephane replied over the comm. "Output and seismic readings are in line with past eruptions. At the upper end of the scale, yes, but she is not setting any records."

"So what do we do?" Hall demanded. Of everyone in the landing party, she had the least experience with unforeseen difficulties during an EVA, and the look on her face, given a slight yellow glow from her visor HUD, was not one of calm.

Shaila watched the flakes and hail swirl over her head. Despite the shelter of the lander, their EVA suits were already covered with a light dusting of white. "I suggest we wait it out. Dr. Durand?"

"Agreed. It isn't harmful, but we won't be able to see well," Stephane said. "Should wrap up any moment now."

"Was the eruption in reaction to the lander?" Conti asked. "Did we trigger something?"

Stephane's eyes darted around the interior of his visor as his fingers traipsed across the keypad on his wrist. "I was wondering that too. Ice thickness is good here. Landing data shows very little in the way of impact—Shaila was actually very gentle about it."

"Actually?" Shaila retorted.

Stephane spared her a quick grin before continuing. "These eruptions, they're not regular. It is not like Old Faithful on Earth. If we had been able to set up our instruments, we may have gotten more of a warning. So I think that—"

His voice trailed off as the stars and Saturn suddenly returned to the sky. They could see the cloud of snow drifting further off, away from the landers. Some of it would return to the surface of Enceladus, to be recycled back into the planet's underground oceans. Some of it would escape the moon entirely and ultimately be pulled into Saturn's orbit, fortifying the rings with fresh particles.

Shaila motioned for the others to stay put as she walked around the lander to face south toward the tiger stripes. Once again, there were stars and a much smaller sun off in the distance; the only change was that the surface was covered in a fresh coating of powdery snow.

"OK, show's over. Everybody up and back to work. Hall, Conti—help Durand get his gear set up so we can have more warning next time. Then you can get your own online. I'll start rigging the lander for fuel exchange."

The four astronauts set about their duties quickly—a few more quickly than intended, given the low gravity. Even more so than the Moon or Mars, Enceladus' weak gravity amplified simple motions beyond belief. A single step could propel the unwary at least three meters, while a full jump could send them dozens of meters ahead—or straight up. Soon, everyone figured out that the slow hop-shuffle that they learned in basic training, the same one Neil Armstrong and Buzz Aldrin developed on the fly one hundred and sixty-five years earlier, would suffice.

A half-hour later, Shaila had finished rigging input hoses into the lander, which required a fair amount of power to keep going. The input hose was heated along its length, as was the interior of the cargo space, so that the water could enter and be transferred to the lander without freezing. Each lander was powered by a small, efficient fusion reactor, which meant they had electricity to spare, which made the refueling op possible in the first place.

"We're rigged," Shaila said as she shuffled over to Conti and Hall, who were working on water-quality testing; they had used a laser drill to bore into the moon's crust, in an area where the ice was only a few hundred meters thick. "How's the water?"

Conti looked up, a frown on her face as data danced across the inside of her visor. "Quite a few complex organic chemicals in here," she said. "Almost as many as you'd find on Earth. Didn't expect that. Even a few that look like broken-up strands of proteins."

"You saying there's life here?" Shaila asked, taken aback.

"No, I'm not seeing an actual life form…yet," Conti replied. "But the way things are going, I wouldn't be surprised if they're down there. Probably closer to the core—otherwise, they'll get sucked up and blown out the tiger stripes."

"You think they're smart enough for that?"

"No, Commander, proteins aren't smart, but nature has a way of making it work," the doctor replied. "Chances are, if there's life down there, it's pretty simple—microscopic at best, single-cells at worst. And they'll breed closer to the heat. They float off, they'll die, freeze and get broken down to the molecular level by the time they reach the crust."

Shaila nodded. "So we'll do the DDP, then?"

Conti stood up and smiled. "I'll come back with the next refueling op and let it loose."

The Deep-Dive Probe was a device the size of a small refrigerator, fueled by nuclear batteries and packing enough sensor equipment to rig an entire ship. Powered by small fins and a propeller in back, it was designed to swim in whatever liquids they came across—petrocarbons on Titan and water on Enceladus, in particular. The probe would plant an antenna on the surface of the moon and another at the refueling hole bored by the laser drill. That would allow *Armstrong* to keep tabs on the little submarine as it dove deep in search of…life.

Pretty heady stuff, Shaila thought. *Are we really going to find the first evidence of life outside Earth? At least, on our side of the fence?*

"So what's all this o-chem gunk going to do to our fuel quality?" Shaila asked, directing her question at Hall.

"Not a lot," Hall replied, tinkering with her own sensors. "I'm worried more about the salinity levels here—they're pretty high. I'm thinking we might want to do filtration on the surface here instead of on board. Otherwise, we'll have to make a lot more trips in order to refuel."

Burning salt water in the engines wasn't the end of the world, but there was an increased chance of buildup in the nozzles as the super-heated water—and salt—burst through them. A few parts-per-million of organic chemicals wouldn't do much, but high salinity could create a huge maintenance headache. If too much salt built up, critical systems could be corrupted. Thankfully, the emergency refuel ops package on board included filtration devices to render Enceladus' water perfect for fuel—and drinking. But they were on board; portability to the surface was an open question.

"All right. Let's load up while we're here, see how much filtration we'll need to do. We'll flag Houston and see if they have ideas on rigging filtration down here," Shaila said. "Can I get in there to drop the hose?"

A few minutes later, the lander's cargo hold began to fill with water. Shaila wished she could see the water, but there weren't any windows into the cargo area. She hoped they didn't suck up a space microbe or something—it would be just her luck to discover life on another world, only to torch it out the back end of the ship.

"Durand, report," Shaila said. "We'll be filled up in a few here. Where are you?"

Stephane's voice came in clearly over the comm. "I'm closer to the tiger stripes. No seismic activity for now, so I'm taking a closer look. Amazing to see the water bubble up and freeze. It's like watching cold lava."

Shaila smiled; he was a geek through and through, despite everything. "All right, but start heading back. We're going to launch at 14:30, give or take."

By the time the cargo hold was full, Conti and Hall had wrapped up their experiments, and Stephane could be seen bounding toward the lander in 10-meter strides. *Probably didn't want to get into trouble with the EVA commander,* Shaila smirked to herself. Stephane at least had the forethought to start skidding to a stop while at least 100 meters from the lander, though he still grabbed onto the edge of a wing to fully arrest his movement. "I cannot wait to come back!" he panted as he righted himself. "The stripes, you have to come with me to see them, Shay!"

Shaila shook her head at him, amused. "Just get in the car," she quipped. "Let's not be late for dinner. I'm famished."

Stephane gave her a wink and picked his way through the snow to the lander's ladder, climbing up to the top to join Conti and Hall, who were already making their way inside. Shaila gave the lander a final visual inspection before joining them, sealing the airlock behind her.

"All right, strap in," Shaila said. "Let's get this place warmed up." She flipped a switch on her board. "Lander One to *Armstrong*, we're ready for liftoff, over."

"Roger that, Lander One," Becker replied. "We'll roll out the welcome mat. You're cleared for liftoff."

Shaila gave her vertical thrusters a tap, followed by a hint of power from the forward engines, and watched the moon slowly fall away. Given how easily the snow on the surface kicked up, not to mention the low gravity, she wanted to ensure the lander was well away from their ongoing experiments before hitting the gas. It took about a minute for the lander to float about a half kilometer away from their landing area. That's when Shaila kicked in her vertical thrusters a bit more, nosing the craft upward and giving the main engines a sustained burn.

"Escape velocity achieved," she reported. "We'll see you in about forty minutes, *Armstrong*."

Shaila ran through her checklist one more time, out loud—it helped her concentrate. "Seals good, internal temperature steady at 20 degrees Celsius, atmospheric pressure holding." She turned to the rest of the team. "I say we're in good shape if you want to take those helmets off."

"Thank God," Stephane said, quickly reaching for his helmet latches. "I hate this thing!" He pulled it off and ran a gauntleted hand across his face. "And the visor, it gives me a headache. I wonder—bleh!"

Shaila turned to see Stephane's face contorted in disgust, his tongue out. "What?"

"I taste something horrible!" he said. "Gross and salty and—"

Conti sat up straight. "Oh, shit! The water! It melted! We're covered in it!"

Shaila looked down and, sure enough, saw damp areas on the outer layer of her suit, and a puddle of moisture around her chair. "And…is that a problem, Doctor?" she asked nervously.

Conti looked flustered. "I don't know, Commander. I mean, I didn't see anything particularly dangerous in the samples we took, but the computer is still working on some of the more complex chemicals. "

Stephane started to look panicked. "So did I just poison myself or something?"

"No, you didn't," Shaila said sternly, as if she could order it to be so. "He didn't, right, Conti?"

"Probably not. There certainly wasn't anything in those samples that would require quarantine, and the lander's sensors would've picked up anything wrong by now," the doctor said. "Meantime, I'm having the ship computer run a full diagnostic on Stephane to be sure."

Shaila nodded. Each EVA suit was wired with medical sensors that would probably detect anything immediately wrong. "All right. Stephane, get your helmet back on and seal up. I think that'll have to be standard procedure until we figure out a better option."

Stephane swore in French as he reached for his helmet again, but quickly snatched up a pouch of energy drink and downed it before he put it on. "What an awful taste," he said as he sealed up again. "I hope I will not grow another limb or something from that."

Shaila fixed him a quick grin as she adjusted course for *Armstrong*. "Oh, I don't know. That might be useful."

October 12, 1798

"Sighting! Three points to starboard! Unidentified!"

Captain Weatherby broke off his conversation with the Countess St. Germain and her son and raced toward the railing, glass in hand. "About bloody time," he groused, peering off into the Void, just to the right of Saturn and her glorious rings.

There it was. A small, white Ovoid—the egg-shaped ships used by the Xan, given such a name by the Admiralty because, Weatherby assumed, calling them "Eggs" seemed quite disrespectful to the powerful Xan civilization. The Ovoids moved with no discernible means of propulsion or attack, yet were capable of impressive speed and, Weatherby was sure, even more impressive destruction.

"I imagine we have some time yet," Barnes said from Weatherby's side. "They seem quite far off."

Weatherby snapped his glass shut. "Fifteen minutes at most, I should say."

Frowning, Barnes peered through his own glass. "That fast, sir?"

"Indeed."

Weatherby turned back toward where Anne and Philip were standing. "Do they know we're coming, do you think?" the boy asked.

Young Philip's words hung heavy over the quarterdeck of the *Fortitude* as the officers all fixed the Xan vessel. They had passed Titan's path several hours ago, but only now had espied the usual Xan customs vessel. Usually, the Xan were much quicker to intercept Earth vessels—especially ones unexpected and uninvited.

Since time immemorial, the Xan found the company of others besides their own kind somehow abhorrent. They had escaped human contact until Sir Francis Drake's fabled expedition to the Jovian moon Callisto during Elizabeth's reign. Callisto was a kind of colony for the creatures now known as Xan; they made their primary homes upon the very rings of Saturn. Upon meeting Drake, the Xan warned against any further contact, and barred humanity from voyaging to Saturn itself.

That is, until the early 1780s.

Following the events surrounding HMS *Daedalus*, upon which Weatherby served as a very young second lieutenant and Anne took passage, the Xan had sent their first ambassadors to the courts of men. These fully robed, masked creatures, nearly nine feet tall, must have seen something of promise, for they began to allow the nations of Earth (and offworld colonies) to send ambassadors directly to Great Xanath, which is what these creatures called their homeworld.

Since then, perhaps a dozen ships each year had traveled back and forth to Saturn with the express written permission of a Xan ambassador. Another hundred or so tried to do so without such allowance; most were turned away with naught but stern words. A few more aggressive interlopers ended up giving those stern words their menace through their unfortunate example, for their ships were simply never seen nor heard of again.

Weatherby fervently hoped he and his ship would not add to that catalogue of misfortune, and he felt he had at least a handful of cards he might play. He simply needed a playing partner, and at long last, there was one to be had.

It had been six long hours since they skirted past Titan, said to be the Xan's true homeworld, now a blasted hulk of a sphere shrouded in poisonous fumes. At the time, most of Weatherby's wardroom seemed discomfited by the captain's refusal to beat to quarters, feeling that if the Xan opted to take umbrage, they might at least have a chance of escape.

Weatherby actually laughed at this. These young men came into the service at a time when the Xan seemed to be simply another nation, and Saturn just another port of call, albeit one of striking rarity. Weatherby knew better. They would enter Xan space peaceably, with no weapons armed, and no men ready to do battle. If the Xan took offense, their preparedness, or lack thereof, would not make the slightest difference anyway.

"They know we're here, have no doubt, Philip," Weatherby said, with a slight smile in Anne's direction, one she returned in kind. "We can only hope that the French haven't poisoned their attitudes toward us."

"And if they have?" Barnes asked as he joined his captain. Of all the officers aboard, he was the most surprisingly sanguine about the perils of visiting Saturn uninvited. In the weeks since their battle in the Rocky Main, the ship's acting first lieutenant seemed reaffirmed in his belief in his captain. And now, it seemed, he was not questioning Weatherby, but rather posing the question solely to allow the captain to answer it.

"We yet have a friend or two among Saturn's rings," Weatherby said. "And I feel confident that they shall not fire upon us so long as our guns remain stowed."

Anne nodded toward the fo'c'sle. "It seems your Dr. Hawkins is quite enamored of all this. His glass is practically stuck to his eye. He's been taking notes for hours. And," she noted conspiratorially, "he seems to have actually gained some color upon his face."

Weatherby turned forward to see Hawkins practically leaning over the railing of the fo'c'sle, straining to catch a glimpse of the oncoming Xan ship, pausing only to take notes within a small book in front of him. Weatherby had a similar journal once, and the memory, combined with Anne's proximity, made him feel young once again. "I should hope he keeps a weather eye on that book of his, lest it end up somewhere unexpected," he said.

Anne laughed at this, as Weatherby had hoped. "Francis told me all about your journal," she said. "Amazing that they could read it upon the other side. He was, however, reticent about its contents."

"Oh, you know how these things are," Weatherby said casually. "The incoherent ramblings of a second lieutenant: lost, lovelorn, too young and too timid for his rank."

"Well, he's aged well enough at least," Anne said. "The timidity may have lessened as well, at least somewhat."

Weatherby smiled most fondly at this, and silence passed between them for a moment until he noticed Barnes shifting his weight next to him, looking most uncomfortable and anxious. Reddening under his collar, Weatherby turned his attentions back to the matter at hand. "So, my lady, have you had truck with the Xan since that time?"

Anne seemed unfazed by the change of direction in discourse, and indeed seemed amused by it, as she always did. They had already discussed this in private, but she grasped quickly that Weatherby's query was for those around them. "Francis served as the first ambassador to Saturn from the Holy Roman Empire for two years, starting in 1786. I accompanied him, as did Philip, who was but two at the time."

The boy looked down and shuffled his feet, seemingly embarrassed by his mother's mention of him. He was, Weatherby thought, such a perfect reflection of his age. Curious, intelligent and proud, yet so easily whipsawed by the merest word from anyone.

"And what can you tell us of our destination, my lady?" Barnes asked. A few of the junior officers and midshipmen on the quarterdeck began to lean toward them somewhat.

"We shall likely dock at the moon we call Mimas, which serves as their main port facility," she said. "There is a most curious lake there, quite circular with a cone-shaped island in the middle. They say it was created by some rocky impact ages ago. But the port itself is likely nothing outside your experience, beyond the self-moving carts, of course."

"Their carts move by themselves?" one of the midshipmen gasped.

Anne turned and smiled at the boy, who was no older than Philip. "They do. There is a driver, as our carts, but there is a series of buttons and levers which control the direction and speed of the cart. They are powered by engines, not pulled by animals."

The boy blinked at her as if she had just spoken in Chinese. Barnes gave him a whack on the shoulder and sent him back to his post. "And from there?" Barnes asked.

"We will be directed to the Earth quarter of Mimas, along the edge of the lake," Anne replied. "That is where all men must dwell when they are around Saturn. From the ambassadors' quarters to the hostels for sailors, you will be confined to this quarter and this quarter only. The gates of the quarter are heavily guarded, and those who would seek to explore outside it are rendered unconscious at the gates themselves, and returned to their quarters with no memory of how they arrived."

"So how did your husband conduct his business if he couldn't leave?" Hawkins asked. He had joined the group a few moments prior from his perch on the fo'c'sle.

"The Xan came to us," she said simply. "If we required their attention, we would pass a message to one of the guards at the gate, and they would come to visit us within a day or so. They would also hold events and entertainments for us on a regular basis, including musical performances. I remember those most fondly."

Weatherby nodded at this; he remembered the Xan voices as being beautifully harmonic, as if two voices were speaking at once, with one voice conveying factual words with simple melodies, and the other singing emotional harmonic undertones to the first. A musical performance given by the Xan would be something indeed.

"Two more vessels sighted!" came a cry from the tops. "Same as the first. Two points to larboard and dead ahead."

Once again, the officers aboard raced toward the rails to take a look at the newcomers, both of which were closing in upon the *Fortitude* with amazing speed. Weatherby glanced at Anne, who now looked somewhat worried. "One would have been enough," she said. "Three is...."

"A problem," Weatherby said. He turned to Barnes. "I want the men to assume their battle stations. We will *not* beat to quarters, there are to be *no* marines sent to the tops, and we will *not* run out the guns until I give the order. No one is to run, to shout, to hasten in any way. Given that, I want us ready to run out and fire as soon as possible. Go."

Barnes turned and immediately waved over the officers still upon the quarterdeck, and they scattered a few moments later, walking with an odd mix of alacrity and forced casualness. Weatherby would have laughed at the sight if there weren't three Xan vessels of unknown capacity bearing down upon him.

Two minutes later, there were men walking all over the ship. The marines had taken stations along the railings of the ship on either side, their guns casually slung over their shoulders. They might have been far more effective from the tops, but two score armed men climbing the rigging would be far too noticeable. Weatherby could feel the vibration of wheeled guns moving about under him, and hoped that this would not be detected by the Xan and their strange, wondrous alchemical engines.

The Xan, meanwhile, had closed to within no more than three hundred yards. They also positioned themselves at difficult angles to the *Fortitude*'s guns, making it impossible for Weatherby's ship to get off a meaningful shot without tacking first. Given the Xan ships' speed—they easily closed several miles in but a few minutes—it was unlikely those shots would ever be fired.

"Attention, HMS *Daedalus*," came a melodious voice that seemed to emanate from nowhere yet permeated the Void around them, filling the air and their ears with a fusillade of sound with angry, martial harmonics, as if a German opera company had suddenly declared war. "You will stop your preparations to fire at once."

"Damn!" Barnes hissed. "How could they tell? Sir, shall I...?"

The first lieutenant was truly taken aback to see his captain smiling. "Do as they say," Weatherby said. "And reassure the men. We are quite safe here."

Once again confused, though more trusting this time, Barnes quickly hurried off to pass the word, leaving Weatherby smiling at Anne, who smiled back in turn. "This isn't the *Daedalus*," she said simply.

"Which means they know I'm aboard, and possibly you as well, and they are likely well-disposed toward us," Weatherby said. The captain took up the ship's speaking horn and directed it at the nearest Xan ship. It seemed a futile gesture, but Weatherby knew they would hear, somehow. "Our most sincere apologies to our most gracious hosts," he shouted. "We are HMS *Fortitude*, and we seek an audience with the British ambassador to discuss matters of a most urgent nature."

A few moments later, the reply came back, with the belligerence replaced by a certain warmth of tone. The words, however, were not as welcoming. "Prepare to be boarded."

Weatherby and Anne exchanged a look; neither had expected this. Indeed, they would likely be the first people to see a Xan enter or exit one of their vessels. And there was no record of any Xan stepping aboard an Earth vessel—not even the ambassadors sent to Earth, for no one knew how they traveled there. Weatherby raised his horn again. "We shall be most delighted to receive guests," he ventured.

The next ten minutes saw the *Fortitude*'s officers prepare an honor guard along the gangplank—an unarmed one, which made the whole affair even more unusual. Combined with the sight of a large, silvery-white, metallic *egg* drifting to the very side of the ship and hovering there in the Void, the whole thing seemed almost comical. "I guess the egg came first," one of the mids whispered to the bosun, causing both to chuckle softly as they waited for whatever would emerge from the Ovoid.

The outline of a portal—one at least ten feet high—soon appeared along the smooth wall of the Xan ship, and Weatherby ordered the gangplank extended to it. The outlined portion of the hull then recessed into the egg, then slowly rose, revealing a solitary figure inside, dwarfed by the doorway.

Weatherby gaped. "I will be damned," he whispered.

Slowly, a man—a human being, to be precise—emerged from the Xan ship and began slowly walking across the gangplank as the hatch behind him closed. He wore the finery of a nobleman and the star of a Knight of the Garter, which looked most incongruous given the situation. His hair was grey, and he walked with the halting, lurching gait of the older gentleman whose heart and body remained strong, even if the knees were a little weak.

"Permission to come aboard, *Captain* Weatherby?" the man said.

Weatherby's grin could not have been wider; his best card had already been played on his behalf, it seemed. "Most assuredly granted."

As the bosun whistled him aboard, the English Ambassador to Saturn, Baron James Morrow, former Admiral of the Royal Navy and commander of a number of its ships—including the late *Daedalus*—gave his former lieutenant a bear hug. "I cannot tell you how relieved I am that it's you here, Tom!" he said, his hands on his protégé's shoulders. "I would've had a much harder time convincing anyone else of this madness!"

Weatherby looked at him quizzically for a moment. "There's much more to this, isn't there."

"Quite so, Tom, quite so," the ambassador said. Then he caught the sight of Anne St. Germain out of the corner of his eye, and it was Morrow's turn to be utterly surprised. "You?"

Anne smiled and walked over to give Morrow a hug of her own. "It is most wonderful to see you, sir," she said.

"Yes, quite," Morrow replied, giving the girl a hug in return, then quickly disentangling himself. "I must ask, however, your purpose here."

"Because of my husband," she said, her voice growing concerned.

"Because of your husband," Morrow replied simply.

"I know not what he has done, or what he aims to do, but from all that we have learned, I must…question his path and his choice of friends," Anne said, struggling for the words. "We have never troubled ourselves in the conflicts of nations, and I would be most aggrieved if he had started now."

Morrow studied her a moment, then nodded and turned back to Weatherby. "And you…oh, Hell, I'm not going to even ask you to vouch for her," he said with a grandfatherly wink; in that moment, Weatherby was reminded of Franklin himself. "Come, then. We have much to discuss. Weatherby, make sail and follow these ships in."

Weatherby smiled and crossed his arms over his chest. "Excuse me, *ambassador?*"

Morrow shook his head with a rueful grin. "I suggest, *Captain,* that we set a course to follow our escorts. We won't be going to Mimas."

CHAPTER 11

June 19, 2134

N ot very subtle, are you, Maria?" Harry quipped. He leaned back in his chair and smiled broadly, which made Diaz want to reach out and choke him. It also worried her that the presence of four government operatives didn't seem to faze him a bit.

"And you are?" she retorted, doing her best to be casual as she slid into the chair across from him. "Seriously, what's up with the mastermind thing? Did we reach the boss level in the hologame?"

Harry looked puzzled at this. "Maria, what the hell are you talking about? You're the ones coming in under false pretenses."

Before she could reply, Greene tapped her arm briefly, showing her a datapad; their sensors and communications were entirely blocked, with an exceedingly complex quantum encryption password needed to operate anything in the room. "Mr. Yu, you do realize that the circumstances that brought us here, and the complete electronics blackout you've imposed, are major question marks."

"Dr. Greene. I've missed you on HV. Loved your holoshow," Harry said. "What circumstances are these?"

Greene looked to Maria briefly, who nodded that he should go on. "An unusual degree of Cherenkov radiation was detected from this site," he said. "I'm sure I don't have to tell you what that might imply."

Harry nodded, his smile dwindling. "I was on Mars. I know what that means. There were only a few of us left on base when everything went down."

"So what'cha doing now, Harry?" Diaz said. "Trying to break through and say hi to the guys on the other side?"

"Using a fusion power plant?" Harry retorted. "If that were the case, there'd be a couple hundred portals to alternate dimensions all over the world. We'd be crawling with English Navy guys. Or sentient kittens. Whatever."

Diaz smirked. She almost missed sparring with Harry. It reminded her of a much simpler time, when all she had to manage was a tiny, backwater mining op on Mars. "Here's the thing, Harry. Your new conglom is listed as one of the backers of the *Tienlong*," she said.

Harry poured himself a cup of coffee from a thermos on the conference table, offering some to his guests with a look; there were no takers. "Yeah, Total-Suez is backing the Chinese on this one. You here to tell me JSC would've been better? We lost the bid to ExEn."

"*Tienlong* wasn't supposed to go to Saturn," Greene said. "They were registered as a Jovian survey."

Harry shrugged. "You ever work with the PRC, Doctor? They change the deal-terms all the time. If they didn't have a massive space op and serious cash, they'd be impossible to work with. We were only told after launch. Totally worth it though."

"Dammit, Harry, they nearly damn well ran *Armstrong* right into Saturn," Diaz growled, leaning in toward him. "Jain's on that flight. Durand, too."

"Due respect for your kids there, Maria, but that's not my problem," Harry said, meeting her gaze steadily. "We got our corporate specialist on board, and he's gonna survey and claim whatever he feels is appropriate, wherever the Chinese take him. You got a problem with the way *Tienlong* is behaving, you take it up with Beijing."

"There's also the matter of Teotihuacan," Coogan added.

Harry turned to glare at the young man. "Teo-ti-what? Who *are* you, anyway?"

"Some of your conglom's gear was found at an Aztec ruin outside Mexico City, Harry," Diaz said. "It was channeling ambient Cherenkov radiation."

"Why would someone do that?" Harry asked. His face was the picture of annoyed innocence.

"Maybe to distract us, maybe to reach out to the folks on the other side."

Shaking his head, Harry stood up and began to pace the room. He always had a nervous energy to him, enough to make it tough to tell when he was being evasive or when he was just being himself. "So because it's my con-glom's gear, you think I'm behind it. Same with the Chinese ship, because I can freakin' control Beijing's space ops from my office here."

Diaz shrugged, but inwardly groaned. Laid out like that, it did seem somewhat circumstantial. "Harry, you know what happened on Mars. We have to be sure there are defenses in place before we try to replicate it."

"Don't have to convince me, Maria. That was scary shit," Harry said, softening for a moment. "But right now, all I got are four people who, I assume, aren't with the IAEA. Which means you've fried the Corporate Protection Act seven ways to Sunday. So what do we do about it?"

"You convince me that you're clean on all this, and help me figure out why your gear is out there at a site like Teotihuacan," Diaz said firmly. "You do that, I'm officially off your case."

Harry smiled, his edge back. "Sorry, but I don't have to do any of that. Since you're not an IAEA inspector, and I'm pretty sure none of you are here at the behest of the Egyptian government, I think I'm just going to have to kick you out and call it a day."

"Harry," Diaz warned as she stood up. "I don't know what you're up to, but—"

He cut her off with a wave of his hand. "I wasn't the bad guy two years ago, and I'm not the bad guy now. I got a plant to get running here, and a Saturn mission to monitor. So if you'll excuse me, Maria, I'm done. These gentlemen will see you out."

"That's it?" Diaz said as the office door opened. Four security officers entered. They were armed with the latest in semiautomatic weapons—de-cidedly not non-lethal.

"That's it," Harry said. He turned to the holoscreen on his desk and swiped through some text. "Special Corporate Charter Law, section 5, sub-section B, paragraph 3: No governmental force beyond standard industry regulators will enter into corporate holdings unannounced, nor will they invade a corporation's privacy beyond that which the corporation is legally required to disclose.'"

Diaz watched as the men fanned out across the room. Mercenaries, likely ex-military. Damn.

"I'll be in contact with the U.S. government to file a formal protest with regard to your actions today," Harry said. "Now get out and have a nice day."

Diaz looked at the guards, then back to Harry, who had already settled in behind his desk, dismissing them from his mind entirely. "All right. Let's go."

October 14, 1798

In retrospect, Finch should've known word of the expedition would have reached the oasis before they did.

The French, after all, were nothing if not indiscreet in their activities in Egypt. They went everywhere in numbers, they were brash and loud, and despite Napoleon's claims to be a friend to all followers of Muhammad, they treated Muslim tradition as inconveniences at best—and something to tamp down upon at worst. Their reputation had spread throughout lower Egypt as invaders and interlopers, no doubt aided by the retreating beys, who had headed south and west as the French pressed on.

That the news would follow the caravan routes should have been anticipated. Indeed, Finch was completely unsurprised at the two hundred mounted warriors now facing them across the desert plain, with the trees of the oasis faint upon the horizon behind them in the morning light. The French were exhausted from the night's travels, and outnumbered more than two to one besides.

"We should attempt a parlay," Finch told Berthollet quietly. "These are Bedouins, and they guard their oases jealously. We should make a truce, and pay the tax they will undoubtedly desire."

"Payment?" Berthollet snorted. "They have swords and horses. We have rifles. We should slay two-thirds of them before they even reach us! Do they not know this?"

"Do you wish to be welcomed or scorned?" Finch countered, growing testy. "We may be welcomed as simply another caravan, or we may be seen as enemies of Islam and the vanguard of another Crusade. The other tribes will spread the word of what happens here."

"The other tribes are a fractious lot," Berthollet said dismissively. "Some of them will welcome us."

"Me against my brother, my brother and I against my cousin, my cousin and I against the stranger,'" Finch quoted. "You're the strangers here."

Any further debate was cut off as four of the horsemen began riding toward the center of the plain. Gathering Finch and the French military commander with a wave, Berthollet kicked his horse forward to greet them. Shaking his head, Finch spurred his camel forward, the creature's loping gait keeping pace surprisingly well.

Minutes later, they reached the center, facing four Bedouins dressed, in their way, to impress. These worthies wore long robes and headscarves, and used patterned silks as sashes and belts. All carried wicked-looking scimitars, and they also had firearms—likely to be a rarity amongst the rank and file, but worrisome enough.

"Who among you speaks a civilized tongue?" the most garishly dressed among them demanded, in Arabic.

Finch raised a hand in greeting. "I am the *murshid* Andrew Finch, of Cairo, and I speak the tongue of the Prophet. In the name of Allah the Merciful and Just, I bid you greetings and hopes for long life and prosperity."

"In the name of Allah, I greet you," the Bedouin said curtly. "I am Sheikh Karim bin Abdullah al-Siwa. Your name is known to us, *murshid*, and there is honor attached to it. So why is it you travel with these Franks?"

Guilt by association, it seems. "You do me honor, Sheikh Karim. I travel with them on a quest for knowledge, not conquest. If you know of me, you know I am a scholar. My companions are as well, and we seek naught but rest at the oasis, and the opportunity to research the ruins we may find there."

Sheikh Karim looked over the shoulders of the Europeans toward the troops behind them, all of whom had weapons ready. "Scholars do not carry swords and guns, *murshid*."

Finch smiled, but inwardly cursed himself. He had an alchemical admixture that would do much to ease negotiations, making his words more amenable to all hearing them. And the damned vial was among his possessions in one of the wagons behind him. He was too damned young for senility. "The desert is arduous, especially for those unused to it. And there are those, as you are aware, who are not as noble and generous as your esteemed tribe, who would waylay caravans without provocation. Thanks be to Allah, we did not encounter them in our journey here, but we thought it best to be prepared."

"Finch," Berthollet hissed, shifting in his saddle. "What are you saying?"

"He's asking why a group of scholars has soldiers with them," Finch said sotto voce. "I'd prefer it if we got through this without loss of life, *monsieur*."

Berthollet grimaced. "Not likely," he said, kicking his horse forward. "You there, Sheikh. That is your name, yes?" he asked in French.

"It's his title," Finch said.

"Fine. Sheikh, you will stand down. We mean to explore around this oasis, and we will not be denied," Berthollet said loudly. "Finch, tell them."

Finch rode up next to Berthollet. "Damn you, *monsieur*! Will you not allow me the chance to do this properly?"

Berthollet sneered toward the Bedouins. "Why should we? They live in tents and know nothing of philosophy, truth or science. They should be grateful we're here!"

At this point, Sheikh Karim rode forward from the rest of his party. "Not grateful," he said in heavily accented French. "We know philosophy. We know Allah. You do not. You will leave. Now."

"Oh, bloody hell," Finch muttered. The Bedouins may be nomadic tribespeople, but some of the better-off tribes sent their foremost sons to Cairo and, in some cases, Istanbul in order to learn more of the ways of the world. Sheikh Karim was likely among them. "My esteemed Sheikh," he said in Arabic. "I must apologize for this man. You must know how the Franks get when they are out in the desert sun for too long."

Sheikh Karim stared wide-eyed a moment at Berthollet, then suddenly burst out laughing, as did those with him. "You know, *murshid*, that would explain much!"

"It explains but half, Sheikh Karim. The other half has something to do with wine and smelly cheese," Finch added.

He was rewarded with more laughter. "Very well, *murshid* Finch," the sheikh said finally. "If they pay the tax, they are welcome to the oasis so long as their soldiers remain in a camp to themselves. You and your scholars will be under my protection, and will not need them in the ruins. But know that it is because of you I extend this courtesy, and these Franks must behave like civilized men while here."

"A moment, honored Sheikh," Finch said before turning to translate for Berthollet. "Honestly, it's the best deal we'll get that keeps everyone alive."

Berthollet frowned. "And what if I do not care if they die?" he said quietly.

"Then the next tribe that comes here will set upon us. And then the next.

And we'll eventually run out of these half-starved boys you call soldiers. And then we'll die as well," Finch said quietly, but with steel. "Now, unless you feel like condemning us all to death today, *monsieur*, I'm going to accept his offer."

Without waiting for a reply, Finch turned back to Sheikh Karim. "Honored Sheikh, we are prepared to accept your most kind and generous offer, but I have one question. What if some ill befalls us that requires weapons whilst we are away from our men? By the grace of Allah, this will not happen, but there are sheikhs out there far less enlightened than yourself."

Sheikh Karim seemed all too ready with a reply. "Then you may all camp at the ruins you seek, and I will accompany you myself, *murshid*, to ensure your safety!" he said with a broad grin. "I have often wondered of these relics. I played amongst them as a child, and could never discern their writing."

Finch smiled. This had turned out better than he might have thought. "Then you are most welcome, Sheikh Karim, and may Allah keep you." He then turned to Berthollet and switched to French. "We're in. And the sheikh there knows the ruins well and has agreed to act as a guide."

Berthollet's eyebrows rose. "A guide? He knows of the temple?"

Finch smiled. "He knows of ruins, *monsieur*. I don't think he understands their significance. Sheikh Karim will guide us to the ruins."

"I suppose this is the best of a bad situation," Berthollet grumbled. "Perhaps it is better to get them to work for us than to shoot them and do the work ourselves." With a perfunctory nod to the Sheikh, Berthollet turned and galloped back to his countrymen. Karim turned and did the same, leaving Finch there in the middle with Jabir, who had dutifully ridden with Finch into the parlay.

"Well?" Finch asked him.

The young man shook his head sadly. "The Sheikh thinks he's getting hostages, and Berthollet thinks you've tamed the Bedouins," Jabir said. "How long can this last, *murshid*?"

Finch turned his camel around and plodded back toward the French line. "Hopefully long enough, Jabir. Find us a place to make camp between the French and the Bedouins, preferably a bit out of the way.

"Just in case things deteriorate."

June 19, 2134

Shaila smiled as she rapped on the glass on the door to sickbay. Smiling and waving, she hit the intercom button with the other hand. "How's my favorite scientist under glass?"

Inside, Stephane gave a half-smile, half-grimace. He was in bed, looking extremely bored, wearing standard-issue hospital wear. After reporting to *Armstrong* on Stephane's taste of Enceladus, Nilssen ordered Stephane quarantined while Conti did a more detailed analysis of the particulates in the water. "Quarantine is the most boring thing ever," he replied.

Shaila's smile grew broader. "Hey, at least you have access to all your Enceladus data," she said. "Plenty to study there."

"Yes, but I don't have access to you," he grumbled.

"Well, you have work to do anyway," she replied. "How's the analysis coming?"

Stephane picked up a datapad and began tapping on it. A moment later, the glass between them filled with data points. "Everyone's interested in the biology, but nobody's paying attention to the geology," he groused.

Shaila looked over the data. While she grasped perhaps a fifth of it, tops, she understood that the geology wasn't behaving as predicted by years of satellite survey data. The cryovolcanism had some odd patterns to it, centered along the southern pole where they landed. "Did we do this?"

Stephane shrugged. "I don't know. I am trying to account for every possibility, but I need more data. I should get down there again."

"Not until Conti clears you," Shaila replied.

"And where *is* my doctor?" he groused, folding his arms across his chest. "I have things to do!"

Shaila knew Conti was pulling triple duty, hustling down to the moon with each load of fuel water, coming back to check on Stephane and doing data analysis in the meantime. Meanwhile, Stephane was into his fifteenth hour of a 36-hour quarantine, and by all reports, his good humor was wearing thin by the hour.

"I just got back from a fuel run. Conti put the underwater probes in," Shaila said. "She's pretty excited about seeing what's under there. Said the data will be coming back soon."

Stephane tossed the datapad onto the bedside table with a bit more force than was necessary. "I should be down there. Stupid! How could I be so careless?"

"Hey now," Shaila said. "A few months on Mars doesn't make you an EVA pro. Don't beat yourself up."

"True, I have my countrymen for that," he replied testily. "Have you seen this?"

A new chart flashed in front of Shaila—an instant poll, showing that 52 percent of people in France were upset that Stephane opted not to be the first man on Enceladus. *Probably because I'm a Brit,* Shaila thought.

"Hey, you still have 45 percent who thought it was sweet," she said brightly. "And I did too. You really didn't have to do that."

"No, I didn't," he agreed, which prompted Shaila to take a physical step back from the door.

"Hey, I didn't ask you to," she said defensively. "That was your call, not mine."

Stephane glared at the door, but seeing her face, relented. "I know, I'm sorry, Shay. I'm just frustrated being in this little cage."

Shaila considered giving him a talking to, but opted against it. If she were stuck in medical while everyone else was exploring a brand new world, she'd be pissed too. "It's OK," she said. "I really did appreciate it."

"Like I said, you don't always get a chance to give a woman a world," he replied, his customary grin returning. "And as for the poll, you know us French. We will debate everything we can a million times."

"Yeah, I know the French all right," she said, her smile tentatively returning. "You should get cracking on a preliminary report. Houston's been pretty understanding, but we want you to make sense of some of the cryovolcanism before too long."

Stephane gave a salute from his bed. "*Oui*, Commander. I am on it."

Shaila turned and walked off, still slightly discomfited by Stephane's outburst. They had been through a lot together over the past two years, and he almost never got snippy with her. Even when all hell was breaking loose on Mars—even when he had an 18th century pistol pointed in his face—he didn't get pissed. Scared, sure. But angry? No.

"How's he doing?"

Shaila stopped abruptly, right before she plowed into Nilssen, who looked at her with bemused concern.

"Sir," she said, unconsciously straightening up. "He's cranky as hell, but he'll be OK once he's released. How's the water works?"

"On target," the commander said. "I was just looking for you. Wanted to get a second opinion. What do you make of these?"

Nilssen handed her a datapad. On it, there were strings of complex carbon molecules—proteins, if she remembered her organic chemistry correctly. "From the water?" she asked.

"Yep. These readings just came in from Conti's submersible. Pretty damn complex if you ask me."

She nodded and handed back the datapad. "More than anything I've seen," she agreed. "You wondering where the line is?"

He nodded. "Does this constitute life? Or do we need to find something that actually moves? I mean…it's close. Damned close. Anyway, I think we need to have Conti grab some deep samples then get back up her to put 'em through their paces in the lab. If we can get that nailed down here, we'd –"

The intercom hummed to life, interrupting the captain. "Nilssen, Jain, report to command at once." It was Hall, who was serving as duty officer while Archie piloted the lander. Even geriatric engineers didn't fly all the way to Saturn and not want a shot at walking on another world.

Nilssen tapped his datapad once. "We're here, Liz. Report."

The datapad showed Hall's face, looking creased and worried. "Houston got some signals from our Titan survey sat they wanted to show us."

"Show us," the skipper ordered.

Hall's face disappeared, replaced with an image of the Chinese ship in orbit around Titan. Houston must've re-tasked the satellite to keep a close eye on the *Tienlong*, because the imagery was stunning. She was a very different design from *Armstrong*, eschewing an outward wheel in favor of an internal centrifuge for sleeping. That certainly saved on space and energy, but the crew would require a lot more gravity rehab when they got home.

A small lander, not dissimilar to *Armstrong*'s own craft, pulled away from the *Tienlong* and, once clear, fired its engines toward Titan.

"You think they have the same electro-mag shielding?" Shaila wondered.

"Hard to say," Nilssen responded. "I'll ask Houston to keep an eye out."

The lander streaked toward the planet, and the satellite's camera dutifully zoomed it on it—the onboard A.I. was pretty good. "Tracking shows the lander's heading for a strange spot," Hall chimed in. "Somewhere near the northern pole. Our surveys show there's not much there. None of our target spots are within 500 kilometers."

"You think we missed something?" Nilssen asked her.

"Makes me think they know something we don't know," she replied.

Shaila and Nilssen traded a worried look. "Ask Houston for as much detail on that area as they have. Suggest you ask your conglom as well. Thanks for the heads up." Nilssen cut off the comm and let out a sigh before turning back to Shaila. "God damn it. ExEn's going to be clamoring for us to get over there ASAP. Where are we on fuel?"

Shaila tapped a few keys on her tablet. "We're at 18 percent. Won't have enough for a burn to Titan for at least a day or two. Besides, we need to get Stephane down there to finish the geology survey. Tell ExEn that and they might hold off."

Nilssen smirked. "I'll do my best. Tell Conti to clear him soon as she can. I stopped in on him a few hours ago and he looked like he was ready to chew through the door. That's one pissed-off geologist."

CHAPTER 12

October 15, 1798

In all his years in the service of King and country, Thomas Weatherby had been privileged to see some of the most fantastical things the Known Worlds had to offer the enterprising soul. He had plumbed the jungles of Venus to find evidence of lost civilizations, tasted the ice of Europa, explored the mines of Mercury. He had watched Finch save men from the very brink of death, watched others have their lives snuffed out with naught but a moment's notice.

He had even seen the future, once upon a time—*a* future, perhaps, one of many, but the future regardless—in which invisible energies paralyzed the unwary, pieces of glass could summon encyclopediae of information at a moment's notice, and a Hindu woman could be an officer in His Majesty's Royal Navy.

None of these things, not a single one of them, could prepare Weatherby for the rings of Saturn. In grandeur, ancient Rome paled in comparison. In intricacy, the greatest clockworks the Great Art could devise were for naught. In sheer beauty, Weatherby could think of only two instances in which he was left as humbled and joyful. The first was when he laid eyes upon his daughter for the very first time. The second….

"You look bewildered, Thomas," Anne whispered as they stood upon the quarterdeck of HMS *Fortitude*, the city-rings of the planet stretching out nigh-infinity.

"I truly am," he replied quietly. "Had I a poet's gift, I could begin to do it justice. As it stands…"

No more needed be said, and the two watched as the rings began to differentiate and become patchworks of different neighborhoods—if a neighborhood of similar character and architecture were to be the size of France or Spain, perhaps! The spires of these buildings seemed utterly small at first, but scale was misleading here, for although Saturn loomed large indeed, these were no mere townhomes. They were individual Babels, all reaching for the sky.

They also reached downward, for the rings themselves were set exactly upon their own gravitational axis. Whether this was a peculiarity of Saturn's rings themselves or a great working created by the Xan, Weatherby did not know. Nor did he care, for it was simply marvelous to behold. It was as if a child glued two towers together at the base of each, and hung them in the Void with millions of their fellows.

As *Fortitude* drew closer, all aboard could see that these structures were linked by an innumerable series of pathways, bridges and, for want of better words, gangplanks—if such spans as could hold entire carriages could be called such. These were necessary, for each building was anchored to a boulder or series of boulders—the materials of Great Xanath's rings themselves. Weatherby could see that many of the larger stones had been hollowed out—by what agency, he could only dream of—and made inhabitable. They were complete with windows and portals, linked to bridges across and to the towers both above and beneath them.

And such towers! Some made of polished stone that seemed to glow in the starlight and the Sun's rays, reflected from Saturn's face. Others seemed to be rough-hewn indeed, as if they were somehow made to grow, rather than cast or carved by the hand of any intelligent being. There were metals as well, gleaming and sparkling…and by God, were those *glass*? Entire buildings made of windows?

Inside those windows, no matter the building, lights glowed. As the shadow of Saturn fell across the rings off in the distance, Weatherby could see nothing but those glowing window-lights, as if there were a tiny ribbon of steady stars stretching around the gigantic world. Some of those stars moved as well, darting amongst the shadows and into the light. Conveyances, like the Xan Ovoids, or perhaps something else entirely. None seemed to close upon *Fortitude* and her three Ovoid escorts as they approached the rings. Perhaps their path was cleared by Sir James' allies.

"We have been cloaked," Morrow said as he touched his ear briefly. There was, it seemed, a tiny bit of something lodged in that ear—a device of some kind that Weatherby assumed allowed the ambassador to talk to the Xan.

"Cloaked, my Lord?" Anne asked. Her son, Philip, was by her side and looked squarely at Morrow's ear, with the utter lack of circumspection reserved for the very young, very old or very carefree.

Morrow smiled. "We have known, my lady, that the Xan had various unknown means of detecting ships coming to Xanath, of course. That's why none were able to approach until after '79. Those means include, I am to understand, a wide variety of alchemical and electronical senses, both living and mechanical."

"Living…monitors, sir?" Weatherby asked, his eyes finally dragged away from the rings.

"Yes, Captain Weatherby," Morrow replied, still seeming to relish his protégé's rank after three days' voyage together. "There are those amongst the Xan who have taken alchemical mind and body training to extreme lengths—so much so that they are said to be able to project their senses outward.

"And as for the mechanical, you had best ask someone else," Morrow continued with a broad smile, "for I understand damned little of it. What of your Hawkins, Captain? Perhaps he might explain."

Weatherby looked down upon the main deck, where Hawkins was busy scribbling away in a notebook—and looking most pale and wan, as if the ring-cities of Saturn/Xanath were apparitions that would carry him hence at any moment. "I think we may prevail upon him later, if you don't mind, sir," he replied. "I've found it best to give the doctor both time and warning to gather his thoughts before asking his opinion."

Morrow barked out a laugh. "One of those, then. Do you miss Finch much?"

"Dr. Hawkins is a most capable alchemist and surgeon, Ambassador," Weatherby said loudly. He then lowered his voice to a bare whisper before adding: "And yes, most definitely."

"Excuse me, Captain," Philip interrupted, "but I do think Dr. Hawkins might benefit from a few texts I've had the good fortune of reading recently. Perhaps I might discuss it with him?"

Weatherby smiled at the boy, even as Anne's face turned a most charming shade of red. "You are extremely intelligent and most diligent in your studies, young man, I have no doubt," Weatherby said with a smile. "But Dr. Hawkins is the ranking alchemist upon this ship. I doubt very much he would take kindly to a boy recommending academic work to him, even if said boy is the son of two legends of the field."

Anne raised her eyebrow at the captain. "Goodness, sir...*two* legends? What makes you think I belong in such august company as the Count St. Germain?" Her smile, of course, made such a question much softer, and told Weatherby much of her true opinion.

For his part, Weatherby slowly drew his blade from his scabbard. "Nearly twenty years, my lady, and this blade has naught a scratch nor pit upon it. I've seen other blades given a similar treatment since you gifted me with this, and there are none that have been its equal."

"Well, then, it's obvious you've kept it in a closet, or perhaps at the bottom of your sea chest," Anne playfully retorted.

"You know full well he hasn't," Morrow chided. "Why, I remember in '81, there was a boarding action 'round Io, and this young man here—my first lieutenant at the time—hacked through..."

Morrow's reverie suddenly stopped as his hand flew to his ear. "A moment, then," he said quietly.

Anne and Weatherby looked at each other, bemused. "I'm rather glad you still have it, sir," she said, nodding at the blade.

"It has saved my life many times, my lady," he replied with a small smile as he sheathed it once more.

Several quiet and unusually awkward moments later, Morrow spoke up once more. "We remain cloaked, but we must find harbor soon. I suggest more sail, Captain, and follow the Ovoid to the left. The other two will create something of a diversion for us as we dock."

Weatherby immediately walked over to his acting first officer, who had the watch and was standing near Wilkes at the wheel. "Mr. Barnes, full royals and stud'sels immediately, if you please. We need every stitch of canvas we have. And we are to follow the Ovoid furthest to larboard." The captain then turned to Wilkes. "If he takes us right between these very buildings, it is your duty to follow him precisely. Call out whatever you need and we will see it done."

"Aye, sir," Wilkes said, straightening with pride, for there were precious few times even a senior seaman as he could order officers around. "I'll trail him to Hell and back if need be, sir."

"I pray it won't come to that," Weatherby said drily. "It seems our friend is taking us to the rings' underside. Down six degrees on the planes!"

As the ring-cities drew closer, Weatherby turned out to be prescient indeed, for the Ovoid began to drift toward the outermost buildings. Through his glass, Weatherby could see individual Xan inside some of the buildings, though it was too far to make out their features. They were large, Weatherby knew, and their heads had some sort of growths upon them, be they rather thick strands of hair, or something more…tenticular.

Suddenly, Weatherby's glass grew blurry. He pulled it away from his eye to inspect it, but saw that the entire ship was now surrounded by a kind of unnatural haze. Weatherby turned to Morrow, who simply nodded. "Part of their cloaking, Captain," Morrow said. "While we are undetected to their eyes, it also serves to mask their true visage from us."

Weatherby turned back to his wheelman. "Can you still make the Ovoid well enough, Wilkes?"

"Aye, sir, 'tis odd," Wilkes said, staring straight ahead at the Ovoid as it maneuvered. "Crystal clear if you look right on her, but turn your head a bit, and she's a blur like all else. I'll be able to keep steady with her, sir."

Weatherby peered over the man's shoulder and saw it was just as he described. "Very well, then, Wilkes. Steady on." He then turned to Morrow, Anne and Philip. "How utterly disconcerting."

The now-blurry ring cities grew closer by the moment, and Weatherby ordered the ship to rotate—a maneuver involving positioning the planesails in opposite directions—so that the ship would be oriented properly for docking on the rings' underside ports. If there were indeed such contrivances as ports, though Morrow assured the captain that there would be "approximation enough."

Fortitude soon entered the city proper itself. There was space aplenty between buildings, akin to that of a modest river, so that the ship could sail between without incident. Indeed, the lines of buildings seemed quite straight, even through the blur of the Xan cloak. Weatherby hoped that they would not have to turn suddenly, for the "streets" of this odd city were aligned in a massive grid. The Ovoids were incredibly maneuverable, but a 74-gun ship-of-the-line decidedly was not.

Thankfully, it seemed Morrow's Xan allies had taken this into account. "Seems a cave or something up ahead, sir," Wilkes said. "The Xan ship seems to be heading straight for it."

Weatherby looked to Morrow, who simply nodded. "Follow her in, Wilkes," Weatherby ordered. "Mr. Barnes, take in sheets and braces, mainsail and planes only. We must be prepared to stop as best we can inside."

As it drew closer, the cavern Wilkes spoke of looked rather like a massive barn, complete with peaked roof, though the composition of its roof and walls were of a grey flatness. Indeed, compared to the ornamentation Weatherby had spotted briefly, before the cloak came down, and from prior experience on Callisto and elsewhere, there was little of the typical Xan artistry to be found. "This must be some sort of…military facility?" he asked Morrow.

"The Xan do not have a military, and would be greatly offended if you suggested such, Captain Weatherby," Morrow said quietly. "They do, however, have self-defense capabilities, as they call them, which to my eyes look not unlike military forces. Whatever the label, this is indeed a kind of dockyard for the Ovoids and the like."

Weatherby nodded. The Xan took immense pains to present themselves as a peaceable, highly-mannered race of beings, though their history showed them to be otherwise, at least in the past. These were the mighty, fearsome warriors that destroyed the planet Phaeton, reducing it to the rubble that now consisted of the Rocky Main, and razed the lush world of Mars into the rust-red deserts of today. So shocked they were at their own savagery in the defeat of the Martians and their warlord Althotas, the Xan laid down their arms and structured their society in such a manner as to keep all martial tendencies buried under layers of politesse and ceremony.

Fortitude slowly drifted into the "self-defense" dockyard, which was a marvel in and of itself. Indeed, Weatherby had never been in such a massive covered structure. Inside were several platforms, most of which had several Ovoid craft tethered to them. A longer platform lay dead ahead, and there were large, cloaked figures there, waiting with lines in hand—the first Xan Weatherby and the *Fortitudes* had seen on their voyage.

Weatherby had thought to order further action upon the sails, but there was no need, for it seemed the strange alchemical technologies of the Xan had matters well in hand. With little effort, the ship drifted to a very gentle stop alongside the platform. The lines the Xan threw to the shocked and incredulous seamen aboard *Fortitude* were practically ceremonial in nature. The gangplank that seemed to materialize between the platform and the ship needed no anchoring, either.

"Captain, your ship is the first of any flag to make port here," Morrow said with a small smile. "I can only pray it's not the last, for I think we have need of the Xan, and more importantly, they have need of us. Shall we?"

Morrow and Weatherby had already agreed that they would meet with the Xan representatives who asked them hither, and that the Countess St. Germain and young Philip would accompany them. All others would remain aboard *Fortitude*, upon pain of court-martial, for while there might be many who would seek out the wonders of such a unique place, it was highly likely that it would only result in nothing short of an interplanetary incident.

The four members of the delegation, then, proceeded across the gangplank, with Anne taking Weatherby's proffered arm, until they were met by three Xan. These ten-foot-tall beings were draped head-to-toe in drab, voluminous robes and cowls, their faces wreathed in shadow, with the barest hint of motion inside.

"Ambassador Morrow," the lead Xan sang in the peculiar harmonies of his people. "It brings me great joy and pleasure to see you again, though I fear there are circumstances involved that I regret to say may cause you a degree of concern, and I apologize for it."

Morrow smiled. "There is no apology necessary, Representative Vellusk, especially when I am met by such a warm and generous friend as yourself," he said, echoing the labored gravitas and manners of his host. "May I have the great honor of introducing my long-time friend, Captain Thomas Weatherby of His Majesty's Ship *Fortitude*? You may recall, your excellency, that he was with me aboard *Daedalus* those many years ago, and was instrumental in the positive outcomes of the Martian incident."

At this, the robes of all three Xan fluttered in unusual and odd ways, and Weatherby could only hope these signified something positive. As it turned out, they did.

"We know your name, Captain Thomas Weatherby, and it is much celebrated amongst the Xan who know it, for your bravery and skill preserved a peace we had long sought to keep," the Xan called Vellusk sang, notes of excited major-chord harmonies echoing in his voices. "I am deeply, truly honored to be the one to welcome you, good sir, to the great ring-cities of our homeworld of Xanath."

Weatherby cast a glance at Anne, who smiled and shook her head in muted disbelief. Nearly twenty years on, he could still dependably rely upon her to keep him well-grounded indeed. "Representative Vellusk," Weatherby intoned while performing a deep bow. "It is I who am humbled and honored to be welcomed by your esteemed…selves…here in this…place. I am most happy to be your guest…here."

Similar introductions were made with Anne and Philip, and Weatherby tried not to be overly chagrined at how even the boy managed a more well-spoken greeting than he. After several minutes of intricate formalities, at which Morrow showed a patience Weatherby had never seen while under his command, the combined party walked through a door in the wall and into a corridor, lit by glowing orbs of light on the ceiling, positioned every twenty feet or so.

Weatherby smiled. The first time he encountered such orbs was with Dr. Franklin, those many years past, who was thrilled to discover that the Xan's alchemy had harnessed the power of electricity itself for their lighting needs. What might the old puffer think of this place?

Lost in thought as he was, Weatherby was startled slightly when the group arrived at a massive door, some fifteen feet tall. Of course, to the Xan, it was likely just an entryway like any other, though here too the lack of ornamentation was evident. There were a few Xan characters upon the flat grey surface of the portal, but little else save for the silvery oversized knob. One of Representative Vellusk's compatriots opened the door for them, and Weatherby found it led to what could best be described as a meeting room. There were tall tables and chairs for the Xan, and slightly shorter ones for the visitors from Earth. All seemed well made and comfortably appointed, though in a minimalist fashion.

As he took his seat, Weatherby wondered if they had imported children's furniture into this "self-defense" facility solely for the purpose of providing seating for he and his fellows.

A moment later, three other Xan entered through a side door to join the already large group. Two were dressed in simple robes and walked in behind a third, one whose robes and hood were adorned with a variety of sigils and markings, some of which looked quite similar to the alchemical sigils Weatherby had seen in the Royal Navy's manuals.

Morrow quickly rose to his feet in the presence of this worthy, and so Weatherby followed suit with all due haste. "Administrator Sallev," Morrow said with a deep bow, "you honor us greatly with your presence."

The ornately dressed Xan bowed back. "As do you, Ambassador," he said. "I thank you for bringing your fellows here as well, particularly your Captain Weatherby. As you said, it is good fortune he is the one to have come to us in this hour. We have much to discuss."

The next ten minutes were spent over tepid tea and a raft of introductions and pleasantries. Oddly, Vellusk brought up the sport of cricket, which apparently he had learned of from the Xan's nascent diplomats and thought to be one of the finer pinnacles of human achievement. Weatherby was forced to admit having participated in a handful of matches, and was quizzed as to his particular abilities. The Xan, it seemed, relished detail, and Vellusk in particular seemed enamored of the minutiae of culture, though Administrator Sallev seemed almost impatient with the idle conversation—surprising, given the Xan predilection for manners and ceremony.

Finally, the talk turned to the business at hand. "So it appears you were most perceptive and correct, Ambassador Morrow," Sallev said. "I am most glad that the English pursued this renegade French ship, and that it was none other than Thomas Weatherby himself sent to stop them."

Morrow and Weatherby traded a sidelong look; the latter had told the former of the ignominious origins of this chase across the Known Worlds. While both men had great respect for Nelson, neither bore him great love, either. "We were most fortunate that Captain Weatherby was the one to arrive," Morrow agreed neutrally. "Perhaps you might update the captain, Administrator, as to what has transpired?"

And so the administrator did, without the excess of formalities Weatherby had feared he must endure: A week prior to the arrival of *Fortitude*, the Xan's alchemical-electrical methods discovered an Earth ship on a direct course for great Xanath. However, much to the Xan's consternation, this ship was able to cloak itself—much as *Fortitude* was kept from prying eyes—just as the Xan's self-defense forces had arrived to investigate. However, the great scryers amongst the Xan did catch a glimpse of the French tricolor, as well as the name *Franklin* prior to the ship's disappearance. Despite the Xan's best efforts, the ship's whereabouts remained unknown, which further increased their anxieties.

Of course, Weatherby could understand the consternation that erupted at this, and easily inferred the source. The Xan jealously guarded their space, and unannounced vessels that simply disappeared into the Void would aggrieve them to no end. Plus, it implied that the Great Work of humanity was starting, in perhaps some small ways, to approach that of the Xan themselves. Reports from Morrow himself, and many other ambassadors besides, pointed to a growing schism within Xan society with regards to humanity's increased presence in the Known Worlds, as well as the appropriate Xan reaction.

And so the Xan's dilemma became clear. Should word spread of a human "invasion," though it be one ship, the Xan would likely take a hard stance against Earth. There were a small portion of Xan who wished nothing more than to return to their old war-like ways, with humanity as the target of their long-simmering wrath. This prompted still others to fear that humanity would be a catalyst that would drive the Xan away from their peaceful ways—and that such a catalyst should be contained...or removed.

Administrator Sallev—administrator of whom or what, Weatherby could not say, though Morrow seemed to attach nigh-monarchical importance to the title—seemed to be of the mind that violence would beget violence, and that the Xan should stay out of human affairs; hence, his joy at finding a human vessel in pursuit, for thus the Earthmen would take care of the issue, and leave the Xan still in peace, perhaps to remain so at least a short while longer.

"That is why we cannot help you overmuch," Sallev concluded. "We wish for you to find and apprehend your adversaries, but we cannot be seen as taking sides or interfering. We officially take no positions in the wars of mankind, and many of us, myself included, fear that entering combat against you would result in the awakening of our old martial rage—to the great detriment of all the Known Worlds."

"Do we know, then, why the French are here to begin with?" Anne asked.

"No, my dear lady, their course told us nothing of their aims, I am most sorry to say," Sallev responded. "They seemed to be heading straight for the Main Administrative Complex responsible for all Xan affairs, but nothing has been reported amiss since then. They could be anywhere."

"Have you searched the Earth Quarter?" Weatherby asked. "For even a cloaked ship might wish to show up in port, or at least its men might."

"We have, but to no avail," Sallev sighed musically, with a few slow notes of saddened discord.

Weatherby sat back and thought a moment, his mind reaching back to his very first encounter with the Xan, upon Callisto. "There is more to this," he said quietly. "There is something that has vexed me since '79."

He looked to Morrow, who nodded sagely. "I told you Captain Weatherby had a fine mind, Administrator," he said. "As I have said in the past, it is possible that the French are being aided by those among your people who may disagree with your peaceful approach to mankind."

Anne and Philip looked perplexed at this, but Sallev merely slumped back in his massive chair. "As you requested, my friend Ambassador, we conducted an investigation into our partisans. There has been…increased activity," Sallev sang mournfully.

Morrow nodded. "As I thought. Just as there may have been a handful who aided Cagliostro in his awakening of Althotas by giving him access to the Sword of Xanthir back on Callisto, we may now see that there are those Xan willing to aid the French in whatever fell task they've set themselves."

"And our society and our peace of millennia will be torn asunder," Sallev cried softly, echoed by mourning minor chords from his fellows on either side. They sat in silence like this for several moments, with only the music of the Xan's pitiable sorrow filling the small room.

Then Sallev's chest exploded in a burst of fire and green blood.

Weatherby bolted to his feet and drew his sword in one smooth motion—but felt a hammer-blow to his back that sent him flying over his small table and onto the floor. Struggling mightily against the pain, he turned to see a Xan.

And by God, it was a Xan in full fury.

One of the guards that had accompanied them into the room had thrown back its cowl, featuring a face most surreal and dangerously expressive. The creature's head was long and drawn, bulbous at the top, thin at the chin, topped with long, black ropes of braided hair that seemed to move of its own accord. Its eyes were white pools with horizontal slits of inky blackness, set against its light blue skin. There were but two small holes were a proper nose ought to be. And on either side of the creature's chin was a mouth. It had two.

And they were both smiling with what could only be described as other-worldly malice.

Weatherby made to stand, but the Xan fired a weapon at him. It was all the captain could do to jump and roll away, and the weapon's discharge—God only knew what fell energy it fired—lanced into the floor with a crack-hiss and a bright light.

And then it was gone, out the door, leaving Vellusk and Sallev's two compatriots calling out in staccato bursts of disharmony and fear. Sallev was clearly dead, as was the second guard. Morrow and Anne were on the ground and appeared to be unharmed.

"Philip?" Anne asked, looking here and there. "Philip, where are you?"

Weatherby cast about as he gathered his feet. The boy was nowhere to be found. And a look of sheer terror grew upon Anne's face.

That was all it took for Weatherby to rush out the door, running in the general direction of the disharmonic screaming that now echoed through the halls.

June 20, 2134

"Goddamn it, Maria! There's a limit to the kind of ops we can cover for!" growled Admiral Hans Gerlich, head of the Joint Space Command and, as of two years' ago, Earth's response to extradimensional incursions. DAEDA-LUS was his baby. And it was getting spanked.

Diaz nodded at the holoscreen in front of her, her head bowed, dejected. "I'm sorry, Hans, but you know as well as I do that there's more to it than the story Total-Suez is feeding us."

"So show me the data," Gerlich demanded, his features getting redder. "Because if we don't have any evidence of malfeasance, Total-Suez is going to make a stink about this, and we'll either have to buy them off with some massive asteroid contracts or give them free rides to Jupiter and Saturn until we're both retired."

"How long can you stall them?" Diaz asked, looking up. "I need more time here."

"A day, maybe two. And if there's nothing there?"

She frowned. "Then print up their round-trip tickets. But I swear, it's there."

"Thirty-six hours. Then you come home and we start making amends with Total Suez. Gerlich out."

The holoimage winked out, to be replaced just as swiftly by the image of Major Coogan walking into the room. "New orders, ma'am?"

Diaz leaned back on the sofa of the well-appointed luxury condo the team had appropriated, courtesy of Egyptian intelligence. "Just running out of time. How's the analysis?"

"We may have struck on something, if you want to take a look."

Diaz pried herself off the sofa and joined the rest of the team in the dining room, which had been converted into a conference room. The resort at least had the latest toys, which meant holoprojectors on demand pretty much everywhere in the place, along with SmartSurface tech that could present data on any flat surface, horizontal or vertical. Thus, at the moment, the dining room was awash in information, from schematics and spreadsheets on the walls to 3D holomodels of the fusion station on the table.

"How we doing?"

Greene looked up. "Maggie may be on to something," he said, though he didn't look particularly excited..

Diaz arched her eyebrow at this. "Didn't know you were good at this science shit, Captain."

"Neither did I, ma'am," Hutchinson said stiffly. "But even a jarhead knows when there's an extra pipe coming out of the sink."

Hutchinson pulled up a schematic and, with a few flicks of her hand, enlarged it so that it covered an entire wall. "This is the main trunk line, right? It goes out to the substations, and from there, all the individual buildings in the area. This," she added, pointing to a small line coming out of the reactor itself, "goes somewhere else. And it wasn't on the schematics the company had on file with the IAEA."

Diaz blinked. "So they're diverting power from their own project?"

"Maybe. It disappears after only about a foot, but…well, Dr. Greene can explain it better," the Marine captain said.

Greene still seemed nonplussed, but dove in anyway. "So you can shield a power line from sensors, right? But by building this line so close to the main reactor and drawing it off prior to the main trunk line, that foot or so is too close to the reactor to be properly shielded. So that's how we found it. It's not a dead end. It leads…somewhere."

Diaz stared at the wall-screen for a moment. "All right, I'll bite. Where?"

Coogan walked up and, with a wave of his hand, batted the schematic aside, leaving a large-scale map of the area in its place. On it, there were literally a million points of light. "Process of elimination. First idea was to remove all power sources with known links to any power plant in the area." This was done with another wave, leaving perhaps several thousand lights remaining, spread almost evenly across the land. "Now, in this part of the world, there are many people who use their own portable generators. Now whether they use solar or gas or thermal or fusion, each has their own unique characteristics, so we were able to run some cross-referencing checks to eliminate them."

Another few waves, and there were but three points remaining. "And so we have three. One is, of course, the power plant we visited, because it's not hooked up to the grid yet," Coogan said. "This one here is in the center of town, the local hospital. We think it's simply too new to be included in the records. It may have its own power source that isn't registered and, if it's deep enough, doesn't show on remote sensors.

"And that leaves this," Coogan said, pointing to a spot about 125 kilometers out of town along a back road, pretty much smack dab in the middle of the desert. With another gesture, he expanded it to show it was a small village with a population of roughly two thousand. "This is Siwa," he said.

Diaz sighed and turned to Huntington. "Home of your oracle, right?"

Huntington nodded seriously. "Yes, ma'am. The untraceable power emission is coming from the ruins of the oracle temple."

"And so you think that Harry ran a massive trunk line 125 klicks through the desert without anybody noticing," Diaz said, sounding very tired. "It's a nice try, Mags, but you'd have to run the line underground. You'd have to burrow through—wait. Son of a bitch."

Greene nodded. "Yuna's experiment. Took me a minute, too. That's the only reason I think we might be onto something."

Two years ago, on Mars, Shaila and Greene had stumbled across a homebrew underground particle accelerator—used by acclaimed astronaut Yuna Hiyashi to generate enough power to break through to another dimension.

Yuna had used mining equipment to send particles zipping through solid rock, creating a circle around McAuliffe Base that was more than 100 kilometers in diameter. And even if Total-Suez wasn't replicating that exact experiment, Harry Yu's experience running the mining ops would give him passing familiarity with any kind of equipment that could burrow quickly and efficiently underground.

"So he could not only drill through, but he could also lay an accelerator there, couldn't he," Diaz said, half-asking.

Greene decided to answer anyway. "Depends on what the experiment is. If you're atom smashing, you could do a parallel track, or smash 'em head on. Or, perhaps even scarier, this could be just one length of a truly massive accelerator, but that would encompass most of Egypt, along with parts of Libya and the Sudan. I think the world would notice if that happened, but I suppose you never know."

Diaz expanded the map more. "Looks like a lot more people could live here," she noted.

"When they started building the resorts ten years ago, there was a lot of immigration," Coogan said. "Up until then, it was like 25,000 people."

The general gave a wolfish smile. "So you get everybody to up and move, leaving the ruins there for…well, hell, Huntington. You did the research. What's there?"

"This was the site of the ancient temple of Amun-Ra, dating back to the 26th Dynasty of Ancient Egypt. Alexander the Great went all the way there from the Nile back in 331 B.C.E. in order to gain the blessing of the Oracle to become a true Pharaoh of Egypt," the Marine officer said matter-of-factly. "It's worth mentioning, I suppose, that it was somewhere in Egypt where Alexander is said to have come into possession of the Emerald Tablet, which supposedly somehow contains the highest secrets of alchemy."

Greene shook his head sadly at this. "Legends and folklore, Captain. You have a nearly vacant town where you can safely do underground experiments without the world noticing. That's more than enough."

"Either way, I got more than enough physical evidence to get a move on," Diaz said. "So whether we find outlaw tech or alien alchemists, I'm good either way. Huntington, get us ready to roll. I'm going to go make Hans Gerlich say sorry to me."

Two hours and one half-apology later (Gerlich still wanted evidence, after all), the four of them rode into the quiet and largely abandoned town of Siwa. It was nearly 3 a.m., and there were very few lights of any sort still on; even the handful of streetlights were either on the fritz or too weak to cut through the gloom. Thankfully, the moon was nearly full, and without trees or other obstructions, shone beautifully across the town. There were a handful of vehicles, many of which were old enough to be called vintage. Diaz wasn't a gear-head, but even she knew that the one with the cloth roof and a horse on the grill was well over a century old, and would command a high price back in the States. Here, it was merely useful.

The four team members got out of their vehicle a few kilometers from the ruins. Coogan and Greene carried advanced sensor packages that, ideally, would help them find the source of the power; Coogan had even programmed his glasses to overlay electrical flows across his field of vision, which he then fed to Diaz' datapad and via satellite for the DAEDALUS team in Washington to monitor and save.

Diaz and Huntington walked behind them, each armed with a machine pistol as well as a microwave emitter—a "zapper," in common parlance. These handheld weapons emitted a short burst of microwave energy that prompted searing pain and unconsciousness in the target without causing any physical damage. The only aftereffect was the memory of feeling as if one's nervous system was on fire.

They had decided to park well away from the main tourist entrance to the ruins, which stood apart from the village among a rather impressive stand of palm trees, still drawing water from the ancient oasis. As they approached, they could see the shuttered souvenir stands and food stalls growing more numerous; the oracle temple was pretty much the only draw for the town now, especially since the formation of Siwa Bay—it wasn't even necessary as an oasis any longer. Here, there were a handful of lights on, but it was still far too late, or perhaps too early, for activity on the streets beyond a couple of rats and a stray dog.

The tourist entrance itself was well locked, and there was a tall stone wall around the ruins themselves. Diaz called up the most recent satellite image—all of three hours old, thanks to Coogan—and found the service entrance. She led her team around the wall, brushing past the palms and a variety of small buldings, until they quickly arrived at a pair of chain-link gates, secured with more chain and a padlock, and featuring razor-wire on top. With a nod from Diaz, Huntington made short work of the padlock with a laser cutter, and the four dashed inside and made for the cover of a couple of Dumpsters.

"Guys?" Diaz whispered. "Which way?"

Coogan looked across the facility, minute lights dancing across his glasses, while Greene flipped through pages on his datapad. "The independent power source seems to be coming from under the ruins," Greene said finally. "It looks like we'll have to find our way down inside."

Diaz frowned; clambering through an Egyptian national treasure in the middle of the night was not exactly ideal. "All right. Huntington, pull up a map of the ruin and take point with Coogan. Deep as we can go."

The young Marine tapped commands into her datapad, and a moment later, her own glass had lights flickering across its surface. With a few smooth hand motions, Huntington laid out their course across the plaza in front of the ruins. She stuck to the shadows, leading the team through a maze of outbuildings, souvenir stands, and interactive kiosks, until they arrived at the entrance itself and, with the help of Huntington's laser cutter, made their way inside.

The temple complex was, at this point, a ruin sitting upon a plateau overlooking the trees and oasis. It was wide open to the night sky, with half-standing walls and cluttered pathways. Here and there, signs in Arabic, English and French pointed out a particularly interesting or important feature, but otherwise, they could have simply been in a construction site anywhere in the Middle East; it was easy to forget the stones were more than 2,500 years old.

Huntington quickly led them into the ruins, and took a series of turns, left and right, before reaching an opening in one of the more structurally sound parts of the ruins. There, a simple chain bearing the Arabic words for "Do Not Enter" stretched across what appeared to be the entrance to a tunnel. Nodding, Huntington waved everyone inside and, out of habit, replaced the chain behind her before taking point once more, leading the team down a sloping corridor that caused even Diaz, the shortest of the group, to hunch over.

"Getting closer to the power source," Coogan whispered.

The group walked on in relative silence for about ten minutes, occasionally ducking low-hanging stones and, on one occasion, crawling about fifty meters before the corridor widened out again. Diaz looked for evidence of more recent stonework, but could see none. A few taps on her datapad confirmed it—the erosion patterns were consistent with stone cut in the time before Christ.

Huntington made a turn and came to a halt, just as her flashlight went out. Her left hand flew up to stop the others. She took a step forward...

...and was seemingly swallowed by the darkness. A moment later, Diaz heard a thump. Then silence.

"Huntington!" she whispered loudly. "Report!"

Then Diaz felt the blinding heat-pain of a zapper targeting her, and all else was forgotten before she herself blacked out.

CHAPTER 13

October 15, 1798

As it turned out, the best place for the French to make camp was within the very ruins of the temple itself. This suited the men quite well, as the palms surrounding the ancient rubble were filled with insects and snakes, and at least one man had to be treated for a poisonous sting that, if not for the rapidity and skill of Finch's response, might have slain him.

But there were causes for concern as well with regard to these arrangements. For one, Finch worried that the French soldiers would carelessly damage some part of the ruins, and possibly something of immense historical import; he had pleaded with the French commander to allow for a complete survey before the men moved in, but was overruled by the commander's insistence and Berthollet's apathy.

That said, the commander had his own concerns. Yes, the ruin kept his men safe from the wild animals of the oasis. So too was the temple on high ground, and thus easily defensible. However, they were not only surrounded by dense foliage, but also by the Bedouins, who could easily surround the place, especially if reinforcements were nearby.

Finch, for his part, set up camp just outside the ruins, on a stony bluff overlooking the palm forest. He and Berthollet agreed that such a camp would serve nicely as an intermediary position between the French and Bedouins. Of course, if the two sides came to blows, Finch would be caught in the middle, so he took a very active role in ensuring there would be peace on both sides.

And that meant entertaining Sheikh Karim bin Abdullah al-Siwa. Far more than the French, the sheikh was a most jovial fellow, and fond of the wine the French had brought with them despite Islam's prohibitions against alcohol. He was also insatiably curious in the way of those who know enough to know they know little indeed.

"I am trying to remember, *murshid*, but I do not think there are any other tunnels beneath," Sheikh Karim said on this particular evening. "There are other openings into the ground, yes, but these are caved in. It is hard to say whether they would be passable."

Finch nodded and translated for Berthollet and the others. It was as they feared, for they had spent the last four nights hoping that any of the existing passages in the ruin would lead down into the temple complex. But the most they found was an ancient larder, full of dust that may once have been grain. There was also a recipe for beer, written on a rotting papyrus in the Greek language, that Finch hoped he might someday try to recreate. But that was all.

"Very well, then," Berthollet growled. The Frenchman had lost at least five pounds since arriving at Siwa, largely due to his insistence upon wearing the fine waistcoat and breeches of a gentleman, even in the heat of the day. Some of the other savants had traded their garb for those of the Bedouins, and were now attired as Finch—and more comfortable besides—but Berthollet would have none of it. "How are we coming along with cataloging the blocked passages?"

"There are eight we might explore, though carefully," Finch replied. "There is no telling the state of these further inside, of course, but they seem to be the next logical venues."

Thankfully, with the help of Sheikh Karim's boyhood memories, three of these passages could be checked off the list, for the cave-ins were fresh—the Bedouin leader remembered exploring them as a child, and the chambers were shallow. Of the remaining five, teams of soldiers and savants simply got to work digging and reinforcing the walls and ceilings as best they could.

"Do we have any sense at all of what we're looking for, *murshid*?" Jabir asked Finch in Arabic one evening as the French began to dig. "No old maps, no inscriptions, nothing?"

Finch smiled as they walked between excavation sites, ostensibly supervising. "Not a single thing, though it would not surprise me in the least if

Berthollet knows more. Of course, knowing the stubbornness of the French, they will simply dig into every possible hole in the ground until they find something. Barring that, they will dismantle the ruins brick by brick."

The boy scowled. "This cannot be good, then. What if they disturb the spirits below? Even the *djinn* can be shown the grace of Allah the just, the merciful, but I do not wish it to fall to me to show them."

Finch regarded the boy carefully, and saw that beneath the joke, his eyes held genuine worry. "Leave them to me, Jabir. We already have avoided mischief with the Sheikh, have we not? I will keep these Franks out of trouble."

Jabir nodded somewhat unconvincingly. Finch wasn't entirely convinced, either, but what could he say?

"Dr. Finch!" came a voice from the other end of the ruins. "Dr. Finch! *Venez vite, professeur!*"

The Englishman sprinted across the encampment, Jabir in tow, and pinpointed the source of the shout to one of the caved-in tunnel areas. There, Dolomieu was clambering out of a sharply sloping tunnel. "Andrew! I think we have found something!"

"How long is it?" Dolomieu smiled. "It twists and turns and goes down quite a way. I thought it best to find you and Dr. Berthollet before continuing."

"And most wise of you to do so," Berthollet rumbled imperiously, having followed the commotion. "Are we sure of this, Deodat?"

The young geologist laughed. "Of course not, *monsieur*. But it is the best tunnel we have found here. Shall we find Sheikh Karim and ask his opinion?"

Finch and Berthollet both turned to look for the Bedouin leader, but he was nowhere to be found at the moment. "No need," Berthollet said quickly. "Have ropes, lanterns and helmets brought to us. Dr. Finch and I shall go in together."

While not about to argue, Finch was mildly surprised. He expected his role in this place to be more consultative—which he rather liked, as the French would be doing the bulk of mucking about in the ground, while he would simply review and comment upon their findings.

On the other hand, Finch figured, he was perhaps more expendable than a Frenchman in Berthollet's eyes. Smirking slightly at the thought, Finch grabbed the lantern he was offered and secured a line around his waist.

"Do you wish me to go with you, *murshid*?" Jabir asked, more worry in his voice.

"No, Jabir," Finch responded in Arabic. "I want you to go to Sheikh Karim and tell him of this. I also want you to ask him, on my behalf, to stay closer next time, so that his people may be properly compensated for what may be found here."

At this, Jabir stared in disbelief. "If the Sheikh cannot be bothered, why do you wish him compensated?"

Finch grimaced. "Now is not the time for questions. Do as I say."

Jabir nodded and jogged off, somewhat sullenly. The boy didn't understand.

At the mouth of the tunnel, Berthollet stood waiting. He added a khaki frock coat to his attire, making him look like a rather preposterous amalgamation of gentlemen-scientist-explorer-professor who clearly had spent little time outside a classroom. "After you, Dr. Finch," he said.

Expendable, Finch thought with a smile and nod to Berthollet. "Come along, Deodat. Please be sure I don't get a headache from these rocks!"

Together, Finch and Dolomieu went down into the tunnel, with Finch in the lead. They were followed by Berthollet and three soldiers acting as... porters? Guards? It was difficult to say, and Finch was annoyed at the clamor they made.

Yet Dolomieu was right—this tunnel held promise. It sloped downward and doubled back upon itself in a very orderly manner, roughly fifty-five feet before each turn. It was delightfully systematic and, aside from a few crumbling areas here and there, surprisingly sound aside from the entrance, which could readily be blamed on the structures that, at one point, may have existed above it.

"This seems rather small for a temple entrance," Dolomieu noted on the fifth turn.

"More likely a back entrance," Finch replied, lantern in hand. "No carvings on the walls, just wide enough for one man to fit comfortably. Something for servants, perhaps, or a private route for the priests themselves."

They continued down until they came to an unadorned arch, fitted with the lintel stones common in many, more recent Egyptian ruins. "Later dynasties, before the coming of Ptolemy," Berthollet said. "This makes sense, given Alexander's visit."

"Well, I doubt he signed his name in the guest book," Finch quipped, "so let us see whether this is really the place first."

The archway opened into a small room fitted with rotting wooden shelves, coated in cobwebs and a thick layer of dust. Indeed, one of the soldiers reached out to touch one and saw nearly an entire eight-foot section of woodwork collapse, which earned him a stern rebuke from Berthollet in scathing French. Any goods here were likely taken long ago.

Finch cautiously went further into the room, looking around carefully. The walls had some carvings upon them, the first they had seen since entering the tunnel, and Finch slowly walked over to see if he might discern their meaning.

A crunch underfoot quickly drew his attention to the dusty floor.

Crouching down carefully, Finch saw that he had stepped upon…a bone. And from his lower vantage, he saw that the floor was littered with them. They looked quite human.

"Bloody hell," Finch muttered, brushing away the dust that coated a nearby skull. The remains came from a person of small stature, though Finch knew the ancient Egyptians were generally smaller than modern men. As he turned the skull over in his hands, he saw there was a hole at the very top of it, roughly an inch wide, with a corresponding hole in the base under the palate.

His eyes grew wide, and he turned to see his compatriots spreading out further into the room. It was exactly the worst thing they could be doing. "Back to the door! Now!" Finch commanded. "Everyone, move!"

The scream from behind him, however, told him it was too late.

June 20, 2134

While Shaila wished the Chinese would land in a petrochemical morass, there was little anyone aboard *Armstrong* could do about the *Tienlong*'s foray onto the surface of Titan. Several hours had gone by, and there was no word, officially or otherwise, on their landing. Odd, given the Chinese propensity for trumpeting their space exploration efforts across every media imaginable.

Shaila sighed as she scanned through the latest data burst from Houston. She'd sent an e-mail to Diaz earlier, updating her on the Chinese movements and asking for some intel help, but the general was incommunicado. It was pretty early in the morning in the eastern United States, though, and she couldn't begrudge Diaz some sleep. The rest of the data burst included private e-mails, which Shaila dutifully routed to their recipients; technically, she was authorized to read any of them she chose, as no doubt folks in Houston had already done, but after months in space together, it seemed an egregious violation of what little privacy they had.

Except…why was Stephane getting an e-mail from JSC's chief medical officer?

Her finger hovered over her datapad. Did Conti ask for a second opinion? Did Stephane? Shaila checked the e-mail header and saw Conti wasn't included on it. She knew he was growing increasingly grumpy at his confinement, but still, it would be a pretty little interpersonal clusterfuck if he'd gone over the head of the ship's medical officer and captain. There were rules for that sort of thing, and if Stephane thought Conti was being unreasonable, he should've gone to Shaila first, or if he was understandably uncomfortable doing that, then Nilssen.

Shaila thought back to the crew's occasional poker games; Conti was a horrible player, and Stephane—whose latent competitive streak came out at the card table—always threw a hand or two away so she could win something. Shaila thought it was gallant and charming. Hell, he was probably the friendliest, most forthright person she'd met in JSC.

By opening the e-mail, Shaila would be asserting her rank over Stephane—a first. She never thought she'd have to.

Grimacing, she stared at the datapad for several seconds longer. Finally, she forwarded the e-mail along, unopened. Then she left her quarters and headed 'round the ring toward medical.

"Commander."

She turned to find Archie climbing up one of the access tubes into the common room, which she had just left. "What's up, Archie?" She tried to keep annoyance out of her voice, but even to her ears, it didn't sound entirely successful.

Thankfully, Archie didn't notice, or just didn't care. "We gotta work on that desalinization process we got going on down there on the surface," he said. "Damn water's still coming up with boatloads of crap in it."

"Define crap."

"About 50 percent more than I'm comfortable with," he replied, holding out a datapad to her. She took it and saw that the mineral content was about 15 grams per liter—half that of Earth's oceans, but a far cry from fresh water. It wouldn't be an issue for drinking water, since the ship's purification systems were already filtering grey water and waste, but the ship's engines was another story.

"What do we need to get down to?" she asked.

The engineer smirked. "None would be great. I'd settle for a gram."

Shaila handed the datapad back. "So how do we do that?"

Archie pulled up a schematic on his pad and held it up to her. "If we took all our spare filters from our crew filtration system, we might get enough decent water to get us to Titan. The depot ship has enough replacements for the rest of the mission."

Shaila frowned. "How close are we cutting it if we do that?"

"Houston would probably know that down to the hour, but I figure we'd get by. Maybe we shave a week or two off the mission. Mimas is boring, anyway. Just a big Death Star crater."

"And if we burn the salty water?"

Archie threw up his hands and rolled his eyes dramatically. "Possibly nothing. Possibly we see some corrosion. Worst case? We lose an engine and have to do some serious jury-rig work. The depots have parts, but I'm too old for that shit."

"Engineers," Shaila muttered with a grin. "Tell you what. Rig me a small-scale version of this with a couple of filters. Run some tests on the water we have up here. If it works, we'll go to Nilssen and make the case. I'll take a look at the system we have in place down there on my next run to see if we can tweak it. Deal?"

"Sure. I'll ask Houston to run some simulations, too. If their test engines crap out on them, you'll have to tie me down before you pump that shit through my reactor," he grumped.

"Don't tempt me."

Archie barked out a laugh and, with a wave, headed off down the ring toward the crew quarters. Shaila turned back toward medical, a slight sinking feeling beginning in her stomach. She really hoped she was wrong about it all.

She entered and walked over to quarantine, peering through the window.

Stephane wasn't there.

Shaila glimpsed down at her chrono. Five minutes. *Five goddamn minutes?*

She walked over to Conti's desk and called up the comm panel. "Jain to Durand, respond."

Nothing.

"Jain to Durand, respond," she repeated, sounding annoyed.

Still nothing.

Finally, the comm panel flickered to life. "Command to Jain, Hall here."

Shaila stabbed at the holobutton. "Go ahead."

"Heard your comm. Stephane's not in medical anymore."

"No kidding," she replied. "Why wasn't the door locked?"

"Does it even have a lock?" Hall replied.

Shaila looked at the door. "No idea. Where's Stephane?"

A pause. "Looks like he's in Cargo Two, EVA prep."

What the hell? "Copy. Let me know if he moves. Jain out."

With that, Shaila dashed out of medical toward the common room once more, dialing up Stephane's e-mail as she went. Screw privacy—the man just left medical quarantine without authorization.

Then she stopped in her tracks, because he didn't.

"AS PER YOUR REQUEST, JSC MEDICAL SIMULATIONS SHOW NO POTENTIAL HAZARDS. QUARANTINE IS LIFTED," the e-mail said.

Shaila shoved her datapad into her pocket and clambered down the ladder into zero-g. So it was nice that those weird proto-proteins didn't get him sick or anything. But there was still a long talk to be had about chain-of-command issues. And picking up the goddamn comm.

She launched herself out of the access tube and down the length of the ship like the practiced astronaut she was, hurtling past storage compartments and the lander bays....

...so quickly, in fact, she nearly missed Stephane, dressed in a pressure suit, loading equipment into one of the landers.

"Hey!"

She grabbed a handhold to arrest her flight and launched herself toward Lander Two. There, she saw Stephane loading large crates into the cargo area of the craft.

"*Cheri*," he said, smiling. "I'm free at last!"

Her first urge was to literally pick him up and toss him out of the bay, but the look on his face stopped her in her tracks. He was smiling, cheerful as usual…but the circles under his eyes had gotten a little darker, and there was a very thin sheen of sweat on his forehead.

"What are you doing?" she demanded, for lack of anything more coherent to say.

"I've been released from quarantine," Stephane said happily as he continued loading crates. "I want to be ready for the next landing."

"You look like shit," she said flatly. "Conti's on the surface. She didn't clear you."

Stephane gave one of his signature shrugs. "She's busy. I felt better, so I asked the people in Houston to let me free. They agreed to do it. What's the problem?"

"The problem is you should've come to me or the colonel first," Shaila said, trying not to snap at him. "There's rules for this sort of thing."

"Ah, I wondered, but you know me and rules," he said, giving her another grin. "You are all very busy, and I didn't want to get in your way because I was feeling…what is it? Cooped up. A little lonely, too. Besides, I have been going over the data from our preliminary sensors. There is something going on."

Shaila shook her head, as if trying to clear it. "Something going on?"

Stephane pulled his datapad from his suit pouch and called up a holo-image. "The fluctuations in the subsurface water currents are developing new patterns. There is even more of a flow to the tiger stripes than when we arrived. Plus," he added, calling up another image, "if these readings are correct, the density of the flow is increasing. There are far more particulates in the current flows, as if the moon's currents are dragging more…stuff… up to the surface."

Shaila grimaced at him for several long seconds, even as he stowed his pad and continued to load the lander. "Why am I just seeing this now?" she said finally.

"Because I just made sense of the data and put it into these simulations a half hour ago," he replied reasonably, nigh obliviously. "And again, you are all so busy with the water transfers. You realize, I didn't see a soul in medical for the past eight hours? Frustrating." He stopped and looked up. "Yes, I should've made a report first. I'm sorry, Shay. I want to get down there. You have been on Enceladus, what, three times already? I was there once, and I'm supposed to be the expert!"

Shaila regarded him steadily for several seconds before reaching for the comm button beside the lander bay door. "Jain to Hall. Where are Nilssen and Conti on their run?"

Hall was quicker on the draw this time; Shaila wondered if she'd been eavesdropping. "They took off about 15 minutes ago. Should be back soon."

"Roger, Jain out." She closed the comm link and turned back to Stephane. "How bad could this get, if these water flows continue?"

"We haven't had a cryovolcanic eruption in a while. When we do, I think it will be very big. But I won't know more until I get down there."

"Are we in danger?"

Stephane smiled. "Unless we are right on top of them, I doubt it. It will be a very big show, no more. But we should be sure our equipment is protected, and our landing sites should be further away, I think."

After a long pause and a fair amount of internal back and forth, Shaila decided. "Here's what's going to happen. You finish loading your gear, and I'll notify the colonel and Conti about your release from quarantine. You and I are going down to the surface together. On the way, you're going to write up a thorough report on all this stuff you just told me, and you're going to make it sound like getting your ass back down there is mission critical. When you're done, you're going to suffer through a metric shit-ton of me yelling at you for being such a bonehead right up until we land. Then you're going to get your ass in gear and do what you need to do. Clear?"

"*Oui*, Commander," he said, sounding sheepish. "I'm sorry."

Shaila quickly launched herself out of the bay and back up toward the command center. Even as she did, a small smile crept onto her face. Stephane had been pretty good about protocols and duties and such on the trip out to Saturn. But he was always an eager one to get out there and *do* things. It was part of the attraction.

She'd just have to school him on how not to be an idiot now and then.

October 15, 1798

Weatherby hurtled down a plain gray corridor, sword in hand, hoping that the plaintive, dissonant cries of startled and upset Xan would continue to lead him to his quarry—and to Anne's son, violently taken by what could only be a Xan partisan of some stripe.

There—another scream, particularly deep and alarming, with a fusillade of contralto notes. Weatherby darted right, then left, and came into a wide area with a vaulted glass ceiling—and with many cloaked Xan singing, and occasionally screeching, loudly. But there were also several exits out of this massive place, rather like a covered courtyard with a strange plant-like… thing…in the middle, a million shades of purple with swaying tentacles and broad fronds that looked like feathers. It nearly stopped him in his tracks.

Thankfully, some of the Xan were already gesturing toward one of the exits, and they seemed too genuinely alarmed to be anything but truthful. Thus, Weatherby ran off in that direction, praying for the continued honesty and good graces of the majority of the Xan.

At least one of them, however, would meet his sword if he had any say in the matter.

The captain burst through the door into another corridor, one that he could clearly see led to a pair of glass doors and, beyond that, the ring-city itself. Humans were never allowed into the cities proper; Weatherby thought briefly he was about to precipitate a rather messy incident, but reassured himself that the Xan's actions would be considered far more grievous.

Someone else had apparently drawn the same conclusion, for he heard a distinct clopping of booted feet behind him. He turned—and saw Anne, tears streaming down her face, hands clutching at her skirts, in rapid pursuit of her son.

"How?" Weatherby panted as he attempted to speed up, for Anne was about to overtake him. She merely shot him a distraught look, one that folded his heart and seemed to give him a second wind. Of course, Lady Anne, the Countess St. Germain, would have the alchemical means to be in fine form—or even at the very peak of human endurance and strength.

The two threw open the glass doors and ran out into the city, prompting a chorus of gasps, both melodic and dissonant from passer-by. Ignoring them, Weatherby and Anne dashed into what appeared to be a garden plaza, suspended between various towers and linked by numerous walkways of gleaming white material. Above them loomed glass and metal reaching dizzying heights, while to their right, the clouds of Saturn loomed across half the sky.

They stopped and cast about, looking for their quarry, and were rewarded with a very monotone, very *human* shout off in the distance. "Philip," Anne breathed. A split second later, she was dashing down the Xan's queer walkways, her skirts in hand, and a Royal Navy captain on her heels desperately trying to keep up.

In the distance, Weatherby could see Philip literally tucked under the arm of one of the Xan guards from the meeting room—the one that likely assassinated Administrator Sallev. The Xan moved fast, but not overly so, for his gait was lumbering and Philip, brave boy that he was, struggled and squirmed mightly, going so far as to beat the Saturnine alien's back with his fists.

Then the Xan guard jumped…right off the path and straight down.

Anne screamed and seemed to go even faster, while Weatherby, having looked down earlier, had a sense of what might have happened. Splitting off the main path, Weatherby loped across a bridge-like structure until he was over the great empty space between buildings that seemed to pass for Xan "streets."

As he drew his pistol, Weatherby saw he had guessed correctly, for the Xan and Philip had landed in some kind of conveyance—nothing short of a carriage without wheels, horse or apparently engine—that was now flying toward him, driven by a second Xan accomplice.

One shot.

Weatherby aimed…and fired.

The driver slumped forward, and the vehicle—which looked like half an egg split end to end, hovering of its own accord—began to slow. But it did not stop.

Cursing under his breath, Weatherby tucked his pistol back in his belt and prayed his timing would work. He could see the Xan guard shoving his injured compatriot out of the way in order to drive the vehicle with purpose once more.

Weatherby clambered up onto the railing at the side of the walkway, with a web of walkways far below, and only the Void beyond. He saw the strange conveyance pick up speed, judged the distance as best he could…and leapt.

His timing was dreadful. He managed to grab the very back of the vehicle by some kind of shiny, mirrored protuberance, one that seemed to be unable to support his full weight. Weatherby kicked and groped and tried to clamber aboard the open vehicle, only to find that he had miscounted the number of Xan therein.

There was at least one more, towering above him now, with terrible smiles upon each of its mouths. In its hands was a long staff of some kind, aimed squarely at Weatherby's head.

Weatherby lashed out with his sword, neatly slicing the Xan's staff in half, which caused it to spark in the alien's hands. This prompted him to fall backward into the carriage once more, giving Weatherby the opportunity to drive his blade deep down into the carriage itself, using it as an impromptu handle to haul himself upward…

…and apparently causing a severe malfunction, for smoke quickly began to billow from the hole made when he withdrew his blade.

Distracted by this, Weatherby finally turned back toward the front of the flying carriage, only to be faced by a furious Xan once more. The creature dispensed with any sort of pleasantry, and quickly dispensed with Weatherby a second later, slapping him with a backhand that sent the captain clean off the vehicle and into the air.

He fell.

Glass, steel and light hurtled past him as he realized this would be his last moment. He thought of his daughter, his precocious, loving Elizabeth, who would now be orphaned entirely but would, he was sure, thrive in his sister's care. He thought of his late wife with sadness and forgiveness, for her and himself both. He thought of his friend O'Brian, and of Anne, and how he failed them. More thoughts, jumbled together, flew through his mind, pierced by the occasional disharmonic gasp from the walkways he fell past.

Oddly, it occurred to him he was falling quite a long time, even for the heights at which he started.

Then his stomach lurched, and suddenly he felt as if he were falling *upward*. And for some reason, all of the Xan around him seemed to be upside down.

Then he fell back down again, in the opposite direction until his stomach twisted a second time, and the sensation of falling upward returned, though for a lesser amount of time.

The gravity horizon—that's what Finch once called it, he remembered.

Saturn's ring-cities were set directly upon the gravity plane of the planet itself, and thus the city was built in two directions—up and down. Weatherby determined he must have fallen straight through the gravity horizon and was now bouncing back and forth through the different fields of pull. Eventually, he would even out.

And so he did, finally slowing to the point where he could lay hands on a walkway and pull himself upward to his feet.

That prompted more screams and screeches, as the Xan here were utterly unaware of the happenings several hundred feet above them. Indeed, Weatherby considered, albeit briefly, that he was likely the first human these worthies had ever seen. A Xan falling from the skies and landing in Brighton might warrant a similar reaction from even the friendliest of Englishmen.

"I'm sorry," Weatherby said pensively. "I did not intend any alarm."

His speaking, sadly, created much more ruckus, and soon he was surrounded by several dozen Xan, all singing and crying in a perfect discord, one that grated severely on Weatherby's nerves. A few in the crowd tried making gestures that seemed peaceful, while at least one of the Xan appeared angry, its movements quick and seeming violent.

Then Weatherby felt massive hands shoving his back, sending him staggering forward. He turned to see a hooded Xan screeching loudly, with intense minor chords. Others approached him, their hands outstretched, cooing melodically, while a pair of Xan stood in front of Weatherby apparently to protect him. The songs grew louder, and the belligerent one who pushed Weatherby began to shove others away, stepping toward the object of his ire.

Suddenly, the crowd's attention was drawn away from Weatherby by an approaching noise, an urgent and harmonic staccato coming from another of the Xan's flying carriages—this one with strange markings upon it. Two Xan were inside, wearing medallions Weatherby had seen amongst those in the self-defense complex, and Representative Vellusk was with them. The crowd quickly dispersed, with the most angry of the Xan seeming to move away at the fastest pace.

"Captain Weatherby, are you all right?" Vellusk sang as the vehicle came to a stop.

"Quite so, surprisingly, thank you," he replied. "The boy? Philip?"

Vellusk's voice took on a sorrowful harmony. "Lost, for now."

Weatherby frowned. "Please, if you would, can you take me back to Ambassador Morrow? And locate the Countess St. Germain as well?"

The Xan gestured as a door materialized and opened on the side of the conveyance. Weatherby got in and sat, and the carriage soon whisked its way up into the skies. In any other moment, Weatherby would've marveled at the sights around him, and at the speeds at which he flew. But his thoughts now were inward, grappling with a death cheated, a mission given another chance.

"We cannot take you back to our facility," Vellusk said apologetically. "This incident has already caused a crisis amongst our people, one that is unparalleled in memory."

Weatherby nodded. "I understand. My ship?"

"Your *Fortitude* has been directed to the Earth Quarter, where your ambassador and your woman will meet you," the Xan said.

"And the boy? Surely you can track him."

"It would appear not," Vellusk replied, seeming as though its pride was wounded slightly. "The *arkasht*—the vehicle you damaged—left a trail of smoke behind. But this quickly dissipated. And the partisans may have the means to cloak themselves, much as we cloaked your entry and exit into the city itself."

Weatherby leaned back into his chair, oblivious to the wonders of the city around him. There were so many things to consider, to worry about—what the French were planning, what the Xan partisans might do, how the Xan would react to the humans in their cities—but there was but one thing on the captain's mind, and it was the look on Anne's face as she desperately ran after the creature that had taken her son.

The boy was somehow key, for if the partisans were simply looking for a prisoner, they would take the ambassador, or the Countess, or even himself. No, a boy was no bargaining chip, Weatherby realized. The Xan partisans needed him for something.

The French ship was cloaked. As was the vessel the partisans were using.

The Count St. Germain was with the French.

"Sir," Weatherby called up to Vellusk, who was sitting in front of him. "We must make all haste. I fear we may have little time."

The representative seemed to nod—or at least, moved its head in recognition of Weatherby—and soon the open carriage began to…close, much to Weatherby's surprise. It was not the collapsible roof found on some more modern carriages on Earth. Rather, the walls and ceiling of the vehicle simply seemed to materialize around the seats, encasing all the passengers securely, with a window upon the front of the vehicle.

For all the world, Weatherby felt as though he were in the inside of a chicken's egg, writ large.

Then the vehicle sped forward at an amazing speed, hurtling through the buildings on either side and away from the ring-cities entirely. With a deft twist, the vehicle was upright and heading for Mimas at speeds *Fortitude* would be well challenged to match. Perhaps at full sail, Weatherby considered, with a very light complement and no cargo....

Then the vehicle sped up yet again, and Weatherby was left to wonder silently, and with a degree of concern, at the Xan's strange alchemy and technologies. Thankfully, he did not have long to be weighed with such thoughts, for the small Ovoid quickly approached Mimas, and the circular crater-lake where most of the Earth ships docked when visiting Xanath. Indeed, compared to the ring-cities, the little harbors of Lake Herschel seemed entirely Earth-like.

The Xan piloted the vessel down to the lake, opening the roof once more and allowing Weatherby to enjoy a cool breeze. Having not noticed it before, he now felt that the air around the ring-cities was seemingly hollow in comparison, as if it were as highly regulated and crafted as the city itself.

The egg deposited Weatherby at a long dock, which was empty. "This is where your vessel will make harbor when it arrives, Captain," Vellusk said. "Ambassador Morrow and," the creature paused a moment, "*the* woman are waiting at the harbor-master's office. I will return to you as soon as I have more news."

Weatherby nodded and did his best to stumble through thank-yous and pleasantries that he hoped would be at least polite, if rushed. He then strode the length of the dock and into the small building, where a very young Royal Navy officer bolted to his feet and saluted smartly.

"Lieutenant Underwood, at your service, sir," the officer said. "The ambassador and countess are waiting for you." With a nod from Weatherby, the young man rushed from behind his desk and opened a door, leading to a small inner office.

There, he saw Morrow and Anne, sitting, with the former consoling the latter. Anne looked up, a wan hope upon her tear-streaked face, and Weatherby's heart ached at the sight of it.

"I am sorry, Anne," he said simply. "I tried."

She nodded quietly, giving him a small smile of gratitude despite the tear that fell across her cheek at the news. "I know you did."

Morrow stood and offered his hand, which Weatherby took. "'Twas a brave effort, sir. And one that may yet win us favor in some quarters," he said.

"I shall leave that to you, my lord. At the moment, my concern is for the boy, for I feel he is truly the key to all of this," Weatherby said.

"How?" Anne asked plaintively.

Weatherby sat down next to her, automatically taking her hand in his. "Anne, if the Xan partisans wanted a human hostage, they had England's ambassador within their grasp. Or a Royal Navy captain. Or you, a Countess and the wife of one of humanity's greatest alchemists. They chose Philip. This could not have been an error."

"Why him, then?" Morrow demanded.

"I can think of but one reason: They know the Count St. Germain is here, and is with the French. The only question is whether these rebel Xan seek to use him to influence the Count and the French to do their bidding against the greater society, or..." At this, Weatherby cleared his throat. "Or, they acted upon the Count's bidding, and we must hold that the Xan partisans are in league with the French."

Anne stared at Weatherby with perhaps the hardest look he had ever endured. Her eyes bore into him, seeming to seek some kind of flaw in his logic. This lasted several long, difficult moments, until finally she looked down at her hands. "It is the most reasonable explanation," she said softly.

"Agreed," Morrow said, with no little sympathy. "Either way, we must conclude that St. Germain is working with the French and the Xan partisans, whether by his own free will or, now, under threat of harm to the boy. Now...all we have to do is bloody well find them."

CHAPTER 14

June 20, 2134

Darkness.

That, and the desire to vomit.

Gingerly, and quietly, Diaz started moving. Her hands and feet weren't bound, which was one in the plus column. Wherever she was, it was utterly pitch black, which went in the minus column. Her tech gear and weapons were gone. She wondered whether getting contact-lens HUDs was a smart idea after all, but figured it was easy enough to put a jammer in a cell these days. In fact, given the hard, stone floor and the dust, it was very safe to say she was in a cell.

The minus column kept getting bigger.

She struggled to sit up, cross-legged, doing her best to ignore the vertigo and nausea—aftereffects of the zapper. That's when she heard a groan from behind her, off to her right.

Chances are, it was another member of the team. Or a pissed off bear.

"Report," she said quietly.

"Captain Hutchinson reporting, General," came a voice almost directly to her left. "Feels like we got hit with a zapper. I have no weapons or tech, ma'am."

"Roger that, Maggie," Diaz said. "Who else is in here?"

"I'm here," Coogan muttered—he was the one behind her. "That was awful."

"No kidding. Where's Greene?"

There was no response.

"Greene?"

Nothing.

"All right. Anybody near a wall?" Diaz asked.

Coogan was, and soon Diaz and Hutchinson managed to crawl over to him. They then started moving in either direction in order to get the dimensions of the room—and to find Greene. The room was roughly five meters on a side, with a single door. While the room seemed to be part of the temple ruins complex, the door was metal and quite new, and thus very, very secure. Even if they started in with belt buckles and whatever else they had, it would take days before they could chip away at the stone around it.

And Diaz figured someone would be around to get them before then.

Meanwhile, Greene was nowhere to be found. Even after the three teammates crawled around the entire room in a grid pattern, they found nothing.

"Why would they keep Greene?" Hutchinson wondered.

"He may have had a reaction to the zapper," Coogan offered. "Perhaps he seized up."

Diaz smiled despite herself, and was glad nobody could see it. "He's been zapped before, Jimmy. I doubt it."

"Then it's his technical expertise," Huntington said evenly. "Somebody's doing something down here. Maybe they need him."

"Maybe," Diaz replied. "Most folks think he retired from his show and hit the beach. Of course, if Harry's here, then he'd know Evan's resume back to front."

They speculated a bit longer before it started seeming a bit futile. There was only so much a dark, empty room could provide before even the most harebrained idea got stale. So they sat.

And waited.

Hutchinson started doing some light calisthenics—not a bad idea, really, Diaz thought. Not enough to get winded, but enough to stay ready, much like an athlete riding an exercise bike between periods in a game. Stay warm and alert. Soon, Diaz joined her. Coogan, meanwhile, sat against a wall and seemed to be scratching something on the floor. Might have simply been nerves. The young officer lived with his visor and data feed 24/7. With their tech gone, digital withdrawal could become an issue.

Fatigue started to set in after a while. They had all taken an energy boost prior to leaving—it was after midnight when they headed off on the road to the ruins, after all—but that was starting to wear off, and it had to be nearing five or six in the morning.

When Diaz started hearing snoring from Coogan's corner of the room, she figured she'd have to start a watch schedule. Being the boss, she took first watch, allowing Hutchinson to catch some sleep. She wished she had thought to bring a manual chronometer, or at least something that ran on chemical batteries. She had no idea when to wake Coogan up for his watch.

Maybe she didn't need to. It was highly unlikely that someone would just open the door and shoot them on the spot. Not impossible, of course—maybe someone needed to get orders from on high before pulling the trigger—but when Diaz thought about who was on high…

She knew Harry didn't have it in him. Most corporate executives didn't. Hell, there were a few in the *Fortune* 500 with enough firepower under their command to take out a small country, all in the name of corporate security. But with a bare handful of exceptions, none of them had military or police experience. None of them wanted it. They had *people* for those sorts of distasteful things, and even then, with some of the most lenient corporate laws in history, corporations could not, in fact, get away with murder.

Especially when it came to a ranking general and a world-famous scientist.

Diaz was startled out of her reverie—had she been dozing?—by the sound of metal scraping across metal. A small grate opened on the door, allowing light to pour in the room briefly, blinding her. Something crashed to the floor—more metal, and some plastic, perhaps—before the grate slammed shut again.

"Hey! Hey! Get back here!" Diaz said, rushing the door and pounding on it. "I am a United States military officer! I demand to be put in contact with my embassy!"

Nothing. Even the footsteps receded quickly.

Diaz felt around on the floor and discovered exactly what she expected. A metal tray, some pre-packaged food, and some plastic water bags. She nudged the others awake and doled out the food and water. Jerky, peanut butter, crackers, apples. Real basic rations, probably something that fell off an Egyptian army supply truck at some point.

They ate. Hutchinson was a vegetarian—funny how Diaz never grokked to that before—so Diaz and Coogan traded her jerky for extra peanut butter and apples. The water bags were generous enough to keep them hydrated for several more hours.

Of course, there was one problem with hydration….

Thankfully, the water bags were fully resealable, and when emptied they provided an easy enough solution for the inevitable. Hopefully, Diaz thought, they wouldn't be in there long enough to need further innovation in that regard.

"No Greene," Hutchinson said, a little sadness in her voice.

"Nope, not yet," Diaz said, keeping her voice neutral. "He's probably spilling. That's fine…if they caught us, they probably figured out enough anyway. Our stunt at the plant didn't help matters to begin with."

Coogan sighed. "I remember watching his shows for years. He was entertaining."

"Enough with the 'was,' Lieutenant," Diaz snapped, a little more forcefully than she intended. "All we know is that he's not here. Hell, maybe he escaped, and the cavalry's on the way. Let's stick with what we know."

Silence reigned after that. Lunch came and went, followed by an old hospital bedpan. Nobody felt like making use of it, but a corner was nonetheless designated for it. Diaz felt like dozing again, and didn't bother setting up watches. It was so damned quiet, any movement would probably wake them up in a heartbeat.

Diaz genuinely felt bad about Greene. Yes, he pushed her—hard—to do more experiments. "Real science," he called it. Admittedly, she may have sold him a bill of goods on that front. He had a top-rated show, book deals, you name it. And she lured him to the DAEDALUS team by promising he'd get his shot at a world-shaking discovery. Instead, they focused on defense, rather than extradimensional exploration. It was the right call, of course, from a security point of view. She firmly believed that. But even though he disagreed, loudly and often, he followed orders. His work was helping keep the world safe from crazy-ass people like Yuna Hiyashi and that Cagliostro guy—and their puppeteer, the ancient Martian warlord Althotas.

In all honestly, Diaz probably wanted to open the door again as much as Greene. But she kept it to herself. Security had to come before exploration. Maybe Greene was right in that DAEDALUS needed to play more offense, less defense. Certainly it seemed Harry—or whomever he was working with—was pretty busy doing just that, and everyone else was left scrambling to catch up. And without the safeguards and common sense Diaz felt her team brought to the table.

Sounds from the other side of the door jarred Diaz out of her reverie, bringing her to her feet; she could hear Hutchinson doing the same from the other side of the room. Keys jingled, locks clicked.

"Close your eyes," Diaz ordered. "Wait a few seconds before trying to open them."

Diaz did just that as the door opened, and felt the light from the space beyond hit her eyelids. Even that was painful, but impatience won out over practicality, and she squinted her eyes open just a bit.

There was a human figure at the door, with what appeared to be a couple more behind it.

"Bring all of them," someone said….someone who sounded a lot like…

"Greene?" Coogan asked.

Men entered the room, grabbing Diaz, Coogan and Hutchinson by the arm, pulling them out.

"We have a problem with the experiment," Greene said. "We need to access BlueNet. But I don't have the clearance to access it from here."

"What experiment?" Diaz demanded, anger coursing through her as the worst-case scenarios that had been playing through her head were confirmed. *Goddamn it, Evan.*

"The one Total-Suez is running," Greene said matter-of-factly. "They're knocking on the door…but the door is knocking back. Hard."

October 15, 1798

Finch rushed to the door of the underground chamber, only to find it had slammed shut with a disturbing sense of finality. In addition, three-foot spikes had sprung up from the floor in front of the portal, and the scream was the very last breath of one of the French soldiers—a boy, Finch noted, barely older than Jabir.

"Don't move!" Finch cried out. But he went unheeded, as another soldier made a mad dash to the door on the others side, only to see it slam shut. The man quickly jumped backward—just in time to avoid a second set of spikes springing up from the floor with a jolt.

"What is this, Finch?" Berthollet demanded, as if mere indignation and seeming authority could countermand the impersonal nature of the crisis around them.

"A trap, obviously, *monsieur*," Finch snapped. "If this was indeed a back entrance to the temple, then it was only for the priests to use. There is likely a mechanism to use to hold all this in abeyance, so the priests could cross unscathed."

"So we must find it!" Berthollet said. "By the doors, most likely."

Finch got on all fours and began to crawl carefully toward the door from whence they had entered. He inspected the floor carefully, looking for odd-shaped stones and cracks in the masonry from which further dangers might erupt. He also paused to look at the walls and ceiling—the skeleton he had inspected had a head wound, and Finch fully expected further mechanisms to come into play.

Finch heard a shuffle behind him. "For God's sake, don't move!" he shouted.

He felt the floor shift under his right hand, and deftly moved it—just before another metal spike shot upward.

"*Le plafond!*" a soldier cried out.

Finch looked up…and rolled. Two more spikes landed right where he had been.

Then he felt the ground beneath him vibrate once more, so he quickly rose to his feet—as two more spikes erupted from the ground.

The door was but ten feet away. He had to chance it.

Finch dashed across the room and pressed himself against the corpse of the impaled French soldier—for it stood to reason that no more spikes would fall or rise in a spot that had already claimed a life. He saw the man's eyes shift toward him—dear God, what a horrible way to die—but forced himself to turn and gauge the rest of the room.

Berthollet stood his ground, looking about, seemingly ready to move if the occasion called for it—but not a moment before. Dolomieu had moved to the other door; perhaps a smart move, but one that should have waited, for it was likely the geologist had tripped the spikes that imperiled Finch. The two remaining soldiers stood stock-still, and seemed to be praying most fervently.

Finch found himself hoping their prayers would help.

He turned his attention to the door. There were various sigils and pictograms marked along both sides. He looked for something larger-than-average, at least the size of a thumb-print, and at the level of his hand at his side.

Nothing.

"Deodat! Anything?" he called out.

"No, Andrew! I am at a loss. I would think it would be easily reachable, and yet I can find nothing!"

Finch frowned and looked across the room. None of the furniture was made of stone or was otherwise permanent. The shelves were wooden and particularly low-slung.

Low....

Finch stooped down and ran his hands up either side of the door.

There. A large pictogram of an eye. How appropriate. Finch drove his thumb into it.

And the doors opened once more, while the spikes receded into the floor. Beside Finch, the French soldier fell to the ground, a torrent of blood washing over the stones from where he was impaled.

Finch nonetheless checked the man, but he was truly dead now. Rising, he gingerly walked over to Berthollet. "Proceed carefully to the door, and do not, for the love of God, touch anything," Finch ordered.

The group quietly made for the door, in the kind of tip-toed rush one sees in comedies on the stage. Finch was the last one through, and closed the door behind him.

"What if others wish to follow?" Berthollet demanded.

Finch frowned. "They must go through the room regardless. Better to reset the traps, now that we know how to disarm them, than to see whether any other mechanisms are triggered by leaving the doors open."

Berthollet nodded after a moment, brusquely conceding the point. "How did you know where to look, Doctor?"

Finch cocked his head behind him. "From what I've seen of mummies and ruins from ancient days, the Egyptians of yore were at least a half-foot shorter than we are, perhaps more. So the disarming mechanism must likewise have been lower."

Berthollet smiled. "Well done, Dr. Finch! Lead us onward!"

Most assuredly expendable, Finch thought as he resumed his place at the head of the column. Idly, he wondered if someone would bother giving that poor boy a proper burial at some point, or if the legacy of French exploration would be littered with the corpses of dead soldiers. The fruits of the French Revolution, it seemed, were still distributed quite unevenly.

The corridor they had entered had several doors upon either side. Most were wooden and infected with rot, and the small rooms beyond—likely the priests' or servants' chambers—held piles of rotted wood, cloth and papyrus. Finch wondered at this for a moment, until he realized they were far enough underground so that the oasis' water-table could come into play. Thus, unlike the desert tombs he was used to exploring, there was just enough water in these ruins to affect the air and wood—and potentially ruin any treasures worth having.

The end of the corridor featured another door, more ornate than the last, with wood banded in brass and, perhaps, gold as well. Finch halted the party and conducted a thorough search of the portal, using his multi-colored glasses to find any imperfections, using a tiny brush to clean minute bits of dust from the masonry, and running his fingers gently across the entire surface. Behind him, he could hear Berthollet huffing slightly in impatience. Finch was quite ready to tell him to test the door himself, but thought better of it.

Finally, Finch tried the door, which opened easily. He then looked closely at the floor on the other side, as well as the walls and ceiling, before allowing the rest of the group entry. At this juncture, Finch believed it quite safe, really, but he had always held to the mantra of making oneself appear as indispensable as possible. Especially when expendable.

"Light!" cried Berthollet. "We need light!"

The two remaining soldiers began breaking out additional torches, while Finch adjusted his lantern so that it would shine particularly bright, as well as forward. The room appeared to be quite large, the walls adorned with a wide variety of pictograms. Finch recognized some, including those said to represent Amon-Ra, which were of particular prominence. Unsurprising for Egypt's late period of antiquity, prior to the rise of Ptolemy.

The center of the room held a large, low altar. Finch had half-expected it to be similar in construction and size to the one he had seen on Mars, those many years ago, but it was nothing like it, and Finch found himself slightly relieved at this. While it would be an incredible find, it would also be one full of portent, and perhaps not for the good.

The group quickly spread out to conduct a thorough examination of the room. Finch could see Dolomieu looking assiduously at the floor and ceiling, as well as the massive double doors at the far end of the chamber. Good—the geologist was applying Finch's methods already. And that left Finch to make for the altar straightaway.

Berthollet had the same idea.

"I believe this is the main temple," the Frenchman said.

"It stands to reason," Finch said neutrally.

Berthollet ran his hands across the top of the stone altar, which had maintained a relatively smooth surface despite the intervening centuries. "Perhaps another trigger?" he muttered.

Finch wracked his brain, trying to think of alternatives. This was a ceremonial chamber, not one for storage. There were no signs of cabinets or shelves, nothing that could be locked, so keeping sacred relics in here would require a permanent guard. That would be incredibly inefficient, and certainly would create a need for wholly reliable servants. If nothing else, the trapped back entrance told Finch a great deal about the ancient priests' ability to trust.

Simply put, any secrets the Egyptians wished to preserve would not be kept here openly. But where, then? Finch was sure the rest of the complex would bear clues, but that was days and days of work. Finch was many things, but exceedingly patient was not among them. And neither were the Franks.

"The Vatican archives said nothing of this," Berthollet muttered to himself in French as he continued to run his large, thick hands over the altar—now the sides, where there were numerous carvings.

Something in that struck a chord with Finch. The Vatican.... His thoughts turned to the trappings of the Holy Church and its cathedrals, how they were built, and what secrets they kept. A moment later, Finch was on all fours, looking closely at the floor under the altar, flipping through the lenses on his ocular device.

There.

Directly beneath the altar piece was a large, square block of stone in the floor, at least two-and-a-half feet per side. There was a small indentation within it, a hole that likely fit some sort of lever for moving it.

Of course, it would be trapped to hell and back.

"Deodat!" Finch called. "What have you found?"

The geologist jogged back toward the altar. "There are mechanisms upon the main doors, Doctor. I have managed to disable them. There are also, I think, many places where spikes or some such may fall or fly from the ceilings and walls. There is something here, certainly."

"I couldn't agree more," Finch replied. He turned to one of the soldiers. "I have need of your musket and your bayonet, young man."

The soldier immediately sought to hand over his weapon, but was stopped by an outstretched hand from Berthollet. "What have you found?" he demanded of Finch.

Finch smiled. "A possible trap, which may lead us to the prize we seek."

"Where?"

"No, sir. I will disarm it or trigger it as safely as I can, but you will leave it to me, or else you may doom us all," Finch said.

Berthollet started to grow red in the face. "Dr. Finch, this is uncalled for. We have treated you with naught but respect and camaraderie! Why now do you endanger this?"

"I endanger it before you do, sir," Finch said coolly. "I have served you well, but I will not have you and your men about, potentially causing more chaos. Those are my terms. Otherwise, you may attempt this as you like."

It was, of course, something of a bluff. It would not take Dolomieu all that long to deduce what Finch had found. Triggering it might cost the lives of more soldiers, but that did not seem to bother Berthollet overmuch. In the end, Finch was counting on the fact that Berthollet would be as impatient as he.

"Very well," Berthollet said gruffly. "You may proceed."

Finch nodded. "Accord," he said. "Now get out. Wait in the corridor."

Berthollet paused a moment, then nodded at Dolomieu and the two guards, who proceeded back into the corridor. Finch could feel Berthollet's eyes boring into him from the doorway as he began his preparations. Of course, Finch knew the reasons behind Berthollet's reticence. Finch would be the first to discover whatever treasures the ancients kept there, and Berthollet seemed quite keen on keeping him in the dark as long as possible. If practical, forever.

Finch turned his mind to the task at hand. The stone would open toward someone standing behind the altar. There was a space there roughly large enough for one man to enter—or jump in, should something go wrong.

Finch searched the altar in vain for some sort of safety catch, like the one in the back entrance, but to no avail.

He then considered his options. His first impulse, to use a bayonet as a lever, seemed quite foolish now, as it would leave him standing and exposed. A rope and pulley, perhaps, to pull it open while he stood at length? Better, but there was no guarantee of safety. Indeed, the only safe place seemed to be directly under the altar, where the presumed trapdoor was housed. For if a priest were to be threatened, he could open the hatch and then duck under the altar, avoiding whatever hell would be unleashed upon his enemies.

Finch opened his pack and pulled out a small case—a portable alchemical laboratory, perhaps one of the finest available. Laying it out on the altar, he mixed several ingredients, including Ionic sulfur and an extract from an acid-spitting plant from Venus, then boiled them quickly using a burner and a portable fuel admixture of his own devising. A few drops of Europan water cooled the resulting liquid just as quickly as it boiled.

With his potion ready, Finch quickly stowed his lab in its case and tucked it under the altar. Crouching, he then carefully chanted a final prayer over his creation and poured it along the cracks in the masonry, then splashed it across the massive stone. Finally, he pulled out another of his own creations—a small stick of wood with phosphorus and sulfur at the end—and scraped it across the side of the altar. It immediately created a small flame at the tip, which Finch then applied to the center of the stone.

The stone caught fire quickly and began to disintegrate as if it were made of mere paper—which, thanks to Finch's alchemy, it very nearly was. Beneath, he could see a number of ritual items—and a package roughly two feet to a side, wrapped in thin bandages seemingly made of a kind of leather.

Then the room went mad.

A deep rumble permeated the floor, while stones and rocks fell from the ceiling and metal spikes flew from the walls. It was a gigantic death trap.

And Finch was quite wrong—the underside of the altar was not safe, for a pair of very large spikes flew from the back of the chamber straight for where he stood…

…except he had already thrown himself down through the flaming stone, and was crouched inside a hole no more than three feet deep. He saw the spikes pass overhead, and hoped fervently the altar wouldn't collapse upon him.

He saw just how wrong he was when a stone fell from the underside of the altar itself—a final check against would-be thieves, of which he was now one.

There wasn't enough room to duck. Finch reflexively raised his arms, feeling the lancing pain as the stone—a foot wide and nearly as thick—crashed into them.

And then all was black.

June 20, 2134

Lander Two gently eased into the snows of Enceladus with barely an impact; Shaila smiled despite herself at how good she'd gotten at low-gravity landings. Plus, most of her vitriol had been spent during the hour-long trip down to the moon's surface, as she ripped Stephane a new one before he even finished with his report. At one point, he had to plead with her to let him complete it before he could begin answering her questions. Even though they were largely rhetorical in nature—as in, "What the fuck were you thinking?"—she gave him just enough respite to get his work done.

Barely. By the time Shaila fired up the landing sequence, Stephane seemed suitably chagrined. In fact, Shaila worried she might have overdone it, because he was almost too quiet as he looked out the side window at the snow-covered world.

"All right," she said as she powered down the engines. "You clear on why everything you did sucked so badly?"

"Yes," he said, smiling weakly.

She stared at him for a long moment, gauging him. He seemed almost crestfallen. "Right, then." She leaned over and kissed him on the forehead. "Don't do it again. Let's get out there."

A few minutes later, they were clear of the airlock. Stephane began unloading crates, while Shaila went to work on the water desalinization unit. She had the schematics on her datapad—putting them up on her HUD would've distracted the hell out of her—and she began poking around it to see if there was any way of getting it to suck up less salt and particulates.

"You OK over there?" she asked Stephane over the comm.

"I am," he replied. "Moving over to the tiger stripes now. The seismic alarms are still in place. I will report in regularly, I promise."

"You better."

Shaila began taking apart the desalinization unit. Once she pulled out the main filter, a cloud of salt particles followed, spraying into the space around her and drifting off ever so gently. There was just too much in Enceladus' water for the system to keep up. Someone would have to be replacing filters every few minutes to get the kind of clean water Archie needed.

Unless....

"Jain to Durand, come in."

"I'm not there *yet*," he responded, sounding miffed.

"Whatever. Question for you. If we let the water sit a while before filtering, would some of the salt and particulates move to the bottom?"

"Not enough," he replied. "It is in solution. Some of the heavier particulates, yes, but the salt? No. To get fresh water out of salt water, you have to...ah! Boil it!"

Shaila smiled. "See? You're a bright guy. Thanks."

She closed the link and hop-skipped back to the lander, the DIY part of her brain clicking along nicely. The only heat source they had was the laser drill they used to release the sensor-bots into Enceladus' undersea oceans. The drill would be overkill if used on freestanding water; it would vaporize it instantly, along with whatever else they were using as a container. But if she aimed it at the ground, well away from the tiger stripes, she could burrow through the icy crust of the surface and into the salty oceans below. Both the ice and the water would be turned to steam...which they could then try to capture. It would likely cool quickly, even in the insulated hoses used to channel water into the lander's cargo bay. Boom—instant, pure water.

Shaila picked up the drill. The problem was, of course, that the drill ran on battery power. It was heavy-duty enough so that it would probably only last five minutes on a charge—nowhere near long enough to get a decent amount of pure water in the tank.

Multiple batteries? Probably weren't enough onboard the ship to make it worthwhile. But the lander's generator could probably feed the drill for much longer. She began calling up the lander schematics on her datapad, cross-referencing them with the drill schematics she put up on her HUD.

Twenty minutes later, she had her solution. She could install a conventional power-plug onboard the lander, then rig a cord between the lander and the drill. Gin up a stand of some kind, then seal the whole thing off so that the steam would be contained, rising to the top and trickling down as pure water. Thankfully, the damned drill was certified waterproof, given its use on an ice moon. Hopefully that particular JSC contractor was on the ball.

Shaila stowed the drill back in the lander, feeling rather victorious. They'd probably be delayed another four to six hours while they got their gear rigged, but once things got going, they'd be able to get some high-quality fuel aboard.

Then she noticed the crates still in the lander. They were Stephane's instruments.

"Jain to Durand, come in," she said.

"Durand here."

"You forget something?"

A pause. "Not that I know of. What did I forget?"

"Most of your gear is still here in the lander."

Stephane laughed through the comm. "Most, not all. I am running with some ideas on these flows. I will be back soon for them."

Before she could respond, Shaila's HUD came up with an urgent comm alert. "Hang on, Stephane," she said. "*Armstrong*, this is Jain. I copy."

"Jain, you and Durand need to get up here ASAP." Nilssen said. "We got a distress call from *Tienlong*."

"Say again?"

"You heard me. *Tienlong* sent a distress call. We need you up here with all the clean water you can bring. Move it."

"Roger that. Jain out," she replied. "Stephane, you hear that?"

"Yes, I am coming."

An hour and fifteen minutes later, Shaila docked Lander Two back aboard *Armstrong*. It had taken a couple of stern exhortations to get Stephane moving; he nattered on excitedly about water flows and particulates and undersea currents throughout the trip back to the ship, so much so that Shaila found herself almost forgiving him for his earlier craziness.

Once out of their pressure suits, Shaila and Stephane entered the common room, where Nilssen had convened the crew. "All right, let's go. Archie?"

"Nothing more on comm, except this message," he said. He hit a button on his pad, and the holoprojector above the table flickered on. Shaila immediately recognized the UN-standard code for spacefaring vessels, including status reports on engines, life-support, personnel and cargo. Before she could dive in, the audio came on. "This is Chinese ship *Tienlong*. We are making a distress call. We have personnel on Titan. Requesting assistance. Repeat, this is Chinese ship *Tienlong*, with distress call. We have personnel on Titan and we cannot find them. Over."

The room was deathly silent.

"It's on a loop," Archie said finally. "We tried pinging 'em back. Nothing. Not detecting anything more from Titan right now. No comms, no engine signature, nothing. Like they just said their piece and shut everything down."

"Visual from our sats?" Shaila asked.

"They're not in position. Won't be for another twelve hours," Nilssen said. "By that time, we could be well on our way there, only to find they're just fucking with us. Or they're all dead. Nice thing is, we're still getting the automated feed from the depot ships. So if they're in shit-shape and try to break in for supplies, we'll know about it."

The comm signal pinged through the room, sending everyone looking to their datapads or HUD visors. "Packet from Houston," Shaila said. "The Chinese have officially reached out to JSC to request assistance as well. Captain's discretion as to whether we do it."

Nilssen smiled. "Nice to have someone to blame. Archie, how fast can we get to Titan?"

"It's not about how fast, it's about the goddamn fuel," Archie replied. "Tanks are 34 percent full, enough for a good solid burn for a quick transit orbit. But it's mostly that salty crap. I don't have simulations back yet from Houston on what it'll do to our systems."

Nilssen pondered this. "Which is worse? Fast burn or slow burn?"

Archie scowled at him. "Doesn't matter. Either could fuck up our engines."

"Could?"

The old engineer leaned back in his chair and rubbed his eyes. "Look, we'll get there. We'll make orbit. The ship won't blow up. From there, we'll have to see just how long it'll take to get our engines back to normal. If we just have to scrub salt out of the engines, a day or two. If we have corrosion, could be weeks. Worst case, I'd have to cannibalize the depot ship engines. At least they're the same model."

Nilssen turned to Shaila. "Jain, set a course for Titan. Soon as you get nav data for a transit orbit, go for full burn. Let's get there fast. We'll plan out our ops on the way over. Dismissed."

Shaila got up and checked the time—it would take a few minutes for Archie to give the green light before she was needed at the controls. So she followed Stephane down the hallway to the science lab. He looked pale and wan at the conference table, more so than before. "You OK?" she asked gently, putting a hand on his shoulder.

He turned and smiled weakly. "I don't know. I mean, I feel fine, but…I'm just tired. I'm getting new data from the sensors I dropped, but I'm still trying to figure out how the currents under Enceladus should work, and I'm coming up with nothing," he said as they entered the lab. He flopped down in front of a workstation and waved up a holomodel of the little world. "You have these currents here, all swirling around the tiger stripes, as if they were rushing up to greet us when we arrived. And yet if you look at gravity, core temperature, all of it, I can't find a reason."

Shaila smiled. "You will. You're smart like that."

Stephane shook his head. "I don't know, it's like Mars again. I'm seeing things that shouldn't be there."

"Any blue?" she asked, using their private code-word for Cherenkov radiation—the blue glow that preceded or accompanied much of the quantum fluctuations on Mars two years ago.

"No," he said with a touch of pique. "It would be easier if there were."

"All right," Shaila said. "Don't work too hard." She bent down to give him a kiss on the cheek…and his skin was cold and clammy. "You *sure* you're all right?"

"I'm fine," he said curtly, spinning the holomodel in his hands, seemingly lost in thought.

"Have Conti take another look at you. That's a serious, don't-fuck-with-me order," she said, a small grin breaking through.

He nodded with a weak smile, then turned back to his work.

CHAPTER 15

October 15, 1798

If you were a French ship trying to hide from the most advanced civilization in the Known Worlds, where would you go?" Weatherby muttered as he turned over pages of charts upon the desk of his cabin, absently nodding at Gar'uk as the Venusian offered him a glass of claret.

Once *Fortitude* had arrived on Mimas, Weatherby had called together his officers, along with Lord Morrow and Lady Anne. Each man (and one woman) held charts and maps of the Saturn/Xanath system. Unfortunately, such maps were woefully incomplete due to the Xan's secretive nature. And there were sixty-four moons circling the massive world—any one of which might provide some form of harbor. Some of these were not even charted properly.

"Most of Xanath's moons are agricultural centers," Morrow said. "The Xan are exceptionally industrious when it comes to farming. The scale of their farms is mind-boggling. With so many millions of them in the ring-cities, I'm told it's all they can do to keep up. It's quite important to them."

Weatherby nodded. "Then let us forget those, for the *Franklin* would dare not risk such important areas. What else?"

Barnes cleared his throat awkwardly. "My lord and lady. Captain Weatherby, sir. Are there any moons around Saturn...excuse me, Xanath...that even the Xan do not visit? Ones upon which there is no civilized presence at all?"

Weatherby looked to Morrow, for the ambassador was the most likely to know, but the latter man shrugged. "I should say nearly every bit of habitable land among these worlds is in use," Morrow said. "The Xan population is quite numerous, said to number in the billions. I have heard they have even begun importing foodstuffs from Callisto simply to make ends meet."

Barnes grimaced at this. "Yes, of course, my lord. But are there any places which are specifically prohibited? Perhaps due to an unreasonable environment?"

"Or perhaps for cultural reasons?" Anne said, growing interested. "Callisto is, in essence, a penal colony used to house those who have lapsed from the Xan's peaceful philosophies, is it not?"

Morrow leaned back in his chair, deep in thought. After a moment, he spoke one word: "Titan."

Looks were exchanged around the room. Titan was said to be the Xan's true homeworld in ages past. Once a veritable Garden of Eden for the Saturnine peoples, the Xan's early martialry resulted in a near cataclysm for the entire race. The Xan were forced to emigrate hastily from their first cradle as the very air and land became poisonous in the wake of their dread sorceries and fell machines.

Or so it was said. As with most things about the Xan, rumors were plentiful, while facts were in short supply indeed.

"From what I understand, there is a basic problem of breathing," Weatherby ventured. "Of course, it would be an ideal place to make harbor, but how long could they last?" The captain turned to Dr. Hawkins. "Then again, they have Earth's foremost alchemist among them, do they not? Could he provide a working to ameliorate such concerns?"

The ship's alchemist shuffled a bit and looked at his feet before responding. "I dare not attempt to quantify what the Count St. Germain is capable of, in terms of the Great Work. The Countess would be better suited to that task, I think. But there are workings in the *Royal Navy Manual* which provide aids to breathing underwater, as well as in harsh climates. With the right materials and some foreknowledge of the exact nature of Titan's air, even my poor skill might create something to sustain us, at least for a short time."

Weatherby caught Anne nodding in agreement before turning back to Morrow. "The Xan, I imagine, would be quite indisposed to our presence there, no?"

"Under normal circumstances, I dare say they'd shoot us from the Void without hesitation," Morrow agreed with a wan smile. "However, circumstances are far from normal. There are those who are howling for the complete dismantling of the Earth Quarter, and others who would see us track *Franklin* down at any cost in order to preserve the civil peace here. If enough of the latter remain in positions of authority..." The ambassador stood up, bringing the rest of the room to its feet. "If you'll excuse me, I believe I need to send a communiqué to whatever friends we have left."

Weatherby nodded as Morrow took his leave. "The rest of you, continue searching. We shall need a catalogue of every single potential harbor the French might employ without leaving Xanath. I don't care if it's a mighty moon or the simplest, smallest boulder. We must find them. Mr. Barnes, coordinate our efforts. Dismissed."

The rest of the *Fortitude*'s officers filed out of the room, except for Gar'uk, who began clearing the table and putting the charts and papers in order as best he could. The Venusian was barely literate, and at times Weatherby found himself searching through Gar'uk's rudimentary filing system for charts or papers. It was a small price to pay, he felt, for the little lizard-creature's loyalty and care.

Weatherby turned to Anne, who did not move from her seat at Weatherby's right hand. "How are you, my lady?" he said softly.

She favored him with a sad smile. "A perfect wreck, of course."

"You do not show it."

"It shall do Philip no good for me to collapse into hysterics," she said simply. "I will find my son and my husband. And if Francis is involved in these schemes, I assure you, Tom, he and I will have words."

The steel in her voice assured Weatherby that more than words would be exchanged. In that moment, she looked fully capable of ending the Count St. Germain's very life with her bare hands, let alone the mystic sciences she commanded.

"We will find your son, Anne," he said, quietly but firmly. "I will not rest until he is returned to you."

Anne rested her hand upon his for a moment. "I know. I thank you for it." They held each other's gaze for several moments, which were not the least bit uncomfortable for either. "You've become the man I hoped you'd be, Tom."

Weatherby smiled. "'Tis better late than never, I suppose. Perhaps one cannot appreciate the best course until having sailed through a few gales."

"Spoken like a true sailor," she said as she rose from her place. "I shall go assist Dr. Hawkins. If we are to make for Titan, or any other blasted place, we may need the workings he spoke of."

Weatherby rose with her and watched her depart. Nineteen years were but a moment in the great histories of the Known Worlds, and they seemed shorter still in her presence.

Four hours later, Morrow reported that the Xan had given *Fortitude* permission to travel to Titan—but not without condition. "We are to be escorted, firstly," the ambassador said as he and Weatherby walked the maindeck together. "Three of the Ovoids will join us. For one, Titan remains something of a sacred enclave—a reminder of their past barbarism, so they may be disinclined to repeat it."

Weatherby could not help but smile grimly. "It seems as though it isn't working quite well."

Morrow gave him a narrow look. "You've spent too much time in the company of that scoundrel Finch."

"My apologies, Ambassador. Do continue."

"The second reason for the escort is that the more warlike factions within Xan society have begun to splinter from their government," Morrow said. "It would seem that the arrival of the *Franklin* may have prompted the first stirrings of insurrection. I fear that the self-defense forces may be unequal to the task, especially if the partisans are willing to shed more blood as easily as they slayed Sallev."

This stopped Weatherby in his tracks. "So we may very well be attacked."

"Quite possibly, yes," Morrow said, not without sympathy.

Weatherby looked around at his ship as the men prepared for departure. Stores were being hoisted and laid into the hold below. The men were scrubbing decks, coiling ropes, finishing up minor repairs.

"What are these Ovoids capable of?" Weatherby asked worriedly.

"I can't honestly tell you, but I've asked Vellusk to impart whatever knowledge of their alchemy he can to your Dr. Hawkins and, of course, Lady Anne. Whether he feels comfortable doing so remains another matter. How long until you're ready to depart?"

Weatherby cast a quick glance around. "Three hours, no more."

"Then they have three hours to find a defense," Morrow said simply, placing a hand upon Weatherby's shoulder, where his captain's braid now hung heavily. "I'm sorry, Tom. We must stop them. The stakes are too high if we do not."

Weatherby nodded soberly. "The French escape with whatever they've sought. St. Germain's alchemy may be put to terrible use. And the Xan descend into civil war—and may yet target Earth." He took a deep breath. "We haven't much time. If you'll excuse me, sir, I believe I have much work ahead."

June 21, 2134

To Greene's credit, he insisted on bringing all three of his former colleagues with him. Diaz was the only one who could retask the BlueNet satellites—if that was in fact what he wanted—without going through a huge security gauntlet. Coogan and Huntington were worthless in that case, but Diaz figured whomever was pulling the strings here would know she wouldn't play ball unless she was absolutely sure they were OK.

As the team marched through the ancient hallways, Diaz had tried engaging Greene in conversation, to no avail. She had no idea if there was a gun to his head here, or if he'd turned, or...any of it. The stakes were real enough; Diaz noted that the guards accompanying them were armed with real honest-to-God automatic weapons. No zappers here—these were serious rate-of-fire weapons used to kill. Indeed, as Diaz got a closer look, she realized they were M19A7 assault rifles, made in the good old U.S. of A. *Christ. Figures.* Seemed the only thing America did these days was export weapons and warfighters.

As far as she could tell, it looked like someone had moved into the lowest levels of the Siwa ruins and made themselves at home. The corridors were of the same sandstone-brick as the upper levels, but there were power and comm lines strung along the upper walls and ceiling, and most of the doors had been replaced with strong metal ones, probably 3-D printed on site. Most everything there, really, probably came from an industrial sized 3-D printer powered by a portable fusion reactor.

When they turned the corner, Diaz realized that last bit was pretty off-base. They had to have had a *lot* more power.

Greene led them into a massive chamber filled with an astounding mix of archaeological artifacts and the most technologically advanced workstations money could buy. The workstations—there were no fewer than fifteen people working the holocontrols—all faced a glass wall; behind it, Diaz could see the side of a massive tube, at least three meters in diameter, that went off into the walls on either side. Before the tube was....

"Is that an altar?" Huntington asked quietly.

Greene turned and actually smiled. "You were right, Maggie. We're in the temple of the Oracle of Amun-Ra. This is where Alexander the Great got the Egyptian priesthood to confirm his divine heritage. But right now, we have bigger problems."

Diaz nodded. With her attention drawn away from the scale and complexity of the room, she could see the people inside it moving quickly, talking fast, sifting through reams of data on the fly. "You hit a snag," she said simply.

"That's why they captured us," Greene said, heading to the front of the room where a large console stood right in front of the glass wall. "There's enough dead ends between here and the surface to ensure you wouldn't find this facility no matter how long we snooped around; that's why I was allowed to even bring us here. But as we were poking around, they had the cascading problem, so they decided to grab us in case they couldn't get it under control."

"You were allowed?" Huntington said. "That means you've been at this a while with them."

Before Greene could respond, someone shouted from across the room. "Dr. Greene!"

They turned to find an elderly African man walking toward them wearing a rumpled suit and loosened tie, his hand extended and a massive smile on his face. "Dr. Greene, do we have the BlueNet codes yet?"

"Not yet. But we need them. Maybe you could explain to the general why," Greene said, turning back to Diaz. "This is Dr. Gerald Ayim of the University of Dar es Salaam. He's the deputy lead investigator on this project."

"The older man nodded and addressed Diaz. "We're trying to replicate the Mars experiment, but each time we ramp up the particle collisions, the resulting energy flows aren't channeling properly. They're bleeding off and threatening to make the entire collider unstable."

Diaz folded her arms. "I fail to see how that's my problem. And if he's the deputy lead, who's in charge?"

"I think you figured that out already, Maria," Greene said, looking down briefly at his shoes.

"Your vacation," she said simply. "You were gonna come here."

"It's real science, Maria. We're so close. And the funding, you have no idea. This team could do it. We could break through, write the greatest chapter in human history. Right here."

Greene's eyes shone with excitement, but Diaz wasn't buying it. "And Total-Suez is footing the bill. Still not seeing how that's my problem."

Looking a little uncomfortable, Ayim chimed in. "In order for this to work, we needed to channel the ambient Cherenkov radiation from around the world. You discovered some malfunctioning equipment in Mexico. However, even with all of our equipment in every hot spot you can imagine, it's not enough. I suppose if we had more than nine months to get it done…but we didn't."

Diaz looked around. "You did all this in nine months?"

"Prefab, Maria!"

She turned to see Harry Yu walking into the room, trying his best to seem professional while suppressing a very large grin.

"Jesus, Harry, you're a son-of-a-bitch," Diaz said.

He nodded. "Yeah, probably. Anyway, we started on the collider three weeks after they hired me. After that, it was pretty easy to ship it here and set it up. Thankfully, Dr. Greene here was pretty excited to join up, even if he had to do it on the sly. The man's a genius. He got the design worked up faster than you could believe. We had to do some joint-ventures with Billiton to get the tunneling done, but we made great progress in a short time."

"How much tunneling?" Coogan asked, a look of intense curiosity on his face.

Harry's smile finally broke out. "More than three thousand kilometers." He pulled out a holopad and a map of Egypt sprang into being. A giant circle was superimposed over nearly a third of the entire country, stretching from the Mediterranean coast to the Cairo suburbs to the southern deserts—and back to Siwa. "When you have drills that can vaporize their way along at 45 kilometers an hour, it doesn't take very long. The hard part was ensuring they were making a perfect circle. It's the single most powerful accelerator in history. If this can't open the door, nothing can."

Greene nodded. "But the problem is, we're still having focusing issues. Nowhere near as much as we had on Mars, but if there ambient tachyons out there, we want to get them into our chamber. And that means focusing all the latent Cherenkov radiation we can onto this site. And that's where we need your help."

"You know I don't have a handle on the science as much as I'd like, but I'm pretty sure BlueNet's not going to help," Diaz said. "It's designed to detect radiation, not focus it. I—" She stopped and looked hard at Greene. "You son of a bitch."

The physicist merely shrugged. "I knew that if the DAEDALUS team ever did what we're trying to do here, they'd need a means to focus tachyons just like we do now. And since I had sign-off on the tech, I added a couple of things to the spec. I was hoping to do it with *you*, Maria. Really. But it wasn't happening."

Diaz' eyes bored into Greene like a laser drill. "Yeah, damn shame. But far as I'm concerned, you can take this whole project and shove it up your ass. You aren't getting my satellites. Period."

Ayim quickly grew animated. "You don't understand. We began a new experiment before you arrived, and I'm afraid that without the additional stabilizing influence from BlueNet, we could see a runaway cascade effect. I don't think we have the capacity to contain and redirect that much energy. The matter-antimatter collision could destroy the entire city above!"

Harry nodded. "We need you, Maria. We can make this work. We just need your help."

Diaz gave him a wolfish smile. "Nice try. Just pull the plug on the damn thing and call it a day. Sure, you'll probably wreck your gear, but too bad. Otherwise, you're going to endanger the lives of everyone here. Even you aren't willing to do that, are you, Harry?"

"Of course not," Harry snapped. "Can you imagine the lawsuits? But if it's lives you're worried about, Maria...."

The guards around the DAEDALUS team suddenly pointed their weapons at Diaz, Coogan and Huntington.

"Always knew you were a bastard," Diaz said quietly.

Harry ignored her. "Dr. Greene, let's get to work. Set up a link to the BlueNet control network and have General Diaz here provide you with all the necessary passwords. If she doesn't, then we'll flip a coin and see which one of her officers gets hurt first."

Harry stalked off, leaving Greene and Ayim looking at each other uncomfortably. Diaz saw Greene's hand shaking as he held a datapad full of numbers.

"You don't have to do this, Evan," she said as gently as she could muster. "Shut it down. You open the door, you have no idea what'll come through."

Greene looked at the floor, then at his pad, and finally up at Diaz. "I'm sorry." He gave a sigh. "We'll need your command codes in about fifteen minutes."

As Greene walked off with his colleague, Diaz saw him start to smile as they discussed their data. *Real science.* Looked like it wasn't that tough a decision for him after all.

October 16, 1798

The first thing Dr. Andrew Finch saw was his apprentice, Jabir, hovering over him and wiping his brow. The boy looked worried and altogether haggard. Any further contemplation was cut off by a searing pain in his head.

"Christ!" Finch moaned, wincing. "What happened?"

At this, Jabir actually smiled. "You are awake!" he said in Arabic. "Allah be praised."

"Why wouldn't I be?" Finch groused, but then events came flooding back into his memory. The altar, the explosion of traps. The stone that fell upon him....

Finch looked down at his forearms, which were swaddled in bandages. As the pain in his head cleared, he could feel the throbbing ache in his arms. "How bad?" he asked.

Jabir sat up and wiped his hands with the cloth. "Both your arms were broken, and you suffered a blow to the head," he reported. "If not for your arms, your head would have been crushed. For an old man, you are quick when you need to be."

The patient smiled despite himself. "I assume the French brought me out of there?"

"Your friend Dolomieu and one of the soldiers carried you out," Jabir confirmed. "Berthollet, they say, treated you there in the temple, though whatever working he may have done was very little to my eye."

"I'm surprised he spared any time at all," Finch said, gingerly sitting up despite the pain. His arms protested, but not overly so. "You healed the bones?"

At this, the boy's face lit with pride and accomplishment. "We did not have some of the more esoteric ingredients you prefer, *murshid*, but I made do with what you had in your portable laboratory. They will be sore a few days, I think. Your head was another matter, of course."

Finch nodded, and immediately regretted the reflexive movement as another wave of pain seared through his skull. For all the curative wonders of the Great Work, injuries to the head remained something of a mystery to all but the highest masters of the *vitalis* school. Finch had postulated that the mind was such an important and nuanced organ that it simply required more time—or greater understanding—for the mystic sciences to be truly effective.

"What have I missed?" he asked.

Jabir shrugged. "The French are very busy, *murshid*. They brought something up from the temple, but whatever it is, it remains with Berthollet. From what I have seen, it remains in the old doctor's tent, with his *savants* visiting him there, then running off with papers and notes to do more work."

Finch shook his head sadly; his chess match with Berthollet was not going well at all. "What of the temple?"

"None are allowed down the passage to see it, not even Sheikh Karim, and he has tried to go below many times, only to be turned away," Jabir said. "The French left your things down there, and I had to beg your friend Dolomieu to retrieve your portable laboratory so I could treat you. He is a good man, your friend. He is worried, and I know not why."

Finch reached for a glass of water on the small table next to him, taking a sip and gauging his surroundings. He was in the tent he shared with Jabir, and his apprentice had managed to create a more comfortable bed for him by seemingly acquiring every spare pillow and blanket the French brought across the desert. He then picked up a small mirror, seeing a very pale, tired man with a bandaged head in the reflection.

"You've done very well," he said finally. "I thank you, Jabir. You are a fine alchemist."

Jabir's grin threatened to overrun his entire countenance. "I have a fine teacher, thanks be to Allah," he said. "And...oh, there is one thing I forgot.

The French have brought a very large wooden box into Berthollet's tent."

The French alchemist's tent was, naturally, palatial compared to all others in their company. It had an actual bed, as well as a table that could comfortably fit four for supper. But, still…. "How big?" Finch asked.

"Nearly as tall as I am, and just as wide. They carried it from one of the supply wagons."

No wonder we traveled the desert so slowly! Finch thought. "They've found something, I'll wager. Something quite impressive, no doubt."

"Do you think they will show you what they have found?" Jabir asked.

Finch barked out a laugh, and winced immediately thereafter from the pain. "No! No, I think that unless they feel there is more under the ground, they have little use for me now. Berthollet will hoard his knowledge, as most alchemists so foolishly do. And it will do him no good, or get him into trouble of the absolute worst sort."

Jabir nodded gravely. "I fear these ancient things, they may be an affront to Islam."

Finch reached over and patted the boy's shoulder. "I know. I fear they may be an affront to everything. Go now and find Dolomieu. Tell him I am awake and wish to thank him. Let's see what he'll tell us."

Jabir immediately bowed—as well as one could in a cramped tent—and dashed off, leaving Finch to lean back in his makeshift bed and further gauge the extent of his wounds. The bones in his arms, it seemed, knitted quiet well; Jabir always had a knack for curatives. His head would likely be tender for a few more days, but overall, he considered himself quite fortunate.

Except, of course, for the fact that the French likely made an impressive find—or rather, he made an impressive find on their behalf, and then had the damnable luck of injury, which conveniently got him out of their way.

A few minutes later, Dolomieu entered the tent and beamed at Finch. "You, sir, are entirely fortunate, you know!" He held up a bottle. "Let's celebrate your return to us!"

Finch smiled. "I was just contemplating my luck before you arrived, Deo. Come, sit and pour some of that wine. I'm to understand you've been quite busy of late."

Dolomieu sat near Finch and poured two glasses. "Not I, my friend. I have been allowed to make some further explorations of the temple below, but the real work has been above ground, with your find."

With a rueful chuckle, Finch took a glass and saluted. "Make no mistake. It's Berthollet's find. I may have had something to say about it had I not been injured, but since I was…."

The Frenchman nodded and dropped his head slightly. "Yes, he has been very cautious with it. Even I don't know what it is. He had me check the room once more for any un-sprung traps while he examined it. All I know is that it's somewhat bulky, and wrapped in leather straps. He took it directly to his tent, and that's the last I saw of it. Only a few of us have been granted access to him since, and he brought the stone into his tent as well."

"The stone?" Finch asked innocently, though he knew there was something to it. Dolomieu had always been a talkative sort, and that was precisely the trait upon which Finch relied in that moment.

Dolomieu's face turned red. "Pay no mind. Something he brought from Cairo with us," he said quickly.

"Deo, come now."

With a sigh and a swig of wine, Dolomieu relented. "In the early days of our expedition, before the Battle of the Pyramids, some of our scouts near the town of Rosetta came across an artifact—a stone with ancient writings upon it. There were hieroglyphs, yes. But also in ancient Greek, and another language we do not know. Syriac, perhaps."

"On the same stone?" Finch marveled.

"Indeed. We believe it is from Ptolemaic times, when the Greeks ruled here. If it was some sort of message or decree to the populace, written in each language…"

"…then it is the key to unlocking the hieroglyphs of ancient Egypt!" Finch exclaimed, ignoring the throbbing in his head. "That is an extraordinary find, Deo!"

Dolomieu smiled. "It is indeed, my friend, and Berthollet has had our language experts at work upon it since. Indeed, the supply wagon held not only the stone, but the two men assigned to decipher it. They have been at it for weeks."

Finch took a slow slip of his wine as his mind raced. There were said to be many alchemical—no one dared say *magical*—artifacts from the days of the Pharaohs still left undiscovered in Egypt. But this find was no mere artifact. It was something written.

A book.

"I can think of at least two finds that might require such extraordinary labors and extensive precautions," Finch ventured. "You know of what I speak, Deo."

The other man's eyes widened. "Surely not," he said. "Those are legends, Andrew. There are plenty of finds to be had in Egypt without resorting to…to…fairy tales!"

"Perhaps not," Finch allowed, seeing that his friend had passed his little test. Deo had no clue what the French dug up—but then, Finch was likewise well in the dark. "But then, Alexander managed to find this place following the flight of a hawk, or so they say."

Dolomieu smiled at his friend. "I'm sure it is an excellent find, whatever it is. If it is indeed the Emerald Tablet, I'll be sure to let you know!"

"Or *The Book of the Dead*," Finch added. "Either or, of course."

"Either or," Dolomieu agreed, quaffing the remainder of his wine. "And now, my friend, I must go attend to the excavations once more. I expect you to stop lazing about as soon as you can!"

Finch sent him off with the usual pleasantries, and let his mind wander. The tablet and the book were indeed the stuff of legends—but then, so were the ancient Martians. As he learned on Mars, the gods of old were in fact representations of Martian culture—or even individual Martians themselves—from before their destruction by the Xan. At what point, he wondered, does myth become history? Or history drift into legend?

Whatever Berthollet found, there would be some alchemical use for it, Finch had no doubt. He was quite sure that the history of Alexander shown to him on the journey was but one piece of the puzzle, and Berthollet likely had more in his possession from the Vatican archives. They would not have risked all across the burning sands to simply find collectibles or curiosities.

Finch was writing in his notebook when Jabir entered the tent once more. "What did you learn, *murshid*?"

"Only how much more I need to know, which is quite a lot," Finch said as he scribbled. "They've found something here, and God only knows what." He ripped the page from his book, then folded it carefully. "Hand me the sealant."

Jabir handed over a small vial, and Finch dabbed the liquid all around the edges of the paper whilst chanting in Latin. He then took up the pen of his little envelope and wrote something in Arabic upon it.

"Deliver this only if I am in any sort of peril, and only at the last possible moment," he said quietly. "Until then, make sure it does not leave your person."

Jabir eyed the paper suspiciously. "What is it?"

"Insurance."

CHAPTER 16

June 21, 2134

The *Tienlong* was an ungainly ship, at least when compared to the graceful lines and elegant ring on *Armstrong*. The Chinese survey vessel was blocky, ungainly, and reminded Shaila of old Communist-style architecture—blunt, unadorned, and altogether too serious.

And there was no one aboard answering the comm.

They tried everything, from old-style radio transmissions to using the ship's running lights to transmit Morse code. The *Armstrong*'s sensors lashed the *Tienlong* every few minutes, but couldn't penetrate the radiation shielding built into the hull of the ship. *Tienlong* represented a very different philosophy of space-faring. It wasn't much longer than *Armstrong*, but it was much bigger inside. They brought all their food and fuel along with them. The artificial gravity was generated by a spinning crossbar of hull in the middle of the ship, providing two distinct areas of gravity on either end of the section. The rad shielding was achieved through ultra-dense polymers sandwiched into the hull, rather than electromagnetic shielding systems. At least the Chinese still believed in preventing asteroid collision; the *Tienlong* boasted a pair of microwave emitters to reduce incoming rocks to dust.

Shaila studied the ship carefully from the cockpit of Lander Two, waiting for clearance to depart. Stephane and Hall were busy loading up their gear in the back; technically, they were going to the surface of Titan to conduct a search-and-rescue mission, likely followed closely by an investigation into Chinese activities there. But it made zero sense not to include the *Armstrong*'s corporate sponsor and planetary scientist. Hall was surprised to find that the Chinese had sent only one lander, and that it had landed well away from the most promising hydrocarbon deposits on the entire moon. That seemed to pique Stephane's interest, as he quickly became interested in what *was* there. The Chinese had landed in a mountainous region near the northern pole, away from the large and impressive lakes that dotted the area. It was utterly unremarkable at first glance—which meant it warranted a second glance.

As Shaila went through her preflight checklist, her thoughts kept coming back to Stephane. He'd spent the better part of their transit orbit either in the lab or in his little-used quarters. The orbit duty roster meant that they didn't have down-time together—not uncommon during long spaceflights, when the captain regularly shuffled shifts and duties to pair up different people—but for the past several months, Stephane's quarters were simply a place to store clothes; he was a social creature, and when he wasn't in the common areas, he was in Shaila's quarters, even while she was on duty.

Her thoughts were interrupted by the comm. "Lander Two, you ready to go?" Archie asked, seemingly annoyed.

"Lander Two prepared for launch," she replied, scurrying to flip the final few switches, lost as she was in her reverie. "Stephane, Liz, let's get on board."

Her two colleagues floated down from the hatch above. Stephane took the seat behind Shaila's, leaving Hall to ride shotgun. Shaila tried not to let it get to her.

"Lander Two and *Armstrong*, this is One," Nilssen called from the other Lander. "We're ready over here. I want everyone's runtime vids and audio linked to the recorders. Whatever happened, we're going to want to have proof."

Shaila acknowledged the order briefly. While she ferried Hall and Stephane to the surface, Nilssen and Conti would head over to *Tienlong* to render aid as needed—and again, investigate just what the hell was happening. Archie would stay aboard *Armstrong* to babysit both operations while continuing to run diagnostics on his precious engines to see just how much damage, if any, their orbital burn had done.

Lander One would take about ten minutes to head over to the *Tienlong*, and probably another ten to ensure it was safe to dock and open the hatch. After that, the commander and medical officer would see what surprises the ship had in store for them. Shaila, meanwhile, would take nearly ninety minutes to reach the surface of Titan. There, they would land about a kilometer from the Chinese lander, which everyone hoped would be a safe distance from…well, they didn't know. Safe distances simply seemed prudent.

"Clear for launch," Archie said. "Go get 'em."

"Roger that, *Armstrong*," Nilssen replied. "Landers One and Two, launch."

Shaila gave the lander's seals one final look, then disengaged the docking clamps. A moment later, both ships were free of *Armstrong's* shielding and peeled off in different directions. Shaila did a full burn for Titan's northern pole, while Nilssen crept toward *Tienlong* cautiously, with near-constant sensor sweeps all over the Chinese vessel.

"No movement in any of the windows," Nilssen reported. Shaila kept his channel open so they could hear and see them—a small holo feed was tucked into the corner of their HUDs. She could see Hall paying close attention, while Stephane seemed to be content looking out the window at the clouds of Titan below, though when she turned back, Shaila could see streams of data flowing across his HUD. *Work is good*, Shaila thought. *Get him in gear again.*

"You'd think they'd notice us by now if they were in there," Conti said. She had a point; Shaila could see that Lander One was close enough to the Chinese ship that they could make out faces in the windows. At that distance, Shaila knew *Armstrong's* proximity sensors would be going off madly, and since *Tienlong* still had lights on, it was pretty likely the sensors still had power. So it was more likely that there was nobody aboard to see them—or they were simply in no condition to reply.

"All right," Nilssen said over the comm. "Docking ring looks solid. Thank God for international standards. We're going to try to link up."

Shaila kept one eye on the vidfeed as she piloted Lander Two over the russet-orange clouds of Titan. The cloud cover was impenetrable, which made things a bit easier—she'd be wholly distracted tearing her attention from one vista to another. As it was, Shaila was quite content to let the computer do most of the flying; she watched the vidfeed intently.

"Docking engaged. We have good seal," Nilssen intoned. "We're linked up. Conti and I are going seal up until we're damn sure there's nothing wrong with the environment aboard the Chinese ship. Transmitting standard docking and rescue protocols now. Jain, status?"

Shaila started at the mention of her name, engrossed as she was in the holodrama projected onto her helmet visor. "Jain here. All systems nominal. ETA forty-three minutes to designated landing site. Over."

"Roger, Jain," Nilssen said. "No response to transmissions. I even had Conti knock on the hatch a few times with a wrench. Assuming this vessel remains in distress, as per relevant sections of the U.N. Space Charter, and engaging manual override for entry. Everyone read that?"

"Roger that, Lander One," Shaila responded.

"Roger, Lander One," Archie added, surprisingly formal. "Confirm your declaration. Go for manual override." Of course, Shaila thought, the whole thing was being beamed direct to Houston, and would be sent to the Chinese as well. Even Archie couldn't be that flippant when teams of international lawyers would likely review every millisecond.

Shaila could see Nilssen's suit camera on her visor now as he opened the lander's hatch, then proceeded to enter the manual protocols to open the *Tienlong*'s hatch as well. The hatch responded after a moment, opening up into a well-lit space. Nilssen floated upward into a very industrial-looking corridor, linked with storage cabinets and handholds. Unlike JSCS ships, the Chinese were never much for aesthetics.

"All right," Nilssen said, sounding pixelated. The vidfeed likewise began to stutter and stall. "Going to…nothing…above…"

Then the feed went out entirely.

"*Armstrong*, we lost them," Shaila said. "You still got 'em?"

"It's the damned rad shielding on the Chinese boat," Archie said, sounding flustered. "Trying to compensate now. I'll get back to you."

The comm line went dead, and Shaila turned to Hall, who merely shrugged. Behind them, Stephane continued to analyze streaming lines of data, punctuated by a variety of images that flashed across his HUD rapidly.

Their course began to take them over the cloud tops, and Shaila took over the stick from the computer; she knew the computer would compensate if needed, but she liked the sense of control. If they were going to be the first JSC astronauts on Titan, she wanted the landing done her way, warts and all.

"Lander Two, this is *Armstrong*, come in."

"Lander Two here, Archie. What's up?"

"Vidfeed still down, but Nilssen wanted me to let you know that they're aboard and fine. He also asked if you're armed."

Shaila sat up a bit. "Say again, *Armstrong?*"

"Skipper wants to know if you're armed, Jain," Archie said, sounding both worried and put out. "He's got two dead astronauts and one critically injured over there, and looks like three are just missing. Gotta assume the assailants are gonna be down on Titan."

Shaila looked over at Hall, who was doing a middling job of not looking scared, and back at Stephane, who for once seemed to actually be paying attention. "We have zappers," Shaila replied. "That's it."

"Then keep your distance," Archie said. "Skipper said one was killed with what looked like a close-range laser blast."

"And the other one? The survivor?" Shaila asked.

There was a pause. "Some kind of blade. They were murdered," Archie said.

October 17, 1798

Weatherby was quite unsure as to which was the stranger sight: watching the two Xan Ovoids on either side of *Fortitude* as they escorted her along the Void-paths between Mimas and Titan, or the ten-foot-tall robed figure walking the maindeck of his ship, poking his head into every hatch, often walking right between his crewmen, pausing to look each in the face even though they could only stare into the Xan's alchemically-created blackness under his cowl.

"Curious fellow, isn't he, sir?" Barnes said diplomatically, though his tone was anything but.

"Representative Vellusk is our honored guest, Mr. Barnes," Weatherby said simply. "And we have the singular honor of having a Xan aboard ship, possibly for the first time in human history. So unless he starts actively injuring the crew or endangering the ship, we shall allow him space for his...eccentricities."

"Of course, sir," Barnes said. "Perhaps someone should offer him a tour below decks as well? He could have a bit of space, as you say, sir, while also having someone along to explain things and, perhaps, keep him out of the men's way."

Weatherby turned and smiled at his lieutenant. "A splendid idea, Mr. Barnes! I'll take this watch. Go and offer your services to Mr. Vellusk."

Barnes' mouth opened and closed a moment before he finally managed to stammer out a reply. "Of course, sir. Thank you, sir."

Weatherby watched—with more than a touch of amusement—as Barnes tentatively made his way to the maindeck, where Vellusk was busy peering down the bore of a 9-pound brass cannon. Bowing repeatedly, with his hand over his heart, Barnes spoke to the Xan at length, likely conscious of their overweening politesse, before the Saturnine creature began nodding and bowing in return. A moment later, they had disappeared belowdecks.

"That wasn't nice, Tom," Anne said from behind him, where she had been sitting and looking starboard toward Saturn. He turned to see her actually smile slightly—which had been his objective, for she had continued to be utterly miserable, and rightly so, since her son's abduction.

"It will do Mr. Barnes good to engage in some minor diplomacy," Weatherby said matter-of-factly. "One day, he may command an expedition to the Xan in his own right."

"Or an armada," Anne said, her smile fading. "I shudder to think what may happen should the partisans win out. These creatures destroyed an entire planet whilst we were barely civilized."

"They have lost their taste for war," Weatherby said, with more conviction than he felt. "They are out of practice."

"Tell that to Sellev," Anne said harshly. "There is reason we have an escort, Captain."

Weatherby bowed slightly, unwilling to press the matter. "Of course, my lady."

Any more words were cut off by a shout from the tops. "Ships sighted! Three points to larboard!"

Weatherby rushed over to the left side of the quarterdeck and pulled out his glass; sure enough, there were four white dots in the distance that moved across the starfield quickly. He made a note to commend the watchful topsman for his attentiveness—he doubted he would have noted such faint movement until they were much closer.

"Beat to quarters!" he shouted. "Topsmen aloft! Gunners prepare but do not run out!" He turned to find one of the midshipmen below, moving up toward the quarterdeck. "Mr. Fyfe, find Mr. Barnes and tell him to secure our Xan guest in the cockpit before taking his post."

"I'll go with him," Anne said, quickly moving down the stairs. "That's where I'm heading anyway."

This time, Weatherby didn't even question her. Progress, of a sort, he thought.

"How many?" Ambassador Morrow asked as he climbed up to the quarterdeck.

"My Lord Ambassador, might I suggest –"

"How many, Captain Weatherby?" Morrow interrupted.

For a moment, Weatherby wondered how many battles he would lose upon his own quarterdeck before he'd return to Earth. "Four. Ovoids, from the look of them."

Morrow nodded. "No doubt our escorts are aware as well."

"No doubt," Weatherby said. "You realize, my lord, if my ship is fired upon, I will return fire."

"And so you should," Morrow said with a gentle smile. "If these partisans are intent upon revisiting the Xan's violent ways, we should present them with what they may face. But if I may, Captain, I suggest restraining yourself should they fire upon our escorts."

"Are they not our allies?" Weatherby asked.

"They are, yes, but it would create a fair amount of difficulties in diplomacy if you were to aid them," Morrow said.

Weatherby smiled at this. "Well, then, My Lord Ambassador. I have no doubt you will be up to the task." He then turned to another of the mids. "I want the guns loaded, but we shall not run out until I give the word. When I do, I want the men to run out, aim, and fire as quickly as possible. Go."

The young boy ran off, leaving Morrow staring at Weatherby with a look of amused consternation. "You enjoyed that, Tom."

"Why, my lord, I've no idea what you mean," Weatherby protested, his growing grin betraying his feelings.

Two minutes later, all divisions reported ready. Meanwhile, *Fortitude*'s escorts began drifting ahead slightly, widening out from the ship as well, while the four incoming Ovoids began a series of odd maneuvers, swirling about and among each other until it was hard to track a single one as compared to its fellows. Which, Weatherby considered, was likely the point.

"What can we expect?" Weatherby asked Morrow.

The ambassador was busy looking through a borrowed glass, and it struck Weatherby that the old admiral still cut quite the figure on the quarterdeck of a ship. "They're fast. You'll want to fire a scattered broadside well before they're in range, with the hopes of catching one of them—which means you'll likely want to be sure your escorts are out of range."

"And how shall we tell them apart?" Weatherby asked.

Morrow grinned slightly. "I anticipated this. Should you engage, you will begin to see splashes of yellow and black upon the hulls of our allies—an alchemical trick that their fellow Xan will be unable to see, let alone duplicate."

"Neatly done, sir," Weatherby allowed. "What of weapons?"

"That I cannot say, because I did not know the Xan had weapons of the sort that could kill a creature in the manner in which Sallev was slain. Normally, they simply use various lights and gasses upon an Earth ship that ventures too close, rendering the crew unconscious. They then put the ship to rights, usually by sending it on a direct course for Earth."

"Seems harmless enough," Weatherby said. "Unless they've come up with something new."

"The attack on Sallev required premeditation. The partisans have been planning this for some time. It stands to reason they may have equipped their ships with something a bit more forceful," Morrow said.

Suddenly, the escorts upon either side of *Fortitude* sped ahead, likely to engage their fellows. Weatherby tensed at this, and quickly found himself upon the rail, looking ahead with his glass like an eager mid—the eager mids being right behind him, doing the same thing.

Then there was a flash of light, and one of their escorts exploded into a million fiery shards.

"That's new," Weatherby muttered before turning to the watch officer and shouting, "Full royals and stud'sels!"

The men upon the tops quickly moved to unfurl *Fortitude's* chase sails. Moments later, *Fortitude* began to speed up…considerably. More, in fact, than she ought to in the Void. They soon began to close upon the Xan Ovoids.

"Tom?" Morrow asked.

"Our sailwood stores," he replied. "Hawkins found an old case study in which sailwood might be consumed quickly in order to give a ship a profound increase in speed for a short time. When it became apparent we might engage actual Xan craft, I ordered him to prepare as much as he could and apply it to the royals and stud'sels."

They closed faster still, while three Ovoids moved to engage. Weatherby considered their whirling attack pattern for a moment. Then inspiration struck. "Full forward on the larboard plane, full back upon the starboard plane!"

And with that, *Fortitude* began spinning wildly upon her axis—so much so that it became difficult to focus on anything except the deck itself. Weatherby quickly told the watch officer to maintain course as best he could, and shouted for all the midshipmen to accompany him before rushing down to the maindeck and, below to the upper gun deck, where a surprised Barnes greeted him. He quickly explained his plans, then moved to the lower gun deck and explained it again, before rushing back to the quarterdeck, panting for want of air. The mids remained below.

The Ovoids would be in range in less than a minute…and out of range seconds after that.

Weatherby felt Morrow's eyes upon him, but there was little time to explain—and besides, for the first time in his career, he wasn't actually obliged to explain anything to Morrow whilst the two shared a quarterdeck.

Closer…closer….

"FIRE!" Weatherby shouted.

Upon the two gun decks, four midshipmen began to run, from the very fore of the ship aft, their hands extended. As they ran, they tapped each gunner on the head.

And a fusillade of fire sprang forth from *Fortitude*'s hull. Between the spinning motion and the second-by-second firing, the ship was suddenly surrounded by a barrage of alchemical cannon fire.

The Ovoids had nowhere to go. Green-glowing shot ripped into two of them, sending them spinning off into the void. A third was nicked upon the widest part of its hull and began spewing smoke from the affected area.

And as quickly as it began, *Fortitude* sped past, out of range. The crew staggered about as the stars of the Void whirled around them, with Saturn spinning past every few seconds. A few of the men, and at least one midshipman, rushed to the railings to relieve themselves of their last meal. Weatherby turned aft to track the Xan vessels, only to see Morrow shaking his head and chuckling to himself. "By God, that was something," the old man muttered to himself, and Weatherby could not help but allow a small smile to creep out. But there was work yet to be done.

"Reload and prepare to fire again! Same pattern!" Weatherby shouted from the quarterdeck. "Bring planes amidships and stop this damned spinning! And give me a report on our remaining ally!"

The ally, as it turned out, had managed to render the fourth partisan ship inert somehow, and rejoined *Fortitude* upon the starboard side, resuming its escort duty. Lookouts reported no attempts by the remaining partisan to give chase, either. Nonetheless, Weatherby ordered the men to remain at quarters for a full hour afterward, and even after that, he kept the guns loaded—dangerous, perhaps, but less dangerous, he felt, than being caught unawares by more Xan ships.

Or *Franklin*. The French were still out there, somewhere. And Weatherby was determined to find them.

June 21, 2134

Diaz couldn't help but notice that Evan Greene was happier than a pig in shit. It made her want to punch him in the face.

Diaz, Coogan and Huntington were sitting at vacant workstations toward the back of the temple-cum-laboratory, guarded casually by two soldiers. Hell, they probably were mercs, since Total-Suez would probably would have declined bringing its own security forces into such an illegal experiment, and Diaz doubted Harry would bring in the Egyptian Army to the site. Either way, while the guards didn't have guns *on* the two officers, the weapons were ready enough to be a sound reminder of the lack of escape routes.

On the bright side, someone brought her team some decent food; apparently, they had even set up a cafeteria. How the *hell* this whole operation was set up beneath an Egyptian national treasure…it was beyond Diaz' comprehension. Someone, somewhere would answer for all this.

Starting with Harry, followed closely by Greene. There was no doubt in her mind that he was indeed playing ball. He and his colleague, Dr. Ayim, were laughing and joking as they worked, and although Diaz was no scientist, she had been around enough data on this type of experiment to know they were getting close to a breakthrough.

Harry walked up and sat on the edge of Diaz' desk. "It's time, Maria. We're going to need those codes."

"Not happening," she said simply.

Harry looked over at the guards, who approached the three officers, weapons pointed. "Don't make me do this, Maria. We're trying to do something extraordinary here. Something you and your team should've been doing in the first place."

"You didn't see any of the shit that went down on Mars, Harry. I did," Diaz said, though technically she was out of commission for the worst of it, thanks to an errant musket ball. "I'm not letting you give them a chance at round two, right here on Earth."

"What about Saturn?" he asked cryptically.

"What about it?"

To her surprise, Harry's face became grave. "Something's happened aboard *Tienlong* in orbit over Titan. Two dead, one critical, three missing and apparently on the surface. *Armstrong* just arrived and sent landers to investigate."

"Your crew died? How?" Diaz demanded.

Harry looked at his feet. "They were attacked. The skipper's the one who's alive but critical. He and the science officer were cut open with some kind of blade. The engineer was hit with a short-range laser, though we have no idea how that happened. They weren't carrying laser weapons aboard ship."

Diaz considered this. "That makes no fucking sense."

"I'm formally requesting that the Chinese government turn over the command codes of the *Tienlong* to your people. I want to figure out what's going on up there as much as you do. And I know from experience Shaila Jain's pretty damn determined when she wants to be."

"So you help us out 'round Saturn on one hand, and on the other hand, you hold us captive here with guns to our heads," Hutchinson said. "'Big damn hero, sir.'"

Harry laughed. "Show's been canceled for more than a century, and every goddamned body in JSC knows it by heart. And yeah, that's what I'm doing. Because I need this experiment to run successfully, and I need to find out what happened to my people on *Tienlong*."

A tech interrupted Harry. "Sir, it's time."

Harry nodded and turned back to Maria. "The experiment has already reached critical. If you don't give us the codes, we won't get the BlueNet satellites online in time to stabilize the tachyon field. And this whole thing blows up. Literally."

Diaz' eyes narrowed. "You're bluffing."

Harry looked up at one of the guards, who immediately put a gun to Huntington's head. The Marine officer stiffened in her chair a moment, then relaxed and closed her eyes. "I'm ready," she said simply.

"Brave," Harry remarked, with a twinge of sympathy. "But it won't matter in about ten minutes. We need BlueNet or all of Siwa goes up in smoke. The codes, Maria." He offered her his datapad.

Maria Diaz was a soldier, first and foremost. She knew Huntington would sacrifice herself. Coogan, too. Diaz would do the same if it came to that.

But all those goddamn people on the surface didn't have a choice in the matter. She did.

Diaz snatched the pad from Harry's hand and entered the codes. "I swear to you, Harry, I am going to fucking ruin you for this." She threw the pad back at him, which he nearly fumbled before getting two hands on it.

"You made the right call," he said. "Sorry it had to come to this. But we didn't know this place would have the kind of random ambient energy it does. We need to stabilize it." He punched a few buttons on the pad and, a moment later, one of the larger holoviewers at the front of the room showed the entire BlueNet satellite network. It was firmly under Total-Suez' command now.

"So there was some Cherenkov radiation already here, then," Coogan said evenly. Good trooper, Diaz thought, getting the bad guys to talk.

Harry nodded. "It flared up out of nowhere early into our survey, nine months ago," he replied. "We had a low-level hit prior to that, but it just suddenly burst out there like a beacon. We sent a team down, and they were able to get into the ruins—apparently, a Chinese tour group got lost down there right around the time of the flare-up. They must've triggered it."

"Triggered it? How?" Diaz demanded.

"Beats me. I'm the funding here," Harry said. "Talk to Greene. He helped pick the site."

With that, Harry turned and walked back toward the accelerator to begin consulting with Ayim…and Greene.

"It's happening again," Diaz said quietly.

"Ma'am?" Hutchinson asked.

"Too many coincidences. They're knocking on the door here while everybody goes batshit up there. There's more going on. I think this experiment's gonna work, and it's gonna go badly," Diaz said. She turned to Huntington and gave her a small smile. "You all right, Mags?"

"Yes, ma'am," she said, allowing her shoulders to slump slightly. "I would've understood either way."

"I know. I'm proud to have you here."

They sat silently a moment until Coogan cleared his throat, a bit too dramatically. "Do you have orders, ma'am?"

Diaz turned to him. "Fuck if I know. I'm hoping that when they get BlueNet online and get it stabilized, we'll be able to make a move somehow. Just be ready."

They looked up to see a soft white glow start to emanate from behind the glass. Greene and Ayim were flipping through holodata quickly, sending status reports and readouts to one another as a hum started to permeate the room, sending small motes of dust down from the ancient ceiling.

A number of alerts flashed across various holoscreens throughout the room, including the one at Diaz' station. BlueNet's satellites were now focusing ambient Cherenkov radiation directly overhead—potentially bringing additional tachyons to bear on the collider, which had just fired off a new round of particles. Three billion to start—with billions more launched every second.

The glow began to intensify…and began to turn a light shade of blue.

Diaz saw Greene pump his fist, and her heart sank.

CHAPTER 17

October 18, 1797

Finch walked through the surface ruins of the Siwa oasis in the cool evening breeze, hoping he might talk to some of the *savants*, or at least Dolomieu once more. A few soldiers continued the excavation work in various places, but their hearts did not seem in it. They exchanged looks, the occasional Gallic shrug, and kept digging. Such was their lot, it seemed.

Yet there were indeed few of them, and as Finch continued his meanderings—his first time out of the tent since the incident in the temple below—he realized something had changed. Yes, there were still guards at Berthollet's tent, and at the temple tunnel as well. A few others were enjoying a meal around their campfires. But the *savants*...

Where were the *savants*?

Finch spied a soldier walking alone between tents, and made for him. This time, he remembered his favorite elixir, placing a dab of it on his tongue quickly before approaching the man.

"Citizen!" he called out. "Could you help me a moment?"

The soldier stopped and turned, a smile upon his face. "Dr. Finch! You are well? We heard you were injured."

Finch gave his best smile. "I am, thanks to your fellow citizens who carried me out of that tunnel. But pray tell, where is everyone? I had hoped to dine with my fellow scholars this evening, but there seem to be none about."

"You are most welcome to dine with us, Doctor!" the soldier said a little too jovially, leaving Finch wondering if he had included too many Venusian extracts in the charm elixir he was using. "But the *savants*, they have gathered below, in the temple, at the request of Citizen Berthollet, along with many of the soldiers. I am surprised that you, of all people, have not joined them."

"Ah, well, yes. I had thought we were meeting somewhere up here first, of course," Finch said, hoping he sounded convincing. The *mentis* arts would only take one so far, after all. "I shall find them below then. I thank you, Citizen. I promise, we shall dine another night!"

The soldier bowed slightly and went upon his way once more, while Finch turned and went back to his tent. Jabir was not there, instead likely in pursuit of his own meal, so Finch hastily scribbled a note in Arabic for him, gathered his portable laboratory and a couple of needful items, and left once more, making for the entrance to the temple.

It was no surprise at all to see it guarded by four soldiers, and some of the more menacing ones at that. Berthollet, it seemed, was taking no chances.

Finch reached into the satchel at his side, pulling out a working of his own design, housed inside a hollowed-out chicken egg. It was a trick Weatherby had suggested back in '84, when they were serving together and found themselves in need of clandestine tools.

Hiding behind a tent, Finch carefully took out his egg, peeked around the corner, and then lobbed it at the feet of the guards, before ducking back out of sight.

One of them let out a quiet, muffled "What?" before all became silent.

Finch approached carefully, waiting for the yellow mist to clear in the night's breeze. The four guards were unconscious upon the ground. One began to snore, much to Finch's chagrin. He quickly rolled the man onto his side, despite his still-aching arms, and was rewarded with silence once more. They would be asleep for four hours, which Finch hoped would be adequate.

He quickly but carefully made his way down into the tunnels, and was surprised to see torches at regular intervals along the walls. Berthollet's men had done yeoman's work in making the tunnel easier to traverse in a mere two days. Likewise, the first room Finch had encountered, the one with the spike traps, was not only open, but swept clean. Finch nonetheless hesitated at the door, thinking of the poor young man impaled by a spike who died before his eyes, but he soon stepped tentatively through the room. Whatever was there had been fully disarmed, it seemed.

Forging ahead, Finch began to hear the low hum of conversation ahead in the temple. He looked about, wondering if someone would come up from behind him most inconveniently, but there was nothing for it. He pulled out a second eggshell, hoping he would not need to use it—or if it was required, that he could use it quickly enough before an interloper raised the alarm.

Quietly stepping forward and keeping to the shadows whenever possible, Finch managed to arrive at the doorway to the temple undetected. He could see nearly all of the *savants* there, including Dolomieu, mingling with at least two-thirds of the garrison and all of the officers. None of the Bedouins, not even Sheikh Karim, were in attendance. The onlookers were talking in excited, hushed tones, occasionally glancing up toward the altar. Shifting his position, Finch crouched low and peeked around the corner to see what the fuss was about.

Immediately, he saw that Berthollet had missed his calling, for it was quite apparent that the Frenchman's heart was not in alchemy, but rather the boards and lights of the stage. The last time Finch saw him, he was the perfect picture of a French gentleman. Now, standing there before the altar, he was nothing less than what one might expect of an Egyptian priest.

It had never been Finch's wont to engage in the more theatrical aspects of the rites and rituals inherent in the mystic sciences. Questions that humanists had begun asking around the time of the Reformation had been clearly answered—ceremonial trappings and entreaties to God and His Angels (or, perhaps, to other beings) were unnecessary to perform the Great Work adequately. The prayers and props had purpose, of course, in that most of them served as mnemonic devices and guideposts for more complex workings, but it had been generally agreed upon by most scholars of alchemy that the praise of God, while laudable, was not strictly required.

Egyptian mythology of ages past, of course, made no mention of Allah, or Christ, or even Jehovah. From his studies and experiments, Finch knew these ancient rites included exacting religious requirements. Finch felt he could safely discern what was truly important—whether it was a particular mineral or an exercise designed to focus the Will—from the merely ostentatious. He had done so many times in the past, and naturally felt quite confident in his abilities, even when faced with a new and potentially dangerous working from the days of the ancient Egyptians.

It seemed Berthollet, however, would take no chances. He was as methodical in this as he was in most things. And so it was that the tall, portly Frenchman was now attired and purified as a Pharonic priest of old. In Finch's opinion...it was not the best of looks.

As would be ancient custom, Berthollet could not wear wool, nor leather, and had but a skirt of linen around his ample waist, draped down to just above his ankles. Around his shoulders was a cape made of leopard skin, obtained at excruciating cost after the French had scoured the nomad tribesmen around the ruins. The skin was mottled and of poor quality, and smelled rather badly besides. It compared poorly to the jewelry and accoutrements he wore, likely salvaged from elsewhere in the temple.

What Berthollet was *not* wearing was hair. His final preparation had been to shave.

Everywhere. Finch knew this was also a requirement of the ancient priesthood, but it was a singularly unflattering look. If not for his dread concern about Berthollet's aims, and the nature of his find, Finch might have found it laughable.

Observing the crowd once more, Finch saw that each person in the room was given a small copper disc with a hieroglyph carved upon it. Berthollet did not seem to wear one, but given his likely role as the rite's enactor, he might not require it, Finch thought. Of course, Finch himself wasn't wearing one either, and he knew not whether to be very worried or exceedingly grateful.

Finch's musings were interrupted by Berthollet. "Let us begin," he intoned.

The room fell silent, and the entire assemblage looked to the altar as one.

And that's when Finch spied the wrapped bundle upon the altar itself, surrounded by a variety of ritual paraphernalia. It was the very bundle he discovered under the altar.

With solemnity, Berthollet began taking the leathery bandages off, unspooling them from what appeared to be a rectangular item, all in black. The Frenchman neatly piled the wrappings off to one side, then took the item in both hands to raise it above his head. "Behold!" Berthollet cried out. "*The Book of the Dead!*"

"Oh, dear God," Finch whispered from his hiding place.

The Book of the Dead was one of two legendary items from Egyptian antiquity, the companion to the Emerald Tablet. The latter was considered the foundation of alchemy itself, compiling all ancient knowledge of the Great Work that would bring light and life to the cosmos.

The *Book*, on the other hand, was the Tablet's opposite. Where the Tablet was light, the *Book* was dark. Where the Tablet dealt with the arts of life and matter, the *Book* was said to detail the workings of the spirit world... and the dead.

And now Berthollet had it. Furthemore, the Frenchman did not seem to want to simply deliver his prize to his patron, Napoleon. Not without delving into its secrets first. The translators must have been working through the night to provide Berthollet the means for whatever he planned to do next.

Finch realized, with a sense of dread, he had no idea what Berthollet would do. He was not only losing the chess match, but was playing blind besides.

"We are in the West, among the Field of Reeds," Berthollet intoned, his arms wide, reading not from the *Book*, but from sheaves of papers beside it—the translation, most likely, courtesy of the Rosetta stone. "We implore the spirits of *Duat* to come forward. We offer the comforts of the living once more, and the means to shatter the bonds of exile, so that you may return. You may leave *Duat*, the land of the dead. You may come forth by night, from Upper Egypt to the very sea. You may call upon the darkness to give you strength, so that the daylight can no longer drive you back to the underworld!"

Finch cast his gaze across the room. The Frenchmen present looked bemused, for the most part, though one soldier clutched a crucifix in his hand at these words. Finch felt his pulse begin to quicken, and his stomach start to churn.

"I call you forth from the Field of Reeds," Berthollet said, picking up a bundle of reeds off the altar. "I shall light a beacon to guide you on your journey!" With that, the alchemist dipped the reed-tips into a bowl of oil, then used one of the candle flames to light them on fire. The reeds burst into flame, and a sickly green flame at that; a half-dozen treatments that could produce such an effect, but Finch could not make sense of any of them in terms of the ritual. Who was Berthollet calling forth?

Berthollet then took up a small straw model of a boat, complete with a small human figurine inside. "These are the ferries that took you to *Duat*, to forever dwell away from the world. See the ferrymen now…and take these boats as your own!" Berthollet used the spear head to pierce each of the figures aboard the boat, casting them into a brazier to the right of the altar.

The ritual's purpose hit Finch's mind like a thunderclap. Berthollet was not performing a ritual to contact the dead, or to raise a particular person.

He was setting the stage for an invasion.

But *from where? Duat,* the afterlife itself?

Lost as Finch was in his own thoughts, the hand that clamped down on his shoulder made him jump. He turned to find one of the French soldiers there, with a pistol pointed under Finch's chin. "Move," the man said gruffly.

Finch clutched at his egg-grenade, but the soldier was canny, and snatched it from him quite deftly. Defeated for the moment, Finch slowly proceeded into the chamber, catching Berthollet's eye in the process.

The Frenchman looked startled at first, but quickly broke into a wicked grin. "I should have known you'd find a way to join us, Dr. Finch." Berthollet waved for the guard to bring Finch closer. "Come, then. You may stay here, with me, and see this working unfold. Watch as I discover the power of the ancients!"

The soldier shoved Finch toward the altar, keeping the gun pointed at the back of his head. Casting about, he saw no avenue of escape.

With a flourish and a shout, Berthollet grasped the book in both hands. And between the altar and the crowd of onlookers, the air itself began to shimmer.

June 21, 2134

"I swear to God, I'm going to sue the Chinese from here to Earth and back," Hall said as Lander Two pierced the clouds over Titan. "Of course, if they didn't file the official claim before it hit the fan for them, so much the better."

Shaila couldn't help but look at the ExEn executive askance. She knew such talk was a charade, an unconscious mask for Hall's increasing discomfort over the fact that they were flying straight for people who murdered their fellow crewmen. But still. "That's one way to look at a search-and-rescue op," Shaila chided. "I assume you have the claim paperwork already done."

"I'm literally gonna send it from the surface of Titan itself," Hall confirmed, missing the sarcasm. "It'll be a running stream. Whatever I fly over and see, I'm claiming for ExEn."

"That's the spirit of exploration," Shaila said. "*Armstrong*, this is Lander Two. We've cleared atmospheric burn. Over."

"You're cleared for landing, Two," Archie replied. "Your vidfeed and data stream is fine. Skipper's comms are still minimal. He says good luck and be careful."

"Roger. Thanks, Archie," Shaila said. "Stephane, what are you getting on sensors?"

Shaila could've asked Hall for the reading, but she wanted to hear Stephane right now, in this moment. He'd been quiet the whole trip, immersed in data, eyes darting over his HUD. "The Chinese lander isn't giving off transponder signals," Stephane replied. "I'm scanning for titanium and coming up with a hit in the same general area we identified from orbit. It's actually pretty close to some interesting geography. Some very deep canyons carved by hydrocarbon flows."

Shaila smiled. That sounded a bit more like him. "Roger that. I have the coordinates."

Just then, the lander lurched as it entered the lower atmosphere. Shaila grabbed the stick and eased around the worst of the turbulence until the lander broke into the clear.

And Titan took their breath away.

They arrived in a very mountainous region, with rocky hillocks and peaks on either side of the lander, with a valley beneath. A large smooth lake of purplish hydrocarbons spread out beneath them, and they could see a river leading out of it and heading down through the valley, linking up with tributaries snaking down through the mountains.

Everything had something of an orange-honey cast to it due to Titan's atmosphere. Combined with the purple of the liquid hydrocarbons, the whole image had a kind of warmth, even though the outside temperatures would be intensely frigid—so cold that the liquid ethane, methane and propane soup below could actually freeze solid in some parts, and would be intensely viscous throughout—more like a tar pit than a lake.

"My God, it's stunning," Stephane said quietly.

"Sure is," Shaila replied, oddly gratified just to hear him talking. She quickly shunted the thought out of her head. Stephane would perform, as usual. She'd have more time to talk to him and figure things out later.

A small alarm went off in the cockpit—the lander's sensors had located the Chinese vehicle 50 kilometers ahead. Shaila cut the engines and opted to glide in as best she could. Given Titan's extremely low gravity—just 14 percent that of Earth—it took five minutes of lazy circling before she felt she had lost enough momentum to justify thrusters. She finally put the lander down a little more than a kilometer from its Chinese counterpart. They could get there in a couple minutes thanks to the low gravity, but it was far enough so that they wouldn't be surprised if some knife-wielding Chinese astronaut came at them.

Surprisingly, Shaila thought, *that wouldn't actually be the strangest thing I've encountered in space.*

Everyone gave their suits a final check before Stephane opened the lander's tiny airlock and headed out onto Titan, the two women following on his heels. Shaila briefly thought there should be some kind of historical note to be made—Hall was the first American on the moon, Shaila the first Briton and JSC astronaut, Stephane the first Frenchman—but under the circumstances, it seemed a bit much. "Jain to *Armstrong*, we've left the vehicle and are on the surface. Streaming our sensors and video. Over."

"Roger, Jain," Archie replied. "Stephane and I are watching your position carefully. No life signs, no electronics other than your own. Proceed with caution."

"No shit," Hall replied. "Thanks for that."

The three *Armstrong* astronauts took tentative steps toward the Chinese lander, with zappers in hand. Their sensor pods, strapped to their backs, provided readouts on their HUDs, overlaying the alien terrain with a wide variety of datapoints. While it was nice to note the exact chemical compounds found in the Titanic river next to them, they were both more focused on the lander ahead.

With one exception. "Claim filed," Hall said with a hint of pride. "Here's hoping they didn't have time for paperwork."

Once again, Shaila thought to snap back at Hall for the flip attitude, but when she glanced over at the corporate exec, she saw that Hall's eyes were darting about nervously, and her hands were fluttering over her suit controls. Everyone had their way of coping, Shaila thought. Maybe that was Hall's.

"Sensors showing the lander's been idle at least six hours," Shaila said, noting the thermal readings off the Chinese lander's engines. "*Armstrong*, what's the best guess we have on survivability for top-line Chinese environment suits?"

A few moments later, Archie came on line. "They're pretty nice, actually. They even carry drinking water and recycle waste-water. Manufacturer says eight hours."

Shaila gripped her zapper. "All right, then. They're still here, likely still active. Roger."

Carefully, the three astronauts arrived at the Chinese lander, going in from the right-hand side, away from the windows—and the engines. Unlike the landers on *Armstrong*, the Chinese lander was environment-suit only; it didn't seal up to preserve its shipboard atmosphere. The Chinese would've had to have worn their suits on the entire trip.

That would explain why the doors were wide open.

It didn't explain the copious brown dust spattered and scattered across the floor of the lander.

Shaila's sensors and HUD identified it as dried, frozen human blood.

"Do you think it's a survivor from the *Tienlong*?" Hall asked quietly; she was receiving the same sensor information as Shaila.

"Not likely," Shaila said as she did a quick sensor sweep of the lander. No weapons found—no compartments labeled "weapons," either. "They don't have airlocks on these, so they had to enter the lander already in their suits. If someone was attacked with a suit on, there wouldn't be this much blood in here."

Shaila switched her comm channel. "*Armstrong*, this is Jain," she said calmly, even as her hand tightened around her zapper. "I think the bad guys are down here with us."

October 18, 1798

Piercing the cloud-cover above the blasted world of Titan proved to be more than even the Countess St. Germain could manage. There were no ships 'round the world itself, so Weatherby ordered *Fortitude* into the clouds near the poles—with the hope they could pull out quickly and make for the Void should they find naught but land beneath them.

"I assure you, Captain Weatherby, your chances of striking land this far north are exceedingly small," Representative Vellusk said, his melodic voice rife with apology and concern. "I should not wish any damage to such a fine vessel."

Weatherby smiled the tight smile of someone doing his very best to be diplomatic. "And I assure you, Representative, I appreciate your advice more than you know. The maps you've supplied us will be most useful indeed once we reach the surface."

Vellusk nodded and made a polite, cheerful sounding melody before turning forward once more, taking in the operations of the ship as the crew prepared to make keel-fall. Out of the corner of his eye, he caught Barnes smiling in his direction, which he allowed to go unremarked upon. It was, Weatherby supposed, only fair.

Hawkins and Anne had worked through the night to alter the ship's lodestones so that the air aboard would remain breathable, for Vellusk and Morrow were quite clear on the matter of Titan's air; it would kill almost instantly. They were still attempting to create a portable lodestone of some sort that would provide protection from the poisonous fume on an individual basis, so that members of the *Fortitude*'s crew might explore on foot—something the French and their Xan partisan allies had likely already considered.

With the apologetic reticence typical of the Xan, Vellusk had suggested they approach the largest set of ruins upon Titan's surface. The fact that it was quite near the northern pole made the decision easy. Apparently, in the early years of the Xan's explorations, they too were confined by the Sun-currents at the poles when it came to venturing off-world, so it made sense for their ancient homeworld to house particularly impressive settlements close to those points.

The descent was unremarkable—indeed, one might call it completely bland, even though *Fortitude* would be the first English vessel to make keel-fall upon this particular moon of Saturn. The orange clouds remained stubbornly thick and monotonous for the vast majority of the fall...

...until *Fortitude* finally broke through the clouds, and a strange, alien vista opened up before them, sending hundreds of men to the sides of the ship.

The land below was a dark orange, combined with smatterings of red-brown streaks among the hills and mountains, while the waters themselves were dark, almost purplish in hue. There was no vegetation to be found—mere rock and sand.

It was a barren, beautifully terrifying waste.

Fortitude splashed down without incident, seemingly without making a ripple in the dark, wine-colored seas. The liquid below them seemed thick as stew, and if it were not for the strong winds that whipped the clouds above past them at a great pace, they might be mired in the muck for quite some time. Even at full sail, however, they would barely make half their typical speed upon a normal ocean, for the seas seemed to cling to the ship's hull, leaving dark purple stains upon her sides. Vellusk assured Weatherby that the "waters" of Titan would not damage *Fortitude*, but he remained nervous—so much so that Gar'uk kept trying to ply him with a glass of port to soothe his mind.

Once the ship was secured and upon its proper course, Weatherby finally turned to the guests upon his quarterdeck. To his surprise, he found Anne and Morrow standing upon either side of a seated Vellusk who appeared to have his hands upon his head, hunched forward, his body shaking.

"My lord?" Weatherby said quietly as he moved to Morrow's side.

"He is overcome," the old admiral whispered back. "He is one of the very few of his people to visit their ancient homeworld and see the wreckage that their past wars caused."

At this, Vellusk stood up abruptly, and Weatherby was reminded once more of the keen hearing these creatures seemed to exhibit. "I must apologize, Captain, for such a display of emotion upon the command deck of your vessel. It is unbecoming."

Weatherby looked up solemnly into the creature's cowl, where he could see faint movement but little else. "Representative, it is I who would apologize. Humanity's troubles have led you here, and for that I am sorry. I hope we may find our errant cousins so that you may leave this place behind quickly."

At this, Vellusk seemed to stand taller. "Your kind would not have come this far if it were not for those among the Xan who seek conflict and war," he sang, determination and forcefulness creeping into the forlorn melodies. "I can only hope that being here will remind these partisan fools of the cost of the violence they seek to embrace."

Weatherby nodded and murmured some words of understanding and respect that, he hoped, would suffice for such a portentous moment, then excused himself to return to his cabin. Whilst he was a fine commander, he knew there was much more to be learned of diplomacy, and despaired at times he might ever come up with the right words at the right time in critical situations.

He collapsed into a chair and saw Gar'uk had placed the port upon his table. Finally giving in, he took a swig and enjoyed the sweetness of the wine, and the slight burn of alcohol. There were various races of Venusian whose skin colors changed with their moods; while Gar'uk was not one of these, Weatherby often felt his valet could read his mind just as well as if his own flesh changed tone.

The knock on his door came all too quickly. "Come!" he barked, frustration quite near the surface.

"A bad time, perhaps?" Anne asked, poking her head through the door.

Weatherby managed a small smile. "Never. Please, come in. Something to drink?"

Anne came through the door, closing it behind her. "No, thank you, Captain," she said, taking a seat across from him. "Dr. Hawkins and I have progress to report on the breathability question."

"Breathability," Weatherby smiled. "Alchemists rather enjoy making up new words, don't they?"

She ignored his aside. "By the time we make port at the ruins, we shall have four devices ready. These should provide protection against Titan's air by creating enough normal air for us to breathe. Vellusk assures us he has his own means."

She held up a belt of some sort, along with what appeared to be a shallow cup. "This goes around your face, while this mask"—she held up the cup—"will go over your nose and mouth. We will likely also need sealed eyeglasses to protect our eyes."

"Is that all?" Weatherby said, eying the device with no small amount of skepticism. "We shall look like perfect monsters ourselves."

Anne frowned. "It is the best we could manage," she said.

"I'm sorry, my lady. I am…these will be quite fine," he said tiredly. "I fear the weight of these events has made me melancholy."

"Understandable," she replied, her voice softening. "You seek not just

Philip, and your lieutenant, but also to stop the Xan themselves from descending into war and barbarism. At least my own goals are simpler."

Weatherby looked upon her with fresh eyes, and found his strength starting to return. "You are quite right, and my own goals should be as simple. We shall rescue Philip, and O'Brian as well, and put a stop to whatever the French are doing. The rest is moot at this moment. I am sorry to trouble you, my lady."

To his great surprise, she actually smiled. "You are no trouble, sir. No matter what happens, you will always have my gratitude."

Another critical moment was at hand, and the words escaped Weatherby once more. "Anne…"

"We must find my son," she said simply, rising from her place. "Should we do that, we may yet have more to discuss, you and I. In the meantime, to whom shall I give the other two devices?"

"Two?" Weatherby asked, confusion in his voice. One look from Anne dissolved this quickly, however. Of course she would be coming. "I'll have Barnes find me the best two marksmen aboard. That will have to suffice."

"What of Vellusk? And Morrow?" she asked.

Weatherby sighed, but managed a smile regardless. "Unless they can find means to breathe on their own, they're staying here. I can only afford to have one person aboard who refuses to take orders."

"You've never given me orders, sir," Anne said sweetly.

"I should rather face the entire French fleet than make an attempt to do so, my lady," he replied.

As it happened, Morrow was unwilling to argue the matter, while Vellusk did indeed have his own means of managing Titan's poisonous air; the fact that the Xan did not share this with Hawkins or Anne was, Weatherby felt, worthy of mention, but Morrow talked him out of making his feelings known. The Xan seemed quite intent on keeping their higher knowledge from mankind, no matter the cost. Weatherby wondered idly if they would sacrifice the whole of their society for it in the end. Was humanity such a threat? Or were they more afraid of themselves?

Find Philip, Weatherby thought. *Find O'Brian. And to hell with the Xan!*

Meanwhile, Barnes had selected two men amongst the marines aboard—a tough veteran named Sgt. George Black, and a young Scot, Gregory Mac-Clellan, who was said to be the finest shot aboard. Weatherby vaguely remembered the young man regularly coming back with game whenever the crew went ashore. They both would do well, he was sure.

Making port on Titan would largely depend on spotting *Franklin* before *Fortitude* was spotted in turn. Weatherby posted multiple lookouts and pored over the maps Vellusk supplied. He opted to come in from the sea, toward dusk and with lights doused, so that he might sneak close enough to launch a boat with the landing party aboard. *Fortitude* would tack away and out to sea, then make for a spot behind a promontory a few miles away. Anne carried with her an alchemical signal rocket that would bring *Fortitude* back—guns ready to fire upon the *Franklin*, if need be—that she believed could pierce the dense, sickly fog.

Yet as *Fortitude* slowly sailed toward the ruins Vellusk had suggested, all was dark and incredibly silent. The winds remained in their favor, but there was an odd lassitude to them, as if filling the ship's sails was a bothersome chore, rousing the breeze from its funereal slumber. The sea was altogether too still, and the massive 74-gun ship barely seemed to make a ripple in the thick, noxious waters as it passed. When Weatherby ordered the lights doused, it became difficult to make out the fo'c'sle of the ship from the quarterdeck, let alone anything more.

To Weatherby's surprise, Dr. Hawkins came up with a solution to the problem on his own volition, presenting the captain with a pair of exceptionally bulky glasses with large tinted lenses and a variety of straps.

"As soon as we made keel-fall, I thought it best to make an attempt at a working to help the lookouts," the doctor said with a small smile. He also looked slightly healthier, as if the events of the past few days somehow invigorated him. "It took some doing to account for the particulars of this dreadful air, but by treating it as a poison to be excised, rather than something to pierce with mere vision alone, I was able to come up with a solution. The Martian sand-beast venom extracts infusing the glass—"

Weatherby held up a hand to stop Hawkins, but granted him a smile by way of recompense. "It is no doubt a most efficacious working, Doctor, and one I urge you to submit to the Naval Alchemy Board upon our return. In the meantime, bring it forward so you may instruct the fo'c'sle lookout on how best to use it."

"Of course, sir. Thank you, sir," Hawkins said, excusing himself and picking his way forward with surprising alacrity and dexterity.

Weatherby turned to Anne and Morrow, who were with him upon the quarterdeck. "It seems our Dr. Hawkins is the only one who might find Titan agreeable."

It was but a few minutes later that a shout came from the fo'c'sle. "Land ho! Come about hard to starboard! Brace for impact!"

Immediately, Weatherby turned to the man at the wheel. "Do it! Now!"

The man started whirling the wheel around, and Weatherby instinctively joined in, even as he looked up at the sails. "Tack in sheets and braces! Weigh anchor!"

Fortitude's timbers groaned as she suddenly came about, while the anchor fell with a loud splash. Weatherby had no notion as to how close they were to land, but the tone in his lookout's voice made it plain enough—they were too close indeed. When the wheel suddenly went stiff, Weatherby knew he had done all he could.

"Tom!" Anne shouted.

Turning, he saw her pointing to larboard—at the shadow of a massive outcropping of rock. A moment later, a scrape and crunch of wood beneath them jarred the ship. Thankfully, *Fortitude* kept moving, and no more terrible noises were heard as the massive rock drifted aft into the fog once more.

Weatherby turned to Barnes, who looked quite unnerved and mortified. "Mr. Barnes," Weatherby said, patiently but loud enough to command the man's attention. "Get someone below to assess the damage." Barnes simply nodded and hurried off. At least he was responding to orders faster, Weatherby thought, though his decorum still needed a bit of work.

With the wheel secure, the anchor chain becoming taut and the ship slowly grinding to a halt on the Titan seas, Weatherby rushed forward toward where his lookout, a young man of perhaps no more than sixteen, stood looking to larboard with Hawkins' contraption upon his head. He looked like half his skull had been replaced with that of a giant insect, so cumbersome and odd was the doctor's working.

"You there," Weatherby said. "What's your name?"

The man turned and immediately saluted, looking quite nervous. "Tully, Captain Weatherby, sir."

"It was not your place to give an order upon my ship, Tully," Weatherby said. He waited a moment before putting a hand on the lookout's shoulder.

"But I'm damned glad you did. Well done. You've earned an extra ration of grog for a week."

Tully smiled broadly with evident relief. "Thank you, sir! I figured it best to say what I said, sir."

"And you were right to do so. Now, allow me to borrow that device a moment, if you please."

Tully pulled at the straps holding Hawkins' glasses to his head and handed the device to Weatherby, who had the man hold his hat in return. He then managed to strap the strange lenses to his eyes, with only a minimal amount of consternation and but one epithet.

And when his eyes focused, the world changed.

The fog was gone, and Weatherby could plainly see the setting Sun, the first twinkling stars of night, and the beauty that was Saturn and its rings. Before him was land—the shores of Titan itself. Looking aft, he saw just how close they had come to running aground, for the outcropping of rock was quite large and would have easily stranded them upon Titan.

"*Two* weeks extra grog, Tully," he said quietly. "Well done indeed."

He then focused upon the shore behind the outcropping, and was doubly amazed, for it was the ruin of a city like no other he had ever seen.

The buildings were tall—easily fifty floors upon many of them, and they would have been stacked straight and true if not for the ravages of war and millennia of ages upon them. There were streets, and machines upon them, all covered in rubble from the ruined buildings. Gaping holes in walls and grounds spoke of terrible engines of pure destruction. The coast itself was lined with wharves and docks, many of which were half-collapsed.

Weatherby thought back to the cities upon the rings of Saturn, and to the settlement on Callisto he visited many years prior. These buildings seemed far less elegant, with more stone used in their construction. Some of the sloping tiled roofs reminded him of the architecture of the Orient he had seen once while on a voyage to China. Other elements seemed more akin to Greek temples, the design of which had since been widely appropriated by Europe's capitals.

On the whole, it was a disturbing mix of exotic, alien workings, combined with hints of Earth's ancient past. Or did the ancient past contain elements of Xan architecture?

No matter, for the ruins remained formidable, stretching from horizon to horizon. Somewhere in there, perhaps, was the Count St. Germain, but it would be as if searching for a thimble in all of London.

"I hope that bloody Xan has a map," Weatherby muttered.

CHAPTER 18

June 21, 2134

The accelerator was working perfectly. To Diaz' untrained eye, it was almost *too* perfect.

She'd reviewed enough of Greene's experimental data from Mars to know what kind of Cherenkov levels to expect as the particles continued to smash together and generate more energy. Up until now, they had been unable to sustain more than a few milliseconds' worth of radiation even approaching Yuna Hiyashi's fateful work two years ago.

Here, though, with BlueNet focusing all of Earth's ambient Cherenkov energy on the Siwa site, they were sustaining high levels for a second or two at a time—and the amount of radiation was rising as well as growing longer in duration.

She looked over at Greene, who remained at the front of the room, working with Ayim. He was still smiling, but every now and then a look crossed his face. *He sees something. Something off,* Diaz thought.

"Ma'am," Coogan said quietly.

"Yeah?"

"Underneath the main accelerator core, behind the glass," he said, nodding with his head. "Does that look right to you?"

Diaz leaned over Hutchinson to look down the main aisle of workstations toward the front of the room. Under the old ceremonial altar in the temple, right where the collider sensors were stored—something was glowing a very soft, pale blue.

"Oh, boy," Diaz said. "Not good."

She turned to one of the men guarding her. "I need to talk to my guy up there. Now."

The guard looked puzzled. "No, you sit."

"No, I don't sit," Diaz said, standing. Huntington and Coogan rose with her. "You wanna have a shoot-out with all this gear in here? Be my guest. I'm walking up there to talk, that's all." And with that, Diaz turned and strode toward the front of the room, her two officers walking behind her, side-by-side. Behind her, she could hear the two guards arguing in Arabic as they followed. That was fine. She didn't care if they tagged along.

Passing rows of surprised techs and scientists—well, the ones who weren't buried in holodata were surprised, at least—she walked straight up to Evan Greene and tapped him on the shoulder. He turned, and his eyes widened, as if he expected Diaz to beat the shit out of him right then and there. Tempting, but there were bigger problems going on.

"Under the altar," Diaz said quietly.

Greene turned back to his holodata. "I know. It shouldn't be there. It's giving off more than 57 percent of the Cherenkov generated in there. It's as if it's supplying additional power to the accelerator process, but we aren't actually seeing any power spikes. Just the radiation."

"Theories?"

Greene paused. "General, I'm sorry, but I'm not reporting to you anymore."

"Dammit, Evan," she hissed. "These are my people down here. Mags and Jimmy, people you've worked with. Are we in danger here?"

Greene looked down momentarily before turning back to Diaz. "I don't think we're the only ones at this particular quantum space-time inflection point."

"Shut it down," Diaz said, urgency underlying her best calm command voice.

"No," he said. "This is what we've been waiting for. This is why it's working. We can't shut it down now." A momentary surge of blue light washed through the room, drawing their attention away from the data, before Greene continued. "We're getting all we're going to get from the particles, but Cherenkov levels are still increasing, even as our own power levels off. Whatever's under that altar is generating it. I think it's the key to the other side."

"And look what happened the last time that door opened," Diaz said. "We were invaded. Literally invaded by another dimension. Please, Evan, shut it down."

A sudden click behind her right ear made her tense up. It was a very familiar sound to a soldier.

"Back to your seat, Maria," Harry said. She turned to see her guard pointing his weapon right at her head, with Harry beside him.

Diaz tried to plead her case. "Harry, you have energy here you aren't controlling. Maybe that's the key to this, sure, but where's your safety measures? Hell, did you even bother looking under the altar?"

"Actually we did," Harry replied. "That was the source of the latent radiation in the room. That's why we built the reaction chamber right on top of it. And I don't want to control it. I want to open it up. And keep it open." He turned to look at Greene and Ayim, who were now busy going through a new set of holodata. "Gentlemen, let's get the barriers in place."

Ayim looked over at Harry—and the gunman—with a concerned look on his face, but ultimately used his hands to sweep away the holodata he was looking at, replacing it with a holo control board. A moment later, machinery on either side of the altar began to whir into motion. A pair of what looked like giant brackets arose from either side of the altar and began extending, ultimately locking together and surrounding the altar on the horizontal axis. A moment later, these were joined by vertical brackets.

"What the hell is that?" Diaz demanded.

Harry smiled. "What's the use in opening the doorway to another dimension if you can't put a doorstop in it? Damned if I know all the quantum mechanics behind it, but that there, my friends, is our doorstop. That's what's going to let us go back and forth, stake our claims to what we find on the other side, and not only make history, but a ton of money in resource extraction."

Diaz grabbed Harry's arm and pulled him around, prompting the gunman next to her to raise his weapon; she didn't care. "And what happens if this whole area floods with energy you can't control? What if there's something on the other side that wants to come over and seriously fuck with us? What if it's Althotas? I have no doubt you know *exactly* what happened on Mars."

Harry looked the gunman off and actually smiled at Diaz. "Of course I saw the holos, Maria. I know what happened. Hell, we built off that. We just had to wait for their knock on the other side. As for protection," he said, pointing to the sealed-off altar, "I can drop a meter of steel all around those brackets. I can vaporize anything that comes through if need be. I can blow the entire altar. Hell, I can take out Siwa if I have to, if it gets that bad. I mean, shit, Maria, I'll do a lot for profit, but I won't risk the *whole* damn planet. But if we can make this stable and get in and out of there regularly, we don't have to go to freakin' Saturn to find new natural resources. We just hop across."

With that, Harry nodded at the guard, who glared at Diaz and her officers and motioned toward the back of the room. Diaz turned crisply on her heel and strode toward the back of the room once more, with Coogan and Huntington trailing behind slightly, looking over their shoulders at the increasingly numerous flashes of blue light flooding the chamber.

"Resource extraction," Diaz muttered as she flopped back down into her chair. "He thinks he can go over there with zappers and machine guns and take their oil. It's the 20th century all over again."

"So it would seem," Coogan said very quietly, out of the guards' earshot. "I'm not an expert, but I glanced at their holodata during your conversation up there. They seem to be quite close to a breakthrough. We'll need to act soon."

Diaz turned to Huntington, who was scribbling idly on a pad of paper.

Not quite idly, however, as Diaz looked over at the scratch marks. The seemingly random bunch of lines were in fact a map of the room they were in, with lines of crudely-drawn flowers marking the rows of desks, a little cloud and rainbow marking the altar-chamber, and swoopy, squiggly lines pointing from two stars in the back toward a variety of happy faces and, in one instance, a unicorn.

It was a tactical map. Huntington had split the room into fire zones. If they could overpower their guards and grab their weapons, they could clear a path for one of them to reach the holocontrols and maybe shut everything down.

"The unicorn?" Diaz asked with a slight grin.

"Your old pal Harry, ma'am," Huntington replied. "Thought you'd like that."

Diaz saw taking out Harry was her responsibility in Huntington's plan. "It's very sweet of you, Captain. I might take this home to show my kid."

"Home's the idea, ma'am."

Diaz turned to Coogan. "You think you could put a wrench in their works?"

Coogan's eyes shifted around, as if he was casting about for data in his now-missing HUD. "Since they're linked to BlueNet, I could simply power down the satellites. If we're fortunate, I might be able to cut power entirely. But introducing that sort of instability…it could blow up in our faces quite neatly."

"Sad to say, but we may have to consider this facility a loss if it means shutting this down," Diaz whispered. "We have to do whatever it takes."

Both Coogan and Huntington nodded soberly, and Diaz felt a small twinge of pride and sadness inside.

Suddenly, a massive, intensely bright blue-white light flooded the room, accompanied by the sound of sirens and klaxons a moment later.

Once her eyes adjusted, Diaz peered toward the front of the room.

Between the brackets, the collider chamber was gone.

In its place were three men. One was an old, pale, fat guy dressed like an Egyptian. Another was dressed in an antiquated soldier's uniform, and was pointing a flintlock pistol at a third man, dressed in a combination of traditional Arabic robes and 18th century clothing.

Despite what seemed to be some serious ravages of time, Diaz recognized the third one.

"Finch?"

The alchemist Dr. Andrew Finch looked up, and his brow furrowed a moment. And then confusion gave way to a look Diaz knew well from her years of combat training.

It was the surprised look of shit going down wrong.

October 18, 1798

What the bloody hell was that? Finch thought to himself. For a brief moment, he had caught a glimpse that was both incredibly foreign and yet strikingly familiar—a group of people, dressed in odd clothing, standing in the room about ten feet in front of the altar, surrounded by glowing numbers and massive banks of machinery.

And two of those people seemed quite familiar. Finch began scouring his memory, but quickly remembered where he was and what he was doing. It was all related, snapping into place in a flash of terrible insight.

"Berthollet, stop," Finch said quickly, turning to the costumed alchemist next to him, who was busy chanting at the altar, reading from *The Book of The Dead* while his audience sat before him, enraptured. "You must stop this. Now!"

Berthollet did nothing of the sort, except move his right hand nigh imperceptibly in Finch's direction, prompting his captor to shove his musket directly into the back of Finch's head. The French alchemist continued his ritual, even as the scene before them—was that really that Diaz woman?—flickered in and out of reality. It didn't matter, of course, for the appearance of strange people in the midst of a ritual such as this would most assuredly bode ill. In fact, the edges of that scene looked rather familiar.

The edges were of darkness—a blackness so pure and miasmal that it seemed to absorb life and energy itself from around it. He had seen that darkness on Mars two decades past, and saw what came from it.

"Berthollet!" Finch shouted. "No more, damn you!"

Finch lunged forward for the *Book*, but found hands grasping at his arms. His guard had been joined by another, and they were pulling him away from the altar even as he sought to put an end to the occult working that, now, he was sure would threaten far more than those in the room.

"Berthollet, he will come through!" Finch yelled, still trying to press his case. "You are being played the fool by a power you know nothing of!"

The Frenchman merely smirked as he chanted.

And the image flickering before the altar began to grow more substantial. Clearer, aside from a particular, peculiar shade of blue. Finch could recognize the small, flat machines some of the people in the image carried about. These would carry information, along with buttons and switches made of light. These would....

...act in concert with Berthollet's working.

"It's happening again," he whispered to himself.

Tendrils of blue light started to snake out from around the edges of the... portal, for want of better language for it. For it was a door, Finch knew. And those tendrils, reaching out like strands of blue hair caught in an unfelt breeze, represented some sort of trouble, though he knew not how.

He would not wait long for an answer.

June 21, 2134

While Stephane and Hall stood watch outside the Chinese lander, Shaila did a thorough survey of the ship itself. It appeared to be in fine working order. She didn't know the codes necessary to fly it—the Chinese were big on security, and she knew each astronaut had a code to key open pretty much everything, from e-mail to flight controls—but she imagined she could hot-wire it if necessary. She suppressed a twinge of jealousy, actually, since the Chinese lander seemed more robust and technologically advanced than the ones they had on *Armstrong*, even with ExEn as a major backer. Of course, the Chinese government had been a monolithic enterprise for nearly two centuries, while the E.U. and U.S. could barely put together a joint mission without squabbling over the bill for catering the planning meetings.

"All right, all clear in here," Shaila said, climbing out of the lander. "Figure we have two options. We wait for them to come back, or we go find 'em."

"I vote B," Hall said. "All this waiting around makes me nervous."

"I agree," Stephane added, sounding surprisingly calm. "Whatever they're doing, we must find them doing it."

"All right. *Armstrong*, you copy all this? We're heading out to find the lander astronauts."

Archie came on the comm a moment later. "Roger that, Commander. You be careful. I've spotted Nilssen and Conti on board *Tienlong*. They've given me a thumbs-up through the cockpit window, but damn if I can't get a signal through all that crap they got layered on that goddamn ship."

"Keep trying," Shaila said. "Link us up to them if you can get a signal through, and keep sensors on both teams. I want as much heads-up as possible if we get more people milling about down here. Jain out. Now," she said to Stephane and Hall, "how do we find 'em?"

"Footprints," Stephane responded. "I saw some boot prints heading off that way, toward the canyon walls. The tread wasn't like ours. And there aren't too many other people out here, are there?"

Shaila rapped Stephane's helmet and smiled; at least his head remained screwed on well enough. "Good eyes. Let's go."

They began at a shuffle, then started leaping when the mystery treads grew further apart. It seemed as though the Chinese astronauts—there were indeed two sets of tracks—knew where they were going, or at least had some killer sensor gear, because there weren't any turn-backs or dead ends. The tracks led directly toward the canyon wall, with little detour.

The JSC astronauts leapt across a small river of liquid hydrocarbons and landed on the opposite bank, right up against the canyon wall—and that's where the trail stopped. They doubled back and checked both banks of the river, but to no avail. The only possible trail was up a high mound of rubble—one that hadn't shown up on maps of Titan made prior to their mission.

"Rock slide?" Hall wondered aloud. "Maybe they got buried?"

"Our survey images are just three months old," Stephane said. "There's not enough erosive activity for this. This may have been created by the Chinese."

Shaila eyed the rubble pile, which stretched more than fifty meters up the side of the canyon wall. "You know, is it me or does it look like a ramp?" she muttered.

"It's the only path they could've taken," Stephane agreed.

The three began leaping up the strewn rocks, while worry nagged harder at Shaila. If they had the means to reduce a canyon wall to rubble, then the Chinese had them severely outgunned. Even if it was just standard drilling and mining gear, Shaila knew those kind of tools could be put to terrible use on people.

They got to the top of the pile, and…there was nothing there.

"What the hell?" Hall said. "Now what?"

Shaila noticed a ledge about ten meters above them. "Ropes, you think? Or just a jump?" she asked, pointing.

"You first," Hall said with a smile.

With a glance at Stephane, who simply shrugged, Shaila hunched down… and leapt.

The canyon wall flew by in light gravity, but she ended up having to reach out with a gauntleted hand to catch the lip of the ledge. Once done, it was a one-handed job to pull herself up and onto it. Immediately, her zapper went out to cover her surroundings.

There was a small crevasse in the canyon wall. Her suit lights illuminated a pathway deep into the mountain.

It was a cave.

"Fuck, I hate caves," Shaila muttered. "Get up here, you two."

To Shaila's surprise, Stephane made the jump with ease; she was always on him about his physical training during the voyage out...maybe he'd finally taken her up on it? It had been a busy few days, certainly. As for Hall, it took two leaps, but she managed to get up to the ledge. The crevasse seemed just big enough for a suited astronaut to squeeze through. Or was it? Shaila saw more rubble by her feet, and wondered if the Chinese had opened things up a bit to go inside.

"Why would someone go into a cave on Titan?" Hall wondered. "I mean, there's good stuff all over the place. No need to excavate for resources."

"Depends what you're looking for," Stephane said, taking the lead and edging into the crevasse. Shaila followed suit, her zapper before her. She chided herself for not taking point, but there was no room to maneuver around Stephane as he gingerly moved down into the narrow cave.

Shaila could hear Hall moving into the opening behind her, and not without difficulty. "Something I should know, you two? Was this in some super-secret mission briefing?" she said crossly.

"Not that I'm aware," Shaila said with a little pique. It served to mask her own insecurities and fears. Flashbacks to a certain lava tube on Mars sprang unbidden into her mind. Rocks rolling uphill...a giant wall...

The three astronauts proceeded down the raw, rocky corridor, which led into the side of the canyon. Occasionally, tiny shafts of light were seen high above—openings between rock walls that let a bit of sunlight in.

Then the corridor grew more uniform.

"Shaila, this isn't normal," Stephane said. "This rock's been...carved."

"Roger that," Shaila said neutrally. "Reading a slight increase in Cherenkov radiation. *Armstrong*, you copy that?"

Silence.

"*Armstrong*, this is Jain, come in. We are reading Cherenkov radiation. Please respond. Over."

Nothing.

"Might be too deep inside," Hall offered.

"Maybe, or perhaps it's something else," Stephane said. "I feel like...this is something we've seen before, yes?"

Shaila swallowed tightly and focused on the path ahead. "We'll see. Keep moving."

The walls, meanwhile, continued to get straighter, until it felt like they were in a building rather than a cave. Thankfully, there was room now for Shaila to maneuver around Stephane, which she did without comment and which he allowed. She caught a glimpse of his face, and he looked... different. Not scared—she'd seen scared. He was wide-eyed, sweating inside his finely-calibrated pressure suit, looking inscrutably intense. Honestly, he was beginning to creep her the hell out.

The walls continued to evolve as they walked, and the rough contours seemed to start forming patterns as they proceeded, like weather-beaten... runes. Carvings.

"*Armstrong*, this is Jain. Come in. Repeat, come in. Where the hell are you?" Shaila said.

Still nothing.

"Increased levels of Cherenkov radiation," Stephane reported. "Something is here."

Shaila felt a quiet vibration through her boots, and a split second later, a warning popped up on her HUD. The vibration was consistent with a laser drill used in mining operations.

A moment later, a blue flash came from down the corridor, and all their sensors went haywire—Cherenkov radiation, among many other types, along with a very small seismic shift.

"Shit. Double-time," Shaila said as she bounded down the corridor. *Dear God, it's happening again.*

Suddenly, the corridor opened up into a room.

It was about the size of a small holomovie theater, roughly 20 meters at a side. There were more carvings along the walls—Shaila couldn't help but notice they were of a very different style from those she had seen on Mars— and a large platform at the front roughly two meters high. There was a very small opening in the roof, which was another 20 meters up, which let in some dim, orange-tinted light.

And at the far wall, near the platform, two pressure-suited astronauts were clearing rubble away from something.

Shaila decided not to stand on ceremony. She lifted her zapper and fired.

One of the two astronauts went down, and the other turned in shock.

He was holding a laser drill in one hand—and a large, ornately carved green slab in the other.

Then he fired the drill.

"Down!" Shaila cried out.

Shaila dove to the floor in front of her, bouncing off the flat stone surface in the low gravity, then rolling over toward the wall for more cover. She saw Stephane hit the dirt opposite her. Her HUD showed that Hall had retreated back into the corridor somewhat to escape the fire. Smart girl.

An explosion of pebbles and dirt centimeters from her face told her the guy with the drill was still busy. She rolled the opposite direction and fired blindly. She had one, maybe two moves left. It wasn't a big room, but big enough for a smart guy to make the most of it.

Then the laser stopped.

Looking up, Shaila saw the Chinese astronaut—the characters on his suit were indeed Mandarin—looking down at his drill. "I think I hit the laser," Hall said from behind her. "Meant to hit *him*."

"Still works," Shaila said. "My turn."

She raised her zapper, but the Chinese astronaut had already dropped his drill and was on the move, literally jumping across the room in a single bound with the slab tucked under his arm.

"Hall! Incoming!" Shaila warned.

Stephane got there first, pushing himself off the floor and using the low gravity to hurl himself toward the door—and right at the Chinese astronaut. He grabbed a foot, then grappled upward until he had a hand on the man's backpack, yanking him backward and sending them both flying back into the room.

The two men rolled to a stop, the slab flying out from the Chinese astronaut's arm. With a shove, Stephane got out from under him and scrambled toward where the slab had landed. It was translucent green, as if carved from a massive emerald. And there were more carvings on it.

Those, Shaila saw with a flash of recognition, were very much like the ones she saw on Mars.

"Stephane! Wait!" Shaila cried out.

Heedless, Stephane reached the slab and picked it up.

And the room was suddenly bathed in an impossibly bright blue light.

When her eyes cleared, Shaila looked to see Stephane standing up and holding the slab, looking down at it and running his gauntleted fingers across its surface.

And Shaila's comm suddenly burst into life.

"Jain, goddamn it, come in!"

Shaila shook her head and moved her zapper to cover the Chinese astronaut, who remained prone but was staring at Stephane intently. "I'm here, Archie. We have two Chinese astronauts here, one zapped and the other captured. Report."

"Nilssen and Conti found everyone aboard *Tienlong* dead. And there's blood everywhere. Someone wrote something in Chinese on one of the walls—in blood. Can't get it translated yet because of the comms. These guys are batshit crazy."

"Roger that," Shaila said, a sinking feeling in her stomach. "They came for something down here. Some kind of tablet thing. I—"

Stephane looked up at Shaila and smiled, completely derailing her train of thought. "It's time," Stephane said, looking down and nodding at the Chinese astronaut, who rose to his feet almost dutifully. And with a dexterity that seemed almost superhuman, Stephane began running his fingers across the green slab in some kind of pattern.

Trembling, Shaila trained her zapper on Stephane. "Drop it. Please."

With a flourish, Stephane tapped on the tablet for a final time, then looked over at the Chinese man. Suddenly, the *Tienlong* astronaut leapt across the room once more—toward Hall, who had come out from cover.

Shaila turned to fire at him, but an immensely strong hand gripped her wrist, twisting painfully. She dropped it and turned to see Stephane looking down at her, his face inscrutably calm...and still smiling.

Hall's scream pierced her headphone; the Chinese astronaut had tackled her and was clawing at her suit. A split-second later and her helmet flew off.

Her scream died instantly. She followed a moment later, the fluid in her body evaporating and freezing instantly, rendering her a husk within seconds.

Shaila turned back to Stephane, tears beginning to well in her eyes. "What are you doing, Stephane?" It was all she could manage.

"This," he replied, holding up the slab in the other hand. "It's time to free them. And my name is Rathemas."

CHAPTER 19

October 18, 2134

How does one melt rock and steel?

Weatherby found himself repeatedly asking this question as he led his small party from the *Fortitude* through the ruins of the ancient Titan city. The streets were broad and queerly uniform, the buildings high and straight. Yet this was a blasted, war-torn place that had seen destructive energies no man could fathom. Rock was reduced to slag. Steel was twisted and melted. Glass and rubble crunched under his feet as he led Anne, Vellusk and his two marines further into the city. Ahead of them, Gar'uk clambered over rubble and ruin with surprising dexterity. To Weatherby's great surprise, his valet had volunteered for the mission, and it seemed his alien body had no need for protection from the poisons in the air. Prior to leaving, Hawkins and Anne had engaged in an animated discussion as to how Gar'uk could breathe there—a discussion that quickly left the ship's alchemist at a loss for words again as Anne engaged in a dizzying array of alchemical speculations.

Vellusk was providing direction for the company, for this worthy Xan had upon him a map of this particular place, though it was at times unreliable due to either misinformation or the placement of ruined buildings that blocked the party's way through the orange fog. Weatherby could not help but second-guess his decision to leave Hawkins' cloud-piercing working with the ship's lookout. Of course, his primary responsibility was to his ship, and he did not want *Fortitude* set upon by *Franklin* or, even worse, any Xan conveyance that may have sided with the partisans who were apparently helping the French.

But only Vellusk seemed to be equipped to see properly, and the creature led them quickly enough through the ruins, taking them uphill at a considerable pace. The rest of them could only see perhaps twenty yards in any direction, which is why Gar'uk took it upon himself to scout ahead as best as he was able. The lack of direction was disconcerting to say the least, and Weatherby was quite sure only Vellusk could lead them safely back to the ship, for he was already lost amid the twists and turns of the city.

"We are close," Vellusk sang, his harmonies taking on a tired, mournful tone. "We make for the ancient Temple of Strength, as it would be called in your tongue. It is upon the hillside ahead."

Weatherby nodded and stole a glance at Anne, who nodded in return. They were both present at a Xan temple upon the Jovian moon of Callisto those nineteen years past; that one was called the Temple of Remembrance, a shrine dedicated to cataloging and atoning for the Xan's warlike ways of the past. Certainly, today's Xan were a far cry from those long ago if this ancient place was dedicated to so blunt a purpose as strength.

But the Xan who had slain Administrator Sallev was perhaps the most rage-filled creature Weatherby had ever seen, and it had shaken him considerably to see it. This was no mindless terror, like a Martian sand beast, but rather a large, powerful, sentient being fueled by bloodlust and power. Worse, there was a fervent zeal in that Xan's eyes, a look all too familiar to Weatherby.

Weatherby looked around and thought the lot of them should be rounded up and sent here, along with more than a few Earth men who seemed to welcome the fortunes of war. The ruins of Titan would make a fine lesson for them.

"Captain," Sgt. Black said, his voice muffled through the breathing apparatus they were forced to wear. The man's voice dragged Weatherby back to the moment. "A word?"

"Yes, Sergeant?"

The marine sidled up closer to Weatherby. "That girl there," he said, nodding toward Anne, who was now in quiet discussion with Vellusk at the party's lead. "Are you sure she knows how to use them weapons, sir?"

Weatherby smiled. Anne had opted for one of the midshipmen's uniforms for their sojourn into the city, as was her wont, he knew. As for the two pistols and smallsword she now carried upon her person… "Sergeant, I would wager she's a better shot than half your marines aboard. She'll manage, I'm sure."

"Yes, sir," Black said, the tone of his voice registering doubt. "But should we be attacked, MacClellan and I may not have means to protect her."

"Then worry about the attackers," Weatherby said. "In the unlikely instance that the Countess requires aid, I shall render it."

The sergeant made his obedience at this, leaving Weatherby to ponder once more as they continued through the mist-shrouded ruins. He had seen Anne lead the men of the *Daedalus* through a Martian desert to do battle with ancient evil. And indeed, thoughts of another frighteningly capable woman entered his mind with these memories. He wondered how the Hindu Royal Navy officer Shaila Jain had fared after their encounter. Nineteen years…he imagined she was an admiral by now.

Vellusk stopped suddenly and held up his clawed hand, prompting the rest of the party to stumble to a halt. Immediately, the two marines had their weapons up and peered through the fog for any threats. And before them, Weatherby could see the ruined stairs of a rather large, pillared and canopied building. A nearly sheer cliff face—no mere hillside to Weatherby's eyes—loomed behind it in dim, shrouded menace.

"Is this it?" Weatherby asked the Xan quietly.

"It is," Vellusk answered in a very odd, harmonic whisper. "And I do believe I have seen a flash of light from inside, though it is difficult even for me to pierce this poisonous air entirely."

"But how?" Anne asked. "We did not see the *Franklin* upon our arrival."

"There are many places where they may have made port," Vellusk responded. "And if they had thought to bring one of our…carriages…with them, they could travel far indeed in a very short time."

"At the ready," Weatherby commanded his party, and the marines—and Anne—followed suit appropriately. Sensing the possibility of violence, Vellusk retreated toward the back of the party, while the redcoats took their place at the point and Gar'uk moved off to the side. His particular tribe of Venusians were considered accomplished hunters, and given the lizard-man's quiet movement and small stature, stealth seemed to be his forte. Weatherby drew his gleaming sword and, with a pistol in his other hand, quietly urged his people forward.

They climbed the steps—no mean feat for the humans, as they were built for the much larger strides of the Xan—and made their way through the ruined columns. The temple was circular and, once, likely domed, though the roof collapsed long ago. The ruins of statuary could be seen in the dim orange light, and there was a raised area in the center of the room that likely served as a central focus of worship.

Quietly, and with a care for their footsteps, the *Fortitude* party entered the temple proper, keeping to the columned sides of the building. Weatherby looked closely, hoping to find any clue as to where the French may have gone—or if they were there at all. The thought that they had acted upon faulty information suddenly cropped up in his mind; if they had, it was likely Philip and O'Brian would be lost to them entirely.

A sudden blast, followed by a whoosh of air near Weatherby's ear and the sound of a musket round burying itself into stone, was both shocking and surprisingly reassuring.

"Return fire!" Weatherby shouted, all pretense of stealth forgotten. He raised his pistol and fired into the darkness, as did the marines and Anne. There was the sound of rapid movement on the other side of the temple—and a short cry of pain.

"Move!" Weatherby ordered.

Quickly, the group dashed across the open floor of the ruined temple, ducking between the larger pieces of rubble. Three more shots rang out before silence reigned—which meant that there were anywhere from two to four assailants before them, depending on how well they were armed. That silence, of course, meant they were reloading.

Weatherby had already sought to reload his pistol while moving, but when he ventured a look toward the direction of musket fire, he saw very little in the dim light. They would have to get closer.

The sound of steel upon rock told him how wrong he was.

Instinctively, Weatherby brought up his blade in time to parry a second blow from the man who had come upon him so stealthily; the man had apparently climbed atop the rubble which sheltered Weatherby from fire, and had just missed splitting his skull. Instead, the man's sword was split in two by Weatherby's alchemical blade. The captain whirled around and lashed out again, and was rewarded by a cry of utter agony as the man's sword arm was hewn clean at the elbow.

Weatherby turned and saw Anne at musket point, raising her hands. They had somehow gotten the better of them all too quickly. Weatherby raised his pistol to fire at the man who threatened her, but the soft cock of a trigger near his ear told him otherwise.

He turned to see a man in the dress of a French naval officer pointing a pistol at his face.

"*Monsieur*," Weatherby said in French, deftly flipping the pistol in his hand and surrendering it to the Frenchman. "We surrender. You will bring us to your commander." He repeated the statement, loudly and in English, for the benefit of his men.

"Your sword," the French officer said in accented English, muffled by the facial apparatus he wore; it seemed the French had canny alchemists with them as well, and St. Germain's involvement was certainly far more likely now. Weatherby frowned, but handed the blade over. Often, surrendering officers were able to keep their swords until such time as they could be handed over to the highest enemy officer present. Then again, most blades could not cut steel in twain.

The *Fortitude* party was rounded up by the French—there were eight of them, as it happened, though some appeared to be recent arrivals—but at this juncture, Gar'uk was nowhere to be seen, which gave Weatherby some small hope that he was racing back to the ship for rescue or reinforcement. Once the French secured them, they were made to march into the shadows toward the back of the ruined temple. There was a large archway there, and they were brought through it into a series of anterooms and chambers. Most were strewn with rubble and ruined furnishings of some kind or another, and they seemed long-ago pillaged of anything valuable.

One such room had another door in it, one that cannily blended into the very wall. A secret door, as it happened, and one that led into the very hillside upon which the temple rested. A small corridor—small, at least, for the Xan, but wide enough for humans to walk two abreast—led deep into the bedrock, which was roughly hewn at first but seemed to become better carved as they progressed.

"Light ahead, sir," MacClellan whispered. And indeed, the familiar flickering of torch-light grew brighter as they progressed. The French began to remove their masks, but a look from Weatherby told his men to keep theirs on.

After another turn, they came upon a doorway which led into what seemed to be a larger chamber. The French officer halted them before the portal, then entered the room and moved out of sight. Snippets of a conversation in rapid French followed.

Weatherby turned to Anne, whose eyes grew wide and jaw became clenched. And in that moment, he knew.

A voice called out from the room, and the guards pushed and shoved the party into the chamber. It was relatively small compared to the ruins above, but had numerous carvings on the walls—ones Weatherby and Anne had seen before on Callisto, at the Xan settlement there.

Inside, a number of men—and three Xan, as it happened, were excavating along one of the walls, away from the door. They were supervised, it seemed, by a tall, strapping man in the clothes of a fine gentleman.

When this worthy turned toward the group, Weatherby saw it was the Count St. Germain, the finest and most powerful alchemist humanity had ever produced. And as Weatherby feared, he was clearly no captive.

He looked quite serious, and spoke with no little compassion. "I am so sorry," he said, primarily to Anne. "I had not thought you would seek me out as you did."

Anne's look was sharper than Weatherby's blade. "Then you do not know your own wife, sir," she spat. "Where is Philip?"

St. Germain glanced over at Weatherby, then turned back in surprise and recognition. "Ah! It makes sense now. What an unfortunate happenstance that they would send you, Mister…Weatherby, am I right?"

"*Captain* Weatherby," he and Anne replied, in unison.

St. Germain smiled. "I'm sorry, I mean not to play with you, sir. I know full well who you are. Our opinion of you, Anne and I, has remained quite high over the years. And word has come to us of your great deeds and valiant efforts on behalf of the English. Sadly, I had hoped our time together would've taught you something of the futility of the affairs of nations, but it's quite apparent that's not happened."

"Where is Philip?" Weatherby demanded by way of response. "And your French allies have several of my men, whom I would see released at once."

St. Germain turned to the French officer and began a new barrage of rapid-fire questions in that tongue. Finally, he turned back to Weatherby. "I'm told your men aboard *Franklin* put up a most ferocious struggle. Only nine remain, including the commander you put in place. They have been removed from the ship and brought here in case we had need of their labor. Which, as you can see, we do not as of yet."

"And Philip?" Anne demanded once more. "I would see him. Now."

"As you wish, madam," St. Germain replied. "Philip!"

A moment later, the boy himself ran into the room toward his father, who nodded over toward Anne. The boy turned...and it was immediately apparent something had changed. He was sweating, his skin was quite pale, and his eyes appeared dark and sunken.

"Mother!" he smiled. "Have you come to see it?"

Anne looked aghast. "See what?" she asked, her voice breaking at the sight of her son.

Philip turned to Weatherby and bowed slightly in acknowledgement. "Father is going to make the finest discovery since the Philosopher's Stone. And we will achieve such enlightenment from it!"

Weatherby's eyes narrowed. "What discovery?"

St. Germain answered for his son. "The Emerald Tablet, of course. The key to understanding the very underpinnings of alchemy as set forth by the ancient Martians millennia ago. And Philip here," he added, nodding toward the boy, "may very well be the key to it all."

Philip smiled, and Weatherby's heart broke for Anne, who could not stifle a gasp and sob. For the boy's smile, it seemed, was not his own.

June 21, 2134

Diaz looked in horror as the tendrils of blue light began to multiply around the edges of the frame apparatus inside the containment chamber. "What the hell is that?"

She turned to her officers, both of whom stared in mute horror. Her next thought was to ask Greene, a mental reflex that didn't reflect the fact that he remained at the front of the room, continuing the very experiment that brought those tendrils into being. Greene, Ayim and their team were working feverishly around the chamber, trading holodata at dizzying rates and shouting at ever increasing levels.

And as for the portal itself, she continued to see glimpses of people through the window, bathed in blue light and looking blurry and distant.

Mostly, it was the guy wearing Egyptian clothing. Finch—was it really Finch?—was nowhere to be seen.

Each time the portal showed an image of…wherever it was, whoever it was…there seemed to be a spike in radioactive activity, and the techs' level of animation rose. Diaz noticed that a few of them started to see the glimpses she was of the other side as well.

So they knew it was a portal, and they knew it was working. But it was also apparent that something was wrong.

"If that really was Finch, then we're breaking through to the same dimension we did on Mars," Diaz said.

"As I understand it, most likely," Coogan replied.

"Excuse me, ma'am," Huntington interrupted. She pointed toward the front of the room, where Harry Yu was gesticulating wildly and yelling at Ayim, who was doing his best to ignore the executive while Greene tried to manage whatever the hell was going on. "Seems your friend Harry's starting to lose his shit."

"Seems like everyone is," Diaz noted. She looked over at the goons guarding them; both seemed to be more focused on the strangeness in the containment chamber than in their charges. "Time for Operation Rainbows and Unicorns, you think?"

Huntington nodded. "On your mark."

Diaz smiled grimly and flexed her wrists and hands a few times. It'd been a few years since she'd gotten into a really good fight. But she kept up with her PT and could still give the youngsters a run for their money. "Remember, no matter what, we've got to get this shut down, in whatever way possible. Jimmy, you're on point for that."

The British officer seemed nonplussed, but nodded. "I'll do what I can, ma'am."

Diaz turned to Huntington and idly held up the piece of paper holding her doodled plan of attack. "As written, Captain?"

"Yes, ma'am," the younger woman replied, visibly tensing.

"Go."

Diaz swiveled around in her chair and lashed out at the kneecap of the guard nearest her, sinking her boot into his patella with a satisfying crunch. The man gasped in pain as Diaz sprang from her chair, uppercut first, connecting with his chin and snapping his neck backward. The guard's head hit the wall, and Diaz' followup hit his trachea to silence any more outbursts. She grabbed the man's weapon and wheeled around toward Huntington, who already was proceeding toward the middle of the room, her target a crumpled, unconscious heap on the floor, with Coogan right behind her. The rest of the room remained, thankfully, oblivious.

Getting slow, Diaz groused to herself as she followed Huntington, weapon at the ready. A couple of techs and scientists toward the back scattered in their wake at the sound of the scuffle, but most were busy contending with whatever was going on in the containment area. There were two more guards near the front of the room, but they were raptly watching the hypnotic dance of blue tendrils along the containment frame's edge. Getting to them would require Diaz and Huntington to pass unnoticed by several workstations and techs. Even with everything going on, that wasn't likely.

Diaz paused just behind a tech, the first she encountered. She held up a hand to stop Huntington, then turned to put the barrel of her gun at the man's neck. "Not a word," she whispered, leaning in toward his ear. "English?"

"Yeah," the man whispered back, already visibly trembling.

"Shut down whatever the fuck's going on here," Diaz growled.

"We can't," he replied. "Don't know how. Energy levels—"

Diaz cut him off with a hiss and a nudge with her weapon, which caused the man to shiver more noticeably. She hoped he'd hold it together long enough for Plan B. "Get those guards out of here and lock the doors behind them."

The tech's trembling fingers tapped out commands on his holocontrols. A few moments later, the two guards, hands to their earpieces, hustled out of the room. Diaz watched as the guy at the controls locked the doors behind them.

"Good boy," she said. "You behave yourself now, OK?"

She was rewarded with a pale, nervous nod. Diaz turned to Huntington and gave a hand signal. They were about to go overt.

Huntington rushed forward and fired her rifle into the air, causing everyone in the room to jump. "All right!" she yelled. "Playtime's over. This thing gets shut down NOW!"

The techs all stared at her for a moment, then went back to their work. Trading confused glances, Diaz and Huntington proceeded to the front of the room, where Harry, Greene and Ayim stood looking at them—Ayim and Greene worried, Harry pissed.

"What do you think we're doing?" Harry barked. "Stop shooting up my fucking lab and let us do our jobs."

Diaz kept her weapon trained on him and did her level best to resist the urge to shoot him where he stood. "Tell me what the fuck is going on."

Harry glared daggers at her before finally nodding over at Ayim, who replied. "We've cut all power to the accelerator, but the chain reactions are continuing and power levels are rising. The…artifact…in the floor is somehow fueling it. As for the effect around the containment frame, the glowing is a Cherenkov byproduct of something else."

Diaz turned to Greene. "Evan, get this shut down. Harry, you need to sound evacuation and get everyone out of here except for the people you need in this room."

Harry pulled out a datapad and punched a number of commands into it. "Fine, have it your way. Evan, shut it down."

Before Greene and Ayim could even begin to huddle again, another massive blue-white flash came from the containment area. As her eyes settled and focused, Diaz could see the guy in the Egyptian clothing once more, his arms wide and mouth moving.

But the tendrils…they were bigger. And they were growing longer, and swaying more. There were hundreds…no, thousands of them.

"Evan, what *are* those?" Diaz asked.

"We have no idea," he said crossly as he began to swipe through holodata alongside Ayim. "Right now I need to see if we can—"

"Radio signals!" one of the techs shouted. "I'm getting an unknown radio signal!"

Ayim stared back at the tech. "We're shielded down here. How can we get a radio signal?"

"It's coming from the containment area," the tech replied, pointing at the chamber and glowing blue frame. "Running a match algorithm now."

Harry turned to Diaz. "You think your pals on the other side invented radio somehow in the past two years?"

Greene interrupted before Diaz could respond or shoot Harry. "Signal identified. It's…God, that can't be right."

"Report," Diaz barked. Old habits died hard.

Greene stared at his data for several moments, then his hands flew into the air, rearranging streams of numbers and images, his eyes darting around. "It's...it's a JSC remote survey signal. From a planetary probe."

"From which probe?" Coogan asked.

"According to the manifests, this is the underwater probe *Armstrong* took with them for use on Enceladus."

"How is that possible?" Diaz demanded. "That's a short-range signal."

Greene turned toward her. "The tendrils. They're not just lights. They represent dozens of tiny...wormholes. And they're connecting this frame, this space-time point we've created, with Enceladus. I have no idea how."

There was another flash from the chamber, and Diaz could see the Egyptian guy again, gesticulating wildly, and what appeared to be flashes of light near him or around him as well. He was doing something on the other side that didn't look good. And seemingly in concert, the tendrils began extending themselves toward the thick, reinforced glass that kept the reaction chamber contained.

The first tendril simply extended itself *through* the glass as if it weren't there at all, and began to enter the lab itself, to the sound of numerous alarms and panicked looks. Then another. And another. Soon, dozens of and hundreds of strands of light began poking out of containment, into the room. An alarm sounded, and a few of the techs in the back decided enough was enough, abandoning their stations.

Diaz turned to Greene. "What did you *do*?"

The physicist simply gaped in horror at the sight before him. "I don't know."

October 18, 1798

With a French soldier grasping each of his arms, Finch watched helplessly as Berthollet chanted through his ritual, as the portal before him winked in and out of existence, becoming slightly more solid, and real, upon each visitation. Beyond, he could see the others. For a moment of madness, he thought he recognized the silvery mane of hair belonging to that future-doctor, the one whose name, at the moment, fully escaped Finch's memory.

Finch turned toward the audience beyond the altar, for those present had begun whispering amongst themselves, and not without a sense of alarm. He quickly saw the reason:

The amulets upon the participants' chests. They were glowing blue.

"Let me go," Finch whispered to his guards. "We must flee, all of us. You must see it, do you not?"

But they were not listening. Both wore the copper amulets. Both looked panicked and began to tremble. And when Finch peered closely, he saw the blue glow of the amulets mirrored in the depths of their eyes. Berthollet looked about, and seemed quite lost as he did. He had not completed the ritual. The crowd's murmurs began to take on a certain uniformity, and Finch could see that some had begun swaying back and forth themselves, all while trembling.

They were chanting. And doing so in a language Finch had never heard in all his travels.

"What have you done?" Finch called out to Berthollet. "Can't you see that you've lost control of it?"

"We must continue with the ritual!" Berthollet said, grimacing, as much to himself as to Finch, it seemed.

Finch cast about for something, anything to do, and noticed that the grip of the guards had slackened to a degree. He would have to find the right balance between the guards' lassitude and the potential danger of letting the ritual continue unabated—but Finch had a feeling that Berthollet's efforts were moot at this juncture. Escape was paramount.

Thankfully, another flash of blue light from in front of the altar gave him the chance, for it temporarily blinded everyone near it. Finch wrested his arms from the guards' grip and flung himself backward, performing a surprisingly adept roll that brought him right next to the side door from which he entered.

The guards stood where Finch had left them, swaying slightly and chanting.

"Well, that was easy," Finch muttered.

"The rest won't be," came a voice from behind him.

Finch whirled around to see Deodat Dolomieu. He had no idea whether to ally with the young *materia* alchemist or attempt to subdue him. So he simply waited to see what Dolomieu would do.

As it turned out, Dolomieu simply stood in the doorway, peering around the corner apprehensively. "I made my escape as soon as that portal appeared," the Frenchman said. "What is happening?"

"I've no idea, honestly," Finch replied, opting to move into the doorway for the partial cover it afforded. "I'd say Berthollet has no idea what he's uncovered, and it seems that there are those in the other…dimension, I suppose, or universe…that are doing the same damned foolish thing."

"Which means?"

Finch shrugged. "A door will be opened. Perhaps it will be between our two universes. Perhaps a third will be opened as well. Or more. I cannot say. I—"

The Englishman paused at the latest flare-up of light from the blue portal above the altarpiece. The portal remained the same size and was now oddly square, like the frame of a painting hanging in the ether. But along the edges of the glowing portal, a number of glowing, thin tentacles of blue light began to snake out in all directions. The number grew, quickly.

"What in the name of God?" Dolomieu breathed.

Finch grimaced. "God isn't here at the moment. We must do something."

But it was too late.

With a surprising speed, the strands of light lashed out from the portal toward the assemblage, striking each person directly upon the amulet they wore. And those that wore them began to cry out in pain.

Not knowing what else to do, Finch ran toward the altar, past the two guards who had held him, who were now convulsing up on the floor of the temple in apparent agony. He had to stop Berthollet.

Then it struck him, as he approached, that Berthollet already had stopped. He was simply staring ahead, watching his soldiers and *savants* crying out in horror and torment. "What is this?" Finch heard him mutter.

Finch gave him a quick glance; the French alchemist seemed unaffected by the events around him, and he had not been struck by a tendril. He simply seemed to be in shock. That suited Finch well enough, allowing him to ignore his potential adversary in favor of more pressing events.

The Book of the Dead remained upon the altar, its onyx pages open and blue tendrils seemingly caressing the hieroglyphs upon them. Caressing… and tracing them? Finch blinked several times at this, then grabbed the book and slammed it shut.

As he prepared to run, he felt a ring of pain around his forearm, piercing through the thick bandages he still wore. Looking down, he saw a strand of blue light wrapping around his arm, pulling with surprising strength and,

God help him, with a cold that could only come from the very Void itself. Reflexively, Finch swiped the book across the tendril and, to his surprise, the strange thing dissipated, leaving his forearm aching with frostbite. Had it been a moment longer, he might have lost much of the limb.

Tucking the book under his good arm, relatively speaking, Finch leapt from the altar and made for the doorway, where Dolomieu remained. The look upon the young man's face was one of terror, and Finch could see him looking off behind Finch's back.

Finch turned, and could not believe his eyes.

Those struck by the light tentacles had begun to rise from the floor. They were covered in frost burns and seemed desiccated, as if all fluid and blood had been leached from their bodies. They looked, for all the Known Worlds, like mummies.

And they began to walk toward *The Book of the Dead*, and the poor bastard who carried it.

Behind them, Finch could see Berthollet smiling slightly, even as he feverishly flipped through pages of his notes. Perhaps the bastard had done the ritual correctly after all.

CHAPTER 20

June 21, 2134

S haila watched as Stephane and the Chinese astronauts—the other shook off the zapper surprisingly fast—synched their comms and began to thoroughly record all of the glyphs and carvings in the room. Shaila was made to sit in the furthest corner from the exit, though she didn't know why, since nobody had given two shits about poor Elizabeth Hall. Why didn't they just kill her too?

Something had happened to Stephane. Something terrible. And as she felt her wrist throb—it was severely sprained, if not broken in a few places—she knew she couldn't count on any mercy from whatever he'd become.

She was able to subtly tune into their comm channel easily enough, but they weren't speaking anything recognizable. Even her suit's computer was drawing a blank.

"Stephane," Shaila said, interrupting some kind of conversation. "What's going on?"

The conversation immediately stopped, as did the three pressure-suited astronauts. They turned almost in unison to look at her. The Chinese guys looked surprisingly normal, but Stephane...his pallor was taking on a greenish tint, and his eyes...dear God, they looked horrible. They were blood-shot and the pupils were all too wide. The sweat was visible on his face, rolling down in drops.

"Quiet," Stephane said dully. He then barked something at the two Chinese, who returned to scanning the carvings on the walls. It was slow work, seemingly at a high resolution. They needed something there, but Shaila couldn't figure out for the life of her what it was.

And she realized, she didn't care. Hanging out there was no longer an option. The Chinese guy with the laser drill had it slung over his back, and Stephane had her zapper tucked in a pocket of his suit. They were preoccupied with their scans. She thought about grabbing that green slab that Stephane kept with him, but he was demonstrably stronger than he should be, given the state of her wrist. They were armed, she wasn't. It stood to reason they had to get off Titan at some point. They had the advantage at the moment, so she needed to change the circumstances. That involved her leaving, and fast.

Shaila balled herself up in the corner of the room, tucking her legs tightly under her…and pushed.

She floated quickly across the room, behind the three astronauts, and grabbed her zapper from Stephane's pocket before landing in the corridor. And she ran. Hard.

An explosion of rock on her right, one that sent gravel ricocheting off her sit, gave notice that her presence was missed faster than she had hoped. She lengthened her strides and began using the walls to push off, trying to gain velocity in the light gravity. More laser blasts scorched the rock behind her, forcing her to randomly switch sides of the corridor as she pushed. Thank God it was getting more winding by the moment.

And narrower.

The crevasse. It was a bitch to get into. It looked really, really small now.

Shaila flew toward it at speed, flipping so she approached feet first, hoping that she'd knock some rock loose along the edges. She did, but not enough. Her boots skittered across the surface before slipping into the crevasse, but her angle was wrong. Her backpack caught at the lip, preventing her from sliding through.

"Shit, shit, shit, shit," Shaila muttered as she worked herself around, trying to get through. She looked up to see the Chinese astronaut down the corridor, drill in hand. He paused to take a long shot, and Shaila closed her eyes as she twisted and turned and….

A shower of rock fell onto her visor—and she pushed herself free with such velocity that she flew off the lip of the canyon wall and into the Titan atmosphere, a good 200 meters above the canyon floor. Instinctively, she spread her arms and legs wide, and found that her already slow descent was further arrested. This made sense, given Titan's low gravity and high atmospheric pressure. She could, conceivably, flap her arms and fall even slower.

Shaila saw bursts of red light moving past her; the guy with the laser drill wasn't about to let her go. Thankfully, the range of your standard mining drill wasn't that great. Shaila tucked in her arms and legs and balled up, feeling herself fall faster, at least on a relative basis. She looked up to see the astronaut still taking pot shots from the crevasse opening. Stephane and the other Chinese guy were behind him.

They would be on the move.

Shaila's languorous fall allowed her a bit of time to gather her thoughts. She likely wouldn't have time to sabotage the Chinese lander on her way to the *Armstrong*'s lander. Best she could do would give it a zap and hopefully cause a system or two to reboot. That would have to be enough.

Shaila hit the ground and bounced off her feet—pretty jarring, even in the low gravity—but managed a considerable forward leap in the process. It was a couple klicks to the lander, and she soon managed a good pace, giving her direction enough of a zigzag to keep any possible assailant guessing.

"Jain to *Armstrong*, come in," she spat. "Archie, where are you?"

Her heart leapt in her chest as she got a reply. "Jesus Christ, Jain, where the hell you been? I've been trying to call you."

"Hall is dead. Stephane's been compromised. Give me a report on Nilssen and Conti."

There was a good long pause before Archie came back. "Compromised?"

"Report on the *Tienlong*," Shaila insisted.

"Nilssen and Conti are still aboard. They seem to be all right. They're trying to get systems back online. Comms are still a goddamn mess."

Shaila considered this. "They're gonna get company soon, and—"

An alert on her HUD cut her off. Something was jamming her comm signal. "Identify jamming source," Shaila ordered.

"There is a signal coming from an area concurrent with the location of mission specialist Durand," her computer answered. "The range of the jamming signal is potentially several dozen kilometers, perhaps more."

Shaila swore as she dashed past the Chinese lander, drawing her zapper and firing several microwave pulses into the ship. There was no discernible effect; it was a gamble to begin with. She kept moving. Whatever Stephane was carrying—probably that green tablet thing—it was putting out a jamming signal that was keeping everyone blind on the surface. There was no telling how extensive the signal jamming would be. Just comms? Sensors as well?

When Shaila ventured a glance behind her, she saw the astronaut with the laser drill about 100 meters away, still in pursuit. Stephane and the third astronaut appeared to be heading for the Chinese lander.

He's going with the Chinese, Shaila thought. *And the Chinese killed some of their own crew. This is...*

Her thoughts shifted as she spied her lander ahead. "Begin lander launch sequence," she ordered her computer.

"Signals jammed. Cannot comply."

"Fuck!" she roared. She looked back at the astronaut trailing her. That laser drill could theoretically carve up her lander, with her in it. She'd have to deal with him first.

Shaila began to lessen her pace, dragging her boots in the orange dirt with each leap. It took a while in Titan's microgravity, but she soon found that if she spread her arms and legs wide after each leap, she'd get a bit more drag from the atmosphere. It was a strange form of jumping jacks, comical if not for the situation at hand. The ground blurred beneath her, and even turning to keep tabs on her pursuer was dicey, as she nearly sent her body spiraling out of control. Finally, she saw a large boulder ahead that might give her a chance to arrest her motion and provide cover, so she reached out and laid a gauntlet on it, holding on for dear life until her motion finally ceased and she felt her body begin to float downward. She must've been going at a pretty good clip, because she felt something in her shoulder pull painfully in the process.

Thankfully, her zapper was in her other hand, even if her wrist remained unsteady. She poked her head over the boulder and aimed.

There. About 50 meters away and closing fast. The Chinese astronaut was in mid-leap and readying his drill—the jury-rigged device probably needed recharging after each shot, which gave her the edge.

Shaila fired when he was 40 meters off. And again at 25 meters. At 10 meters, her opponent plowed into the dirt face first, unconscious, leaving a trail of orange dust wafting up into the air.

She zapped him again for good measure. Because...goddamn it, he deserved it.

Shaila turned and leapt the last 150 meters to her lander in just under twenty seconds. She knew that whatever had the astronauts in its grip was also giving them some pretty good strength and stamina; the guy she stunned would be up soon.

She forgot to grab his drill. *Fuck*. She really should've killed him. The fact that she wanted to, and thought so little of the consequences, would probably keep her up at night later. But not now. Not in the least.

Shaila jumped atop the lander and opened the airlock, diving in and starting the cycle. She was also able to begin warming up the lander while in the airlock, thanks to a well-placed holopad control in the lock itself. By the time she was able to enter the warm, breathable cabin, the lander had nearly run through its entire startup sequence.

Vaulting into the pilot's seat, Shaila aborted the non-critical checklist items and got the engines warmed up. She tried to hail *Armstrong* again, but comms were still being jammed. Sensors weren't though; she pulled up a hologram of the area and saw the Chinese lander had already taken off and was heading for orbit.

And there was movement 150 meters away. The guy with the drill was already waking up. Four minutes…usually, zappers required fifteen to twenty minutes recovery time. Her own record was eleven minutes.

Shaila fired up the engines and went for a full-throttle launch. As the lander rose off the surface of Titan, she could see the Chinese astronaut she had eluded just standing there, looking at her lander.

Then he raised the drill to the front of his visor…and fired.

That was the last thing Shaila saw on Titan before clouds enveloped the lander.

October 18, 1798

It said something of the estimation the Count St. Germain had for his wife that she was seated next to Weatherby, her hands bound before her just as his were. Certainly, with the Count never having seemed to be a God-fearing man, the institution of marriage was likewise something for which he had little regard. But Weatherby also felt it had much to do with the utter capability Anne could muster, especially in the face of what was happening with her son.

"What have you done to Philip? Why did you take him?" Anne demand-ed, and not for the first time. To this point, the Count and his coterie of French and Xan allies continued to excavate the room and record the glyphs and images from the walls using sketchpads and pencils. Philip assisted readily in this, paying no heed to his bound mother, nor the captain who had befriended him on the long voyage from Venus.

St. Germain, however, deigned to answer this time. "I had no intention of involving Philip, my dear, until you did by bringing him hence. As I delved into my research, I realized he could well be the key to deciphering our find here. For this is no mere relic we've uncovered. This is the Emerald Tablet! The keystone to Al-Khem, taken from Earth long ago by the victorious Xan to keep humanity from enjoying the light of true knowledge! Once I explained to Philip what we were to achieve, he volunteered most readily for what is to come."

"And what is that?" Anne asked, her voice breaking for the first time. "What would you sacrifice for this knowledge? Our son? Our flesh and blood? All we hold dear?"

St. Germain frowned. "You witless girl. After all we have been through, all we've accomplished together! You, and your Captain Weatherby here, who have seen the face of true evil in the form of Althotas! You know it is but a matter of time before the Martian warlord finds new ways to make his Will felt upon the Known Worlds. The Emerald Tablet is a weapon for humanity and the Xan to use to defeat him fully, once and for all!

"And," he added, his voice softening, "I love Philip as much as you, Anne. Nothing here will harm him. Indeed, he will enjoy a depth of knowledge and wisdom mankind could only dream of. He will be the vessel in which the Tablet's lore is placed!"

Weatherby looked anew at the boy, pale and sweating and grinning with a smile born not of enthusiasm, but of zealotry. The thoughtful boy who walked the decks of *Fortitude*, taking everything in with a glance, process-ing it, seeking its meaning…gone. In his place, a lessened creature, doing his father's bidding without so much as a glance toward the mother upon whom he doted.

"My Lord Count," Weatherby said, "you know full well the dangers of an-cient Martian alchemy. Or have you forgotten the lessons of Cagliostro, who was lured into aiding Althotas while thinking he would usher in a golden age of human knowledge? Does this not sound familiar? And why not select yourself, rather than your son, to be the vessel for this font of wisdom?"

The glare from St. Germain's face would have reduced a lesser man to obsequiousness. "The ritual for unlocking the power of the Tablet requires a knowledge of alchemy only I can approach, with all due respect to my wife," he replied icily. "It also requires a vessel for that knowledge aside from the ritualist. One of the French here might have sufficed, but there remained a question as to strength of Will. There is no such question with Philip, being the son of two alchemists. And I will remind you, Philip volunteered. He drank of the waters of the Pool of Souls, as spelled out in the ancient lore provided to me by these worthy Xan."

The three Xan accompanying St. Germain—all unhooded, their alien countenances in full, mystifying view—made harmonic, excitable noises before continuing with their work. Each of them bore wicked looking swords, fully five feet in length, and some form of firearm of unknown make and efficacy, though the latter was never really in doubt.

On Weatherby's other side, Representative Vellusk shifted in his place and made a mournful sound. He too was bound and captive, and had looked entirely morose since they were taken. "What is he talking about, Representative?" Weatherby whispered as St. Germain returned to his work.

"The Pool of Souls," the Xan whisper-sang. "It is where the souls of the dead are kept, in the depths of the moon you call Enceladus. It grieves me as little else has in life that this man, and worse, these who would call themselves Xan, would violate it."

"There are souls in the very waters of this pool?" Weatherby asked, incredulous.

"All the souls of the Xan since time long forgotten, and of our enemies besides. It had been our hope that those who were violent in the past could one day be redeemed through the time spent with our more peaceable brethren in the Pool of Souls. There, they may together find enlightenment and become one with all Creation."

Weatherby quickly whispered this information to Anne, which sent them both pondering. "If Philip had partaken of these waters, Representative, is it possible that he might carry in him the soul of someone else?" Anne asked.

Weatherby quietly relayed the question to Vellusk. "It is possible," the Xan replied sadly. "The entire moon is covered in ice, with the Pool beneath stretching across the entire surface. But there are billions of souls therein."

"And you said your enemies," Weatherby pressed. "These would include the souls you fought on ancient Mars?"

Something dawned on Vellusk in that moment. "It is possible that your Philip has taken on the soul of a Martian. Or a Xan. Or even more than one of each. I cannot say for certain, but it is possible."

"And the Tablet…" Anne trailed off.

Vellusk leaned over Weatherby, nearly crushing him, as he sought to re-assure Anne. "The souls are inert, my good Countess. They cannot be so easily wakened, even through the Tablet's power. Another piece would be required to empower them without the Xan's consent, and that remains upon Earth, as was our intention when we split them up millennia ago."

And the final piece fell together in Weatherby's head. "This piece, it was hidden in Egypt long ago, was it not?" Weatherby asked.

"Yes," Vellusk sang with a tremulous note.

"The French are in Egypt now. They have invaded. And they are search-ing for something there with a veritable army of alchemists," Weatherby said. "They know of this."

Vellusk was silent under his cowl for several long seconds before replying. "The betrayal of these partisans is even more foul than any had believed," he sang finally, his harmonics taking on notes of sorrow…and anger.

Weatherby turned to Anne and saw she was wide-eyed, tears forming in her eyes. "It is called *The Book of the Dead*. It is the counterpart to the Emerald Tablet. Light and dark, life and death. And I am sure the French have not told Francis of their efforts there, for he would not have let Philip partake of this Pool of Souls otherwise."

"What could happen?" Weatherby asked her.

Anne closed her eyes a moment to compose herself. "If the energies of both are released, those that dwell beyond death could conceivably find new life," she replied. "These items are of Martian origin, not Xan. From what Francis has told me, they were to be the final weapon of the Martians against the Xan. They could…."

She was stopped by a sob which caught in her throat, and turned to look upon her son, who was now taking notes while gazing upon the Emerald

Tablet itself, which now rested upon the large table in the room. It was a bright emerald green—the color of Althotas' skin, if Weatherby's memory served—and seemed to be glowing slightly of its own accord.

"This is Althotas' doing," Weatherby said. "He has everyone in the dark again. The French believe they've found great alchemical power. The Count hopes for the secrets of alchemy. And the Xan…"

Weatherby looked to Vellusk, who replied, "The Xan here, these partisans, believe they will finally have their war, and the means to defeat Althotas at his own game. From there, they may seek to rule over the rest of us—and perhaps the humans of Earth as well."

Before this could sink in, St. Germain began reading aloud from the Tablet itself. Within the room, there seemed to be an impossible, invisible yet wholly palpable shift, as if the very walls suddenly throbbed with power. The alchemist looked up briefly and smiled, then brought Philip over to stand next to him, pointing out something upon the Tablet and whispering to the boy, who nodded excitedly, even as the sweat upon his brow became more pronounced.

"Francis! No!" Anne cried out. "It is a trap! They want you to do this!"

One of the Xan walked over to Anne menacingly and stood over her. He raised his hand, but found it stayed by the count himself, who had to reach high above his head to grasp at the creature's wrist. "No," St. Germain said firmly. "You will not harm her."

The Xan's head-tentacles flared and writhed as the creature's two mouths creased in a pair of awful frowns, but lowered its arm and was satisfied to simply glare at Anne. Weatherby, for his part, began to struggle subtly against his bindings, hoping he might wheedle one of his hands free in time to act.

St. Germain returned to the altar and read another passage, one which Philip echoed and added to, and Vellusk gave a plaintive sound in reply. "It is the language of the ancient Martians," he sang quietly. "We are doomed now."

Weatherby frowned. He would be damned for time eternal if he'd give up so easily. Of course, his options were quite limited.

Then, faintly, he began to hear the faint echoes of shouts from elsewhere in the massive temple complex. The clang of steel. A single, muffled pistol shot. A skirmish.

Weatherby smiled, his hope and faith confirmed. He would never let Elizabeth use Gar'uk as a toy ever again.

"To arms!" he suddenly shouted for all he was worth, in hopes his men were within earshot. "*Fortitude*!" And he leapt awkwardly to his feet and, much to the surprise of the Xan in front of Anne, threw himself into the much larger creature, sending them sprawling to the floor in a mass of limbs and tentacles. It was a poor gambit indeed, but he hoped he would disrupt the ritual altogether, or at least delay it until…something else happened.

The Xan he tackled, of course, was in no mood to allow for delay, grabbing Weatherby by the neck and lifting him bodily off his feet as it stood. "So weak," it sang, with a dread tone and staccato pronunciation. "So terribly weak."

Yet down the hall, the sounds of the fracas increased, and there was another gunshot besides. As Weatherby had hoped, loyal Gar'uk had found the means to effect a rescue, whether the Venusian had alerted *Fortitude* or found the captured men from *Franklin*. He could only hope it would be enough.

The Xan turned to peer down the hall, and Weatherby—spots appearing before his eyes as the creature crushed his throat—curled his legs to him. He lashed out, his boots connecting to the side of the creature's head and one of its mouths.

The Xan gave a loud, atonal squeal that set Weatherby's hair on end, even as it dropped him. The captain tumbled a full eight feet to the ground, but managed to roll and come up upon his knees, where he was able to stand, though not without pain from his landing. He spared a glance toward Anne, who had been shielded by Vellusk's large body. A strange low-pitched sound, like growling and humming simultaneously, emerged from the Xan representative, aimed at the other two aliens in the room, who were now approaching him.

Philip.

Weatherby turned and, his hands still bound, dashed toward the altarpiece. There would be something—anything—there to do, he was sure.

But he was too late.

Philip had begun convulsing, and a blue light began shining from his very eyes, much to the shock of the Count St. Germain, who was shaking the boy's shoulders and shouting his name.

"The French have *The Book of the Dead*!" Weatherby shouted. "They have played you for a fool!"

St. Germain stopped and turned to stare in astonishment at Weatherby, then over toward Anne, who was hidden from his view by the Xan. "Dear God," St. Germain said quietly.

"Stop it," Weatherby insisted, reaching the altar. "Stop this ritual. End it. Do something!"

St. Germain looked around, casting about in his mind for some solution. "How?"

Frowning, Weatherby jumped up to sit upon the altarpiece, then quickly found his feet.

And he kicked the Emerald Tablet off the altar and across the room. If nothing else, he felt it would change the equation.

"No!" St. Germain shouted. "The energies!"

The Emerald Tablet shattered into a million glittering green shards upon the stone floor of the room. And in that moment, Philip screamed.

Weatherby turned to see the young man writhing in pain and clawing at his own face while his mouth gaped open to a nigh-impossible degree. The boy's screams became muffled, as if his very throat was blocked. He began to convulse further.

Then, to Weatherby's horror, a pair of clawed fingers, green and translucent in the dim light, emerged from the boy's mouth and curled around his lips, prying them apart even further. As Philip gurgled and fell to his knees, a face began to emerge—small at first, but growing at a prodigious rate as it squeezed itself out of the boy's body. It had a bald, misshapen head, mere slits for a nose, and a small, lipless mouth that gasped and grinned horribly, showing pointed teeth full of menace.

Weatherby had seen such a creature before. It was an ancient Martian.

Or perhaps the ghost of one, for as the creature continued to pull itself out of Philip's body, Weatherby could see through it to some small degree. A spirit, a shade…one growing quickly as its arms emerged, long and gangly with hands tipped by razor claws. Then the skeletal, emaciated body, and long, muscled legs, which the creature lifted out, one by one, from the gasping boy's unnaturally stretched mouth.

As Philip collapsed to the floor, unconscious, the Martian stood tall… very tall, a full nine feet, rivaling the height of the Xan. Its eyes were black as night, and its skin had a viscous sheen to it, even though its body remained translucent.

"*Two worlds, one soul, soon to be freed,*" the creature intoned, its voice a horrific, buzzing whisper, as if echoed by every soul of every destroyed Martian of old. "*I am Rathemas. And in this world, and the other, I have been reborn. The Pool of Souls will be destroyed. The rise of Mars is at hand.*"

Perhaps, Weatherby thought, his earlier gambit had been especially poor indeed.

June 21, 2134

"*Armstrong*, this is Jain. I'm on approach for docking. Please respond."

The comms continued to be maddeningly silent ever since Shaila piloted her little ship off the surface of Titan. If nothing else, the sensors remained active, which allowed her to track *Armstrong* as well as the Chinese lander…with Stephane aboard.

She also used the time to think. The carvings on the walls down in that room looked nothing like the ones she saw back on Mars. If Weatherby's old journal was correct—and she had seen enough to believe that it was—the other alien race in his dimension were the Saturn-dwelling Xan. It stood to reason, then, that the runes on Titan may have belonged to them. Of course, the potential for another encounter with Weatherby's dimension was one of the reasons *Armstrong* was sent to Saturn in the first place, and Shaila and Stephane were added to the crew.

Stephane…

Shaking her head, she ran through her sensor data from her EVA on Titan. As she feared, the only hits of Cherenkov radiation came when Stephane handled the green slab for the first time. Mars, on the other hand, was overflowing with Cherenkov radiation when the ancient ruins appeared there two years ago. The radiation likely signaled the presence of tachyons, likely the byproduct of the dimensional shenanigans that went down.

No Cherenkov meant no discernible tachyons…which meant either the room down on Titan was firmly in Shaila's dimension, or there was something else at work there. Exactly what was at work, she couldn't say. All she had was a name—Rathemas. It sounded a little too much like Althotas for her tastes.

Shaila's thoughts were interrupted by a blinking light ahead, about thirty degrees to the left of Saturn in her viewscreen. Sensors identified the light as coming from *Armstrong*. A second, dull light right next to it would be *Tienlong*.

Those lights shouldn't be blinking. *Armstrong*'s running lights didn't do that. Unless…

She keyed a series of commands into the computer. A moment later, her hunch was correct. *Armstrong*'s lights were blinking out a signal in good old-fashioned Morse code. *Figures Archie would be old-school enough to think of that.* Shaila quickly had the computer translate, since she had probably missed some of the letters.

JAIN REPLY. Over and over.

She keyed on her running lights and, with the computer's help, sent out a signal: JAIN HERE.

A moment later: CHINESE AT TIENLONG NO WORD FROM MARK COMMS OUT

"Shit," Shaila muttered. That meant Nilssen and Conti were sitting ducks. They'd see Stephane, assume he was a friendly, and probably end up captured or killed. She keyed out a reply: MARK IN TROUBLE WARN HIM USE MORSE.

It took a moment, but *Armstrong* responded: UNDERSTOOD. Then it started blinking again, for *Tienlong*'s benefit: DANGER DANGER. Over and over again. It would have to do.

Shaila overrode the speed governor on the lander and made a bead for *Armstrong*, covering the space in just fifteen minutes. However, it seemed the Chinese lander had done so much earlier—or was just plain faster—for as she approached *Armstrong* for docking, she could see both Chinese landers already attached to *Tienlong*. Shaila momentarily thought about trying to head over to the Chinese ship, but that would require a suited EVA into space, and it wasn't like they'd simply let her in through the airlock if Stephane and his new friend had taken the ship.

The helplessness was almost overpowering.

Shaila hit her reverse thrusters hard and came to a stop neatly under the *Armstrong*'s docking ring. At any other time, she'd be proud of her piloting skills—and concerned about JSC's reaction to that kind of cowboy flying— but right now, she needed to get aboard her ship and find a way to stop whatever the hell was going on.

As soon as the ship hit the docking ring and began the pressurization sequence, Shaila keyed on her internal comm. "Archie, come in."

"I'm here," he replied. "Command center. Get up here."

Shaila bolted out of the pilot's seat and waited impatiently as the ship's mechanisms finished docking. She was out the upper hatch in record time, tossing her helmet and gauntlets aside and hurtling through the length of the ship toward the command center.

She found Archie in there, and he quickly tossed her a visor and comm unit. Once she put it on, she saw he was surrounded by holoimages of ship schematics for both *Tienlong* and *Armstrong*, overlaid atop the view of space around them.

"Where's Stephane and Hall?" he demanded.

Shaila settled into the seat next to him and buckled in. "Hall's dead. Stephane's been compromised. He's working with the Chinese."

Archie looked dumbfounded for several long seconds before he continued on. "Then we got serious problems here. I finally figured out the damn comm issues aboard *Tienlong*, but now we're jammed to hell and back by something else."

"The Chinese dug up some kind of artifact that's jamming all our signals," Shaila replied. "What was the problem on *Tienlong*?"

Archie enlarged the schematic of the Chinese ship, his hands darting through the data with an impressive grace for his age. "Well, I was thinking that all their hard rad shielding was to blame, and that'd be true at longer ranges, but not this close. There's some kind of low-level interference going on in there. If I had to guess, someone jury rigged something on that ship to keep things quiet."

"So they walked into a trap," Shaila said. "Any response from the Morse code?"

"Nothing. I've got cameras and sensors on all their windows and hatches, too. Haven't seen much movement aboard. I—what the fuck is that?"

Shaila looked over to where Archie was pointing, one of the feeds from *Armstrong*'s external cameras, trained on one of *Tienlong*'s airlocks. The door was open...and an astronaut was floating out of it...

...without a helmet.

"Identify," Shaila ordered, her voice tremulous.

The camera zoomed in. It was Nilssen. There was a red mist coming out of a vent in his suit along his abdomen, and up around his head as well. He wasn't moving.

If he wasn't dead, he would be in the next fifteen seconds.

"Good god," Archie breathed.

Shaila sat in stunned silence for a moment. "Any sign of Conti?"

Archie's fingers dashed across the holocontrols. "No."

Their options were growing slimmer, and they still didn't know what they were really facing. But two members of the *Armstrong* crew were dead, including the commander. "Note that Colonel Mark Nilssen is hereby reported dead. As of this timestamp, I've assumed command of JSCS *Armstrong*," she said quietly.

Archie nodded somberly. "Noted," he said hoarsely.

"Fire up the external emitter," she ordered next. "We're going to try to disable *Tienlong*."

"Whoa there," Archie said. "We don't have the capability to do that. It's not like we can independently target the damn thing unless there's an outage in the ship's collision sensor system."

"So unplug the damn sensor!" Shaila growled. "Then we'll manually aim it."

Archie paused a moment, but finally pulled up a series of command codes and prompts. "It'll take a few minutes."

"Work fast. We—"

A new alert stopped Shaila in mid-sentence. Their comms were back online. Just like that.

"What the hell?" Archie growled. "How'd that happen?"

Shaila keyed on the comm. "*Tienlong*, this is *Armstrong*. You are to stand down immediately or we will fire on you. Repeat, stand down immediately and surrender yourselves or we will fire on your ship. Over."

Nothing. It was worth a shot.

"Their dish is turning," Archie reported. "They're cutting off their feed from Earth. Moving it toward…well, hell, I don't know where."

"Track it," Shaila ordered. "Who the hell *else* is out here?"

A new holoimage sprang to life in front of them, tracking the swiveling dish aboard the Chinese ship and the various places it might try to reach. Earth was gone, then the Moon, then Mercury, Jupiter…until the dish finally stopped.

The only world in the solar system in range of *Tienlong*'s communications dish was Enceladus.

Shaila quickly called up all the sensors they had left on Enceladus. All were operating normally. The cameras still showed a pristine white landscape, the underwater probe was still sending back images and data, the survey satellite had a solid orbital view, and the ExEn demolitions unit....

"Who put a demo unit on Enceladus?" Shaila demanded. "That wasn't on the manifest."

Then Shaila remembered. Stephane's experiments.

"*Tienlong* is transmitting," Archie said.

"Jam it!"

"We can't!"

Suddenly, all the surface sensors on Enceladus went blank, along with the underwater probe. But the survey satellite remained online...and what Shaila and Archie saw was nothing short of horrifying.

A massive plume of ice crystals suddenly erupted from the tiger stripes on the southern hemisphere of the moon, stretching out nearly half the diameter of the world itself. It was followed by large chunks of ice being hurtled out into space. The plume grew wider...and wider...until just twenty seconds later, nearly a quarter of Enceladus seemed to be erupting.

Then the entire moon began to slowly, inexorably fall apart. Ice floes spanning dozens of miles broke off from the surface every few seconds in gigantic puffs of snow and ice crystals. Alarms blared through the command center as the survey satellite began to lose orbital integrity—because Enceladus itself was losing integrity. In less than a minute, the moon had broken up into at least two dozen large chunks of rock and ice, surrounded by a haze of snow and ice crystals.

And then a new alert came across the screen. Minute traces of Cherenkov radiation were detected throughout the Enceladus debris field. Millions of them, tiny pinpricks of blue light. Enhanced by *Armstrong*'s computer, they looked like millions of blue flashbulbs going off within the expanding cloud of ice and snow.

Then a blinding flash of white light engulfed the image, and the satellite went dead.

The two sat in the command center, stunned, for at least a minute until Archie finally reached up and trained *Armstrong*'s own telescopes and sensors at Enceladus. All that remained was a slowly dispersing debris field—ice, snow, rock—one that would likely be absorbed into Saturn's rings over the course of the next several decades. "Confirm Enceladus is destroyed," he said quietly, solemnly.

Shaila stared at the images before her. "Confirmed," she replied dully. "Any further Cherenkov readings?"

"Can't get 'em at this range," Archie replied. "We'll have to go there."

Someone else already had that idea in mind, however. Yet another round of alerts and alarms went off—*Tienlong* was firing up its main engines.

"Fuck," Shaila swore. "Where's the emitter?"

Archie went back to work on the reprogramming, his gnarled fingers flying over the holocontrols. "Hang on. I need to…aw, hell. They're leaving."

With a massive burst of engine fire, *Tienlong* quickly sprinted out ahead of *Armstrong*, breaking orbit. The computer confirmed its course; it was headed for the remnants of Enceladus.

Shaila sat bolt upright in her chair once more, her hands deftly moving over the holocontrols. "Setting course for Enceladus. Prepare for main engine burn."

Archie reached out and grabbed her arm. "Can't do it, Shaila."

She turned on him, slapping his hand away. "What do you mean, 'can't do it?'"

"We don't have the fuel," Archie said gently. "We burn now, we won't be able to stop. We'll either burn out of Saturn's orbit or end up circling the planet until we crash into it."

I don't care. That was Shaila's first thought. Frankly, she was willing to plow *Armstrong* right into *Tienlong* if necessary. But *Tienlong* probably had the fuel to avoid *Armstrong*, and as much as she wanted payback, it wouldn't bring back Enceladus. Or Conti.

Or Stephane.

"Set a course to rendezvous with the depot ship," Shaila said finally, slumping back in her chair. "I'll pack all this off to Houston. Soon as we're refueled, set a course for Enceladus."

Shaila unstrapped herself from her seat and floated out of the command center. She wanted to chide herself for not staying with Archie—he was a shipmate, her last shipmate at that, and he was probably just as freaked out as she was—but she couldn't bring herself to be around anyone in that moment.

CHAPTER 21

October 18, 1798

The creature calling itself Rathemas slowly began to take a more solid form, seemingly leaching the very color and essence of the Emerald Tablet from its shards. The Martian looked around dispassionately at the humans in the room, but stopped when it saw St. Germain's Xan conspirators.

"*Bend the knee,*" the creature rasped, "*and you may yet be spared.*"

To Weatherby's great surprise, the three Xan immediately took to one knee before the ephemeral spectre of their ancient enemy. At this, Representative Vellusk let out a plaintive song, a stream of discord and pleading aimed at his fellows. Only one spared him a glance. The others merely made their obedience. Whether this was their plan all the while, or they simply sought to preserve their wretched lives, Weatherby could not say.

Anne rushed to Philip's side, cradling her son's head in her lap where he lay upon the temple floor, tears flowing freely down her face. She looked up at Weatherby and gave a brief nod; the boy remained alive. For how long remained the question.

One man here knew the answer, and Weatherby was quite prepared to drag it from him by any means required.

The captain of the *Fortitude* jumped off the altar next to the Count St. Germain, and in a feat of strength fueled by anger and fear, slipped through the bonds around his hands in order to grab the alchemist's arm and hurl him into the wall behind them. "You, sir, will put an end to this. Now."

Yet the count looked, for once, quite confused. "This was not how it was meant to be," he said quietly. "I know not how this has taken place."

"Egypt," Weatherby replied. "The French have invaded Egypt, and Anne says the counterpart of this tablet may be there. Could that be the cause, then?"

St. Germain's face changed in rapid sequence—confusion, calculation, epiphany…and anger. "The French…I have been played a fool, as have the Xan," he whispered, his voice full of menace.

The count sought to move away, but Weatherby shoved him back against the wall. "Then make this right, damn you! For your son's sake. And her's."

St. Germain shoved Weatherby backward—showing a strength greater than Weatherby's own, despite the count's advanced years—and strode forth before Rathemas. "I have heard your name, creature, spoken of as a curse by the Xan in ages past," St. Germain shouted.

"*And I know yours, son of Earth. My master has whispered it to me in the dark place between places, and with curses that would destroy your mind should you hear them,*" Rathemas responded. "*Yet you have freed me here and now. The time is near, and the worlds move close together. Souls and forms have been brought forth. Bend the knee and be spared.*"

St. Germain just smiled. "I will not. And your time will end before it begins."

At this, the three Xan rose and began advancing toward St. Germain, hearing the menace in his voice. Weatherby moved to interpose himself between them, knowing full well he may only delay, not defeat.

But then a rush of voices came echoing down the corridor, followed quickly by the clamber of men. "*Fortitude!*" came the cry.

And Weatherby smiled. He knew that voice.

Lt. Patrick O'Brian—dressed in the rags of his uniform and looking painfully thin besides—charged into the room, sword drawn, and followed by a handful of the men Weatherby had detailed to the *Franklin* those many weeks past. With them was Gar'uk, darting between their legs, the Venusian's head-frills in full array, his eyes blazing, and a pistol clutched in two small, clawed hands.

"Charge!" Weatherby cried, pointing toward the three Xan, whose alien expressions bore what could only be evidence of surprise.

With a cry, the men of the *Fortitude* surged forward, O'Brian giving his captain a quick grin as he dashed past. But Weatherby had no time to respond, for a French soldier was upon him in an instant, the man's blade slicing through his coat and leaving a thin red line across his chest.

Someone gave the French these orders, Weatherby thought, even as pain lanced across his body. He fell backward, but managed to roll out of the way in time to avoid the soldier's thrust. Weatherby saw his opening, and although it was not a sporting move in the least, he felt the situation warranted it. His boot connected squarely between the man's legs, sending him backward, howling, his sword dropped as his hands moved to protect himself.

Weatherby grabbed the sword and brought himself painfully to his feet to face his adversary, but the man was in no condition to continue; a blow to the head with the sword's pommel was enough to bring about relief from pain and consciousness.

Meanwhile, St. Germain had quickly produced several vials from his waistcoat, and was crouched over the shards of the Emerald Tablet. He poured the contents of the vials over the relic's remains, chanting in Latin all the while. One of the Xan attempted to rush him, but was tripped by Gar'uk and fell face-first onto the stone floor. The Venusian dashed forward, placed his pistol at the Xan's head, and deftly pulled the trigger.

St. Germain's voice grew louder, even as the shards of the tablet began to give off a strange, bluish mist. The alchemist's voice caused Rathemas' head to snap around suddenly, and the Martian's face contorted in hideous anger as his body began to become *more* translucent. Rathemas started to tremble, and arched its back as if in intense pain.

But apparently, the Martian had one final gambit to play.

With a final, terrible cry that would haunt Weatherby's memory for years to come, the creature surged forward toward St. Germain...and into his open mouth, cutting off the alchemist's chant and reducing it to a sickening gurgle.

"Dear God," Weatherby whispered.

St. Germain's eyes grew wide as his body started to convulse and shake. He looked about, his hands flailing, a man at war with his body and mind.

And then it hit Weatherby. Rathemas had been in residence inside Philip. If he were to instead reside in St. Germain, the most powerful alchemist in the Known Worlds....

Weatherby gripped his sword firmly and advanced on the count. As he raised it to strike, he looked into the count's eyes, hoping he was wrong, that somehow the count could overcome this, as he had so many other enemies.

And for a brief moment, those eyes focused, even as his body continued to shake uncontrollably. "Do it," St. Germain said as he choked on his very words, his voice barely recognizable.

Weatherby raised his sword to strike—and a shot rang out across the room.

The Count St. Germain fell to the ground, a round in the side of his head.

Weatherby turned to see Anne, tear-streaked but determined, holding a smoking pistol.

Then a hand grabbed Weatherby's boot.

Looking down, he saw St. Germain, half his skull crushed by the shot, nonetheless grabbing his ankle and slowly, clumsily rising to his feet.

Horrified, Weatherby reacted as only a man with twenty years of service to King and country could. He brought his blade down swiftly, cleaving St. Germain's head from his body.

The grip upon Weatherby's ankle slackened.

St. Germain's headless corpse collapsed to the floor once more, and did not move again. Yet, out of the corner of Weatherby's eye, he believed he saw a curious flash of blue light briefly emanate from the count's severed head. But when he turned toward it, it was gone.

Weatherby moved to help his crew—but they had managed the situation quite well on their own. Two Xan lay dead upon the floor, and a third had surrendered. Representative Vellusk was unharmed, and the two marines that had accompanied them from *Fortitude* had vouched for the Xan official with their fellows, along with Gar'uk, who bravely placed himself in front of Vellusk to protect him.

Philip, however, remained unconscious. Weatherby quickly moved to Anne's side, as she had gone back to tending to him.

"How is he?" Weatherby asked gently.

Anne was trembling slightly, the events of the past few minutes catching up to her. Still, she was handling it better than some officers Weatherby had seen after battle. "There's no telling what his body has gone through, or what the effects may be. But he is alive.

"And for that, sir," she added, "I am forever in your debt."

Weatherby smiled slightly, which she managed to return. "Let there be no debt between us, my lady," he said quietly. He then rose to his feet and addressed his men. "Well fought, all of you! Gather all the breathing masks you can find, and stretchers for the wounded."

As the men quickly set to their tasks, Weatherby went over and gave O'Brian a hearty hug, which prompted a muffled cry from his friend and lieutenant. "Sir, please. I'm in no state!"

Weatherby quickly disengaged, especially after feeling just how thin O'Brian felt in his arms. "Quite sorry, Lieutenant. Your timing was excellent."

O'Brian looked over at Gar'uk. "You've the best damned valet in the service, sir. Makes me think we've done a disservice to his kind over the years."

"I always thought so," Weatherby said. "How did it happen?"

"The *Franklin's* officers posed as mere seamen, sir," he said, bowing his head. "We didn't know. Their scheme cost us nearly our entire prize crew."

"'Tis not your fault, Paddy," Weatherby said gently. "I was distracted by Nelson's politicking. I should've been there." He clasped O'Brian's shoulder. "You did well here. I thank you. Do you know where *Franklin* is now?"

O'Brian shook his head. "She put our party to shore and sailed off. There were other Xan aboard. Their captain met with them often, with and without St. Germain. I fear there may yet be more to this."

Weatherby nodded grimly. "When you're well, you must tell us everything. For now, let's get back to our ship."

June 21, 2134

By instinct, Diaz trained her weapon at the tendrils of blue light sneaking into the lab from the containment chamber, even though her rational mind knew it wasn't really likely she could destroy a series of miniscule wormholes with bullets.

But she had nothing else to do, except look over at Greene and Ayim as they furiously worked to find a solution. "Guys, we need to do something *now*."

The two scientists swapped glowing holodata at a rapid clip, muttering to each other as they went. From their tone and voices, nothing seemed to be going all that well. "Working on it," Greene said absently. "It's that damn thing under the altar. It's acting like a battery. We need to remove it."

Diaz turned to Harry, whose smug anger had been replaced with genuine concern. "Harry, you said you could blow this thing, right?"

He nodded dully. "Thirty-second timer. The whole containment chamber gets vaporized. I—what the fuck is *that*?"

Harry pointed to the containment frame; when Diaz turned, she saw an arm.

And not just any arm. For one, it wore a blue coat with braiding on it…just like an old-time soldier or sailor might wear. And the hand was shriveled, skin tight against bone.

And yet it moved. It was clawing.

"Holy shit. Harry, blow it up. Everybody, time to go," Diaz barked.

Greene and Ayim quickly moved to gather datapads and printouts, while Harry called up a holoscreen and began punching in the authorization codes.

Suddenly, Greene screamed.

Diaz turned to see her traitorous colleague with a look of sheer terror on his face—and a tendril of light buried in his chest.

"Thirty seconds to detonation," an all-too-pleasant female voice intoned from the lab's speakers.

Huntington grabbed Greene by the shoulders, pulling him away from the miniscule wormhole. The string of blue light went with him, stretching further into the room. The physicist began to shake violently, spit coming out of the sides of his mouth, his eyes rolling into the back of his head.

The young officer looked up at Diaz, who eyed the chamber warily. The arm was joined by two more, and she swore she could see a shriveled, desiccated face, its teeth bared, peering through the frame.

"Twenty seconds," the computer said.

"Leave him! Move!" Diaz ordered. "Out! Now!"

Harry needed no further encouragement. He dashed out of the room, Ayim and Coogan on his heels, followed by Diaz.

"Fifteen seconds."

Diaz turned at the door to see Huntington lifting Greene's twitching body onto her shoulder in a fireman's carry. "Captain, I said leave him!"

"Go!" Huntington said. "I—"

Then she too began to twitch.

Greene's body tumbled to the floor as a blue light began to emanate from the marine's chest.

"Ten seconds."

Diaz started to sprint back into the room, but Coogan grabbed her arm and pulled in the opposite direction. "No time, ma'am!"

Huntington looked down at her chest, then looked up, eyes wide…and then began shaking violently.

"Five seconds."

Coogan pulled harder. "General! Come on!"

Reluctantly, Diaz turned and followed Coogan as he ran down a corridor.

Behind her, the doorway erupted with white light, and the ground shook. Dust and pebbles rained down on them.

They kept running.

A huge piece of stone fell a half-meter behind Diaz as she followed the rest down a maze of corridors. Ayim hustled past a number of doors, finally choosing one—a stairwell. They climbed as fast as they could, with Diaz taking Ayim's arm as he began to tire.

Below, fire entered the stairwell and began to move upward.

"Move it!" Diaz yelled.

Another doorway beckoned, one of the reinforced steel ones the Total-Suez people brought in. Diaz wrenched open the door and shoved Ayim inside, followed by Coogan. She dove inside and slammed it shut just as the flames reached her feet.

They were in a large room, dimly illuminated by battery-powered emergency lights. A bright red exit sign hung over another door at the other end of the chamber. In between, inert holodisplays and a variety of artifacts under glass were scattered across the room.

The Siwa museum.

Diaz breathed a sigh of relief and slumped against the wall. Then she felt someone slapping her leg.

"What the hell?" she groaned.

Coogan was busy putting out a small lick of flame on the cuff of her pants. "Sorry, ma'am," he said with a tired, sad smirk. Then he looked around. "Where's your friend Harry?"

Diaz bolted upright, her gun at the ready. Harry Yu was nowhere to be found.

"I swear to God, I'm gonna kill that fucker," she spat.

October 18, 1798

Finch struggled to think clearly as the mass of revenants—for truly, there was no better name—shuffled toward him and Dolomieu. He thought to brandish *The Book of the Dead* before him as a talisman, but managed to dismiss the idea as something that might actually encourage them to move faster.

Then the glowing blue portal before the altar became bathed in white light—and gouts of fire shot out of both sides of it.

A moment later, there were no fewer than five flaming revenants staggering about the chamber, bumping into their fellows and setting them ablaze as well. And those first few unfortunates were slowly disintegrating within the flames.

"A torch!" Dolomieu cried out. "We must have torches if we're to save Berthollet!"

The two alchemists raced into the corridor, grabbing torches from the sconces upon the walls, then rushed forward again, brandishing the flames in front of them. They burst back into the room…

…and found their way blocked. There were still a dozen revenants there, their skin shriveled onto their bones, teeth bared in fell parodies of smiles, eye sockets empty and oozing.

Cradling the book against his chest, Finch immediately shoved a torch into the face of one of them, but had to dodge the grasping hands of several others. He had hoped to cut a path toward the altar in order to reach Berthollet—or if not the man, his notes, for he bore little love for the Frenchman at the moment—but was soon cut off, his back against the wall with Dolomieu at his side, both men swinging their torches in wide arcs in order to keep the dead at bay.

Yet the torches would not last forever…and the dead were already dead. They had nowhere else to go.

Dolomieu was swinging his torch even more wildly, and left himself open to attack. One of the revenants lurched forward and grabbed for his throat, prompting him to cry out and drop his torch. As Finch watched in horror, Dolomieu was carried off by several of the unliving creatures, his screams echoing in the chamber. Finch shouted after him, but to no avail.

Then the sound of musket fire erupted into the room.

Being taller than most, Finch looked past the swarm of grasping hands and sickening faces before him to see Sheikh Karim charging into the chamber with a small number of fierce desert warriors, guns and blades drawn. And right there with them was Jabir.

The Bedouins surged forth as the revenants turned to meet these new foes. Muskets did little to harm them, but the scimitars were quite efficient, especially when aimed for the neck.

Finch pressed the advantage, setting fire to two other revenants then dashing off toward where he last saw Dolomieu. And Finch found him indeed…first his arm, then his chest, a leg, and finally his severed head, the man's face frozen in terror. Finch cried out at the sight, but there was nothing to be done…and still much else to do.

Karim's warriors seemed to have the advantage, leaving Finch surprisingly hale and uninterrupted. He rushed toward the altar, but could find no trace of Berthollet…or the man's notes. Finch quickly looked around the room, but the French alchemist was nowhere to be found.

Finch was shocked, at first, at the man's callousness in escaping such a horrific scene…then reminded himself that Berthollet had very well caused it in the first place. And with his notes still in his possession….

Berthollet had the translation in hand, and Finch possessed the one thing that might tip the scales back into balance—*The Book of the Dead* itself.

Looking about on the floor, Finch spied a rucksack that had been tossed aside by one of the Frenchmen. He quickly grabbed it and stuffed *The Book of the Dead* inside, closing it tightly before slinging it upon his back and making his way to the back of the chamber, where the last of the revenants had fallen to the Bedouin blades.

"*Murshid*, you are harmed," Jabir said, running toward him with his eyes on Finch's arm, which he had cradled toward his chest.

"It's nothing," he replied with a smile. "You're late."

"They took convincing," the young man replied.

Sheikh Karim stepped forward and bowed deeply. "And for that, I must ask your forgiveness, *murshid*. We did not believe this boy's tales at first, even with the note written in your own hand, but now we see the evil that these Franks committed."

"And they may yet commit more. Berthollet has escaped," Finch replied.

Karim turned toward his men and launched into a stream of rapid Arabic. They immediately rushed from the temple, swords at the ready. "He will not go far, *murshid*. And we will have words with him before he is sent before Allah to answer for his crimes."

"If you please, do not to kill him before I've had a chance to talk with him," Finch said. "There is much that happened here that needs clarification."

Karim nodded and bowed once more, then turned to follow his men, leaving Finch and Jabir alone in the temple. The boy was looking at the corpses upon the floor, worry writ upon his brow. "What happened here, *murshid*?"

"I cannot say for certain," Finch said tiredly. "The ritual should have called forth souls, not caused dead bodies to rise.

"And I think," he added, thinking of the tendrils of light snuffed out by fire, "our allies upon the other side kept those souls from arriving on cue."

"But where would these souls have come from?" Jabir asked.

"I'll wager Berthollet knows."

CHAPTER 22

June 22, 2134

The Total-Suez lab underneath the ruins of the Siwa temple was a perfect wreck, but that didn't stop the mass of investigators and technicians Diaz had called in from doing their level best to piece together what happened.

It wasn't looking good.

The energies released from Harry's collider experiment caused the ceiling above to cave in over much of the room, destroying billions of terras of computer equipment, not to mention key pieces of the particle collider. Nearly everything in the entire room carried scorch marks, and the thick walls of the containment chamber were *melted*—along with the first two rows of workstations and a fair number of computers.

The loss of the collider she could live with—Diaz was already considering how to draft legislation to limit this kind of experiment—but the computers housed reams of data, much of which might be lost. The computer geeks seemed to think that the backup drives might be salvageable, but the optical-quantum storage drives were fragile to begin with.

Worse, there were no signs whatsoever of Huntington and Greene. Literally none—not even trace amounts of DNA could be found, though it would take weeks to be sure. It was possible they may have been completely vaporized, but they were already a fair distance from the containment area when it blew.

Yet as the techs carefully worked around her, she was far more concerned about the reports from *Armstrong*. Two dead, one captured, and one…to be determined.

Diaz had seen a fair amount of Stephane Durand after the incident on Mars. They'd traveled back to Earth together, been quarantined and debriefed together (and separately), and both he and Shaila had helped with the initial launch of Project DAEDALUS before reporting for training for the Saturn mission. Straight up, he was a good guy. The whole *Daedalus* incident had given him much-needed focus, and Shaila had kept him grounded. Optimistic, dedicated, a team player.

Shaila had sent along an eyes-only addendum to Diaz, apart from her official report. She believed Stephane had somehow ingested a proto-protein from the water on Enceladus that somehow possessed him. Even Shaila sounded unsure when offering up her opinion, but the millions of Cherenkov hits from the moon's destruction seemed to back that up, as did the miniscule wormholes they had encountered in this very lab.

And then there was the artifact they found on Titan. Diaz couldn't help but wonder whether the green tablet found on Titan may have been linked to whatever it was under the altar that had overloaded the power on the collider within the Siwa temple. And in a bit of this-ain't-coincidence, Coogan discovered that two of the Chinese astronauts assigned to *Tienlong*—their identities confirmed by a chagrined and suddenly cooperative Chinese government— had been part of a tour group that visited Siwa more than nine months ago, likely the same tour group that drew Total-Suez there in the first place.

Finally, there was little doubt in Diaz' mind that Harry's researchers—with Greene's help, damn him— managed to open the door to the other side of the fence, the other dimension where Weatherby and Finch came from. She still wasn't sure whether she truly saw Finch there, but on a whim, she had done a Web search of late 18th century military uniforms. One of the arms she saw trying to claw its way out of the containment frame wore the coat of a French infantry officer circa 1795.

Dr. Ayim—who quickly agreed to assist the DAEDALUS team in exchange for immunity from any charges stemming from the experiment— believed that if there were a pair of artifacts interacting with each other across millions of miles of space on this side of the fence, chances are there was a mirror situation going down on the other side. Preliminary comparisons of the power spikes from the *Daedalus* incident seemed to bear that out—the additional power that overloaded Harry's experiment had to come from somewhere, after all.

Sadly, there was nothing left of the altarpiece in the temple now. Indeed, the DAEDALUS team had their work cut out for them just getting to it, because not only was the ceiling collapsed, but the floor as well. There were no traces of Cherenkov radiation for miles around Siwa. If the computers melted, chances are whatever was under that altar was destroyed.

Diaz walked over to where Ayim and Coogan were reviewing some of the salvaged data from the experiment. "Anything?" she asked.

Coogan shrugged. "Bits and pieces, ma'am. It's going to take weeks before we have a full picture of what we have and don't have." He paused and looked up. "I'm sorry about Maggie, ma'am. I know you were close. And-Greene too, for that matter."

Diaz stared down at her boots. "Me, too. But I can't help but wonder if Evan had a point after all," she said. "I mean, what he did was stupid." At this she looked pointedly at Ayim, who looked extremely uncomfortable. "But that said, I don't think we can afford to just focus on defense anymore. There are guys on the other side screwing around with this stuff—human beings, just like us, probably trying to figure shit out. Maybe this blew up in their face, or maybe they planned it. Maybe that fucking Martian was involved. I don't know. But we need to find out."

"How?" Coogan asked.

Diaz took a deep breath. "We need to find a way to communicate with them. With the guys on the other side."

Ayim actually took a step backward. "You're serious, General?"

"'Fraid so. It's already been proven once that whatever's out there can influence both dimensions. Maybe they did it again yesterday. If we're going to figure this out, we need intel from the other side. And they might need us, too. Soon as you're done with the post-mortem here, that's your next priority. We need to find a way to talk with our opposite numbers on the other side. So long as you're willing to play ball, Dr. Ayim."

The African physicist nodded gravely. "I have seen things here, General, that I cannot begin to explain. Dr. Greene and Mr. Yu did not tell me everything, otherwise I might not have agreed to participate. But now..." He paused, gathering himself. "I will help you, if you'll have me."

"What are you going to need?" Diaz asked.

Ayim looked unfocused, lost in his head a moment. "It's going to require a lot," he said finally. "At least a couple different colliders, better containment, some energy buffering...." His voice trailed off as he began tapping on his datapad.

Diaz couldn't help but smile slightly. "Just send me a shopping list."

She turned and headed out of the ruined chamber, leaving the experts to their job. The thing was, Diaz hadn't told Gerlich about this plan yet.

She wondered if she really needed to. He'd probably just say no.

October 20, 1798

The men of HMS *Fortitude* stood at attention upon the deck, staring up at Captain Thomas Weatherby. Beside him to his right were Lt. O'Brien, looking far better than he did prior thanks to a clean uniform and proper meals, as well as Lt. Barnes, Dr. Hawkins and the rest of the officers behind them. To his left was the Countess St. Germain, her head bowed, and Lord Morrow. In front of him was Gar'uk, ready to assist his captain with the grim task at hand.

And before them, resting on mess tables on the main deck, were the shrouded remains of four of Weatherby's men, draped with England's flag. And there was a fifth as well—the finest alchemist in the history of mankind, the Count St. Germain. Normally, an ensign would be laid over his body as well, but Weatherby knew St. Germain bore no national allegiances—or any allegiances, really.

This was, undoubtedly, the worst duty a captain had aboard ship. And this time, it was one of the most conflicting, for Weatherby's emotions ran a gamut he had hitherto never experienced. The customary sadness and guilt for the loss of his men—those who had died while captive on Titan, as well as those who had fallen in the final melee—was joined by anger, disappointment and dismay over St. Germain's actions.

But he had a duty nonetheless, despite the weariness in his soul and the lingering ache of the wound across his chest. "We therefore commit their bodies to the deep, to be turned into corruption," Weatherby said by heart, not bothering to read from the open book in his hands, "looking for the resurrection of the body, when the Sea and Void shall give up their dead, and the life of all the worlds to come, through our Lord Jesus Christ; who at his coming shall change our vile body, that it may be like His glorious body, according to the mighty working, whereby He is able to subdue all things to Himself."

Weatherby nodded, and groups of four men below picked up the tables and took them to the starboard-side rail, tipping them so that the bodies, weighted with iron shot, slid into the thick, viscous depths of Titan's sea. Only the flags remained.

"In the sure and certain hope of resurrection to eternal life through our Lord Jesus Christ, we commend to Almighty God the souls of our fallen comrades—seaman Thomas Wells, able seaman George Finn, carpenter's mate John Mason, fifth Lieutenant James Floyd Kellogg, and Francis, the Count St. Germain—and we commit their bodies to the depths," Weatherby said. "The Lord bless them and keep them. The Lord make His face to shine upon them and be gracious unto them. The Lord lift up His countenance upon them, and give them peace. Amen."

Weatherby closed the book and led the crew in the recitation of the Lord's Prayer, then nodded toward O'Brian, who gave the order: "Company dismissed."

"Thank you, Mr. O'Brian," Weatherby said with a small, sad smile. "'Tis a good thing to have you back once more. Though I will say," he added, with more volume to his voice, "that Mr. Barnes did a fine job in your stead." As Weatherby had hoped, Barnes smiled broadly at this as he took his station as officer of the watch. "Mr. Barnes, we sail north. Once we are within the aurorae, rig for Void and proceed outward on course for Mimas."

Weatherby turned to look for Anne, but she had already retreated into the great cabin, which Weatherby had readily given up for the use of her and her son, who remained unconscious after his travails.

"You've done well," Morrow said. "Again. You're becoming far too useful, I think. Be careful or they'll make an admiral of you, and all use will be lost."

"Thank you, my lord, but I shall be content to remain captain a while longer, I think," Weatherby replied. "Though I wish we'd be able to find the *Franklin*. From what O'Brian has told me, they remain at large, and in contact with the Xan partisans. He was unable to identify the leader of the French expedition, but I shall do my utmost to find this out, and which parties were behind the venture in the first place. The thought of the French allying themselves with even a small faction of Xan could spell doom for Europe. Perhaps all of Earth. And I worry that they were not, in fact, acting solely on behalf of France. What if other parties were involved?"

"I share your concerns, but more importantly, so do the Xan," Morrow said. "Without the count's alchemy to cloak their movements, the Xan will no doubt find them, and God help them when they do. And I hope the identity of those behind this madness will be made plain soon after."

Weatherby nodded. "Speaking of the Xan, I'm surprised you did not return to Saturn with Vellusk when he departed aboard the Ovoid that arrived yesterday."

Morrow shrugged slightly. "Vellusk needs time. There are factions to be dealt with. This crisis was averted only in part. There remain rifts in the Xan society that may yet be beyond repair. I will go in due course, when Vellusk feels it appropriate. But I will say that the crimes of the Xan partisans here have given him some leverage against those who would take a more active role in our affairs."

"Yes, but there will always be those who will take that role, I think," Weatherby said. "They came quite close. So long as the partisans remain at large, and in contact with the French, I cannot help but doubt the future."

Morrow actually smiled at this. "Then I thank God you remain in the service. If anyone can defeat an alliance of French and Xan, I dare say it's you, Tom."

Weatherby looked at the decking, embarrassed. "You're too kind, my lord."

Morrow reached out to clap Weatherby on the arm. "Call me James." And with that, Morrow took his leave to walk the decks, as was his wont. For his part, flush with embarrassment and pride, Weatherby retreated toward his cabin to check upon Anne and Philip. He found them much as they had been since returning to *Fortitude*—Philip unconscious in Weatherby's own hammock, and Anne in a chair by his side, reading to him.

Weatherby spied the title of the book. "You're reading him the Royal Navy alchemical manual?" he asked, with but a touch of incredulity.

She smiled slightly at the copy of the *Royal Navy Handbook of Alchemical Praxes and Policies* in her hands. "Hawkins had given him a copy to read when we first came aboard on Venus. He'll get it back with some additional commentary, it seems." Anne held up the book to show Weatherby numerous annotations in the margins, made in the boy's careful hand.

"Questions?"

"Improvements," Anne said, maternal pride in ample evidence.

Weatherby took a chair upon the other side of the cot and looked down at the boy. "How fares he?"

To his great surprise, the boy opened his eyes slightly and spoke—weakly, but clearly nonetheless. "He fares well enough, sir."

Weatherby started. "When the hell did *you* wake up?" he asked, surprised enough to fall into the coarse language of the sailor.

"A few hours ago," Anne said. "You were busy with the funeral preparations. Thank you for that, by the way. You did not have to include Francis among your crew."

"He was your husband," Weatherby said.

"Yes, he was, though in the end…I doubt there would've been much to keep us together had he survived."

Surprised at Anne's frank assertion, Weatherby looked down at Philip, who seemed weak but otherwise sound. Gone were the signs of bodily stress seen within the ancient Xan temple, though the boy's eyes showed signs of many questions. Philip no doubt knew of his father's actions, and of what had possessed him. It would take him years to come to terms with all that transpired. It seemed, though, he was in agreement with his mother's assessment.

"The Count St. Germain was my shipmate, many years ago, and he was a fine one indeed," Weatherby said finally, addressing the boy. "To my mind, that counts for a great deal. Yes, he was made a dupe by the French, but he sought to correct his folly in the end." He then turned to Anne, looking into her eyes. "We should all be so fortunate as to have that opportunity to make amends for our errors."

Anne closed the book and favored him with a genuine, heartfelt smile. "You know, we seem to have horrible timing, you and I."

Weatherby shrugged as he stood to make his leave, tousling Philip's hair as he did so. "Perhaps. But I dare say nineteen years is far too long between encounters."

"Will you walk with me on deck, sir?" she said, rising as well. "I wish to see Titan once more before we leave."

Weatherby offered his arm and escorted Anne above decks, where they took a slow circuit around the maindeck. The men saluted smartly when their captain passed, and made a point not to look overmuch afterward. Privacy was a rare thing aboard any ship of the line, and Weatherby felt thankful for his crew's small gift.

"You know, Tom," Anne said quietly. "Francis and I...ours was not a romantic love. Perhaps at first, but long ago and not for long. He was brilliant, and I loved his brilliance. But to say he was a doting husband would not be true."

Weatherby nodded gravely. "There are many kinds of marriages, my lady. I had thought to marry for love. I actually thought I did, but..." His voice trailed off. "I remain saddened my wife was taken from me. In the end, though, I think it suited us both that I was in the service. We were very different. I know now her heart may have been elsewhere while I was away."

Anne let this sink in a moment. "I am sorry, Tom."

At this, Weatherby actually smiled slightly. "I have Elizabeth, thanks be to God. And she is the most beautiful child. I tell you, her mind is always ablaze. So many questions! And if I do not return from sea with a chest full of books for her, I dare say I would be sent back to ship post-haste." He stopped and turned to Anne. "I do hope you get to meet her someday. So long as we can manage to meet again before she's married off!"

"I wouldn't worry so much about that, Captain Weatherby," Anne said. "I dare say you may find it difficult to be rid of me."

Weatherby's heart jumped in his chest. "I should find that a most welcome predicament."

June 23, 2134

Shaila stowed the last of the cargo containers from the depot ship, thinking about the time, less than a week ago, when she was excited about laying in supplies for the voyage home. JSC thoughtfully included all-new meal items for the voyage back to Earth, the idea being it would help break up the monotony.

Shaila desperately wished for monotony now. She'd happily take the longest, most boring flight ever in exchange for reversing the events of the past several days.

But it wasn't going to happen. And she kicked herself for the umpteenth time for wishing it otherwise. Wishes wouldn't make it right.

"Archie, this is Jain. Supplies are stowed. How's refueling?" she asked over the comm.

It took a moment for the crusty old engineer to reply. "We're tanked up.

Think you better come take a look at something, though. Common room."

Shaila pulled herself out of the cargo bay, trying hard not to look at the corner where she and Stephane had their first zero-g experience together. She instead focused on her destination, but even floating through the ship now was off-putting. There was just more bustle, more sounds, with five other people moving around. There were more e-mails and alerts, more voices and movement. Now, it was dead silent. It felt haunted.

Shaila pulled herself into one of the access tubes and crawled down the ladder into gravity once more. In the common room, she found Archie sitting at the conference table, leaning back and looking very, very tired.

"What you got?" she asked, sliding into the chair next to him.

He tapped a few commands on the table; the lights dimmed and the holoprojector sprang to life. "JSC retasked one of the Saturn survey sats to keep an eye on Enceladus since we lost the dedicated sat in the explosion," he said. "They caught this."

An image of *Tienlong* started moving in the air above the table. It approached the debris cloud that was once Enceladus. It had its cargo hatch open.

It then disappeared in the dense cloud of ice crystals.

"What the hell?" Shaila said.

"JSC broke down the image. They had all their hatches open. All the goddamn doors and windows. And they let all that ice into their ship," Archie said.

"The Cherenkov readings," Shaila mused. "Not just ice. Something else."

"Maybe those proteins. Maybe something even weirder."

Shaila leaned back in her chair and rubbed her hands down her face. "Where are they now?"

"JSC says they just went through that cloud, came out the other side, and fired up their main engines on a course toward the inner solar system. Tough to get resolution at this distance, but best guess is Earth."

"It's a plague ship," Shaila said quietly.

"Maybe so," Archie said. "Meantime, we got a long-ass vidmail from your old boss, Diaz, in the latest data packet. She sent it to me, too. I guess I'm in the loop."

Shaila's ears pricked up. "What'd she say?"

"Long story short, they had something go down back on Earth that they think is related. And that maybe your friends from the other side had something go down, too. Honestly, didn't make sense, but I figure you got plenty of time to explain it to me on the way home. We've been ordered back ASAP."

"Our launch window isn't for another month," Shaila protested.

"Yeah, well, *Tienlong* didn't seem to mind. JSC wants us right behind 'em. The way Titan's positioned, we may even catch up by the time they reach Earth."

"And then what?"

Archie shrugged. "Hell if I know. But I'm gonna rig the damn emitter to make it the best goddamn weapon I can."

Shaila nodded. "You got the burn OK?"

"Course is laid in, fuel's good and the depot ship is at safe distance." Archie held up his datapad. "I could punch it now if you want."

"Punch it," she said. "Let's get the fuck out of here."

With a single finger-tap, Archie gave the order. It would take another ten minutes for the ship's ring to stop its rotation, then another few minutes for the reactor to come online for the burn. But within the next half-hour, they'd be slingshotting around Saturn once more, on their way back to Earth.

Shaila gave Archie a pat on the shoulder and climbed up the access tube, heading for the command center so she could take the stick and monitor the burn. She settled into the pilot's seat and put her visor and gloves on. Her vision gave way to a field of stars, with Saturn looming off to her right, the rings stretching out before her. It was a glorious sight, and at the moment, it just made her feel numb.

An alert popped up on the starfield in front of her: INCOMING TRANSMISSION.

"Real time?" she asked, incredulous.

CONFIRMED.

Her heart started to beat faster in her chest. "Accept transmission."

A holographic image superimposed itself onto the space in front of her. It was Stephane.

He looked even more horrible now—pale, sallow, sweaty, with nearly black circles under his bloodshot eyes. "Stephane," she whispered.

"No," he said, emotionless.

Shaila blinked. "What do you mean, no?"

For a moment, it looked like he struggled to say something. The composure faltered. There was something in his eyes. Then it was gone. "I am not Stephane. I am Rathemas."

"Whoever you are, you've taken unauthorized control of *Tienlong*," she snapped. "I order you to immediately surrender yourselves and your ship upon your return to Earth."

"No."

It was worth a shot. "Where's Conti?"

Stephane looked confused a moment, then seemed to remember something. "The woman. Yes. She is with us now. One of us."

Shaila shifted in her seat. "Right. What are your intentions?"

Stephane answered immediately this time. "Liberation."

"What?"

Stephane shook his head. "It doesn't matter. Right now, he will not let me be until I deliver a message."

Shaila shook her head as if to clear it. "Who? Whose message?"

"This one. The one I hold now."

He's in there. He's still in there! "And what message is that?" she replied, her voice breaking just slightly.

"He…loves you."

The transmission went dead.

She sat stock still for several moments before taking the transmission recording and sending it off to JSC.

Only then did she break down, allowing herself the body-wracking sobs that had built up since seeing his face.

November 12, 1798

Captain Samuel Hood, commander of HMS *Zealous*, looked at his visitor askance and with a great deal of bemused disbelief. Of all the strange and seemingly inane things he had to contend with since becoming commodore of the fleet keeping station at the mouth of Aboukir Bay, this was likely the strangest. Though not inane in the slightest.

"Admiral Nelson did mention you and your…investigations…in his orders to me," Hood said. "But the tale you weave here is, well, it beggars the imagination."

Dr. Andrew Finch, seated on the other side of Hood's table in his cabin, and still covered with the dust of the desert, simply shrugged and pointed to the papers he had laid before the captain. "My notes on *The Book of the Dead* are here, sir, and your own alchemist can attest to their veracity if he's indeed worth his Salt. And the stone from Rosetta with the translation is with me as well."

"And what happened, then, to this book after the incident with *Monsieur* Berthollet?" Hood asked. "For if it does as you say, it would be a dire threat to England, would it not?"

Finch straightened his robes and looked the man in the eye. "The book is no longer a threat, sir. I saw to it myself. Unfortunately, Berthollet evaded capture at the oasis. It's quite possible he died in the desert. Sheikh Karim and his tribe swore oaths to Allah that they would tell me should they chance upon his remains."

Hood clucked his tongue and leaned back in his chair. "These people swear oaths to their God every time they say hello," the captain said. "But… Nelson spoke quite highly of you. And your former commander, Thomas Weatherby, also recommended you to me. In fact, he sent word from Saturn that we should keep a watch for you."

"Saturn?"

"Yes indeed. Captain Weatherby chased a French renegade all the way to Saturn, and uncovered some sort of plot involving the Xan and some alchemical nonsense I'm sure I don't understand," Hood said, reaching into a small chest upon his desk and withdrawing a paper. "His dispatch is here. It's rather lengthy, and he specifically requested you read it."

Finch practically snatched the paper from Hood's hand, and scanned the contents with prodigious speed. "My God…that's incredible."

"So I'm not the only one, then. I thought it quite queer indeed."

"No, sir, not queer at all," Finch said, trying to hide his impatience. "I find this clarifies more than a few questions I've struggled with of late." The alchemist stood. "With your permission, sir, I believe it imperative that I return to England at the earliest possible convenience."

Hood frowned. "Dr. Finch, I cannot spare a ship solely to ferry you home after your hardship in the desert. You're not even in the service anymore."

"That, at least, will change," Finch said. "I feel it time I should take up my commission once more."

At this, the captain actually laughed. "An officer cannot simply resume his commission solely by declaring it. You make it sound as if you're simply changing your waistcoat!"

Finch's last shred of patience finally gave way. "Captain Hood, I require a ship to take me to England. Once there, I will immediately convene both the Naval Board of Alchemy and the Royal Society—and yes, I *can* do that, and they *will* listen. And if I have to explain to Nelson why you failed to help me, or even allow me to return to service simply because of the manner in which I did it, I'm very sure the admiral will make his displeasure known."

Without waiting for a response, Finch rose from his seat and stormed out of Hood's cabin, striding across the main deck and into the alchemist's lab in the fo'c'sle, where his effects were taken when he boarded. Finch had dispatched Jabir to Cairo to check up on his house and possessions, and Finch had already determined on his walk across the ship that he would simply give them to the boy outright. He'd been a fine apprentice, and was quite ready to strike out on his own path in the Great Work. Finch knew he would practice and teach an ethical, respectful style of alchemy. Jabir would be fine.

The rest of the world remained to be seen.

Finch produced a key from his pocket and opened a small chest—the worst sort of thing to carry on any trip through the desert, but security was paramount. Inside, he carefully unwrapped *The Book of the Dead*, running his hand across the pitch-black cover.

The Book of the Dead. The Emerald Tablet. One dark, one light. Two parts of the same thing.

Something, or someone, pointed Berthollet toward Siwa. Of the millions of documents stored in the Vatican Library, he came across the only one that might drive him toward where *The Book of the Dead* was kept. Furthermore, Berthollet's notes were gone—not only from the temple, but from his tent and those of the *savants* as well. There were other forces at play here, there was no doubt, and Finch recognized that while he had the book, someone else may have at least part of the lore within it.

And meanwhile, another part of the French plan nearly succeeded as well. They almost took the Emerald Tablet right from under the noses of the Xan.

Finch thought back to the portal he saw in the temple of Amun-Ra. He remembered the people on the other side. *Two parts of the same thing...?*

Then it struck him, like a veritable bolt of lightning thrown by Zeus himself.

What if the Known Worlds and the other...place...the place from whence Diaz and her people were from, were once part of the same universe? After all, if the warlord Althotas was shunted into a shadow prison in ages past, that "place between places" of which Rathemas described and Weatherby wrote—and bless Tom's prodigious memory for such detail!—it may have been possible that the Xan somehow sundered one universe from another in creating that place. If you create a place between places, after all, it stood to reason that there would need to be two places for it to reside.

Twice now, Finch had seen that other place, a dimension in which technology was ascendant and alchemy unheard of. Calling it coincidence would stretch the bounds of credulity. Althotas could make his Will known in both places. They were linked...and perhaps it was due to the fact that they were once bound together.

Finch stared down at the black book upon his lap. This would not be the end of things, Finch knew. It was likely just the beginning.

EPILOGUE

July 3, 2134

O f all the nations in the Islamic League, Dubai remained the best place to drink your troubles away.

Problem was, Harry Yu pondered as he nursed his fourth Scotch, his troubles outnumbered all the gleaming bottles of liquor behind the immaculately kept bar.

Harry knew he played it fast and loose, sure. That's why he stashed a couple billion terras in Swiss accounts. That's why he had a couple of different ident-chips, which was not exactly legal but certainly attainable. To make money, sometimes you had to take risks. So you did the prep work to mitigate the risks, then rolled the dice.

But this…this was beyond fast and loose. There was a million kilometers of red tape to cut through to arrest a multinational conglom executive— and another half-million if that exec had ties to China.

Maria Diaz had gotten a warrant in just six hours.

Sure, he'd been in contact with Total-Suez. They swore up and down they'd have his back. But they also said he needed to come in, that they couldn't help him unless he surrendered, got the mug shot, did the perp walk. Only then would they pony up the gold-plated legal team. They had to—it was part of Harry's contract. The company, at least, was done letting him play cowboy.

Harry took another swig of Scotch. Hell, the Siwa thing was a good idea. It was *still* a good idea. He just played it too fast. Too loose. He should've had the team do more legwork, more research. But the lure of an unspoiled

Earth—an unspoiled solar system! And actual fucking alchemy!—was too good to resist. Sure, the money was part of it—a large part of it—but he'd be the guy who opened up an entire new market full of resources. Unlimited energy. New scientific breakthroughs. He'd be a star in the business firmament.

"How ya doin', Harry?"

Harry turned to regard the woman who slid into the seat next to him. In his buzzed state, it took a moment. "Huh. You work for Diaz. I didn't think you made it out."

"I didn't," Maggie Huntington replied. "Not all the way. But close enough."

Harry looked her up and down. She had ditched the uniform for a slinky dress, which she wore well, but otherwise she looked pretty bad, almost as if she was hung over. Sweaty, bloodshot eyes, dark circles. Twitchy.

"You here to take me in?" he asked, downing the last of his Scotch. He was glad he went for the good stuff tonight. Might be his last for a while.

"Nope," Huntington said, looking over Harry's shoulder.

Harry turned to see Greene taking the seat on the other side of him.

"We're going to restart the project," Greene said. He also looked like shit. "And you're going to help us."

It was all Harry could do to not laugh in his face. "And if I don't?"

Greene shrugged. "We'll just tie you up, leave you in your room and call Diaz."

"Huh. And if I do?"

Huntington smiled at him, a wicked grin which did very little to make Harry feel better. "Then you get it all back. And then some."

Harry was a good businessman. He could read situations pretty well. The best situation would've been to *not* be found, but that was out the window. And that left…

"I'm listening."

December 4, 1798

"You have a visitor, *mon general*."

Napoleon Bonaparte looked up from his desk and frowned. It was easily past midnight. This was supposed to be the time to work, not receive guests. He glared at his aide-de-camp. "Why would you interrupt me with visitors at this hour?" he demanded.

The aide looked suitably cowed, yet remained undaunted. "I think, *monsieur general*, you will want to see him."

Before the aide could speak further, a man strode past him into Napoleon's study. He was older, and quite thin, wearing cast-off rags and thin sandals. And yet... "My God, Berthollet!" the general exclaimed, rising from his desk. "So thin! I didn't recognize you! I thought you were lost to us!" The two men hugged and kissed each other's cheeks. Napoleon looked closely at his friend...and saw something in his eyes that seemed quite different. "What happened to you?"

Berthollet smiled, and there was a feral quality to it. "Our expedition was lost, General. But out of defeat, I believe I have given you a tool for your eventual victory."

Napoleon retreated back behind his desk and sat; something deep inside him wanted to ensure there was space between him and Berthollet. "Did you acquire the book?"

"No, sir. Not exactly. Did we acquire the tablet?"

"No, we did not," Napoleon said, a hint of disgust in his voice. "The damned English sent that Weatherby fellow, of all people, in pursuit of *Franklin*. He and his Xan allies intervened, though the *Franklin* managed an escape thanks to our friends among the Xan. The tablet was destroyed, the Count St. Germain slain. Our friend wept for days on hearing it. I'm not sure which loss struck him more."

Berthollet only smiled again. "Cagliostro was always an emotional fool. He hoped the synthesis of the book and tablet would restore the power stripped from him by St. Germain. But I think he has served his purpose."

"Oh, really?" Napoleon said. "The only man to have awakened an ancient Martian warrior, the one who guided you toward both the book and the tablet—a fool past his purpose? And what would replace such a resource?"

Berthollet turned and shouted toward the door. "Come!"

Two French soldiers entered into the room, wearing full cloaks. Berthollet ordered their cloaks removed, and they stiffly complied, allowing the drapings to fall to the floor.

Napoleon gasped.

The soldiers were dead.

Their skin clung to their very bones like wet clothes upon a rack. Their eyes were gone, their lips as well. They had various small wounds upon their bodies, and a few larger ones as well. There was no blood upon these wounds, save for flecks of dried blackness. Napoleon could see dried flesh and bare bone where the skin was rent.

"What madness is this?" Napoleon whispered.

Berthollet's smile grew even wider, and more disturbing besides. "No madness, General. The book is lost, but through the notes I kept, I have discovered a way to animate the bodies of the deceased. They are revenants, devoid of soul and Will, but also lacking the need to eat or sleep, and deprived of any ability to feel pain. They follow commands to the letter.

"They are, I believe, the perfect soldiers."

Napoleon stood once more and walked toward the two…revenants, was it? He inspected them carefully, his natural revulsion quashed by the potential he saw. "This is sorcery," he said finally—not as an epithet, but as a question.

"No, General. It is alchemy. The sorcery was in trying to place souls within them, and that is where we erred, and doomed our expedition," Berthollet said. "These men, their souls are at peace. And their bodies remain…a resource, as you said."

Napoleon continued to pace around the two revenants, thinking. "How difficult is it?"

"The working needs refinement. But given two, perhaps three years, I believe we can make this working practical and, more importantly, teach it to others to use."

The general stopped pacing. "That is quite a bit of time, Berthollet. There is a war *now*. We make for the Levant soon."

"What is in the Levant, my general, which Europe does not have? Why rule the desert sands when this"—he pointed at the revenants—"guarantees you the fertile fields of the most advanced civilizations on Earth?"

Napoleon slowly began to nod. "This will take planning."

"Yes, it will," Berthollet agreed.

The general looked the revenants up and down once more. "You can replicate this working, yes? Do you need these two?"

"I can, General. And no, they are not necessary to continue my work."

"Have them destroyed," Napoleon ordered. "No evidence should remain.

We must work secretly, so that when the time is right, our army will take the world by surprise."

Berthollet agreed. Borrowing Napoleon's sword, the alchemist neatly decapitated the two revenants—and they crumbled to dust almost immediately. Useful, indeed.

Napoleon had his aide see to getting the alchemist fresh clothes, food and a bed, and ordered Berthollet to make a full written report of all that transpired. The general then spent the rest of the night wide awake, thinking. Finally, he sent a letter to his brother Lucien, a politician of growing influence in Paris.

There was much to write about.

ACKNOWLEDGEMENTS

There was a time when the first book in this series, *The Daedalus Incident*, was in jeopardy of never getting published—which means you might not have *The Enceladus Crisis* in your hands now. Thankfully, in late spring 2013, Night Shade Books completed the sale of its assets to Skyhorse Publishing and Start Media, which published *Daedalus*; Skyhorse then agreed to let me continue writing in the Known Worlds. Needless to say, there are a lot of people to thank for that.

Tony Lyons of Skyhorse and Jarred Weisfeld of Start Media purchased those Night Shade assets and made Night Shade an imprint of Skyhorse and Start. And that meant I got to see *The Daedalus Incident* and this book out on the shelves. The Science Fiction and Fantasy Writers of America, and particularly Mary Robinette Kowal, looked out for the interests of Night Shade authors during some difficult times. And of course, the crew at the old Night Shade deserves credit for making the sale happen as well. Thank you all for your hard work.

I also want to thank all the folks in the SF/F community for all their support for this series. Hats off to John DeNardo, Patrick Hester, Paul "Prince Jvstin" Weimer and the whole SFSignal crew, Stefan Raets and the Tor.com gang, the folks at io9.com, Justin Landon, Abhinav Jain (Shaila's great-great-grandpa, apparently), the Skiffy and Fanty crew and so many others. And thanks also to so many authors who lent me their digital space to talk about my work, including Mary Robinette Kowal (again!), John Scalzi, Anne Lyle, J. M. McDermott, Heather McCorkle, Bryan Thomas Schmidt and my beer-kin, Chuck Wendig. Also, a shout-out to my agency

Michael J. Martinez

brethren, Michael R. Underwood and Jason M. Hough, for the kind words and encouragement. Really, the whole SF/F community of authors, reviewers and readers has been very welcoming, and I greatly appreciate it.

The team at the new Night Shade imprint has been fantastic to work with. My thanks to Jason Katzman for agreeing to let me play more in this nifty sandbox, to Cory Allyn for excellent editing, and to Ardi Alspach and Lauren Burnstein for yeoman's work on the publicity front.

For this book, I enlisted a couple of beta-readers to help me make sure I was on the right track, and they delivered in a huge way. Many thanks to Andrew Montgomery and Dan Hanks for their excellent feedback. It's a better book because of them.

I want to give a special thank-you to my agent Sara Megibow, who negotiated contracts for *The Daedalus Incident* twice during the transition, then turned around and did a fantastic job on the sale of this book and its forthcoming sequel. And she did it all with great humor and grace. I salute your awesomeness.

And then there's my incredible wife, Kate, and our amazing daughter, Anna. Thank you both for all the love and encouragement. You make the journey worthwhile.

Finally, there are all the folks out there who embraced *The Daedalus Incident* and are reading this now. Thanks for letting me tell these stories.

Michael J. Martinez

ABOUT THE AUTHOR

(Photo by Anna Martinez)

Michael J. Martinez is the author of *The Daedalus Incident, The Enceladus Crisis,* and the upcoming *The Venusian Gambit,* and is a member of the Science Fiction and Fantasy Writers of America. Mike is a former journalist who, when not writing about sailing ships in space, enjoys cooking, homebrewing, and travel, along with all things geek. He lives with his wife and daughter in the greater New York City area.